# chase the dream

# B.B. MILLER & LESLIE CARSON

Cover Design by:
Jada D'Lee Designs

Cover Image by:
iStock Photo

Editing by:
Lauren Schmelz, and Greg—Write Divas

Interior Design & Formatting by:
Christine Borgford, Type A Formatting

*This story deals with issues of domestic violence which may be sensitive to some readers.*

*For all those living in the face of fear, remember, you are strong.*

# chapter one

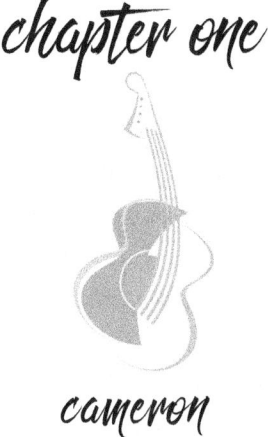

## cameron

"STOP SLOUCHING, CAMERON." THREE WORDS from my mother guaranteed to make my thirty-seven-year-old self feel like an awkward teenager again. "All those years hunched over your guitar haven't done a thing for your posture."

"Lovely to see you too, Mother." I lean in for the obligatory kiss to both of my cheeks, which are clean shaven as requested in the formal email sent from her assistant earlier in the week. The familiar scent of Chanel swirls around me as she leans back with a scrutinizing gaze, looking for flaws.

"You always did look so handsome in a suit," she murmurs in a rare compliment. Apparently, I pass inspection. "This isn't the Armani I sent over, is it?" She purses her distorted lips in disapproval. The collagen and countless face-lifts have been putting up the good fight. Not a single wrinkle on her sixty-year-old face.

She's dripping in diamonds and vintage Versace, and with her hair perfectly styled and sprayed to within an inch of its dyed blond life, she still manages to command the room. The poster model for the billionaire's wife.

The crowd at the Chapman Center for the Arts buzzes around her, all sharks in the water, quietly waiting for their turn to take a bite. A few minutes with Victoria Chapman, the reigning queen of Boston's elite first, and my mother second, can rocket you to exclusive status. You can almost smell the desperation on the high-society wannabes lingering around the fringes.

Cameras flash around us, although this time in a welcome change, they aren't for me. The Thanksgiving concert is the elite event of the year in Boston, produced by my parents in support of the arts center, one of the many charities that benefit from my family's influence and power. Hell, the building is named after them. Even if this is a massive publicity stunt, it's for a good cause. It may be the only thing that actually doesn't turn my stomach about being dragged here.

The money raised tonight and throughout the year supports the arts center that provides opportunities for talented musicians who otherwise wouldn't be available. Everything from programs like the one my band, Redfall, played in Sydney that offers chances for child prodigies to train with symphonies around the globe, to an all-day private high school focused on the arts and a fully funded day care for the musicians who are part of the symphony. I know how much time and dedication it takes to play at this level. It also takes money—something these musicians don't have. The symphony only operates for half the year, and the musicians all need to supplement their income in the off season.

"I stopped wearing the clothes you picked out for me when I was sixteen." She shakes her head slightly before flattening her hand down the lapel of my dark blue suit jacket. "And it's Tom Ford," I add just to rub it in.

She takes a step back as if standing too close to her son is a crime. "How many times do we have to have this conversation? Armani cuts a better suit."

"In your opinion."

"My opinion is the only one that matters, dear." She sounds conceited, but she's not wrong. My mother is practically worshipped in the Boston social scene. She's a staple on every charity committee and endowment fund. She speaks at highly publicized events where she preaches about the importance of giving back to the community. When Victoria Chapman talks, people listen.

She links her arm around mine and turns to flash her practiced smile for the cameras before gliding us through the lobby. The masses part for her as if she's some holy relic to be revered. "There's someone I want you to meet."

I frown, glancing down at her. "I do just fine getting my own dates, thank you."

"Yes. We know." She flashes me a warning glare before her public mask snaps back into place. "Darcy Hamilton." I barely manage to bite back a groan. "Recently single," she continues loud enough for me to hear as we merge into the line for the theater. She nods and gives a finger wave to a few people along the way. "She was dating Benjamin Knight, you know? Of the athletic company? Shoes, apparel."

"I'm familiar," I murmur. "Isn't he worth a few billion?" Sometimes, it's fun to annoy her. She scoffs, taking a program from one of the ushers standing outside our private box seats.

"Please." She leans closer, her voice dropping lower. "He had a gambling problem. Lost half their earnings in one night. It was quite the scandal. I'm surprised you didn't hear about it."

Shaking my head, I lead her to our spot above the mezzanine. Only the best box seats for the Chapmans. All the little unworthy peons scatter below us just where my mother wants them. She's high above where she can reign supreme. "I've been a little busy."

She pats my chest. "It's cute that your hobby can keep you entertained. While you've been gallivanting from city to city in your little band, your father has been working himself nearly to death." Anger has my jaw tightening. If my mother had her way, I'd be chained to a desk beside dear old Dad and my brothers. Another heart attack waiting to happen. The fact that I've worked my ass off establishing Redfall and doing something I love doesn't even enter her mind. I've disappointed her and the family name, and that's a crime for which no amount of penance is ever going to be enough.

"I hate to break it to you, but he's been doing that his whole life. And I don't gallivant."

She waves the program in front of me, clearly not wanting to hear a thing I say. "Anyway, Darcy is lovely. Long blond hair, thirty, on the board at the Children's Hospital Foundation. She was Miss Massachusetts a few years ago, you know. She does Pilates at the club. I've seen her there when I meet the girls for brunch on Thursdays. Her parents own Hamilton Jewelers," she rattles on, sinking down gracefully to a seat at the front of the box.

"You going to tell me how much she weighs, too? Jesus. It sounds like you're trying to sell me one of the horses." Unbuttoning my suit jacket, I take the seat beside her.

"Watch your language, Cameron. Darcy and her mother will be here shortly." Of course they will. I knew she'd try to set me up with some trust fund trophy wife in waiting. Every time I'm home for a visit she does this. You would think by now she would have given up, but my reluctance only serves to fuel her determination.

I'm sure in her mind, having her rebel son married off is good for business and the family name. It would mean she'd get someone on the inside watching me, making sure I don't screw up again. Though, I don't see rehab as a screwup the way she does. It was a necessary reset.

I had started to spiral out of control with our former tour manager, Brodie Dixon, and I was inching from the occasional bump of coke into more dangerous territory. It could have escalated quickly into full-blown addiction, but I checked myself in. I wanted to go through the process, and I'm damn glad that I did. I was close to losing everything I had worked so hard for, and if I hadn't stopped the cycle, things would be very different right now. Enduring a night like this with my mother seems to pale in comparison to the hell I could be in.

I smell her before I see her, a cloud of Clive Christian wafting over me. It's an expensive scent I grew up with, being surrounded by high-society women who wanted to make sure they not only looked rich, but smelled it too. They all have a certain air about them—something that screams refined, sophisticated, elitist.

"Ah, Darcy, Elizabeth . . ." It's hard not to roll my eyes. "You made it." My mother should've been an actress. She actually sounds like she cares about these people. She stands and extends the customary kiss to each cheek greeting, and I stand as well. Even after years in what is considered a raunchy and highly unpredictable rock-and-roll band, the breeding drilled into me comes back easily.

"Cameron, of course you remember Elizabeth." My mother motions from Elizabeth to me as if I'm on display. I don't remember Mrs. Hamilton. Too many carbon copies of her have passed through our doors over the years. None of them are memorable. But I lie because it's what's expected of me.

"Mrs. Hamilton." I incline my head in respect, like a proper gentleman, earning me a few brownie points. *Yes, Mother. I remember every single thing you and your legion of nannies taught us.* Elizabeth looks her fill of me, her eyes widening as I take her offered hand. She can hardly hold it up with the ice rink sitting on her finger—a given when your husband owns one of the biggest jewelry franchises in the world. "Lovely to see you again."

"Oh, you've grown into a fine young man, wouldn't you agree, Darcy?" At least Darcy lives up to the hype my mother was spewing. She's striking in that manufactured, beauty-queen way. I wonder why her mother doesn't have her married off already. Talk about trophy wife material.

Almost as tall as my six-five in her stilettos, she's rocking a form-fitting white sequined gown that barely conceals a pair of fake tits that probably put a significant dent in Daddy's pocketbook. She's got so much makeup on, I wonder what she looks like underneath it all. Darcy, too, is dripping in jewelry—some huge sapphire monstrosity locked around her neck looks like it weighs more than she does. Jesus, woman. Eat a cheeseburger.

"I would absolutely agree," Darcy purrs, holding her hand out. You'd have to be blind to miss her freshly manicured nails, painted blood red, and the bling on her fingers, except notably the one finger she's actually desperate to put something on. "Darcy Hamilton." She's about as subtle as a brick to the head.

"Pleasure to meet you. Cameron Chapman." Her nails trail a light circuit over the inside of my wrist as she bats her big eyes at me. It feels like she's staking a claim, and I don't like it. I move to the side, motioning for them to sit.

"I downloaded your latest album last night." She brushes past me, her voice breathy. "It's brilliant."

"Yeah? Well, you can thank Kennedy for that. He wrote it."

She giggles at this—the usual response for ridiculous women

who don't have a fucking clue how to carry on an actual conversation. Underneath all that glitz and glamor, she's not as far off from the groupies as I'm sure she thinks she is.

I'm not stupid. Between my family's wealth and status and my own stake with Redfall, I'm a catch for a girl like Darcy. I could easily support the ridiculous lifestyle she expects. Plus, I've been blessed with good genes; I have my father's height and jawline, and a body shaped by a variety of sports growing up and years of rigorous playing on stage. I know I'm looking good tonight. The smoldering look she's giving me, like she's imagining what's under my suit, is testament to that.

I snort and shake my head. Darcy's just like every woman I meet, regardless of the expensive dress and glimmering jewels. All they see is my money, my looks, and my fame, not necessarily in that order. Some are attracted to the bad-boy rocker image. None of them give a shit what's underneath. They're all so fucking transparent.

Her hand snakes up my arm. "Maybe you could play something for me sometime." I let her blatant pickup line hang in the air as she sits elegantly. She makes sure the high slit of her dress opens to reveal her endlessly long legs. I curse the no-sex bet I made with our pain-in-the-ass bassist, Matt Logan. I'd actually like to fuck that smug look off Darcy's face. She thinks I'm a done deal, and judging by the expectant looks on our mothers' faces, so do they.

"WHERE THE HELL HAVE YOU been?" My voice raises as I find Katherine—my little sister and favorite sibling—lingering by the bar. In pure defiance of our mother, she's got on a rainbow-colored short cocktail dress that just hits her knees, paired with purple Doc

Martens. Fuck, I've missed her. "You left me with soul-sucking Darcy—"

"Hamilton. I know." She downs what looks like not her first glass of champagne.

"You knew that Queen V was up to something?" I narrow my eyes, but she just throws her head back and laughs at one of the many nicknames we have for our mother.

"When isn't she?"

"A little warning would've been nice there, Kitty Kat." I ruffle her long blond hair, and she nudges me in the side.

"Where's the fun in that? And come on. Darcy is smoking hot. You'd totally do her. So would I."

"She's ridiculous."

"She was Miss Massachusetts. Did Mom tell you? A real-life pageant queen!" She gives a royal wave, flashing me a fake smile.

"Yeah. She mentioned that." I scowl and take a peek over her shoulder in the direction of the box, knowing my time is limited before the vulture descends again.

"Welcome to my nightmare. I've been the target of Mom's bullshit for the last couple years there, hotshot. It's your turn." It's hard to miss the disdain in Kat's voice. Fuck only knows what she's had to put up with. Our mother is stifling at the best of times, and for a free spirit like Kat, it's got to be hell.

"She's got two other kids she could inflict her special kind of torture on. How did they manage to get out of this?"

Kat rolls her eyes. "They're with Dad at some convention in the Turks and Caicos. It's just you and me now, kid." She tips up on her toes and slings her arm around my shoulder, crushing her tiny body against me. How Kat missed the tall gene in the pool, I don't know. She's always been a pint-sized wonder. Family photos—a critical element when you're a Chapman—always had to be elaborately staged so she didn't look totally out of place next to the rest of us. Dad is almost a monster at six-eight. My brothers Brooks, Nathan, and I check in at around the six-five mark. And then, the little freak of nature herself at barely five feet tall on a good day. It makes no sense at all. If she didn't look exactly like our mother did thirty years ago, I'd swear she was adopted.

"I've missed you, jerk," she whispers, giving me a squeeze, and that right there makes the whole trip home and having to endure this farce with my mother worth it.

I tighten my arms around her. "I missed you too, Kat."

"You could've called me, you know?" She folds her arms across her chest, jutting her chin out. Of course, she knows about what I hope is my stint in rehab. No matter how much money you have, some things can't be buried. Fuck knows my parents tried to keep it out of the press, but pictures get out, and flights to Malibu when you're famous and don't have a home there, typically mean one thing: You've hit rock bottom and you've checked yourself in somewhere. "You can always call me." Her eyes search mine, and she grins. "Well, not at two thirty in the morning. I'm not at my best then. But any other time. Call."

She punches me in the chest with that unchecked fury I grew up with, and I chuckle in response. "I wanted to do it myself. Fuck, you've got enough to deal with here without worrying about me, and anyway, I'm good now. Free and clear for over a year." She beams a smile at me. "What about you?" I ask, wanting to change the subject. "Who's your latest victim? Whitney still in the picture?" The fact that Kat is bisexual isn't one that sits well with my parents. The number of times she's called me in tears after getting berated by our mother is staggering.

"Nah. I kicked her to the curb a few months back." A waiter wanders by, and she switches her empty glass out, snagging two flutes of champagne, and offers me one. I shake my head, and she gives me a shrug, downing it.

"Aw." I give her a fake pout. "I liked her."

"You mean you liked the fact that she didn't wear a bra."

I raise both hands up in surrender. "Guilty."

She takes a healthy sip of champagne from the remaining glass. "Men. You're so predictable."

"Cameron?" Nails on a chalkboard would hurt less. I cringe at the sound of Darcy's voice. "There you are."

Kat elbows me in the side. "Damn, she's hot," she murmurs before finishing off the rest of the champagne.

"You date her then. That just might send dear old Mom over the edge."

Kat snorts, watching as Darcy sashays over. There's no mistaking Darcy's critical glare, how she holds herself just a bit straighter. She's sizing up potential competition, looking for weaknesses. She glares at me.

"Darcy, meet my sister, Katherine."

"Sister?" You can almost see Darcy's claws retract. "It's so nice to finally meet you," she says, her voice all buttery soft as if she wasn't just getting ready to scratch my sister's eyes out.

"The pleasure is all mine. Believe me." Darcy misses, or chooses not to acknowledge, Kat's almost indecent perusal of her.

"Victoria talks about you all the time," Darcy adds, like she and my mother are lifelong friends. "I was hoping to meet some more of the famous Chapman crew." How many more hours of this shit do I have to put up with?

"The orchestra is about to start, Cameron," Darcy starts, her voice almost scolding. "Shall we?"

"Oh, we wouldn't want to miss that now, would we?" Kat hooks her arm around Darcy's before she can sink her claws back into me and leads her back to our private box. Kat peeks over her shoulder at me as I follow, giving me a wink. Time to torture our mother. Payback is a bitch.

On a haunting violin intro, the curtains lift, and lights rise in dramatic fashion to reveal the impressive, large orchestra with the infamous Maestro Hoffman conducting. He's related, somehow—my mother's second cousin once removed, or something like that. I recognize the Beethoven piece, having grown up with classical music being a staple in our lives. My mother is a gifted pianist, although I don't think she's played in years. I loved listening to her play when I was little. She was horrified when I started to play guitar, calling it "pedestrian."

Kat has been nattering away to Darcy, trying to keep her entertained, but now that the main event is on, Darcy's attention—or rather her hand—is focused back on me. Her palm rests on my thigh, and if it was any other time or any other woman, I'd welcome it. Now, it feels like a vise, holding me in place, reminding me of all the things I don't want. I try to shift away, and when she doesn't take the hint, I lift her hand and place it back in her lap. I ignore her glare and little huff of indignation. Poor thing. She's used to always getting her way.

I turn my attention back to the stage, to the subtle, rhythmic lines of the second violins. It's not that different from my role in Redfall—supportive and harmonic, seamlessly blending the difficult rhythms of our sound to bring it a texture that's uniquely ours. A lot of people think Kennedy has the hardest job playing lead guitar. I'd like to see them try to master the complexities of mine.

The melodic, sensitive notes, played with passion and commitment, pull me to the edge of my seat, trying to get a better look at the second violin section. In a common placement, they're buried behind the first violins and sandwiched next to the violas.

And then, I get a flash of curly auburn hair that seems to blaze from the overhead lights. I can only catch rare glimpses of this beauty; the sweet curve of her neck, the odd bounce of her hair as she pours her heart and soul out. So much intensity and energy, but in a weird dichotomy, it's like she's deliberately hiding behind the music stand.

Finally, she glances up and I'm treated to gorgeous green eyes, full of fire and concentration as she flies through the piece. A jolt of—something—shoots through me, and even when her eyes return to her music, I'm transfixed.

For the rest of the piece, she plays with a subtle hunger that has me mesmerized, lost to everything but her until Darcy's grip on my arm pulls me back to reality as the entire theater rises to a standing ovation.

With my heart hammering, I stand beside Darcy, trying to get a better look at the violinist, but it's nearly impossible. While the rest of the orchestra stands tall to the audience, her head stays lowered, with her auburn hair cascading around her face and her eyes focused to the stage floor as if she's afraid to look up.

She's dressed in nondescript black, like the rest of the orchestra, a simple, long flowing dress that covers everything, giving nothing away. Her shoulders seem stiff, as if she's terrified to move. Maybe it's her first performance. I know that feeling. I remember mine, and it wasn't pretty. It was a miracle I didn't pass out.

I can't look away from her, even as Darcy tugs on my jacket, trying to coax me to follow her out of our box seats. I can hear my mother's voice like a fading far-off echo, excitedly going on to Mrs. Hamilton about the performance. I almost trip over the step in the aisle, straining to get another look at the stage as the curtain falls.

Following along behind the crowd blindly, I'm in a haze as we move to the lobby. It's been a long time since anything outside of playing our own concerts has affected me like this. It's an addictive feeling, wanting something and having no idea why, but you need it, crave it, want to seek it out. And right now, I need to find that shy auburn beauty. "Cameron?" Darcy's shrill voice breaks the spell. "Didn't you like it?"

"No . . . I mean yeah . . ." I stammer, and Kat looks at me like I've lost my mind. "It was amazing."

"You must be so proud." Mrs. Hamilton gushes to my mother as if she's had something to do with the brilliant performance we just witnessed. "Oh, there are the Wilsons, let's go say hello." She tries to herd us all across the lobby, and I manage to tug from the death grip Darcy has on my arm.

Her eyes snap up to mine, daggers flashing as I take a step away and motion in the direction of the restrooms. "I have to . . ."

Darcy giggles, batting her eyes at me again. It's a little disturbing how quickly she seems to morph from one emotion to the next. Hello, bat-shit crazy. "I'll be waiting," she says in that breathy voice. It's a threat and a promise I don't like.

Kat gives me a not-so-subtle kick to the shin as they start to move off. "You're not leaving me here with them," my sister hisses once they're out of earshot.

"Who said anything about leaving?" I flash her a knowing grin, and she rolls her eyes.

"All right. But you owe me. Big time." She pokes me in the chest.

"You love me, and this is gold for you. Think of how much fun it will be to torture Mom for the rest of the night. You can flirt with Darcy, get Mom all riled up."

Letting out a laugh, she starts to move into the crowd, glancing back over her shoulder. "You still owe me."

NAVIGATING THE BACKSTAGE AREA IS way too easy. I've spent a lot of time in this theater over the years. I know the layout, and I stop at each green room, searching for my violin beauty, but come up empty. She can't have gotten that far.

Muted voices come from one of the small rooms near the exit, and I move toward the sound. My adrenaline fires, anticipation teasing at me. "I'll see you at rehearsal tomorrow, Sam," a woman's voice calls, and I quicken my steps, having the sinking feeling she's slipping away before I can even meet her.

A tall blonde turns out of the room, zipping up her winter jacket before pushing open the heavy metal exit door to the parking lot. A blast of cold air rushes into the hallway as I stop at the room she just came out of, glancing inside. I'm not disappointed.

*Sam.* At least I have a name. There she is, tugging a long dark coat from a hook on the wall, her thick hair cascading around her shoulders. She's turned away from me, shoving a knitted cap on her head likes she wants to hide away under it.

She turns at the loud creak of the hardwood complaining under my shoes. My eyes find hers, wide, terrified, the deepest green. I'm lost, blown away, my heart pounding out a stuttered beat. Her pretty mouth drops open, but she doesn't say a word. A tense silence tugs between us, punctured only by the buzzing of the fluorescent lights on the ceiling as we stare at each other.

I'm not used to the quiet; my life is loud, over the top, chaotic. I get the feeling that may all be about to change.

*samantha*

*HE'S FOUND ME.*

The thought freezes the marrow in my bones. I stare at the giant in the doorway, my fingers clutching at my belt. But then, he smiles, and a long-forgotten warmth steals through my body, thawing my tense muscles. He doesn't look like any of Ray's friends, at least those I can remember. That rough-and-tumble group wouldn't have worn tuxedos even if you paid them. And none of them were this stunningly attractive.

Classically handsome, his face boasts a strong, sharp jawline, and long, straight nose. The dyed-blond tips speckled throughout his short brown hair are incongruous with his refined dress. It's his eyes that really give me pause; a rich, sparkling hazel that seems to reach out to my soul.

"Hi." His voice is low and resonant, with a warm undertone that cuts through the apprehension that is second nature to me now, and making my heart skip a beat. With an effort, I unclench my hands from my belt and grasp the handle of my battered violin case. The weight is comforting, and I step sidewise, hoping to lure him out of the doorway—the only exit.

"If you were hoping to catch Olivia, she just left." I nod toward the door. With her cool blond looks and hourglass figure, Olivia attracts men of all ages. This is hopefully just another of her admirers.

He steps inside, but not enough to clear the way. He's almost a foot taller than me and looks to have a proportionately long reach. "Actually, I was looking for you," he says. My jaw tenses. Maybe Ray found someone new to do his dirty work for him.

"Oh?" There are a few chairs along one wall, but nothing I can use to put between us. I squeeze my case tighter. It's not very large, but it's hard. I know from experience that it can stop a man cold if you can hit the right spot with it.

"My name is Cam, um, Cameron Chapman." He tilts his head,

as if waiting for something. Then an awkward chuckle rumbles in his chest, and he runs a hand through his hair. His fingers are long and elegant, but I can see the strength in them. "I, uh, wanted to tell you how much I enjoyed your performance."

I edge closer to the wall, trying to keep my distance. "I'll pass along your compliment to Maestro Hoffmann." I look up at him through my lashes, taking in the fine cut of his suit and the jaunty way he wears it. Chapman . . . not one of *the* Chapmans, surely? Everyone who's even slightly associated with the arts in Boston has heard of the Chapman family, especially Victoria Chapman, the ice queen who reigns supreme over the family and foundation that supports artistic endeavors in the city. The handsome man before me looks vaguely familiar, but I can't place him among the few haughty members of the family I've seen at previous performances.

"I'd appreciate that. But I meant *your* performance."

The cocky tilt to his head sparks something in me, and the words are out before I can stop them. "Really?" I'm unable to keep the sarcasm from my voice. "You could pick me out over the whole orchestra? You must have some kind of superhero hearing."

I brace myself, mentally cursing my lapse. But instead of the anger I'm used to seeing in response to my snark, he barks out a laugh, startling me. "Point taken. I meant that you played with real feeling—I could see it in the way you held yourself and your instrument. It's obvious that you love what you do."

The sincerity and frank admiration in his expression is both flattering and unsettling. I try so hard to blend in with the orchestra; it's disconcerting to know someone could still pick me out of the crowd.

I can't afford to attract attention.

"Ah, well, thank you, Mr. Chapman," I murmur and tuck a flyaway curl back into my hat. The dry winter air always plays havoc with my hair. "Have a good rest of your evening."

"My pleasure, Miss . . ." He pauses, obviously waiting for me to supply my name. Instinctively, my mouth clamps shut. He may not be one of Ray's trackers, but that doesn't mean he's safe. In fact, considering the way his intense gaze warms my blood and makes my thighs twitch, he's most definitely *not* safe. Despite his obviously expensive suit and shoes, he exudes a masculine allure, a dangerous sexiness, that doesn't fit with the well-heeled, inconspicuous audiences we usually attract.

A sudden ringing from his pocket tears through the quiet, startling us both. I let out a quiet sigh of relief when his attention is diverted. It's like I've been released from a tractor beam. "Oh, um, excuse me," he mutters, pulling his phone from the pocket of his jacket and scowling down at it.

I use his distraction to skirt past him into the hallway. A light, spicy scent teases my nose, and I inhale deeply as I brush his elbow. Good Lord, he smells good. I shove aside the thought, seeing the exit door mere steps away, and hurry to make my escape.

"Wait!"

I gasp when I feel a large hand on my arm. Alarmed, I swing around, case at the ready, to see his surprised expression. He's close enough I can see the amber flecks in his eyes glowing warmly among the mossy-brown of his irises. They're hypnotic.

"Wait," he says, softer this time, and slowly removes his hand, his fingers trailing over my worn wool coat. "Do you have to leave now? It's not even ten. I was hoping I could take you for a cup of coffee." My mouth falls open, and he continues, his deep voice softening, as if he's coaxing a wild rabbit with a carrot. "Or . . . dessert or something? Whatever you want. Have you had dinner already?"

My hand tightens on the push bar, poised for flight. Something in his voice stops me. He seems so sincere, hopeful even. That, combined with his startling good looks, stirs a hunger in me I haven't felt in years. I gaze up into those beautiful eyes, wishing I was someone else . . . that I *could* go for a simple drink with a handsome man and not constantly look over my shoulder.

But I can't.

I tamp down my longing and pull out the words guaranteed to send the tempting Mr. Chapman on his way. "I appreciate the offer, but I need to go pick up my child."

He rears back, his eyes snapping open with the shock I expected. I can practically see his interest die. No one who looks like him and who's possibly related to the illustrious Chapman family would ever get entangled with a single mother, regardless of how well she plays the violin.

Pushing open the door, I close my eyes at the rush of freezing air that hits my face. The door shuts with a bang, leaving me standing in the small parking lot behind the building. Alone.

Of course.

I head for the bus stop on the corner, ignoring the small part of me that hopes he will follow.

THE LUSCIOUS AROMAS OF LAMB stew coming from the Finnegans' apartment bring a smile to my face. Mr. and Mrs. Finnegan own a small grocery on the corner and live in a small apartment in the back of the building. When I answered their ad to rent the tiny apartment located above the grocery, I gained not only a safe place to live, but a pair of pseudo grandparents as well. I adore them.

"Ah, come in, lass, come in!" Mrs. Finnegan opens the door with a wide smile, and I eagerly step into the warmth of their small living room. It's been decades since she last visited Ireland, but there's still a bit of a warm burr to her speech.

"How was Hannah?" I untie and open my coat.

She waves her hand. "An angel, as usual." The dark-haired woman bustles to the kitchen and comes back, slipping a small container into a plastic grocery sack. "I made a little extra for your dinner, Samantha. I know you didn't take time to eat before you left." She gives me a knowing look, daring me to contradict her, and I laugh lightly.

"I didn't have time. Thank you, Mrs. Finnegan. You're a life-saver." Stepping over to their couch, I lift my sleeping daughter into my arms. She's wrapped in a blanket like a burrito, her red-gold ringlets in glorious disarray. My landlady slips the handle of the sack around my wrist. With a practiced maneuver, I carry my daughter, violin case, and sack, and manage to step out of the apartment again without banging anything against the doorframe. Whispering my thanks again to Mrs. Finnegan over Hannah's head, I leave her looking after me in the small hallway and trudge up the narrow stairs to my room.

I finally have to put my case down so I can fish my keys out of my pocket. Safe behind my locked door, I head directly to Hannah's small bed in our bedroom. After tucking her in, I toss my violin onto my twin bed and stand staring down at my angel. Long golden lashes brush her soft cheeks as she dreams peacefully. She is the best thing I have ever done. A reminder that in all the ugliness I've gone through, there's a beautiful angel I can't imagine my life without.

Tiptoeing out of the room, I pull the door almost shut and wearily take my coat off. I hang it on the coatrack next to the door and move to our kitchenette to heat up Mrs. Finnegan's gift in our ancient microwave, not bothering to change out of my concert black. The wood floor creaks as I carry the bowl to our small card table and sit. Staring down at the delicious stew, I think of what a pair of beautiful hazel eyes would look like peering at me across a table in a nice restaurant.

And I let the tears fall.

# chapter two

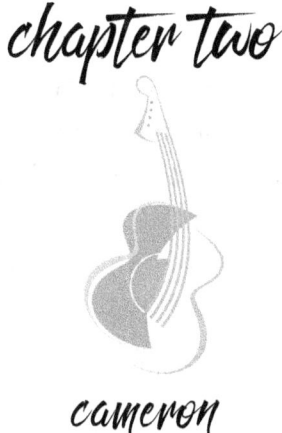

## cameron

"GOOD MORNING, SIR. I WASN'T expecting you for breakfast."
Henry Phillips has been the head butler at my family's main estate
in Boston forever; he essentially runs the place. Always dressed in
an impeccably fitted suit, he's pushing sixty, English, and for some
unknown reason, loyal to the core. Hell knows we gave him and
the revolving door of nannies a run for their money over the years.

"Henry, it's been over twenty years. Are you ever going to
actually call me Cameron?" I toe out of my boots, placing them
on the mat under the Italian imported table as he closes the heavy
door behind me. It's an action engrained into me even after all these
years. God forbid we should get messy footprints on the freshly
cleaned marble floor.

The corner of Henry's mouth twitches in amusement. "If
it hasn't happened by now, sir, I highly doubt it. Can I take your

coat?" In a practiced move, he holds his arm out.

"I know where the closet is. Used to hide in it from time to time, if you remember." Shrugging out of my leather jacket, I move across the marble floor of the expansive foyer. So many memories wrapped up in just this part of the house. The two-story double spiral staircase we used to chase each other up and down, the massive stone fireplace in the sitting room where I would frequently burn Brooks's homework, and the slick, black grand piano where Mom used to play.

Hanging up my coat, I shoot Henry a surprised glance, seeing the stack of boxes piled up against the closed doors of the grand ballroom. They're definitely out of place in an otherwise impeccably clean mansion.

"Forgive the mess, sir. We're starting preparations for decorating for the holidays."

"Have you got the tree picked out yet?" I peer through the stained-glass doors into the empty ballroom. The Chapman Christmas tree is nothing short of legendary. Right up there with the Rockefeller tree. The tree, and our estate when fully decorated, are typically featured in design magazines.

"There's a few I've had my eye on in the western acreage. A blue spruce and Norway spruce. Mrs. Chapman hasn't given her approval yet." I can see the excitement in Henry's eyes. Christmas always was his favorite time of the year, also one of our busiest with hosting parties and fundraisers through the holiday season. The mansion was always full of life and that's the way Henry likes it.

"I'd be happy to help when she finally makes her mind up."

Henry's eyes widen at my offer. "I'm sure the staff and I will have it in hand."

"And I'm sure I can help, Henry. It will give me something to do."

Henry nods, his eyes crinkling around the corners. "Very good, sir. If I may say, you're looking better than you did when you visited last December." Henry knows, as I'm sure the entire staff knows, about my time in rehab. The list of people I've disappointed just continues to grow.

"You may, and thanks. I'm much better now. Clean, and I intend to stay that way." I clap my hand over his shoulder.

"Beautiful words to hear, sir."

"How's your daughter? I think she was getting married the last time I was here."

Henry smiles. "About to make me a grandfather for the first time."

"Ah. More kids running around in your future. Bet you can't wait for that." I give him a nudge to the side.

"Children are a joy you don't fully appreciate until you have them in your life, sir. I'm looking forward to it." I get a flash of my auburn mystery woman at the mention of children. Sam, I heard that other woman say her name last night, and it's been on repeat in my head. *Sam, Sam, Sam.*

She was pretty damn quick to throw out that piece of information about her kid last night. Makes me wonder if it's actually true. Also makes me wonder if I've officially started to lose my mind. I haven't been able to get her out of my head, and that's not normal. Neither is losing sleep over a woman. Curiosity is a damn bitch.

"I'll take your word for it. Where is Queen V?" Henry almost laughs, but manages to hold it back.

"Taking breakfast on the southern terrace. Then she's going to the stables to check on Northern Star. She's due any day now." I had almost forgotten about Northern Star. This will be her last foal, having had a few champion racehorses over the years, and my mother is making a big deal about it.

"Ponies and kids, Henry. You're living the dream."

"That I am, sir. May I show you to the terrace?"

"I remember where it is. Let me know if you want help scoping that tree."

"I will do, sir." He lowers his head, effectively dismissed. On the rare occasions I've brought the guys in the band to the house, they've been mind-blown about the amount of staff we have at our beck and call. Growing up with it, it's my kind of normal, even though I realize it's wildly out of character for most of the population.

I find my mother on the enclosed heated terrace, dressed like she's going to attend a high-society afternoon tea. I recognize the Mozart piano concerto softly playing in the room. My mother looks dwarfed sitting all by herself at the massive table designed to seat twelve people. She adjusts her pearl necklace, leaning up for a kiss to both cheeks. "Mother."

"Darling. I wasn't expecting you. Twice in less than twenty-four hours has got to be a record. To what do I owe the pleasure?"

"Do I need a reason to see my mother?"

"Of course not, dear, but there always is one." She waves her hand in the direction of the hallway. "I'll have Heather fix you a plate." She snaps her fingers.

"I'm good. Just coffee is fine." I pull out a chair beside her, shaking my head at the sheer amount of food covering the huge table. There's enough here to feed our entire family easily, and she thinks more is needed.

"Nonsense. You're skinnier than you should be. You're eating." Sinking down to the chair across from her, I look up to a gasping sound. A twenty-something, starstruck girl in a light gray maid's uniform stands in the doorway. I recognize that look. I've seen it on too many groupies over the years.

"Don't just stand there gaping like a fish, Heather. Have the chef fix a fresh meal for Cameron." My mother's annoyed voice seems to spur Heather out of her celebrity-induced haze.

"I'm fine. Really. Just coffee, if you don't mind." Heather blinks between my mother and me, not quite sure who to listen to.

"He'll have an omelet with the chanterelle mushrooms, Heather, and a side of the Canadian bacon. Try not to let the chef burn it this time."

Heather wrings her hands, her eyes wide as she stares at me like she can't quite believe I'm sitting here. "Before Christmas would be nice," my mother adds, her brow raised.

"Yes, ma'am." A blush blooms over poor Heather's cheeks and she scurries away.

"Do you even hear yourself when you talk to them?" I ask once Heather is out of earshot.

She picks absently at the neck of her expensive cashmere cardigan. "Hear what, Cameron? Honestly, you'd think Henry could find some decent help."

"You'd think you wouldn't be so bitchy."

"Careful. Now tell me why you're here."

"When's Dad due back with Brooks and Nathan from sunning themselves in the Caribbean?"

She purses her lips. "The jet is due back tomorrow, and they're not sunning themselves, they're working at the investment convention."

It's hard not to laugh. "I've been to the house in the Turks and Caicos. They're not working."

"I suppose you're going to tell me that partying in some dingy bar at two in the morning is your definition of working." She levels me with one of her blistering glares.

"You're way behind on your gossip. I haven't done that in a

long time." I pluck a strawberry from the silver serving tray, and dip it into the cream, desperate to change the topic. "How much do you know about the musicians in the orchestra at the center?"

She leans back in her chair. Her eyes assessing, judging as always. "Next to nothing. Why?"

I shrug, taking a bite out of the berry. "You know the band's been doing a symphony series." She glares at me, saying nothing. "I heard something last night that I'd like to explore. That's all."

"I can speak to Maestro if you like. I have an appointment with him this afternoon after his rehearsal to discuss the holiday concert. You could join me."

I can barely contain my grin. The blonde from last night mentioned some sort of rehearsal to Sam. I think my plans for the afternoon just got made. "I'd appreciate it." Heather returns, a tray with a fresh carafe and fine china cups and saucers shaking as she sets it on the table. I wonder how many times we intimidated the staff over the years. The Chapman siblings could be a nightmare to deal with, and while I always try to be polite now, I'm sure growing up I wasn't.

"Thanks, Heather. I'll take it from here." I set my hand next to her trembling one on the coffee carafe. The last thing I need is scalding hot coffee landing in my lap.

She nods. "Very well." She bites down on her bottom lip, blinking at me. "Sir."

Heather makes a quick exit as I pour the coffee, passing a fresh cup to Queen V. "I don't know what's gotten into her," she says. "She was fine when the governor was here last week."

"Yeah? Well, the governor is like seventy-five and not in a rock band."

She huffs, adding a few cubes of sugar to her cup. "How much longer are you going to jaunt around the globe with those boys?"

"We're the number one concert tour on the planet, *Mom*. It's something I take seriously. It would be nice if you did too."

"What would be nice, *Cameron*, is if you could be around to help your father. To help me." Ah, the guilt trip.

"I'm here now, aren't I?" I lift my cup to her, taking a sip. The coffee is amazing as always. Imported beans from Brazil will do that for you. It tastes like heaven.

"Yes. Let's talk about Darcy Hamilton. I think it went well last night, don't you?" Nervous Heather returns with the requested breakfast, thank fuck, setting the plate in front of me. She even manages not to drop it. I cut into the omelet and take a bite. The conversation may be cringe-worthy, but at least the meal is delicious.

"YOU SURE YOU DON'T WANT to take Whiskey instead?" David Adams, who's overseen the stables for years, adjusts the browband on the jet-black stallion. The stallion huffs in response.

"Admiral and I will be just fine." I stroke my hand over Admiral's neck before settling into the saddle. It's been too long since I've been riding. When I was here last year, all my focus was on Dad and getting him through recovery from his heart attack. Now, feeling the cool late November air and seeing the open acres stretch out in front of me, I've missed it. We used to ride all the time. While most kids got bikes for their birthday, I got horses. I played polo for Christ's sake, right through high school—a fact that Sean never lets me live down. I'd never admit to him that I used to love it. It gives me the same rush I get when we're on stage.

"He can be a handful. Just remember that. You sure you don't want your helmet?"

"Not my first time in the saddle, Davey." He smiles at me and shakes his head as I guide Admiral away from the stables.

"Yeah, but it's your first time in a long time. I'll come looking for you if you're not back in an hour!" he hollers. Glancing over my shoulder, I give him a wave and push Admiral into a gallop.

I'm a little rusty, but it all comes back easily. Admiral isn't as young or as fast as he used to be, but he's sired more than one champion racehorse in his day and proves it by picking up speed while I guide him down one of the familiar paths that leads to the river.

Getting lost out here was something I loved. A place where I didn't have my mother breathing down my neck. Kat and I spent countless hours on these paths, talking about everything and nothing. Then there were times when I just came out here to be by myself, where the expectations of being a Chapman were lost, if only for a little while.

These days the expectations are wildly different. There are times where I wonder if I'm getting too old for it all. With Kennedy and Matt settling into a groove with their girlfriends, things are changing in the band. I've never given an actual relationship a second thought. It just hasn't been on my radar.

It wasn't for either of them, but to quote one of Sean's famous Murphy's laws, it's the things you don't expect that turn your life upside down.

I sure as hell didn't expect to be blown away last night. Maybe that has more to do with the ridiculous bet I made with Matty. No sex through the entire month of December. What kind of an idiot am I to take a bet like that? It's going to be a long month.

Sliding from the saddle, I lead Admiral over to the riverbank, letting him get a drink. The river hasn't frozen over yet, but it will soon. I can still see us all playing hockey out here in the middle of winter, and Kat scoring on Nathan for the first time, much to his horror. My siblings may be pains in the ass, but those are memories we'll have for a lifetime.

I wonder what kind of memories my mystery woman has. She seemed guarded, on edge, and that doesn't sit well with me. I'm not going to get the answers from my mother or the maestro, that much is clear, but the thought of seeing her today has me keyed up.

Pulling my phone from my jacket pocket, I scroll through and find Tucker Pearson's number. Our head of security knows things about the band no one else could even dream up. If anyone can shed some light on a mystery, it's him. It only takes two rings before I hear his tired voice.

"What's wrong?" he mumbles.

"What makes you think there's something wrong?"

"Because it's six-goddamn-thirty in the morning."

"Shit. Sorry, man, I'm on eastern time."

"Yeah? Well, some of us aren't." I hear rustling in the background and a woman's faint voice.

"Well, well, well. Do I hear what I think I hear?" My eyes sweep across the open field. There are a few clouds hanging heavy in the distance, threatening to drop the first snowfall of the year.

"Shut up. You hear nothing, got it? She's important, and I won't have any of you ruining it."

"My lips are sealed." Tucker has a girlfriend. Who knew? I guess things are changing for everyone these days.

"So, what has you dragging my ass out of bed at this fucking hour of the morning?" Tucker grumbles and I can almost see his scowl.

"You're good at finding out about people."

"This is true. Wait, what did you do?" he asks warily.

"Nothing." I try not to sound defensive.

"Yet."

I let out a sigh, shaking my head. "Yet."

"Who is she?"

"That's the million-dollar question."

"You've got to give me something to go on, man. I can't help you if you don't give me details."

I feel Admiral nudge me in the back, and I turn to run my hand over his muzzle. "Shit. I don't know about this now."

"If you've woken me up for nothing, so help me, Cam, I will kick your ass the next time I see you."

Looking up to the graying sky, I question my sanity before blurting out, "Her name is Sam. She plays violin at the center my parents fund in Boston."

Silence from Tucker before his voice comes through again. "That's it? No last name, no description? Nothing?"

"It's not like I gave her a physical, Tucker."

"Was she tall, short, what color of hair? What kind of a car was she driving? Do you know where she lives? Give me something here."

"Probably a foot shorter than me. Wavy red hair—not like fire-engine red, more auburn." I hear him chuckle. "She has freckles, green eyes, and she's slim. I didn't see a car. She took off before I could get anything else out of her."

He lets out a huff of frustration. "That's not a whole hell of a lot to go on."

"Actually, one more thing. She has a kid. At least, she said she did."

"Oh fuck."

"Yeah. Oh fuck." Rubbing my hand across the back of my neck, I feel a wave of guilt roll over me. I shouldn't be doing this. I know next to nothing about this woman, and getting Tucker involved feels wrong now. "You know what? Forget I called you."

"Are you fucking kidding me right now?"

"Sorry, Tuck. Call it momentary insanity." I feel the wind pick up across the river.

"I'm so kicking your ass next time I see you," he growls.

DROPPING INTO AN AISLE SEAT at the back of the theater feels foreign. I'm used to being either on the stage or in the coveted box seats. I spot Sam easily, trying to conceal herself again in the second row, that thick red hair giving away her otherwise hidden position.

Just like last night, it's impossible for me not to focus on her with each pull of the bow across the strings and the intensity of her playing; it's captivating. It's obvious she's been doing this for a long time, and she's very good.

Maestro Hoffmann, however, isn't in a good mood, although from what I know about him, that's not unusual. After an illustrious career leading several of the best symphonies in Europe, he's chosen to spend part of his retirement helping out my mother by conducting this, one of the best community orchestras in Boston.

He commands the orchestra to stop, and then he's ranting away, his thick accent bellowing through the theater. His shocking white hair is a mess, sticking up in every direction, and he's panting like he's just run a marathon. You can't knock the guy for being passionate. He shouts a series of words in German, berating some poor trumpeter's lack of timing.

"It's D major, yes? The trumpets should be grand and royal! Not whatever that was!" He hollers more in German as the trumpet player cowers in shame.

"Jordan!" he barks, turning his attention to the string section. "Much better in the second transition. You too, Samantha." I perk up, leaning forward to try to catch a better glimpse of her. She's planted herself out of view, shrouded in mystery again. "Try relaxing, yes? The violin is . . . how do you say? A part of you. Breathe with it. I know you know how to do this." Maestro flails his arms around before letting out an exasperated huff.

"Enough for the day. Come prepared tomorrow or do not come at all!" While Maestro mutters to himself, I watch the orchestra gather their sheet music and a few instrument cases and start to file out in a chorus of hushed whispers. I can see her deliberately move into the fold, her head bowed, hiding that beautiful face almost like she wants to get lost in the crowd. And despite the red flags that tell me pursuing her is an epically bad idea, I know that's exactly what I'm going to do.

♪ ♩ ♪ ♩

## *samantha*

OUR HEELS ECHO IN THE narrow, whitewashed hallway that leads back to the staff areas. "Crabby bastard," Olivia mutters and hikes the strap to her cello case higher on her shoulder. I giggle and shake my head. The good maestro was in rare form today.

"Do you think he realizes that some of us don't speak German?" She waves her hand in irritation.

"I don't think he cares." She huffs in response and follows me into the locker area. I retrieve my bag and look at her in surprise as she locks her case in one of the cello-sized compartments. "Aren't you taking your beast home?"

"Some of us are going across the street for lunch first. You should come with us." She plucks a lipstick from her purse and skillfully applies it without needing a mirror. I couldn't do that in my wildest dreams. "Come on, Sam. You deserve a little fun.

Jacques is going to be there." She's been trying to set me up with the new harpist for a month.

"Thanks, but I'm not hungry." It's a lie, but it's easier than explaining I spent my spare cash for the week on a new pair of winter boots for Hannah. She's at that age where she seems to grow into a new size overnight. "Besides, I've reserved one of the practice rooms. I want to get some time in while Hannah is occupied." One of the godsends about this place is the day care next door. It's another one of the Chapman-sponsored gifts to the arts; musicians can leave their children there at no cost during rehearsals and performances. The day care is also open to others at an extremely reduced cost, but musicians' children have priority. As with other Chapman facilities, it's state-of-the-art—the staff is incredible, the curriculum is stimulating for all ages, and there's even a full-time nurse on site. It's a relief knowing Hannah is safe and well cared for while I'm here. Otherwise, I don't know how I'd make it work.

Olivia's eyes light up. "You *are* going to audition for first chair, aren't you? I knew it!"

Our aging concertmaster, Ivan, is retiring, and auditions for his coveted spot are being held next month. "Don't be ridiculous," I blurt, holding a hand up to stop her, but she isn't deterred easily.

"You could have that spot in a heartbeat, Sam." She gives me a look. "I *know* you're good enough." I usually try to pick times when most people are gone when I practice so I can really let loose. Unfortunately, Olivia surprised me one day, and she hasn't shut up about it since.

"I'm perfectly happy where I am." I give her a breezy smile. "Besides, Albert wants it; he's been sucking up to Hoffmann for months." She shrugs and lets me off the hook . . . for now.

"Aw, come on. Being called concert*mistress* would be so hot."

We laugh and I sling the straps of my tote over my shoulder before grabbing my violin case again.

"I'll see you tomorrow. Have fun at lunch."

"I will. I'll tell Jacques that you were pumping me for information about him." She laughs when I roll my eyes at her joke and give her a wave before quickly making my way past the other musicians and various staffers, keeping my head down. Lively chatter fills the halls of people making plans to get together or comparing notes about the rehearsal. Truth is, I wish I could go with Olivia and the others. It's been forever since I allowed myself to relax and do something on the spur of the moment. Sometimes I miss the days of having a little disposable income.

I give my head a quick shake. Someday, we'll be able to stop running, and Hannah and I will be able to have a normal life with friends, lunch dates, and not having to scrimp for every penny. Until then, keeping my daughter safe is worth any sacrifice. Tucking my disappointment away, I take the stairs to the third floor, and the babble fades away. I emerge into a long hallway lined with doors. Most of the rooms have only chairs, but a few have spinets and two boast grands. I've reserved one of the small rooms on the end.

Soon, I'm lost in Beethoven's violin concerto. The soaring melody soothes me like nothing else, and everything—money troubles, a grumbling tummy, and psychotic exes—disappears. It's a place where no one can touch me. It's just me and the music; my favorite place to be.

Olivia's right. I could easily compete for first chair. It's a position I've held before, and I loved it. It's a daunting role, being the intermediary between the orchestra and the conductor, but I relished the challenge and was successful. Being concertmistress also brings public attention—attention I can't afford. Ray may not recognize my name now, but all it would take is one photo or some write-up referring to the "red-headed concertmistress" and he'd be here in a flash to check it out.

So I rein myself in, play below my ability, and stay in the second tier. It's fine. I like my section mates, and we get along well.

It's safer this way.

A sharp knock startles me, and I screech to a stop—literally—as the bow scrapes across the strings. "Sorry, baby," I murmur to my instrument and turn, expecting to see Olivia's face at the tiny window in the door.

It's not Olivia.

A mass of butterflies let loose in my stomach. "Mr . . . Mr. Chapman? What are you doing here?" A delightful wave of warm leather and spice blasts me as he steps inside without waiting for an invite, and I stare in shock at his presence and his audacity. He's so tall, he actually has to duck to enter the small room. His beautiful hazel eyes seem greener today, picking up the dark forest color of his sweater. He shrugs out of his worn bomber jacket and sweeps a hand through his hair.

"Call me Cam. I, I thought you might be hungry," he says, setting a large sack on one of the chairs. I blink up at him.

"You brought me lunch?" I ask dumbly, looking between him and the bag. He chuckles.

"Sure. Why not? It's lunchtime." He slings his jacket around another chair and sits, gesturing for me to do the same. Numb, I sink into the opposite chair, holding my violin and bow loosely in my lap. "It's just lunch, Sam," he says mildly, as if I'm a skittish colt he's trying to tame. "Your name is Sam, yes?"

"Yes . . . Wait. How did you know my name?" I look at him sharply, alarmed, despite his warm smile.

"Your friend called you Sam last night so I assume that's your name. Unless it's some kind of super-secret code name or something."

Relief eases my tense shoulders and I smile in spite of myself.

"Hmm, okay, but—wait. Stop! I didn't say I'd eat with you . . ." He ignores me and pulls items out of the sack and sets them on another chair.

"Are you saying you aren't hungry?" My stomach chooses that moment to let loose a growl that would put Sasquatch to shame. He hands me a bottle of water, seemingly ignoring my steadily heating face. "I didn't know what you'd like, so I got a turkey sandwich, roast beef, and . . . oh, this is a piece of vegetarian quiche." He points as he identifies each wrapped item.

He pulls the chair with the food between us as a makeshift table. I clutch my instrument to my chest and glance at the window, halfway expecting to see one of the center's staffers. "But we're not allowed to have food up here," I argue weakly, the tempting aroma of the warm quiche wearing down my resolve. Suddenly, the carrot and celery sticks I packed for my lunch have lost their appeal.

"Don't worry. I have an in with the staff." He winks at me, and I can't help my giggle. Not knowing what else to do, I set my violin and bow into the open case on the floor and open my bottle of water. Taking a drink, I hum in gratitude; I didn't realize how thirsty I was.

"Thank you. So . . . *Chapman* . . ." I muse. Against my better judgment, I take the cardboard container of quiche and plastic fork he hands me. "Is that why you have an 'in' with the staff? You're connected to the Chapman family?" Despite the gorgeous image he struck last night in his suit, I can't quite picture him with the stuffy Chapman family. I've seen Mr. and Mrs. Chapman at a distance during a few of our rehearsals. The rest of the family is a bit of a mystery. I know there are four siblings in the Chapman family, but they're never at the arts center. The elder Chapmans are the epitome of high class and old money. Designer clothing, noses in the air, and not a hair out of place. With his heavy black boots, speckled hair, and roguish demeanor, he looks more like the disreputable cousin no one talks about.

It's my turn to be evaluated, as he cocks his head to the side and watches me, a mixture of wonder and doubt on his face. Then his smile returns and he nods. "I'm a distant relation," he says, and then takes a healthy bite out of the roast beef sandwich. He makes a startled noise and sniffs, his eyes watering. "Strong horseradish," he explains, awkwardly trying to cover his mouth as he chews and talks. "Sorry."

I chuckle and wave off his apology as he gives me a sheepish smile. The quiche is delicious, and I have to keep myself from inhaling it. "You play beautifully," he offers, drawing my eyes back to his.

"Oh, thank you." I feel my blush spread across my cheeks. "Do you like classical music? I suppose you must, considering you were here last night."

The corner of his mouth twitches in amusement. "I like all kinds of music. I grew up around classical, but I enjoy jazz, folk . . . and rock."

I hum in acknowledgement and take another bite, feeling the weight of his eyes on me. It feels like I'm being evaluated, but not in the mean-spirited way I'm used to. It's more like he's expecting me to say or do something. It's unnerving.

"So, is that a fashion statement or is your hair naturally that spotty?" I clap a hand over my mouth. I can't believe I said that. His eyes shoot open, and instead of the anger I expect, he laughs.

"I lost a bet," he says ruefully, rubbing a hand over his head. "It's almost grown out, thank God. This is an improvement—I looked like Billy Idol for a couple months. It was hideous."

"I'm sorry—it's not that bad." I instinctively reach out and touch his hand in apology. His skin is warm, and I jerk my hand back as if I've been burned; I peek up to find his eyes sparkling with mirth. "I shouldn't have said anything," I babble, feeling exposed under that tantalizing gaze.

"No worries." He takes a deep breath. "Is Sam short for Samantha?" At my cautious nod, he continues, "Samantha . . . ?"

At this point, I suppose, it would seem odd if I didn't tell him. "McKenzie. Samantha McKenzie."

He holds out his hand, which I automatically take. My hand practically disappears in his much larger one. "Nice to meet you, Samantha McKenzie."

"Likewise." He's not letting go, but the extended contact doesn't feel awkward. In fact, it's rather nice.

"So, where are you from, Samantha McKenzie? I'm not hearing a Boston accent."

His thumb starts a slow, rhythmic circle over the back of my hand, and I can't look away from his gaze. "Um . . . the Midwest." A fresh wave of apprehension rolls over me. *What am I doing?* He can't know where I'm from. No one can.

"Well, that narrows it down." His smile is teasing. "The Midwest's loss is Boston's gain." His words wash over me like a warm caress, and I feel my heart pick up.

The ringing of my phone startles us apart. I immediately excuse myself and tug it out of my jeans pocket. He frowns in confusion at the ancient device as I flip it open and answer.

"Ms. McKenzie? It's Holly at the day care. Can you come, please? Hannah woke up from her nap with a nightmare and she's inconsolable, the poor dear."

"Yes, of course! I'll be right there." I snap the phone closed and jump to my feet, gathering my trash and throwing it into the corner trashcan. When I turn back, he's standing and looking at me with dismay. "I'm sorry, I have to go. My daughter needs me."

Not wanting to see his recoil at the mention of Hannah, I

stoop to secure my instrument in its case and shrug on my coat. "Thank you for lunch. It was very sweet of you." Keeping my eyes down, I'm aware of him hastily throwing things back in the lunch sack. I know I'm being rude, but I can't stop my feet from moving. I skirt around him as he's struggling to disentangle his jacket from the chair and jog down the hallway to the stairs. When my feet hit the bottom landing, I can hear him above me calling my name, but I don't stop. I fly through the labyrinth of backstage hallways, leaving him far behind. As it should be.

"AW, BABY, DON'T CRY. MOMMA'S here," I croon, gathering my sniveling daughter in my lap. Hannah wraps her arms around my neck and takes a shuddering breath, already calming down. Holly looks down at us with a sympathetic smile. She's one of the day care staffers and Hannah's favorite.

"She woke up screaming about 'the scary man.'" She rubs her hand on Hannah's back. "We tried to calm her down, but sometimes Mommy is the best thing."

"That's okay. I'm glad you called me. She's had trouble sleeping the last few nights, but I thought it was just the wind we've had this week." I smooth Hannah's soft hair away from her forehead and press a kiss to her silky skin. "There, baby. Are you feeling better?"

"Was the scary man, Momma." She sniffs, her little voice still trembling a bit. "He was after us. He took Josie, and I couldn't get her."

I swallow, my heart sinking. I hoped she'd forgotten, but I should know better. Hannah is a bright, perceptive four-year-old, and despite my attempts to shield her from the realities of our present, I can't erase our past.

"It was just a dream, sweetie. The scary man is gone." After a few minutes, Hannah has calmed enough to put on her coat and retrieve Josie, the battered rag doll she takes everywhere with her. Holding Josie in a death grip, she allows me to tug on her knit hat with the silly pom-pom on top. It makes Hannah look like a bobblehead, but she loves it.

"Thanks, Holly. We'll be back tomorrow." I lead Hannah by the hand toward the front of the building. Holly nods as she walks along with me to the lobby, but comes to a sudden halt, staring past me in shock. I turn and follow her gaze . . . and my mouth drops open.

"Is your daughter all right? I was worried, since you looked so upset when you left."

I clamp my mouth shut, swallowing my disbelief. "Yes, yes she is. Thank you." The persistent Mr. Chapman shuffles from foot to foot by the front door, looking supremely uncomfortable. But he doesn't leave, and waits patiently while I say my good-byes to the frozen Holly, who can't seem to stop staring at the scruff on his chiseled jaw. I can't really blame her.

He holds the doors for us, and once we're outside, I tug on my own knit hat and swing Hannah into my arms to center myself. Her nightmare forgotten, she's looking up at our tall escort. "Hi. My name's Hannah. I'm four," she chirps with her usual forthrightness. "What's your name?"

He stifles a laugh. "My name's Cam. It's nice to meet you, Hannah," he rumbles, his deep voice making her smile.

"You're really tall! Do you play baskeeball?" This time, he laughs freely.

"No, but I play guitar. Is that okay?"

Hannah nods, making the pom-pom on her hat dance. "It's basketball, sweetie." I tug her cap back in place and head for the corner. "I'm sorry, but I think I need to get her home."

"Let me drive you." He motions up the street, but I shake my head.

"No!" He freezes, looking at me in consternation, and I take a breath. "No, that's quite all right," I say more calmly and gesture toward the transit station across the street. "We'll be fine on the bus." Accepting lunch is one thing, but there's no way I'm letting him know where I live. A frown ghosts across his lips, but he nods in acceptance. The light changes and I start across the street, surprised when he continues to walk with us.

"Can I see you again?" I look at him sharply, surprised to see a faint blush on his cheeks. He rubs the back of his neck. "I mean, can I take you to a proper lunch, or even dinner after your next rehearsal?"

A few other people are standing at the stop, hunched deep in their coats against the winter breeze, their attention on their phones. He looks at them warily before turning to face me again.

"I'm not sure," I answer, flummoxed by his attention. I fully expected him to disappear after I mentioned my daughter again and left him upstairs. But here he is, looking hopeful and handsome. "Look, Mr. Chapman . . ."

"His name is *Cam*, Momma." Hannah says his name like it's second nature and holds her doll out for his inspection. "This is Josie. She's my baby."

"Hello, Josie," he says, giving Hannah a wink. "You're as pretty as your momma." Hannah giggles and buries her face against my neck. I roll my eyes and set my wiggly daughter back down, taking her hand. She's staring up at Cameron like he's her new best friend.

His eyes lock onto mine, and he reaches out to move a lock of hair that had blown into my face with a gust of wind. The intimate gesture makes my knees weak. "I don't . . . I mean, I can't . . ." A screech of brakes announces the bus's arrival, and I automatically steer Hannah to join the line of people shuffling toward the door.

"Samantha," he huffs in frustration. "At least take this." He hands me the bag from lunch. "It's the turkey sandwich and a banana. Maybe Hannah can have it for a snack?"

"Thank you." I look up into his eyes, and he frowns. "I'm sorry. Maybe I'll see you later." It's all I can offer him, and I hate it.

He purses his lips, looking confounded. "I hope so," he says simply and steps back as we mount the steps and the doors close behind us. I find a seat for us as the bus pulls away. Once Hannah is settled, I look out the window, trying to catch a last glimpse of him; a lonely figure shoving his hands in his pockets and hunching against the chill.

# chapter three

## cameron

I RUN MY HAND THROUGH my hair in frustration as the bus pulls away, leaving a cloud of exhaust in its wake. Staring up at the signs that line the sidewalk along the bus stop, I think they might as well be in Greek. Just a maze of lines and random stops. I have no fucking idea where she's going.

I hate this feeling of being out of control. Worse, I hate the feeling of her slipping away again just when I'm starting to get to know her. Seems like she can't get away from me fast enough. The night of the symphony, today at lunch, and now she's gone, only leaving me wanting more. "Fuck."

"Miss your bus, son?" I turn to the sound of the raspy voice, an older man with a cane who remains huddled with a smaller group at the stop. "Damn things are never on time," he grumbles.

"Do you know where that one was going?" I ask, and he grins

a little.

"There're probably twenty stops on that route. That bus could've been going anywhere." I scowl at the retreating brake lights as I watch the bus disappear around the corner ahead. She's gone, just like that, leaving me with an uncomfortable feeling in my chest.

"Thanks anyway," I mumble. The man gives me a crooked smile and shuffles off to the next bus that pulls to a stop by the curb.

"Cameron?" There's no mistaking the surprise in my sister's voice. Kat approaches, bundled up in a long, dark coat with a bright yellow scarf wrapped around her neck, looking at me like I've lost my mind. "What the hell are you doing here?"

I meet her at the corner, a cab blurring past as we stop at the curb. "I could ask you the same thing." I get bumped by a few people rushing to the bus stop. Normally, I'm coordinated, senses heightened to my surroundings because I have to be. Now, I feel like I'm in a daze, totally confused by Samantha McKenzie. One minute she seems interested, teasing me about my hair, and the next she's running for the hills with her violin and her *daughter*. I'm used to women wanting one thing and one thing only from me. There are no mixed messages, no confusion. It's sex—quick, dirty, typically forgettable sex. In the space of an afternoon, I know Sam is someone I'm not going to be forgetting any time soon, and I haven't even touched her yet. *Yet.*

That addictive feeling of anticipation isn't one I'm used to when it comes to women, but it courses through me when I think about Sam. Typically, women want one thing from me. They're happy to go tweet their backstage quickie and move on to the next. We both leave satisfied, but it also feels shallow.

"Ah, I'm on my way to work."

Chuckling, I tug on the ends of Kat's ridiculous scarf. The thing is a mess. It looks like she made it herself. "Sure. *Work.*" I don't think Kat has ever worked a day in her life. Sure, she coordinates the volunteers at the arts center during events, and helps out at the fundraisers, but an actual job? I don't think so.

Kat rolls her eyes at me, motioning back to the day care center across the street. "Yeah. The children's center. You know? The one I run?" I look at the building before focusing back on her. "Sometimes I forget how little you know about what goes on in this family." She reaches up and pats me on the head like I'm seven. I swat her hand away.

"*You* run the day care?"

"Surprised?"

"Kind of, not gonna lie."

"It's worse than that—I fund it, on the down-low. More ridiculous Chapman money put to good use. Queen V was appalled when I told her what I'd planned, until she saw the good press." She nudges me in the side. "You know, if you checked in more than once a year, you'd be surprised what you find out."

"No guilt trips. Not from you, Kat."

She knows she's hit a nerve. "Sorry. Bad habit that I learned from the best. But back to you and why you're at the bus stop."

"Wait. If you run the day care, that means you have information." *Stalker.*

She glares at me. "No way. Not in a million years."

"Come on. Help your big brother out." I sling my arm around her shoulder, and she shoves me away.

"Not even for you. We have privacy rules, Cam. Privacy rules I helped write. No way in hell am I giving you or anyone else any info."

"Samantha McKenzie." I've only just learned her name and already I like the way it rolls off my tongue.

Kat's eyes widen. "Hannah's mom? Hell no, Cameron. In fact, do yourself a favor and walk away. Now."

A gust of wind blows down the street, taking my breath. "Why would you say that?"

"When does your tour start up again, hmm?" Kat folds her arms across her chest, an eyebrow cocked.

"After the new year. We have a couple of months, and then we're on a break for a while. Why?"

"You really think it's a good idea to start playing house for a couple weeks just because you're bored?" Leave it to Kat to spew her unfiltered opinion.

"I'm not bored."

"Really? Is that why you're hovering around the bus stop in the freezing cold? Because you're not bored?"

She ignores my frustrated huff. "Kat, it's just an address. That's all I need, and I'll never ask for anything ever again."

She snorts a forced laugh. "How many times have I heard that?" Some regal ringtone bellows, and she pulls her phone from her jacket pocket.

"Hey, Mom." I can't help but laugh. Of course, she's picked the royal march for Queen V herself. "Yeah. He's with me." Kat gives a slow shake of her head as she listens to whatever our mother is ranting on about. Even through the phone, I can hear the annoyed tone in her voice. "We're just down the street. I'll have him there in five."

Dropping the phone back into her pocket, she levels me a warning glare. "Seems as if you're ignoring your phone, and you're late for a meeting with the maestro."

"Shit. I totally forgot about that."

"What exactly are you up to?" Slinging my arm around her shoulder, I steer her back in the direction of the arts center, darting us around the slower moving people on the street.

"Here's a deal. You tell me about Samantha McKenzie, and I'll tell you what I'm up to."

TURNS OUT, THERE'S A BETTER chance at finding life on Saturn than there is getting any information out of my sister. Whatever she knows, she's keeping it locked up, which only serves to amp my curiosity.

The maestro is another matter. Once he got over being offended at me not showing up on time, he was receptive to the idea of me playing with the orchestra. Showing him footage of one of our concerts in Sydney where we played with the symphony sealed the deal.

We spent the afternoon in his disorganized office, arguing about the pieces for the holiday concert. The maestro is stubborn, and at times wildly erratic. He reminds me a bit of Sean if he were thirty years older. He also thinks the sun rises and sets on Bach's *Christmas Oratorio*. "It's tradition. The people, they expect it," he complained, even whining a bit.

"So, live a little, Maestro. You can still do the *Oratorio*. We're just going to rev it up a bit. Give it a new life so to speak."

He threw his arms up in the air, feigning annoyance, but I could also see his excitement. Artistic geniuses love nothing more than pushing the envelope. It's the reason Redfall has been so successful. We don't want to do the same thing over and over again. "Get outside your comfort zone, Maestro. You really want to play Bach the same way again? For the fifteenth season in a row?" I was throwing him a challenge. I know it works with us in the band if we ever feel we're falling into a rut. We push each other to be better, strive to give the fans something they will always remember. It's not any different for the maestro, and in that moment, I know I had him.

"Fine! Come to rehearsal on Wednesday and don't be late. We will see if I permit you to play with us." He shoved a hand through his wild mane of gray hair in exasperation, but I could see the intrigue in his eyes, his mental wheels already turning. I thanked him and pretended to be in awe of the greatness of the master. In some ways, I am. I'll never be able to conduct the way he does. It's daunting to think about. But, playing with the orchestra, pushing them, maybe pushing *Sam* to try something new? That I have no problem with.

Now, I'm finally at my townhouse in Beacon Hill after finishing up with the maestro, and it's time for a check-in with the guys. I love my place here, and as my dad has always taught us, real estate is a good investment. He should know with the number of homes he and my mother own around the globe. A large chunk of my family's portfolio is tied up in real estate.

The townhouse is a three-story historic brownstone building, in a neighborhood lined with brick sidewalks and gaslit lanterns. On nights like this, when the snow is just starting to fall, it almost feels like I've drifted back in time.

After I bought it a couple of years ago, my mother had it redone by some architectural firm that probably cost a small fortune to bring it up to Chapman standards. The neighbors, whom I rarely see, leave me alone, even when I decide to play the guitar on the back patio, which is probably the best part about this place.

"How's the Chapman mansion and all your minions?" Sean Murphy, our drummer, looks exhausted as we wait on video chat for Kennedy and Matt to join us. Dark shadows hover under his eyes, and he lets out an exaggerated yawn. Sean's in his beloved London for the holidays. If the Brit had his way, we'd tour the U.K.

and only the U.K. all year long.

"Good as always. How's the family? Has Sydney set a wedding date yet?" He scowls at my question, which is why I asked it. We like to wind each other up. Sean's twin sister Sydney's engagement hasn't gone over well. Her first husband—who had been one of Sean's best mates—was killed several years ago during his last tour of duty in the Middle East. It was a tough time; we helped support Sean through it while he supported his sister. Sydney's fabulous, and we all knew that eventually she'd find someone else. Sean did too, but his protectiveness of her has tripled since it all happened. I don't think anyone would be good enough in his eyes for Syd now. He needs to get over that.

"Have I mentioned how much I dislike that twit?" He takes a sip from a Union Jack mug. Poor guy. I almost feel bad about him being awake at two a.m. London time.

"A time or two. But there's nothing you can do about it. Syd's in love."

"Fucking love sucks. Thank fuck you're still with me in singlehood. Kennedy and Matty are sadly lost in the vortex of love."

Laughing hard, I shake my head. "The *vortex of love*? Is this another one of Murphy's laws?" Over the years, Sean has spewed his special brand of advice on life and love to the point where we've started calling his little tidbits Murphy's laws.

"It sucks you in, mate. Deep. Twists you up and spins you 'round until you can't see straight. It's a fucking vortex you'll never get out of."

I grin back at the screen. "We should write a song about it."

Sean rolls his eyes as Kennedy comes into view in the chat window. He's sitting at his grand piano in his house at Bodega Bay. "What are we writing about?"

"The vortex of love," I deadpan.

Kennedy laughs. "Another one of your laws, Sean? Did somebody finally get to you?"

"Shut it. And hell no. That's the way I intend to keep it. Single is fewer hassles."

"Sure. That's what they all say," I chime in.

Kennedy starts singing, adding a country twang to his voice. *"I was minding my own business, swinging high from above, until you pulled me under into the vortex of love."*

"What the fuck am I hearing?" Matt shakes his head as he joins the video chat. "Are we doing a country album now?"

Sean flips us all off. "Grasshopper, welcome to the shit-show. You're late. Busy with the lovely Tess?"

Matt grins, rubbing the back of his neck. "She's here. Come say hi, Cardinal."

Tess appears behind Matt, giving a wave to the camera. She's got her long, black hair pulled back into one of those high ponytails, and she's grinning ear to ear as she drapes an arm over Matt's shoulder. Matty and Tess have been together for over a year now, living together at his place in San Francisco. "Hey, guys. We miss you."

"Don't lie to them. That's not nice," Matt says with a smirk, and Tess gives him a playful smack to his chest.

"Of course we miss you. Don't listen to him," Tess says into the camera.

"As if we'd start now," Sean replies.

"I'll leave you to it." Tess gives us a wave. "Talk to you guys before Christmas."

Matt watches Tess walk away before turning back to his webcam.

"See?" Sean says. "Matty's stuck in the vortex. Can't focus to save his life."

"I can totally focus. I'm here, aren't I?"

"Why are we here, out of curiosity? You know it's the middle of the bloody night, right?" Sean asks, giving his chair a spin. The man never sits still.

"It's time for our check-in, genius, and I've got news."

"Everything okay?" Kennedy frowns. Fuck, it still kills me that I disappointed them. But, through some sort of miracle, they stuck by me through rehab. I'm not sure most people would have. My own family threatened to disown me if I didn't get my shit together. Not the guys. They were right there, supporting me. Outside of Kat, the rest of the family was more worried about the bad press than they were about me. At least that's the way it felt.

"Yeah. I'm good. I'm going to be doing a concert with the symphony here. The holiday series is coming up."

"Is this just something for you, or did you want us to head out for it?" Kennedy asks.

"You'd do that?" I say, a little surprised. We're off for the holidays, in part to get away from each other.

"Sure, if we can make it work. I'll have to check with Abby on what the plan is."

"Vortex victim," Sean whispers. "I'll be there, mate, if you want. Time away from my future arse of a brother-in-law might be a good thing."

"I'll have to—"

"Check with Tess. Blah, blah, blah," Sean finishes Matt's sentence. "Of course you will because the women rule the roost, yes?"

"Don't be a jackass," Matt fires back at him, flipping him off in the process.

"Hey, it's not a big deal, guys," I tell them. "If you can't make it, no problem. It's not like it's TD Garden or something. It's a holiday concert for the Boston socialites. The place holds a thousand people, tops."

"We could at least make a vacation out of it. Maybe go skiing in Vermont," Matt suggests, ignoring me completely.

"Now you're talking, Grasshopper. Bring on the ski bunnies!" Sean roars, rubbing his hands together. "I've never skied before. It's on my list."

"Shocking. We'll get you lessons—you know, on the bunny hill?" I chuckle at Kennedy's smug grin.

Sean leans closer to the webcam. "Why do I get the feeling that means something different than I imagine?"

"Resorts might be sold out this close to Christmas," Matt says. "We should get Nic to take a look."

I shake my head at Matt's offer. "No need to. We have a chalet there."

"Well, look at you, Mr. Moneybags. A chalet in Vermont. La-dee-da," Sean mocks, raising his pinky as he takes another sip from the mug.

"Will it hold us all?" Matt asks.

"Maybe not the Brit's ego, but everyone else? No problem. There're seventeen rooms."

"Jesus. You have got to be kidding me," Matt says, his eyes widening. "*Seventeen?*"

"I remember that place. We stopped in during that first couple of months before we met up with these two." Kennedy grins. I get a flashback of us at barely twenty, hitchhiking across the country in search of the ultimate bandmates. It's lucky we made it back to California in one piece. We've come a long way since then.

"That we did. It's got outdoor hot tubs, fireplaces, too. You get the picture." I shut up, not wanting to sound like I'm bragging. In all our travels together, we've rarely used one the family properties, but the chalet makes sense if they want to make a trip out of it. It's remote and away from the prying eyes of the paparazzi, something

I know all four of us desperately look for now. Plus, seeing the Brit try to learn to ski is something I'd pay money to watch.

"Sounds pretty damn sweet," Matt replies. "When's the concert?"

"The week of the fifteenth. But, I still have to pass the maestro's inspection."

Kennedy laughs. "Think you'll make the cut?"

"Fuck off, and I hope so. I'll text you with the details."

"Solid plan there. Now, let's talk about the epic bachelor party I have to plan for my soon-to-be brother-in-law," Sean says with an annoyed groan.

Kennedy's eyes widen. "I thought you didn't like him."

"I don't. But I figure if I plan it, at least I know it will be legendary. Leave it up to his boring lot, and we'll likely be playing with his *Star Wars* figurines in his parents' basement."

A FEW HOURS LATER, I'M playing my Les Paul, breathing new life into every single classical Christmas track I can find. This is something I know I'm good at. I've studied some footage of the maestro's past concerts, trying to learn his style, where he likes to push his orchestra, but he's almost impossible to figure out. Just when I think I know where he's leading them, he changes it up, doing the unexpected. It makes me even more impressed with how talented the orchestra has to be to keep up with him.

My thoughts drift back to Sam. Having heard her play, I know she's got the talent to be a principal violinist; I'm just not sure why she's not. There's no way the maestro has missed how beautifully she plays. It makes me wonder if she asked to be put in the second string.

Maybe it's a confidence thing. Thinking back to how she hid from the audience during the standing ovation, and how she ducked into the bus earlier today, part of me thinks she's shy. But, then at lunch, I saw little glimpses of something else: a determined, driven, caring woman. That woman wasn't reserved or unsure of herself. That's the woman I want to get to know. The one who doesn't seem to know who I am. Maybe that's why I can't get her out of my head.

♪ ♩ ♪ ♩

## *samantha*

HOLDING HANNAH'S HAND TIGHTLY, I hustle her down our street to the bus stop, arriving just in time. She's clutching her doll in the other hand and singing one of her made-up masterpieces to herself. I recognize the tune as Mozart, but the lyrics are pure Hannah.

*"The puppy has spots, but he don't miiiiiind,"* she sings, bringing a smile to the bus driver's face as we climb on. He seems to be one of the kind ones, thank God. The driver last night wasn't as enamored with my daughter's talent.

"That's nice, sweetie, but use your inside voice, okay?" I ask as we find our seats. She nods and switches to humming, playing with Josie in her lap. I'm blessed to have a sweet-natured and mostly compliant daughter. Not to say she can't throw a tantrum with the best of them, but they're rare. I suppose she's had to learn to go with the flow, considering our transient life the last few years. I'd give anything to be able to put down roots somewhere, for both our sakes, but I don't see it happening anytime soon.

Not until I'm sure Ray's given up. *If* he ever gives up.

I look out the window over Hannah's head, watching the parade of storefronts, brownstones, and schools go by. I like Boston. Chicago was nice too, but I love the history here. I love being able to walk past something modern like Starbucks and then see a plaque on a corner church with a date of 1746. I love walking Hannah through the Commons and explaining the historic figures immortalized in statues. The Boston Children's Museum on one-dollar Fridays is always a surefire hit with her, as is the Franklin Park Zoo. There are myriad kid-friendly things we can do here to expand her world, even on our limited budget.

Speaking of Boston attractions, my thoughts turn for the fifty millionth time to the baffling Mr. Chapman. Shaking my head in confusion, I tuck a renegade strand of hair back under my knit cap. What's his game? He doesn't strike me as the type of man looking for an instant family. There's a strength and confidence about him that's captivating. He's sure of himself, but not in a conceited way. I know the difference now. And, based on Holly's hungry gaze in the day care lobby, I'm sure he's not lacking in female companionship. But I can't deny it; the man is definitely interested. He brought me lunch, completely out of the blue, even hunting me down in the practice rooms to do it, wanting nothing in return. Ray only did nice things for me when he wanted something, or when there were other people around to impress.

I tap the violin case on my lap as I consider the options. Maybe he didn't believe me when I'd first mentioned Hannah and followed me to the day care to see if I was telling the truth. But even once he knew I wasn't just making her up to have an excuse to ditch him, he didn't bail. In fact, he tried to make her smile and laugh. I suppose he could have done it to get in my good graces, but it didn't feel like that. Ray was never interested in Hannah. He didn't want her in the first place and blamed me for getting pregnant. Asshole.

I banish thoughts of my ex with a blink and concentrate on how it felt when Cameron held my hand. A warm flush steals over my cheeks, and I find that I'm running a finger over my lips. Embarrassed, I jerk my hand away from my mouth and stuff it in my pocket. *Stop it, Sam.* There's no good that can come of this.

My heart aches a little as I recall the confusion I saw in his gorgeous hazel eyes. I hated to leave him that way at the bus stop yesterday, but I didn't have a choice. It wouldn't be fair to encourage him. There's no way I can get involved with anyone now. But a tiny part of me also knows that if I thought I'd have even a whisper of a chance of putting down roots with the owner of those eyes, I'd jump at it . . . asshole ex-husband or no.

The bus lurches to a stop, and I'm startled to see we've arrived. "Come on, sweetie." I maneuver my daughter down the aisle. Once on the sidewalk, I ensure Hannah's hat is on firmly and her coat is zipped before we head down the street. She skips alongside of me, her exuberance bringing a smile to my face.

"Momma? Do you think Santa will be able to find us this year?"

My heart stops for a second at her innocent question. "Yes, sweetie, of course he will. Santa knows where all children live."

She nods, satisfied. "Good. Do you think he got my letter about the Hannah doll?"

I plaster on a bright smile despite the misgivings fluttering in my belly. "I'm sure he did. But there were other things on your list besides the doll, weren't there? He might not have room in his pack for everything." Hannah has been obsessed with the American Girl doll one of the more well-off little girls brought to the day care not long after we moved here. In fact, a good portion of the fees I earned from the violin lessons I gave last night and this morning went into a small jar hidden in my closet just for that purpose. But the damn things cost more than a hundred dollars just for the doll itself. Add clothes and other accessories, and you could spend five hundred dollars easy.

I almost have enough for the doll that looks like Hannah, with her blue eyes and red-blond hair. If I can squeeze in a few more lessons, I might be able to do it for Christmas. I sigh and help Hannah over a pile of slush at the curb. Actually, I'll also probably have to perform for a few hours in the Commons for tips next weekend if it doesn't snow again. She'll have to be content with the outfit it comes with for the first year. Maybe I can get her more next year.

We enter the day care, and I let out a grateful sigh at the rush of warm air wafting over my face. It's truly a cold one today. "Hi, Hannah!" I wave at Kat, who's walking over with a huge smile for my daughter. "Hello, Sam," she says to me, as I help Hannah off with her coat and hat. As soon as she's free, she tears over to her friends with only a hastily blown kiss in my direction.

"Bye, Hannah. Have fun, Hannah," I mutter with a roll of my eyes. "Sure, see you around, Mom."

Kat laughs. "They're all like that at this age. At least she let you take off her coat." She takes the hat and coat in question from me and hangs it on one of the small pegs next to the door. "How are you? We haven't had much time to chat lately. Maestro must have scheduled an extra rehearsal today; I didn't think there were any on the books until Monday." Kat is one of the few people here who know my situation. As humiliating as it was, I had to tell her about Ray and the restraining order. He's violated it before, and I wouldn't put it past him to snatch Hannah to get to me. She's my weak link. I would do anything for her . . . and he knows it.

"Yes, although why he thinks we need extra work on the *Oratorio* is beyond me." I shrug. "But I gave up questioning the motives of übercontrol-freaky conductors years ago." She laughs again, and this time I join in.

Kat was—is—wonderful about my situation. The day care center is truly one of the places I feel safest about leaving my daughter. It has a state-of-the-art security system complete with cameras and impeccable confidentiality protocols. Kat Pierce is the manager, but she also takes time to get to know and play with the kids. She knows their parents too, since many of them are involved with the arts center as performers, stagehands, or staff.

We've enjoyed a few cups of coffee in the café across the street in the last few months. I enjoy her quirky style and carefree attitude. But for all her quirkiness, she's incredibly serious about the kids. She also respects my privacy, taking only what I feel comfortable divulging.

Her eyes travel past me toward the window and her smile dims. I turn to see what she saw, but there's just cars passing by.

"What?"

She waves a hand, stifling a secret smile. "Oh, I just thought I saw my brother."

"You have a brother?" She's never mentioned it; she doesn't really talk about her family at all, besides her girlfriends.

"I have three. It really sucks to be youngest sometimes." Her contemplative look is back, although this time I have the disconcerting notion it's directed at me. "What time is your rehearsal?"

That snaps me back to reality. "Now!" I swirl around, heading for the door. "Sorry, Kat." She merely smiles and waves me off.

I hate being late.

"SAM! WHERE HAVE YOU BEEN?" Olivia grabs my hand and pulls me into a doorway out of the rush of bodies heading toward the stage.

"What? I'm only a few minutes late." I sweep my hair back over my shoulder in agitation. "We haven't even taken the stage yet."

"Hoffman's on a tear. Something must be going on," Olivia whispers as we take our places, Olivia over with the other cellists, and I with my second-stringers. I say hello to my neighbors, Peter and Susan, and begin some last-minute tuning. It only takes a few seconds, but I fiddle with my tuning pegs anyway, making sure it's perfect. I look up when Ivan stands to run us through warm-ups, in preparation for Hoffmann. As with most conductors, the man himself would never deign to preside over tuning. After several minutes, Ivan deems us ready and takes his place. While waiting for Hoffman, Ivan goes over some scheduling announcements that I listen to with half an ear. I can't help but scan the back rows of the audience seating, wondering if someone tall and mysterious is lurking in the shadows.

I have no idea what Cameron does for a living, but both of our interactions have started here. Based on his last name and the stunning suit he wore the first night, he must have attended the fundraising gala, but he showed up yesterday out of the blue. Maybe he works in one of the offices nearby? There's a law firm down the block and an investment management firm around the corner. His confident demeanor would fit in either place, but . . . no. He doesn't look buttoned up enough for either of those.

But before I can wonder further, Maestro Hoffmann charges onstage, making Ivan scramble to get out of his way and take his own seat. Our agitated conductor clears his throat.

"As you know, the annual Christmas concert is only a few weeks away. We'll be doing the Bach cantata." I let out a quiet sigh. *Bach's Christmas Oratorio* is a staple during the holidays, and while the piece is challenging, it would be nice to try something new.

If this was six years ago and I was back in my position as

concertmistress with the Denver Symphony, I may have had the chance to suggest we try a different piece. It might be safer playing in the second string, but I can't deny that I miss having input. *Baby steps, Sam.* As wildly tempting as it may be to audition for a more prominent spot in the orchestra, I just can't risk it. The last words Ray screamed at me may have been over a year ago, but I still remember them in vivid detail.

*"I told you I'd find you. Run away from me again and I'll fucking kill you."*

I suppress a shudder, trying to erase the memory of the hatred in Ray's eyes, and the ghost of his fist I can still feel throbbing against my ribs. I wonder how much time it's going to take to wipe it from my memory. I wonder if I ever can.

The sound of Maestro Hoffman's incessant baton tapping has me blinking back to stare at the sheet music that is in front of me. "Focus, Samantha. Try to keep up, yes?" I feel my cheeks heat with embarrassment as I try to avoid his angry stare, and the hushed murmurs of Peter and Susan beside me.

I never zone out. I pride myself at always being prepared for this job. I can't afford to lose it. I whisper an apology to the maestro that he responds to with a purse of his lips. Thankfully, he doesn't belabor my uncharacteristic slip, and soon, we're off to a place where I can push the memories back for a little while longer.

"THIS IS BECOMING A HABIT." I recognize the richness of Cameron's voice, and feel a smile tug at my lips. Knotting the belt on my coat, I turn to face him. He's larger than life in the doorway, the air seeming to crackle between us. *What is he doing here?* I can't deny the thrill that runs through me at the sight of him.

It's at odds with that ever-present cloud of unease and doubt that I can't get away from.

"Did you get lost?"

Stuffing his hands into the pockets of his jeans, he shakes his head. "I'm exactly where I'm supposed to be."

"You work around here then?" I try to sound indifferent, but I don't think it works.

His lips twist as if he's trying to suppress a smile. "Sometimes. I was hoping to see you again."

"You were?"

"I was wondering if you wanted to go to the zoo—with Hannah, I mean. And me. Hannah and me." He rubs a hand across the back of his neck, his gaze so intense it almost takes my breath away.

*Is he actually nervous?* "The zoo?"

"Yeah. The Stone Zoo. They put their Christmas lights up over the weekend and I thought maybe you'd like to go. If you're not, you know . . . busy or anything?" The fluorescent lights buzz in the silence. I haven't been on a date in years, and this definitely sounds like a date—a date I'm not sure I'm ready for.

"You want to go to the zoo?"

"Yeah, I mean I took my nephew there a couple of years ago." He shrugs his shoulders. "He loved it. I thought maybe Hannah would, too."

His offer is tempting—*he's* tempting, but then so was Ray. My throat is dry as I swallow back regret. The truth is, I'm still living the past, terrified to move forward, so I tell him the only thing I can. The safe thing. "It's nice of you to offer, but I have errands to do. Maybe some other time."

# chapter four

## cameron

HER WORDS HAVE MY CHEST tightening because I have a feeling she's lying. There's no way she doesn't feel the pull between us. Sam is definitely a mystery. One I want to unravel. I'm not used to reluctance in women, but there's something else with Sam; a hesitation that doesn't speak to just not being interested. There's also a hunger in the way she's looking at me. Time to call her on the bullshit brush-off.

"It's okay if you're not interested. I'm a big boy. Just give it to me straight." I make a show of palming my hand over my chest, above my heart. "I can take it."

But, Sam's not smiling. She doesn't seem amused at all. Her hand grips the strap of her purse like she's holding on for dear life. "I wish we could go with you, if you want the truth. Hannah loves the zoo. It's just that . . ." Her eyes dart past me into the corridor.

"It's complicated."

Complicated I can deal with. Hell, my life is one pot of simmering complications. She said she wishes she could go, and I'm all about granting her wish. I grab onto the glimmer of hope. "Actually, the zoo is pretty simple." Energy kicks through me as her dark green eyes fix on mine. "A few animals, some holiday lights, hot chocolate." The corner of her mouth quirks up. "The most complicated part is probably the carousel, but I think between the two of us, we can figure it out."

She shifts uneasily while I silently beg her to say yes. The Brit would probably say I'm breaking one of his ridiculous rules, but I'm not ashamed of appearing eager. When I want something, I go after it. And I want Samantha. More than I probably should. "I could pick you up at your place after your errands."

"No!" I lean back at her sharp tone. "I mean, there's just a few things I have to do. We could meet you back here in an hour or so?" Relief floods my veins. Something so simple feels monumental. Sam's not hiding her face or studying the floor. She wants this—time with me—and I intend to make the most of it.

IN THE PARKING LOT OF the zoo, Sam lifts Hannah from the back seat of my SUV, glancing at the lights that line the pathway to the entranceway. Letting out a little gasp, Hannah takes Sam's hand, tugging her forward. "It's so pretty!" Hannah squeals, lifting up on her toes to try to see further inside.

I fall into step beside them. "You know, I hear some of Santa's reindeer are here. Would you like to see them?" Hannah's hat almost falls off her head she nods so fast.

"I take it that's a yes."

Sam's answering laugh is in sharp contrast to how she was on the drive. She seemed more guarded in the car, peering out the window, lost in her thoughts when she wasn't answering Hannah's endless questions about the animals at the zoo.

"I think you're fast becoming one of her favorite people," Sam says as we join the short line to purchase tickets.

"What about you? Am I becoming one of your favorite people, too?"

Heat floods my veins as she looks up at me with a half smile. I bet a full smile from Sam would be lethal. "Buy me a hot chocolate and you might move up the list."

Once inside, Hannah skips along just ahead of us as we stroll through the tree-lined path. It's like we've stepped into the North Pole. Holiday lights glow through the exhibits, and we stop in front of each one while Sam patiently explains the animals.

The Canada lynx is a big hit as it seems to play hide-and-seek with Hannah from behind one of the large tree trunks in its enclosure. "Momma, can we get a kitty?" Those blue eyes of Hannah's blink up at us.

Sam chuckles low. "Not right now, sweetie." Hannah unleashes a pout that tugs at my heart, but doesn't seem to faze Sam.

"The reindeer are just up ahead. Let's go see if we can feed them." It's gotten cold enough that I can see Hannah's breath as she lets out an excited shriek, bounding toward the reindeer enclosure.

"Well done," I murmur, dipping my neck to whisper next to Sam's ear.

"Not my first rodeo. Distractions are a requirement, I'm afraid, at this stage." Somewhere along the path, we've moved close enough that I feel the brush of her arm against mine while we head to the fence. It's just the mildest of touches, but I feel it in my groin.

I lean against the enclosure, watching as Sam helps Hannah feed one of the curious reindeer. Hannah is tentative at first, her eyes wide when a reindeer sniffs at her hand before gently taking the feed. I bet she'd love to spend some time at the stables.

Another girl around Hannah's age joins her at the fence as one of the employees starts giving them some facts about Santa's sleigh. Sam takes a step back, glancing up at me. "She's having fun?" I ask.

"She is. Thank you again for driving us. She'll be talking about this for weeks."

"Will you?"

Sam lets out a breath, looking up to the darkened sky dotted with stars. "I'll be thinking about it for weeks. About you." She brings her gaze back to mine as I close the distance between us, willing my heart to stop racing. "And that scares me."

"Why?"

"Because I haven't done this in a long time. I'm not sure if I even remember how." Her voice is soft, and she takes a shuddered breath.

"There you go making it complicated again. It's easy. You talk, I listen, and vice versa. It's as easy as that." She wraps her arms around her waist, her body tensed. It makes me wonder what she's thinking. Why she's closing in on herself when all I want is for her to open up.

"I'll start. Tell me why you're playing in the second string? You should be in the front where everyone can hear you."

Her mouth drops open. "That's the last place I should be."

"People need to see you, Sam—to see how talented you are. Is it performing? Does it make you nervous?" *I could help you with that.*

"It's not that. It's just—" She tugs her hat down over her hair. "I like where I am."

"And you don't ever think about going further?"

Her gaze flicks to mine. "I think about it all the time."

"Then why—"

"Look at the camera! Say Santa!" A shadow of worry clouds Sam's face, and she bolts past me, back to the reindeer.

"No. No pictures. Please!" Sam's voice is panicked as she hurries over to the photographer who's got a group of kids posed around the reindeer. Sam sets her hand on Hannah's shoulder, gently steering her away from the group. The photographer frowns, lowering her camera.

"You can buy a copy if you like. If you sign the release, we might use the picture online."

Terror flashes in Sam's eyes. *What the hell?* "No. Please. If you took one, please delete it." The words pour out of Sam in a rush as Hannah turns back to watch the reindeer.

The photographer tilts her head, glancing at Hannah. "I didn't, but I can if you'd like to take one home."

"Thank you, but that won't be necessary. Hannah? Let's keep going, sweetie." Sam holds her hand out and Hannah bounces back beside her. I follow along confused.

"You want to tell me what that was all about?"

Sam takes a shaky breath in, shaking her head. "Not right now."

I touch her elbow, stopping us in the middle of the path. "Hey. You can talk to me. What's going on?"

Hannah stops at the exhibit beside us, jumping up to try to look inside. Sam's eyes close, her lips smashed together before she speaks in a hushed tone. "Please, just drop it, Cameron. I can't talk about this. Not right now."

I want to erase the haunted look in her eyes when they open. I want to pull her against my chest and tell her that I'll fix whatever the problem is. I open my mouth, but she takes both of my hands in hers, squeezing, a silent plea. "Please. Let's just enjoy the rest of the time we have. The carousel is right there." She nods her head over to the small merry-go-round that looks magical all lit up. "We can try to figure it out, like you said."

My hands engulf hers, and I try to savor the feeling, even if she's shutting down on me, because I'll take whatever I can get with Sam. "You're using distraction techniques on *me* now?" I run my thumb along the slim curve of her wrist, holding her gaze.

"Please." That one word stabs at my heart and gives me hope at the same time. Believe me, I know how fucked up that sounds. But I'll also never deny Sam anything.

"Okay. Merry-go-round it is."

## samantha

I'VE BEEN IN A BIT of a fog for the last few days. Spending time with Cameron at the zoo opened my eyes to the way things could be. But, it was also a reminder that I have to be careful. Letting my guard down is dangerous. If pictures of Hannah or me ever got out and Ray found them, there'd be no stopping him. Ray said he'd find us, and I can't let that happen. Not when we've finally found a place that's starting to feel safe.

Irritation burns as I lift my violin and bow, heading out to the stage. I wish I was able to enjoy getting to know a man who seems genuinely interested in me. Instead, I'm a constant ball of worry, wondering if I can trust him, having him drop Hannah and I off at the arts center after the zoo instead of at our apartment. The thought of him knowing where we live is too much too soon.

Part of me thinks I should have just turned him down. It would have been easier for everyone. Now that I know what kind of a man he is—how generous, and how good he was with Hannah—it only makes me want more and I shouldn't want more. I'm in no position to want more from anyone.

But, I also can't deny how he made me feel: excited and desired, like I'm lit up on the inside for the first time in years. I smile to myself remembering how he crammed his tall frame onto the carousel, standing on the opposite side of the horse from me like some sentry, ready to take down anyone who dared to come close to Hannah.

I'm so caught up in the warmth of those memories, I almost run into Olivia in the hallway. She hops out of the way with a giggle, and we take the stage together.

"Ivan said a guest artist is sitting in and that Hoffmann is even grumpier than normal."

I groan. "Oh no, not another mystery artist. How much do you want to bet it's his cousin from Berlin that was here in June? That jerk kept coming on to Kayla until she finally threatened to put her bow up his ass."

Olivia bites her lip. "No, I don't think so. I'm not getting a European vibe from what Ivan said." I roll my eyes and move into my row, saying a quick hello to Peter and Susan.

The conversation with Cameron comes back to me as we make last minute adjustments to our instruments. He's right—I could easily have a different position if I wanted to. If I thought we'd be safe, I would do it in a heartbeat.

It's not as if our smaller orchestra gets the attention that the Boston Symphony does—it's one of the "Big Five"—and although I'm sure I could play there, it's just not a risk I'm willing to take.

An excited rustling among the orchestra draws my attention. I hear measured steps drawing nearer on the hardwood stage, accompanied by a few gasps and even a muffled "fuck." Ivan directs a stern look toward the offending bassoonist and smiles at the newcomer, indicating a seat at the front of the stage. I see a pair of scuffed black boots stop near the chair; my eyes widen in shock as I scan up the long denim-clad legs, to the black sweater, to the chiseled jaw and warm smile, and finally to the beautiful hazel eyes locked to mine.

You have *got* to be kidding me.

He's holding an electric guitar in his hand and standing there like he owns the stage. *He's* our guest artist? I blink, trying to remember something, anything . . . Wait, he told Hannah that he plays guitar. I don't think I've ever heard of him in concert circles before. But for Maestro to approve this, he must be good. Who the hell is this guy?

"As Ivan mentioned, please welcome Mr. Cameron Chapman, our guest artist for the Christmas concert." There's the usual polite tapping of bows along with a less usual smattering of applause. The bassoonist who swore earlier lets out an excited hoot, earning a glare from Hoffmann. Among the orchestra members, there's a weird mix of polite smiles and enthusiastic awe. I look to Susan and Peter next to me, but they only give me shrugs. No help there.

"I know this is . . . unusual for us to host an artist of Mr. Chapman's ilk, but I want to assure you that I have every confidence in you and will tolerate *no* distractions," Hoffmann continues in his heavily accented voice, casting a warning look at Cameron, who merely returns his gaze calmly. He adjusts his guitar strap over his shoulder after plugging into an amp, and stands at attention, watching the conductor respectfully. A sly look steals across Hoffmann's face before he faces us, and his eyes dart toward Cameron, as if he's challenging him. "The Bach cantata, from the top," he says imperiously. He raises the baton as we frantically flip pages, not giving us any time, and then, we're off.

Bach's *Christmas Oratorio* has six parts and takes about three hours for the whole thing, but we traditionally only do the first part, the Christmas cantata, for the annual Christmas concert. It is a joyous piece and pure, unmitigated Bach. But now, I feel like I've entered another dimension.

Bach certainly never envisioned having an electric guitar in his toolbox, but if he had, I bet he'd have wanted Cameron to play it. The man is remarkable. Although I get the feeling that Hoffmann is trying to make some kind of a point regarding our guest, Cameron stays right with us, measure for measure. He hasn't faltered once. His countermelody is giving the baroque beauty a new depth, a twist that brings it to life in an unexpected way.

We soar through the piece, and it's a fight for me to keep on task. My eyes keep drifting over to the tall man swaying back and forth at the edge of the stage. His eyes are hooded as he follows the music sheets, his body slouched in perfect relaxation as his fingers fly over the strings. He seems almost one with the music—it's something I can relate to, and it only adds to his appeal.

When we finally reach the end, I'm panting as if I've run a marathon. My cheeks hurt from smiling. It's one of those moments that you love as a musician, when all the moving parts come together in perfect synchronicity, elevating the whole. And seeing my joy reflected in those hazel eyes as they find mine is the cherry on top.

There's a hush as we all bask in the residual energy. Even Hoffmann seems to have gotten whatever answer he was seeking. He simply nods politely once to Cameron and gives us a satisfied smile. "Excellent. We'll go back to that in a moment. For now, please turn to the Tchaikovsky. Mr. Chapman, please join in as the spirit moves you."

BACKSTAGE IS ABUZZ FOLLOWING REHEARSAL. After going over a few more pieces for the concert, we were excused with a recall for the following day. Cameron stalked off after Hoffmann to discuss something, but not before giving me a heated glance I felt all the way to my toes.

"Can you believe it, Sam?" Olivia is vibrating, her eyes bright. "I've never seen him up close before. He's amazing!"

I nod slowly, trying to marshal my rampaging hormones. It felt like he could see right through me on stage, and the sensation ignited something in me that I've been trying to ignore. Tamping down my physical reaction, I try to focus on the cerebral. "He's incredible. Even Hoffmann was impressed."

"Like he'd turn down the chance for Cam Chapman to join us," she scoffs, rolling her eyes. "I'm more surprised that Mrs. Stick-Up-Her-Ass Victoria Chapman let her black-sheep son anywhere near her precious orchestra. I heard his band did something with the Sydney Symphony last year, but I never dreamed we'd have a chance!"

My mouth drops open. "Her son? His *band*?"

Olivia gives me a double-take, and then laughs. "You're kidding, right? *Redfall*, Sam! I know you're all about philharmonic, but please tell me you've heard of Redfall."

My flush is instant. "Of course I have, but . . ." Frantically, I try to recall any of the snippets I've seen of Redfall over the years. There's the lead singer, Kennedy Lane, of course, and the crazy drummer is Sean something . . . and there are two other guitarists . . .

Holy shit.

"My sister and I saw them five years ago playing at Gillette Stadium." Olivia flips her blond hair over her shoulder, oblivious to my sudden anxiety. Her eyes are bright and her smile wide.

"Jesus. He's so much taller in person. And did you see that ass?" She's practically swooning, and I'm reminded of the similar look on Holly's face at the day care. "Oh, there's Kayla—she was going to try to get his autograph. I'll be right back." She darts off to continue her postgame analysis, leaving me blinking in her wake.

This can't be happening. I run my hand through my hair in disbelief and lean against the wall as the stream of musicians flowing down the hall past me turns into a trickle. Of all the people I could have chosen with whom to let my guard down a little—finally—I pick an internationally known celebrity whose lifestyle is plastered all over the internet and gossip magazines. And he's one of the Chapmans' sons? This is ridiculous; I've got to get out of here.

"Samantha?"

The deep voice behind me makes me jump, and I spin around. Our no-longer-a-mystery guest artist is smiling down at me with a mischievous twinkle in his eyes. "What did you think?"

I stare up and find myself drowning in his penetrating gaze. The confidence, the sureness in his stride, the way his fingers flew over the fretboard . . . it all coalesces into a stunning truth.

"You're breathtaking," I blurt.

A shy smile lights his face, and he rubs the back of his neck. "You liked it, then?" He leans on the same wall, facing me. "A bit out of the ordinary for the maestro, I think, but he seemed to come around. It should be even better once I've practiced with you more."

My eyes roam over his face, taking in the slight scruff accentuating his jawline and his straight nose. The shadows in the hallway play over the fine planes of his face, giving him an unearthly allure.

"I've never experienced anything like it," I admit. I blow a strand of hair out of my face; he grins and slowly—as if dealing with a skittish animal—reaches out to sweep the offending curl over my shoulder. Butterflies take flight in my stomach, but I try to ignore them. There's something else I need to know now. "Is it true? Redfall? Seriously?"

His eyes widen, suddenly wary. "Yeah. Did you really not know who I was?"

"Not everybody keeps a catalog of famous rock stars in their head," I snap. "You said you were a *distant* relation to the Chapmans."

He grimaces, leaning back against the wall. "Not so distant, really. Victoria and Louis are my parents."

I shake my head, feeling supremely foolish. I'm also a little pissed off at his deception. Before I can say anything else, there's a flash of a camera phone that makes me automatically cringe away and duck my face against the plastered wall. "Hey, Cam! Er, I mean, Mr. Chapman, can we get your autograph?" Two stage-hands thrust a Sharpie at him, eager smiles on their faces. "Can we have a picture?"

Oh, fuck. I lurch away from them, not waiting to hear Cameron's response, moving faster as I go. I can't afford pictures of me getting out. "Sam! Wait!" Trying to keep down my panic, I break into a trot, my only thought to get my coat, grab my daughter, and hide. But before I make it back to the locker room, a strong hand grabs mine, the force swinging me around and planting me against a solid chest, knocking the breath from me.

"Hey, what's going on? I'm sorry about that. It tends to happen occasionally, but it's harmless."

Oh, if only he knew. "I can't . . . do this. I'm sorry," I stammer. I know I must sound like a maniac. His confusion is verging on irritation, but I can't help that, either. "You don't understand. I can't be in any pictures! I can't risk him seeing—"

As soon as the words leave my mouth, the world drops out from under me.

"*Him*, who?"

# chapter five

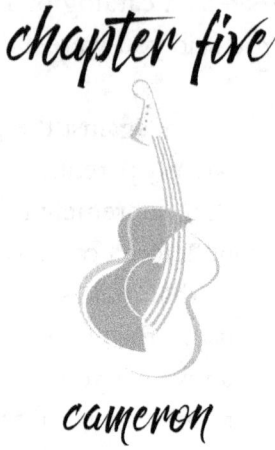

## cameron

"THERE'S A *HIM*?" I TAKE a step back, releasing her arm, my chest tightening. This is why I don't bother trying for anything with a woman that lasts more than a couple of nights, tops. But I didn't expect a *him*. Not from her. She doesn't seem like the type of woman to spend time with one man if she's tied to another one. "Didn't see that one coming."

"It's not what you think," she yelps, her face flushed as she stares up at me expectantly.

"Really?" She shakes her head. "No boyfriend? Husband?"

Her expression darkens. I hit a nerve. *Please don't let there be a husband.* "No." *Thank fuck.*

"Girlfriend? Because I could work with that," I say, trying to lighten the mood. She gives me a nervous half smile. "I know what it is. You don't date musicians? I've heard we can be a royal pain in the ass."

"There's a restraining order," she murmurs, her words so faint I almost can't hear them, but they're like a kick to my gut.

A heavy weight settles between us, threatening to drag us down. I know all about restraining orders, but to hear she has something like this hanging over her head? That explains a few things about her and why she seems so intent on hiding herself away. "Well, that's something I understand. I've got one of those, too."

Her green eyes widen with surprise. "There's a restraining order against you?"

"No. I've got one against a nutjob fan who thought it might be fun to sneak into the dressing room, shred all my clothes, and trash the place after stalking me for a couple of years." I glance down the hall at the small crowd gathering. This isn't the place for a conversation like this. "Something tells me your story is a little different."

Under the muted glow of the overhead lights, she lowers her head, nervously worrying the handle of her violin case. "Just a little."

I squeeze the back of my neck, seeing her starting to shut down on me. This reluctance of hers isn't something I'm used to. It pisses me off as much as it turns me on. But if there's anything I know, it's how to adapt, how to smooth out the edges. It's always worked for me in the band, and I'm counting on it to work now. "How about this? There's a café just down the street. It's quiet. You can tell me all about it."

She peers back at me, and I can tell she's fighting, questioning whether to go with me or not. "It's not something I like to talk about it."

"How's that been working out for you so far, hmm?" Her pretty lips part as if she can't quite believe I just said that. "Sometimes, the not talking about it makes it worse. A little something I picked up in rehab." I like that I can shock her. She's speechless again, looking me over like she can't quite figure me out. "See? Everybody has skeletons in their closet. It's good to clean them out."

I'M NOT SURE I'VE EVER met anyone as adverse to someone doing things for them in my life. Opening the door for her? Paying for a simple lunch? Holding a chair out? I think she'd rather spend an afternoon getting a root canal than let someone try to take care of her. It's frustrating as hell.

Sam's quiet, avoiding eye contact and studying the uneaten sandwich on her plate. She's nervous, guarded. I don't like it. She's been this way since we left the arts center. She kept her hands stuffed deep in the pockets of her jacket, walked with her head down, and tucked her hair under her knit hat.

Hiding, hiding, hiding. I hate every second of it because I know that isn't who she is. That woman who played her heart out this afternoon, who met every chord of mine with one of her own, isn't this skittish, timid shadow.

She lowers her fork to the plate with a resounding clang, finally lifting those bright green eyes to meet mine. There's a mix of worry and excitement living there. This woman is a contradiction. She squares her shoulders almost in defiance as if she's getting ready for a fight. I can feel the lingering adrenaline swimming in my veins the way it always does after I play, and it spurs me on to stop her before she has a chance to give me the brush-off.

"Why don't I go first?" I suggest. She hesitates, her eyes darting away from mine, obviously wanting to say something, but afraid or too stubborn to. "Think of it as a therapy session."

Her lips twist with a half smile. "Therapy?"

"For me. Kind of like a confession." Sam watches me warily as I take a sip of coffee.

"You don't strike me as the churchgoing type." Her soft voice with just a hint of sarcasm wraps around me, giving me hope.

"True, it's been a while. But it's the holiday season, a new year about to hit us. Time for new starts, you know?"

"Kind of like a second chance?"

"Seconds, thirds, hell, I've probably had fifths and sixths. Under the right circumstances, everyone deserves a fresh start." The smile she gives warms me up, makes me raw with need. Keeping my eyes locked to hers, I lean forward, watching her cheeks flush. "Make a resolution with me."

"What would it be?" Sam sets her elbows on the table and leans forward, too. So close that I can breathe in the scent of her skin and can see the tiny freckles that sweep across her nose. I want to count them, kiss them, find out where else she has them.

"To get the past out, right here, right now. Leave it behind where it belongs."

It slays me the way she looks at me with guarded caution. I want her to trust me, to know me, to not have this constant live wire of worry running through her. "What if it won't let us?"

"We'll make it." I can't resist reaching for her hand. It's the lightest touch, my fingers branding a slow circuit along hers. I can feel the little marks and indents left from years of her holding a bow, playing with a fiery need I know she has. "Rehab for me was brutal, but necessary. I was starting to spiral out of the control and I needed a reset. A course correction. My family was more worried about the press and protecting the Chapman name than they were about me. They wanted me out of there as soon as possible so they could bury my dirty little secret. Only it didn't stay a secret.

People found out, and I was just the dumb rebel Chapman—the disappointment of a son who was a fuckup. If it weren't for the guys in the band supporting me, I'm not sure where I'd be. I learned a hard lesson."

"And what was that?"

"Family isn't defined by blood. Those guys, my band-mates . . . I'd take a bullet for any one of them, and they'd do the same. But I lost something, too. My father doesn't trust me. My brothers think I'm a step away from relapsing, because the cycle—drugs-therapy-relapse-rinse and repeat—is a carousel that's hard to get off."

Her eyes darken as she studies me. "I think it matters more what you think."

"Rehab for me was a course correction that I needed. I'm clean, and I'm never going back there again." I hope she hears the truth in my words, because I believe them.

I feel her fingers tighten against mine. "Even though you said it's a cycle?"

"I was in a bad place then. Doing shit I never should've been doing because it made me feel like a god."

"And because you knew it would upset your family." I don't know how she can read me like this, but she does.

"Sounds so juvenile, doesn't it?" I shake my head with a half-hearted laugh.

"I know a rebel when I see one," she says, her eyebrow cocked. I grin at that. "What was so different this time that made you want to stop?"

"I'm not even sure of that myself. A bunch of things, I guess. I'm not twenty-two and an idiot anymore. I don't want to be a strung-out musician who can barely hold it together on stage. Don't want to end up dead like our tour manager because I decided to chase the dragon a few too many times." This time it's her fingers lightly tracing mine, learning them, and sending a jolt of need right to my groin. "I wanted to feel again. I didn't want to be numb anymore." I don't tell her about the nameless whores who go along with the scene I was diving head first into with Brodie's wholehearted encouragement. I don't tell her how I didn't recognize then that he was already lost and looking for company along the way. I don't tell her how it made me feel dirty and sick after. How I wanted to rub my skin raw to get rid of the gritty feeling that ran through my veins. I can't change any of it, and more importantly, it's not who I am anymore.

"Then that's all that matters. Your family should support that. They should support *you*."

I try to shrug it off, but their apathy still burns. "They're not all bad. My sister is a bit different." I smile at the thought of Kat. "She supports me in her own way."

"I'm glad you have her. You need someone in your corner."

"So do you."

Her fingers still, and I feel her stiffen. "And you want to be in my corner?" She has no idea the places I want to be.

"Yeah. I do. Your turn." I squeeze her hand. "Confession time. And then we leave it."

She looks down, studying our joined hands on the table, and I'll take it. I'll take anything she gives me as long as she doesn't bolt again. Even this silence, as painful as it is. "It's Hannah's father," she says finally, her voice clipped. I can feel my blood boil, pumping wildly at her words. *What the ever-loving fuck?* "The one I have the restraining order against."

My jaw tightens, muscles primed and ready to unleash on the bastard whose name I don't even know. I swallow back the lump in my throat. "Her father?" My voice is raw, edgy, some base instinct I don't recognize kicking in. Sam releases my hand quickly, reaching for the fork to take a stab at a tomato on her plate. "Did he hurt her?" I barely get the words out through gritted teeth.

Her chin lifts, her expression hardened. "No. He saved that all for me."

It's like I've been stabbed in the chest, all the air stolen from my lungs. "Sam . . ."

She abandons her fork, studying the table. "It wasn't like that at first. He was kind, attentive, charming. He was like something out of a dream. But that changed. It changed a lot." Her voice is quiet, but she continues, "We'd been married for about six months." She takes a shaky breath, her eyes closing. "We had an argument one night. That was the first time he hit me—slapped me so hard I flew off my feet and fell against the hall table. I think we were both in shock. He spent the night apologizing over and over, but it didn't end there. After that, I walked on eggshells all the time. I never knew what would set him off. It might be his dry cleaning wasn't ready, sometimes it was because I had cooked chicken and he wanted steak." She shakes her head as I try to get a handle on my rapidly spiking anger. I'm gripping my coffee cup like it's a lifeline. "While I was pregnant with Hannah, it stopped, and I thought it was over." Her eyes raise to meet mine, and I can see the hurt, the lingering fear, and it stabs at my chest. "He got worse."

I open my mouth to say something, anything to take that look of sheer terror away from her. Her eyes slide shut, lips pressed together before she says, "Don't. Don't look at me like that. I don't want your sympathy or your pity."

"That's why you're in the second string, isn't it? It's why you were upset about that photographer taking pictures at the zoo. You're hiding from him."

Glancing at me again, I see a spark of determination in those green eyes. "I have sole custody of Hannah and the protection order against him, but I can't let him find us. I can't. We're in a good place right now. I'm doing what I love, and Hannah, she's safe. That's the only thing I care about."

"But what about you?"

She shakes her head. "It doesn't matter."

"Of course it matters. *You* matter. Your life, your happiness . . . It matters."

"You don't get it. She's all that matters, and I'll do whatever it takes to protect her. So this"—she motions between us—"whatever this is. It's not happening. It can't. This is as far as it goes. I don't know how much clearer I can be."

"We have security. The best in the business. I could help—"

"And where was your security when the fan you told me about got into your dressing room?" She cocks her head, her gaze clashing with mine.

Good fucking point. One I don't have an answer for. "That's a long story . . ."

"I can't have a long story, and I don't need or want a protector."

"That's not what I'm—"

Tossing her napkin on top of her plate, she reaches back for her coat, fighting with it as she tries to tug it on.

"Please don't go." Gently, I place my hand on her arm, but she yanks it out of my grasp.

"No. I'm done with men telling me what to do. I lived that way for too long. With a man who dictated what I wore, who I could talk to, when I got fucked. I'm not doing this again." Each word stabs at me. Thank fuck we're at the back of the café and there's no one within earshot because she's ranting, unleashing what has to be years of hurt and anger. "Not with you, not with anyone. Cameron, you've been good to me, and to Hannah, but

I can't be seen with you." She motions to the front of the café. "My being here with you is dangerous. If pictures ever got out and he saw them . . ." She barely suppresses a shudder, and now I'm scrambling. Scrambling to salvage this, to make it right. Now, her reaction to the photographer at the zoo the other night makes sense. She's terrified of this jackass finding her. "He can't find us. He just can't," she whispers.

"Sam, I promise I'm not trying to make your life more complicated."

"But you are! Just you and I having this conversation is making it more complicated."

My heart squeezes at the passion and intensity in her eyes, sparking protectiveness in me I didn't know I could feel. She's strong, but she doesn't need to be alone in this. How can I make her see that? "It doesn't have to be. Look, we're going to be practicing together, right? And everybody needs a friend."

Pressing back against the chair, she lifts her eyes to mine. "Friends? That's what we're going to be?"

"I know, I know. You don't think you're going to be able to keep your hands off me, do you?" I give a fake sigh. "Fine. I'll take one for the team, but only if you're really, really nice to me." I grin at her, borrowing one of our drummer's laws and going for humor in the hopes that under all the hard layers she's built up she can see that I'm trying, that I'm not a threat.

"You're impossible, you know that, right?" she says, her fingers tapping out a rhythm on the table as those beautiful green eyes search my face. She's not bolting, and that gives me hope.

"I may have been told that a time or two."

"SO, HE'S NOT IN BOSTON then?"

Sam looks up at me as we near the day care center. Time is slipping away from both of us. Our conversation, one that's not nearly finished, came to an end when she realized she was almost late from picking up Hannah.

"Hannah's father?"

"No. At least I don't think he is."

"Do the police know about this?"

She huffs, picking up the pace a little, eyes focused on the ground again. "The police, the orchestra's HR manager, the women's shelters. Everyone who needs to know knows about him."

"Wait, shelters?" I touch the arm of her coat, and she meets my eyes. My heart stutters. They've been staying in shelters?

"Yeah."

"Is that where you're staying now? A shelter?"

"Not anymore." Her chin juts out in defiance. "But we have. You do what you have to do."

My chest squeezes. It hurts to think about Sam and Hannah having to go to some cold, dingy shelter to hide away from an asshole abuser. "Shit. Sam."

"It's fine. We're fine, Cameron."

"Hiding away and staying in a shelter isn't *fine*."

She pulls to a stop. "Don't you dare judge me. You have no right, no idea what this is like," Sam hisses, taking a deliberate step away from me, which won't do at all.

I close the distance between us, because her running again isn't an option. I brush a strand of her soft hair behind her shoulder, and she leans forward slightly, her face tilted up to mine. "I'm not judging. I want to understand."

"There's no way you can." If I didn't know I was in trouble before with Sam, the minute my fingers touch the softness of her cheek I do. "And we're leaving it in the past, just like you said, right?" Her hand closes around my wrist, grounding me as my thumb skims her cheek.

I swallow back the knot in my throat. She's not the only one who usually avoids complications. I should just walk away from this, from her. She's right; I'm a complication for her and for Hannah. But I know I can't walk away. Not now. Maybe never. "Right."

"Please, Cameron." Her voice comes out in a cautious whisper. "Please just leave it. He's not worth it." I can't stand to see her like this, to hear the desperate tone of her voice. The only thing I want to do is protect her, take away every awful memory that haunts her.

"Cam!" A high-pitched voice breaks the spell, and I turn in the direction of the sound. We've ended up outside the fenced-in yard at the day care already, and I see Hannah with her banged-up doll, beaming over at us. "Mommy!"

Sam mutters something under her breath before moving to the fence. "Hi, sweetie. How was your day?"

"We had a teddy bear party!"

Sam crouches down by the fence, smiling. "You did? That sounds like fun."

"With cupcakes!" I can't help but grin at Hannah's excitement. The kid is adorable.

"Want one, Mommy?"

"Well, sure, if there are any left, I'd love one."

Hannah leans closer to the fence, trying to whisper, but I can hear every word. "Can Cam have one?"

Sam looks over her shoulder at me. "We'll have to see if he wants one. How do you feel about cupcakes?"

"Best snack ever."

Hannah smiles, her eyes widening as I crouch down beside Sam.

"And if you like parties, wait until you come to mine."

♪ ♩ ♪ ♩

# samantha

"YOU'RE HAVIN' A PARTY?" HANNAH'S face lights up. She grips the fence and hops up and down, making the pom-pom on her hat bob.

"I am." He nods, beaming at her. "And you and your mommy are invited to come."

My eyes snap to his as Hannah exclaims, "When? When? Can we go, Momma?"

He mirrors me as I slowly stand, one hand gripping the fence. "What kind of party are we talking about?"

"It's Saturday," he answers Hannah first, a gentle smile on his lips. When she scrunches up her face with the effort to try and figure out how many days until Saturday, he beats me to the answer. "That's two days from now." She giggles and sways back and forth.

"And it's a Christmas party at my parents' place. We go out and get a tree on the property and haul it back to the house to decorate. There are horse-drawn wagon rides, hot cocoa, and carol singing . . ." He smiles down at Hannah. "And there should be other kids there, too. It's fun."

"I don't think—"

"They've got horsies, Momma!" Hannah gasps, drowning out my automatic demur. Her eyes are practically popping out of her head, and I can't help my laugh.

"We do." Cam nods. "We have lots of them, and you can meet them when you come. You can help me feed them a treat."

"A treat! Like cupcakes?"

I bite back another laugh. "No, sweetie, horses like apples and carrots for treats."

"And sugar cubes," Cameron chimes in, wiggling his eyebrows and making her giggle again.

Hannah peers up at me through the fence, making puppy-dog eyes like a pro. "Please, can we go, Momma? The horsies need me."

I can feel the weight of Cameron's gaze on me, but I keep my attention on my daughter. Irritation bubbles in my gut; I don't appreciate being maneuvered like this. A cold breeze sweeps down the street, reminding me the weather report called for more snow today. "I'm not sure, Hannah. But right now, let's go inside and see if there's a spare cupcake, okay?"

"There is!" She races past the handful of other kids in the yard toward the back door of the day care.

Cameron's soft chuckle brings a smile to my lips. "Does she always have that much energy?"

"You have no idea." I shake my head in amusement. "She's my little tornado." He stays beside me as I walk down to the end of the fence and make the corner toward the front door. I shoot him a look. "You couldn't have mentioned this party during lunch?"

His cheeks, already pink from the cold, turn rosy red. "I didn't think of it then. I didn't mean to ambush you. Please come Saturday, Sam." His deep voice caresses my name, sending a shiver down my back. "It'll be fun. I promise. When's the last time Hannah got to cut down a Christmas tree?"

The hope in his voice dims my irritation. I recall the scrawny tree my aunt and I had bought at a lot in Chicago when Hannah was barely one year old. It was a far cry from the trees my parents and I cut down in the forest when I was small, and I feel a jolt of longing for Hannah to experience it. "Never," I admit. I stiffen automatically when he takes my hand and twines his long fingers with mine, but the comfort and warmth he exudes thaws me almost as fast. Despite my jumbled nerves and worry, it feels . . right.

"Then it's high time for her to experience it." He smiles at me gently as we walk and holds the door for me to enter first. I'm acutely aware he hasn't released my hand. I'm even more aware that I haven't let him go, either.

*Friends hold hands once in a while, right?* I mentally scoff at myself. *Sure they do, Sam, sure they do . . .*

Hannah bounds toward us, a mini chocolate cupcake thrust out in front of her. "They had one left!" she crows in triumph, but then frowns in consternation as she looks between us. "I wanted to get two, but—"

"That's okay, sweetie," I interrupt. "Let's give this to Cameron. He looks like he needs a treat, right?"

She giggles. "Right!" She thrusts it toward him, and he bends to take it with a laugh.

He makes a show of carefully unwrapping it and darts a mischievous look at me. "But I think we can share." He holds the cake out for me to take a bite, tempting me. My eyes shoot open, and I shake my head, until Hannah grabs my hand that's holding my violin case.

"Do it, Momma. It's really good!" she says, those puppy-dog eyes in full force again. Cameron grins, sensing a victory, and he steps closer, raising the treat to my lips. My eyes lock on his as I open my mouth to take a small bite. The explosion of chocolate and creamy frosting in my mouth makes me moan involuntarily. It really is good.

His hazel eyes darken as he stares at me, and when I lick a small bit of frosting off my lips, his breath catches. Suddenly, the background chatter of small children and staff disappear. All I can hear is my blood thrumming through my veins. His hand tightens on mine and he leans closer.

"See? It's really yummy!" Hannah's bright voice breaks through my haze, and I take a half step back, giving her a shaky nod. She tugs on Cameron's pant leg and looks up at him expectantly. "Eat it, Cam."

He blinks, and then grins down at her before popping the rest in his mouth and chewing with relish. "Mmmm, delicious," he tells her. "Thank you. It was just what I needed."

"Hey, Hannah, did you remember your drawing?" Kat's voice precedes her as she comes around the corner from her office. She stops dead in her tracks when she sees our little trio. "What are you doing here?" she asks, her eyes glued to Cameron. I look between them, bewildered by the silent conversation they seem to be having.

"Samantha and I had lunch after practice," he says, his eyes speaking more than his lips. "I'm playing with them for the Christmas show."

"You are?" Her eyes widen in disbelief. "Maestro Hoffmann is letting you play?"

She seems so surprised, I find myself bristling on his behalf. "Cameron's guitar work is amazing. You should've heard the rehearsal. It was extraordinary."

"Extraordinary, huh? Well, that's a word I haven't heard for him yet." She smirks up at him.

Cameron huffs at her teasing and runs his free hand through his speckled locks. "Um, Samantha, meet my sister, Kat."

"Kat's your sister?" I immediately try to drop his hand, but he doesn't let me go. Kat's eyes zero in on our joined digits, and he finally relinquishes his grasp. Then she turns to my daughter and claps her hands with a smile.

"Don't forget your drawing, Hannah," she says. "It's over on the craft table."

"Okay!" She zooms off, leaving the three of us momentarily alone. Kat looks at me with a twinkle in her eye.

"I go by Kat Pierce professionally; it's my mother's maiden name. Sometimes the Chapman moniker gets a bit overbearing." She folds her arms and cocks an eyebrow at her brother.

"So, what else are you two up to today?"

"Nothing," I exclaim. Knowing Kat's his sister has thrown me for a loop. She knows so much about my situation; I hope I can trust her to keep it to herself. "Hannah and I need to catch our bus."

"You mean that bus?" Kat points across the street toward the bus stop, where I see our Number 86 is pulling away.

"Oh no!" I rub my hand across my eyes. I can't believe I let time get away from me—that I let him distract me so much.

"Let me drive you," Cameron says, his eyes imploring. "Please. It's started snowing again; you don't want Hannah standing around in that."

I eye the swirling flakes outside. "You don't have to do that—"

"I want to. Please." He gives me a crooked smile. "Friends, remember?"

Hannah zooms back to us, a piece of paper waving in her hand, and almost crashes into Cam's long legs. "Hey, Miss Pierce! If you're Cam's sister, does that mean you're going to the tree party?" she asks, breathless from running.

Kat's eyes dart to Cam's in surprise, before returning to my enthusiastic girl. "I sure am. It's great fun. Are you going to be there too?"

"Cameron was kind enough to invite us, but we haven't decided yet." I ignore Hannah's pleading look. "I need to work Saturday night."

Before Cameron can reply, a few more parents enter the lobby to collect their children. Kat waves at them, before turning back to us. "Well, I hope you can join us. It really will be fun. Have a good evening. See you soon, Hannah!"

As she turns to the newcomers, I take Hannah's hand and lead her back outside and take her drawing from her. It's a shaky illustration of a small stick figure with yellowish curls standing next to a taller figure with long red hair. A small house-like building is in the background with smoke coming from a chimney and green scribbles that I think might be grass. "It's beautiful, sweetie. Thank you."

She beams at me as I fold it carefully and tuck it in the pocket of my peacoat. Still trying to decide about how we're going to get home, I glance up at Cam's hopeful expression. A whoosh of wind seems to bring the snow down thicker, making my decision for me. "Cameron is giving us a ride home, Hannah. Isn't that nice of him?"

"Really?"

Cameron chuckles in my ear the same time I feel his hand on my back. "I sure am. Let's go."

HANNAH IS HAPPILY ENSCONCED IN the back seat of his midnight blue BMW SUV. She's half-singing, half-humming her puppy song to her doll, lost in her own little world. Cameron keeps glancing at her in his rearview, an amused smile on his lips. She had skipped the whole way to his car, chattering about her day. Cameron made little affirmative noises at the proper times and even asked questions to keep her going. It's so not what I'm used to; Ray would've told her to shut up as soon as we were out of Kat's sight. He only kept up the happy family image when we were in public.

I keep watching for signs that Cameron's attention is just for show, but there are none. He's relaxed and seems truly interested in her ramblings.

Just as interested as he seems in me.

I fiddle with the handle of my case, watching as he turns the corner according to my directions. This is ridiculous. He's a bona fide rock star. Rock stars don't date normal people. They date models, actresses, or other celebrities. Not girls from Colorado who have been on the run from their asshole ex-husbands for three years.

But as I watch him smiling at Hannah as if she's a rare jewel—which she is, of course—and wiggling his eyebrows just to make her giggle . . . a warm, gooey feeling bubbles up in my heart.

"Sam . . ." He pauses, checking to see that Hannah's absorbed in song and looking out the window. "Please come Saturday. It will be fun." His eyes flick to mine and he reaches to place his hand over mine, making my heart skip a beat. "I'll get you back in time for work, I promise. Where do you work?"

"I wait tables and tend bar occasionally now. Full-time in the off season. Teaching violin and playing in the orchestra only get us so far." His eyes tighten at my indirect answer, but he doesn't comment further. Smart man. "Cameron, didn't you listen to what I said earlier?" My frustration building, I take a deep breath and try not to think about how nice his hand feels over mine. Aware of the little ears in the back seat, I lower my voice. "I wish things could be different."

"They can if you want them to be," he whispers, giving my hand a squeeze before returning his hand to the steering wheel. "Besides, it's just one day," he continues lightly. "What could go wrong?" He gives me a quick smile when I huff a laugh.

"Plenty."

We ride mostly in quiet, with only Hannah's singsong murmuring in the back. I finally let myself relax into the soft leather seats and enjoy the heat blasting from the air vents. It's been a long time since I've been in a luxury car. Ray always insisted we own one as part of his image. But instead of wearing it as a badge of his social status, it seems like just a car to Cam. There's nothing pretentious about him. His Levis are worn and his black boots are scuffed. The bomber jacket is made of fine leather, but it's old and obviously well-loved.

Maybe he's right. Maybe things can be different . . . if I want them to be.

"Oh, turn here. Park anywhere." He obliges me and pulls up about a half block away from Finnegan's grocery store.

"This is your neighborhood?" He looks around warily. South Boston has a deserved reputation. "Where do you live?"

I busy myself with gathering my tote bag and case. "Not far." He purses his lips and nods, again accepting my nonanswer.

"Oookay." He reaches into the glove box, plucks out a pen and a fast-food napkin, and quickly scribbles something on it. "Here's my number. Call and let me know what you decide, although I hope you'll come. I can pick you up."

"We could take a—"

"There isn't bus service out there." He gives me a wry smile. "Believe me, you don't want to walk from the nearest stop. I'll come get you. It's not a problem. I *promise*, Sam."

I'm caught in the intensity of his gaze, hoping beyond hope that his promises are something I can believe in. "Cameron—"

"Come on, Momma." Hannah's whine breaks through from the back seat, startling me. "I'm hungry."

Seizing the distraction, I reach for the door handle. "Thanks for the ride. I appreciate it."

"Wait!" He scrambles for his door, but I don't wait for him to come around. By the time he reaches my side, I've got Hannah out and we're standing on the sidewalk.

"Samantha . . . I hate to just leave you standing here in the cold. Are you sure you'll be okay?" Frustration colors his voice, and he rakes a hand through his hair; it comes away wet with melted snow, and he hurriedly wipes it on his jeans.

"We'll be fine. I'll call you tomorrow and let you know if we can make it." He reaches for my hand but I step back and take Hannah's instead. "I promise, Cameron," I add, softening my voice.

A worried frown flickers on his face, but he masters it and gives Hannah a grin instead. "Have a good rest of your day, Hannah. I hope to see you Saturday."

"Me too! I want to see the horsies," Hannah chirps, looking up at me with those eyes again. Traitor.

We stand looking at each other, fat snowflakes falling fast and furious, until he laughs. "You're not going to move until I leave, are you?"

"Nope."

He gives me a grudging smile. "Stubborn woman," he mutters. "Fine. Have it your way."

Shaking his head and mumbling to himself, he circles the car and climbs back in. It feels a little weird to watch him drive away. I catch a glimpse of him looking back at us as he turns the corner, and as soon as he's out of sight, I'm on the move. I hustle Hannah into Finnegan's grocery and quickly up the back stairs to our tiny apartment. While she's taking off her coat and hat, I hurry to the window, just in time to see him drive past below. Ha—I knew he'd try to figure out where we went. His protectiveness warms my heart.

Feeling a little smug, I take off my own coat and hat and busy myself with making Hannah a snack. Once she's happily munching graham crackers and milk, I sink into the one soft chair I own and take in the room. There's the cheap strand of lights I tacked around the window, the worn angel ornament sitting on the bookcase, a smattering of angel and snowman drawings Hannah made at day care, and her stocking hanging on the back of the door—the sum total of our Christmas decorations.

I pull the napkin from my pocket. Staring at the scrawled digits, I recall the hope in his eyes and the thrill that shot through me when he fed me the cupcake. I also remember Christmases past; times of warmth and love and family.

Tears prick my eyes. I was right before; this is ridiculous. But maybe he's right, too.

And for my daughter, maybe it's time to find out.

# chapter six

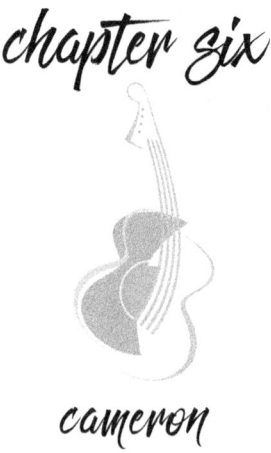

## cameron

SLEEP. WHO NEEDS IT?

Being in a band, I'm used to a lack of it. It's not like sleep has ranked high on the priority list over the years. Sleepless nights with Redfall are due to concerts, parties, and hauling ass from one city to the next, not this bullshit.

Wild scenarios haunt me, each one worse than the last, about the questionable neighborhood I dropped Sam off in, and worse, about Hannah's father, who is obviously the lowest of the low.

This kind of rage isn't normal for me. The guys and I have gone a few rounds before, and I've had my share of fights in the occasional bar or two when we were first starting out, but this? This is something else. Pure, single-minded, blinding rage against a man who doesn't deserve to breathe. I know I need to channel this dangerous energy running through me. Sam has had enough pain to last a lifetime. The last thing I want is for her to see me as a threat.

Inhaling another cup of coffee, I glare at my laptop. You should never google anything. Given who I am, I know this. But I do it anyway. Knowledge is power, so they say. The websites on abuse are terrifying and only serve to light the fire burning through my veins. Words like *emotionally scarred, traumatic injuries, loss of self-worth* rattle around and beat at my head, but they also give me focus. Keeping this bastard away from Sam and Hannah is now my only priority.

Just the thought of someone laying a finger on either one of them is like a knife to the heart. Now, I understand the reluctance, her keeping her face from view in the orchestra. She's hiding. She's hiding from a monster, and I'm going to do everything I can to make sure he never touches her again.

"WONDERFUL TO SEE YOU AGAIN, sir. I'm afraid I didn't know you were coming. You're getting into a habit of surprising me." Henry offers me his practiced smile as I kick off my boots. It's early morning and my parent's estate is already buzzing. A small army works to transform the place into the impressive holiday statement everyone expects. Thousands of strands of white mini lights are being strung on the mature trees that line the driveway, a few delivery vans from a flower shop open at the back where crews carry in an endless supply of elaborate wreaths and holiday centerpieces that probably cost a fortune, boxes of decorations from Saks in every corner of the house. It will be amazing when it's done.

I frown slightly, still annoyed that I haven't heard back from

Sam yet. I told her to call me about the party, and so far, nothing. I've got a hell of a lot of patience, but I think I'll take matters into my own hands today. We have a rehearsal this afternoon and I intend to make the most of it.

"I like to keep you guessing, Henry. Wouldn't want you to get bored here." I shrug out of my coat, bypassing him to hang it up in the closet around the corner.

"Not a chance, sir. If you've come to visit your mother, I'm afraid you've missed her."

I step out of the way as one of the workers scurries past with a large box. "Already?"

"Spa day this morning."

"Ah, that would explain it."

"Yes. The Hamiltons picked her up shortly after seven this morning."

Annoyance creeps in. "The Hamiltons? Darcy and Elizabeth?"

Henry nods. "It's a weekly event for them."

"I just bet it is." I scowl, moving to the living room. I can only imagine what my mother is trying to cook up. Darcy Hamilton at the spa with my mother's undivided attention is a fucking scary thought. "Is Dad back?"

"Yes, sir. Arrived last evening just after nine. He's already at the office."

My jaw clenches. "Stubborn man is going to have another heart attack."

"I made sure he had a good breakfast, and he's only allowed to work until four under strict instructions from your mother."

I laugh at that. "Because he always listens to what she says?"

"In this regard, he does, sir. A scare like the one he had, I don't think I need to tell you that it changes things."

I clap Henry on the back. I know how much he cares about

Dad—about all us. Seeing Dad go through recovery from a heart attack wasn't easy for any us, Henry included. "I know it does. And thank you for looking after him."

"Of course, sir." He looks at me expectantly. "Can I have breakfast made up for you?"

"No, Henry. I actually came to see you."

He eyes me warily. "Me?"

"I need your help."

"How can I be of service?"

"Do we have leftover Christmas decorations?" He looks confused. "Mom still buys new every year?"

"Well, yes. There are some heirlooms she uses every year, of course. The angel tree topper from your grandmother, and a few bits and baubles from you and your brothers and sister, but otherwise, it's a new theme each year, sir. Were you looking to decorate your home for the holiday?"

"I probably should, but no. This is for a friend." *Friend.* I need to redefine that word.

"A friend?" He motions to the wide hallway, leading me around the staircase on the long walk to the east wing of the house. "Do I know him or her, sir?"

So subtle. "Her, and I doubt it. Her name's Samantha." I gaze up at the family portraits hung in stylish frames on the wall. Our family over the years, looking ridiculous in staged photos where we were told what to wear and how to smile. A stoic painting of my grandparents looms large and intimidating in a gilded gold frame when we finally reach the storage room.

Henry opens the door to wall-to-wall metal boxes, all labeled and neatly stacked. The room is bigger than my first apartment with Kennedy, and this is where we store the things we no longer want. "Is there a theme you were hoping for?"

"She has a daughter."

His mouth kicks up to a quick smile, but he's quick to snap back to his usual controlled demeanor. "A daughter? Brilliant. How old, if I may ask?"

"She's four. And nothing too fancy or over the top." Henry hums to himself, scanning the rows of boxes. "If we can just keep this between us for now, I'd appreciate it, Henry."

It's as if I've slapped him when he turns to me. "I would hope that by now, sir, my loyalty to you and your family wouldn't be something you questioned."

"I question a lot of things in my life, Henry, but your loyalty isn't one of them. I just meant to not say anything to Queen V. You know how she is, even if you'd never admit it. And things with Sam are . . ."

He raises his eyebrows. "If I could, I believe the word you're looking for is *complicated*?"

"Ain't that the truth."

"Women typically are, sir. And I apologize for my outburst."

"You think that was an outburst? Do you not remember the fights I used to get into with Brooks and Nathan? Now some of those were outbursts."

He smiles. "I can't argue with you there, and my lips are sealed. You have my word."

"Good enough for me."

He turns back to scan the boxes, stopping at the far end of the room. "Will Santas and snowmen do the trick?"

I smile thinking about Hannah's face when she sees the decorations. "Sounds perfect."

THE ELEVATORS OPEN ON THE top floor of the building my father owns, one of more than a dozen in Boston alone. These places are always sleek and modern, reeking of wealth and entitlement. I hate coming here. I always feel like I'm suffocating.

It should be easier than this to track down Dad and my brothers, but so far, I've struck out. They aren't returning my text messages, which isn't unusual—they're busy men running an empire after all. This is the one place I know they'll be.

Maggie Hughes, my father's trusted assistant for at least a million years, blinks up from behind her ultramodern desk. She's at least sixty-five and shows no signs of slowing down. My father would be lost without her. She's the exact opposite of my brothers' assistants; both of them in their twenties, fresh out of college with implants and dollar signs in their eyes. I'm sure Nathan is fucking his assistant, and even though Brooks is married with a four-year-old son, he's got a wandering eye.

Maggie's silver glasses hang on a little chain around her neck and she slips them on, blinking deliberately. "Wait. I must need new glasses. Is that Cameron Chapman I see? It can't be. There's no way." She's probably the only person who could actually get me to smile in here.

I set a gift bag on the corner of her desk, and her eyes widen. "Godiva, dark chocolate mint. Yes?"

"I always knew I liked you best." She peeks into the bag with a smile. "I think I love you. Marry me."

"If only you didn't already have a husband."

She waves her hand. "He's old and a pain in the ass. I was thinking about divorcing him. Trading him in for a younger model, you know what I mean?" She ignores the phone ringing off the hook. "I should scold you for not seeing you since January. Take you over my knee. Your generation is into that sort thing. You'd probably like it." I laugh as she leans back in her chair with a satisfied grin. "My granddaughter went to your concert in New York this summer. Said you rocked it."

"You should've told me. I would've gotten her backstage passes."

"Over my dead body. I know what goes on backstage." She shakes a finger at me.

"I bet you do."

"Don't get me started. I once spent a weekend with Rod Stewart in London back in the day that rocked his world."

I stare at her for a minute, a few pieces clicking into place. "Wait. You're not Maggie May, are you?"

She grins, turning to her computer and pretending to ignore me. "Didn't your father ever teach you to never kiss and tell?"

"Holy shit. I'll never listen to that song the same way again. Maybe you *should* divorce your husband."

Her smile gets wider. "You wish."

"You're coming to the party on Saturday, right? I'll save you a cup of hot chocolate."

"Haven't missed one yet. Your father's in the executive boardroom with your brothers. He's got a conference call in fifteen minutes."

"Shouldn't need more than that." I shake my head with a laugh. "Maggie May. You're officially my idol." I can hear her laughter all the way down the hall. Unfortunately, the closer I get to the boardroom, the harder it is to breathe. Lines of cubicles surrounded by offices, the constant buzz of phone calls, hushed conversations, millions of dollars being traded and invested. I don't know how my brothers do this. They both say they love it, but I haven't got a clue how that can possibly be true. I live for freedom, for the frenzy of the crowd. Being surrounded by four walls is stifling and seems like a special kind of torture I can't imagine having to deal with day after day.

I can see them through the glass windows that line the boardroom. My dad leaning his intimidating six-foot-eight frame forward, hands flat against the large table, my brothers looking like they're about to get detention. The three of them are dressed almost identically in dark blue suits and ties, fresh tans from a week in the Caribbean sun evident on their faces. I unzip my jacket, my throat tightening just looking at them. They might be tanned, but they sure as hell aren't relaxed. Knocking on the door, I open it without waiting.

"Jesus, you're smarter than that! We don't need another scandal." My father's voice bellows as I step inside the boardroom. The door closes with a loud thud, and they turn in my direction.

"At least his was outside of the building! Son." He gives me his standard greeting of a head nod.

I eye him warily, waiting before crossing the room to take his outstretched hand. That's right. We don't hug. We shake hands, firmly, and with authority and purpose, just like we were taught. With Redfall's tour schedule, it's been almost a year since I last saw him, but that doesn't matter. Even when he was recovering from the heart attack, there were no hugs. Not for him, not from him. "Sounds like I missed one hell of a meeting."

"I was reminding Nathan here why it's a bad idea to have sex in his office with an assistant whose father happens to be a member of the board. Your thoughts on the matter, Cameron?" Dad folds his arms across his chest, staring Nathan down. The wrath of my father is something I know well. That I disappointed him, my family name, and our reputation is something he'll never let me forget, but if one of my brothers is the focus for a change, I'll gladly step aside as the black sheep.

"Can't disagree with you there, Dad."

"See? Even Cameron knows how idiotic it is." I try to ignore the implied insult there. Dad's face is red. That can't be good. He shouldn't be getting worked up like this.

"Because he's the poster boy for committed relationships?" Nathan glares at me.

"I'm not the one having sex with someone who's not my fiancée."

"No. You're the one strung out and making headlines that send our stocks into the tank for weeks," Brooks chimes in like the annoying shit he is.

"Hey! I've been clean for over a year. And I've apologized. More than once."

"Apologies don't mean anything for stockholders."

"I'm pretty sure you've recovered. Don't think you'd be vacationing in the Caribbean if money was an issue. Or am I wrong?" Neither one of them has a response. Of course not. My stint in rehab may have registered a minor blip, but I also know it was short lived.

"Are we seriously going to argue about whose scandals are worse?" Nathan pushes back from the table, stands up, and straightens his suit jacket. "No one even knows about Kaylee." Like that somehow makes it okay.

"Kaylee?" I snort a laugh. "That's cute. Does she sign her name with a little heart at the end?" Nathan squares his shoulders. If it was twenty years ago, and we weren't at the office, we'd already be pounding the hell out of each other. "And something tells me your little assistant's father knows or this conversation wouldn't be happening."

"That's enough, boys." Dad runs his hand through his graying hair in frustration. "I'd prefer we didn't have any scandals, but that ship sailed a long time ago." He cuts his eyes to me before focusing back on Nathan. "I want this dealt with. Quietly, Nathan. Do I make myself clear?" Dad's voice is eerily calm, and just as intimidating as if he was screaming his head off.

Nathan frowns, duly reprimanded. "Yes, sir."

"And Cameron's right," Dad says. "You're engaged—again. You'd do well to remember that."

"How is Ellen?" I just don't know when to shut the hell up. "Did she enjoy the Turks and Caicos?" Nathan frowns in annoyance. "Oh, wait. She didn't go, did she?"

"She didn't want to go," he grinds out, and I see that telltale tick in his jaw he gets just before he typically loses it. Nathan's got a temper on him. Brooks and I used to love to rev him up—of course, back when he was a teenager he was lanky and relatively harmless.

"Right. Because Boston in December beats out eighty degrees and sunning yourself on a beach any day. Maybe the third time really isn't a charm."

Nathan's nostrils flare. He's one to talk about scandals, going on to wife number three and fucking everything in a skirt. He's fallen prey to the temptations of power and wealth just as I almost did to the temptations of the road. The difference between us is I did something about it. "You're a goddamn—" he snarls.

"Enough!" My father's fist hits the heavy boardroom table, silencing the three of us. "Can we not have a day when you three aren't at each other's throats? We've barely seen you all year, Cameron." He turns to unleash on me. "And I know you were on tour, although why you couldn't stop here I'll never understand."

"The tour schedule isn't up to me—" I start, but his blistering glare shuts me up.

"You were in New York, Philly, hell you could've stopped in." His words, his tone, it all cuts me off at the knees. This is new.

Dad's never mentioned wanting to see me before. He's always too busy to care.

I swallow back the unexpected lump in my throat. "I'm here now."

"We're honored with your presence," Brooks says, leaning back in his chair. "How long are you gracing us with it, little brother?"

"The tour starts up again in January, so until then, I guess."

"Just breezing through then. Man, to have your life. You just do whatever the fuck you want whenever you want to." Nathan is pissed. I've heard this from him before, but I make no apologies for my life. I work my ass off, not in the chained-to-a-desk-sixty-hours-a-week way he does, and that's the problem. Why it's always been a sticking point with them is something I'll never understand; Brooks and Nathan never wanted to do anything else but be part of the family business. I wanted to run as far away from it as I could get. It's that simple. That they resent me for forging my own path is always going to sting.

"What the hell is that supposed to mean?" I fire back at him.

Nathan shakes his head. "Nothing. It means nothing." Glaring at each other in the silence that follows is agonizing. The overwhelming urge to bolt flows through me.

"Well, as fun as this little reunion has been, I have a rehearsal to get to. Since none of you are answering your texts, I came to see if you wanted to go for lunch. Maybe we can get together later this week."

"I'll get Maggie to call you," Dad mutters, frowning at something on his laptop, while Brooks and Nathan both bury their noses in their phones. The message is loud and clear, and I don't bother to stifle my sigh. I've been effectively dismissed.

MAESTRO IS ON FIRE TODAY. Snapping orders at the trumpet section, ranting away in German when he doesn't get exactly what he wants. As annoying as he is, this is what I need after that visit to the office this morning. It's distracting, challenging, something to get my mind off my family.

An even better distraction smiles at me as I make a face behind Maestro's back during one of his epic meltdowns. Sam shakes her head, looking down to the sheet music once more. Her cheeks flush slightly, and I know I'm making progress. It's been this way for most of the afternoon. Sam, catching me watching her. Her cheeks heating, her pretty mouth quirking in surprise every time. I don't look away, even though I know she wants me to. *I want her to know I see her.* I see her for the beautiful, talented woman she is.

At least I know she feels something, despite her argument at the café about nothing happening between us, and her reluctance to call me. She looks at me with a bit of curiosity, and a light I haven't seen before. A heat I haven't seen before. That heat speaks to something more than friendship. *Friendship*; we're going to have to redefine that word.

## samantha

THE SCUFFED TOE OF A boot comes into my field of vision as I snap the catches of my violin case closed, and I smile.

"Are you avoiding me?"

I rise slowly and tuck my case under my arm. "Obviously not, since I'm standing right here."

"You haven't called to accept my invitation."

A few percussionists loiter near the door of the cloakroom,

their eyes darting toward us every couple of seconds, and I sigh in exasperation. It was like this all during rehearsal. People's curious eyes followed his every move on stage between numbers.

How can he stand it?

"Let's discuss this outside." I nod to our not-so-stealthy audience. "I need to pick up Hannah in a few minutes anyway."

Glancing at the gawking fanboys, he sighs. "Something I can help you with, fellas?" he asks, causing them to jump and scatter like a flock of startled partridge, mumbling apologies as they leave.

"I suppose that happens frequently?" I ask, amused and a little impressed.

He shrugs. "Eh, it goes with the territory." He helps me into my coat and escorts me out into the cold, the feel of his hand on my lower back making my heart skip a beat. He tugs his scarf up around his neck and watches me do the same. "Well? Will you come on Saturday?"

He falls into step beside me, and I take a deep breath, feeling like when I skied my first black diamond run. "Yes, we'll come." He stops abruptly and stares at me, a wary smile flickering on his lips.

"Really?" At my affirmative nod, he finally lets his smile out. He takes my hand and links his fingers with mine. I like the way it feels. "So, are you going to tell me why you didn't call when you promised you would?" He shoots me a reproachful look through his eyelashes.

"I'm sorry about that." I bite my lip and shift from one foot to the other. "It took me a while to decide."

"Decide what? To trust me?" His quiet accusation hits me in the gut. I pull my eyes from our joined hands to his face, knowing I'm responsible for the disappointment I see there.

"No. To trust myself."

The hurt in his hazel eyes changes to concern. "You can do

both, you know."

I give his hand a squeeze. "I know."

I think I shock him when I accept his offer of a ride home without argument. He keeps shooting me confused looks as we walk my bouncy daughter outside. But he's right; I need to start trusting myself again, and accepting kindness from him is a good way to start.

Hannah alternates skipping, hopping, and walking beside us. She was thrilled to see Cameron again, and it warms my heart to see how readily he interacts with her as she chatters away. When we reach his BMW parked at the curb, he gives her an indulgent grin.

"Guess what," he says, opening the backseat door. "I have a surprise for you."

Hannah's eyes are like saucers. "What?"

He points to the large box on the seat. "Climb in and open it."

She scrambles into the car as I lean toward Cameron. "What did you do?" I hiss in his ear, but he just shakes his head, keeping his eyes and smile on my daughter.

"Momma!" she gasps. "Look!" With an exultant grin, she holds up a beautiful snowman figurine encrusted with glitter. "There're lots in here. Oh, here's Santa!"

I rub a hand over my face. "Cameron . . ." I'm torn. I'm irritated that he did this without asking. I love seeing Hannah's excitement. And I feel guilty that I can't provide this for her myself right now.

He finally tears his eyes away from Hannah, who's carefully digging through her box of new treasures, to face me. "I'm sorry I didn't run this past you first, but I didn't have a way to contact you," he murmurs, the excitement in his eyes dimming. His reminder I didn't call him when I said I would isn't very subtle. "And it's Christmastime. Everyone needs surprises at Christmas." He leans closer, his fingers toying with a button on my coat. "Please don't be angry. I wanted to do this for her, to make her smile. No strings—I promise."

The sincerity in his deep voice touches my heart, and my irritation melts. He's not doing this to get in my good graces or show off. This is just another example of his generous spirit, and it would be rude not to accept. I brush my fingers across the back of his hand that's holding the door open. "I believe you. Thank you, Cameron. Truly."

His answering smile is like the sun coming up.

SATURDAY IS OVERCAST BUT AT least it's not snowing yet. I shift in Cameron's passenger seat, my nerves making an appearance. I think he's gotten used to picking me up on the street corner. He doesn't like it, but he accepts it . . . at least for now. He wanted to carry the box of decorations to my apartment yesterday, but gave up after only a few minutes of haggling. I'm probably being overly cautious, but I just can't go that far yet.

Hannah is practically vibrating with excitement in the back seat. She grills Cameron about the horses that will be there and pats the paper bag we brought with carrots we got from Mr. Finnegan's store this morning. I'm not sure how she'll feel once she sees how big horses actually are, but I'm not going to put a damper on her enthusiasm.

We speed down the Massachusetts Turnpike, passing signs for various country clubs, the buildings becoming fewer and trees more prevalent. A fresh layer of snow blankets the landscape; it makes me homesick. I haven't been back to Colorado for about four years, and I miss the mountains and forests. He takes a turn, and I let myself get lost in childhood memories of building snow forts and learning to ski until I realize what I thought was a little country road is actually a driveway winding through the woods. We come into a clearing and my breath catches when I see the edifice looming ahead.

It's enormous; the perfect example of a mansion. The stone facade is impressive, and the upper stories peppered with paned windows. There must be a hundred rooms in this place. My nerves rocket to DEFCON 1.

Cameron swings around the circular drive like he's done it a million times, but drives past the imposing main entrance and pulls up to one of the smaller outbuildings in the rear. There's a garage farther away that looks like it has bays for five vehicles. The behind-the-scenes area is a beehive of activity; staff dressed in black are unloading crates from a delivery truck and carrying them inside a set of double doors. Beyond that is a glassed-in solarium of some kind and a large patio area dotted with wrought-iron benches, covered in a dusting of snow.

"Here we are." He flashes me a grin, but there's a hint of nerves in his voice. This time, I let him come around and help me out; I need the time to wipe my sweaty palms on my thighs. Now that I know who he is, I expected his family's house to be big, like some of the ski chalets back home. But this . . . this is an enclave of affluence I've only seen in movies or old *House Beautiful* magazines.

He pulls on a beanie and helps me out, shooting me a shy smile when he sees my white-knuckled grip on the door handle. "Hey," he whispers, gently prying my hand free and holding it firmly in his. "It's just a house, Sam. Nothing to worry about."

"Right. Okay." He looks relieved when I manage a smile, and we both turn to the whirlwind that jumps out of the back seat. Hannah is oblivious to my inner turmoil, eagerly looking around with a dozen questions. But when she gets out and sees the huge wagon with two beautiful Clydesdales hitched to it, she's stunned into silence, the bag of carrots clutched in her hand forgotten. Cameron beams at her.

"Hannah." He bends over to speak gently in her ear, and gestures to the wagon's team. "Do you want to give them the treats you brought? I bet they'd like to meet you."

She nods, her mouth still gaping open, and he takes her hand to lead her over to them. He looks relaxed, comfortable in this plush setting. He returns the nods from a couple of the staff members as he saunters toward the horses. It makes me wonder what it was like—what *he* was like—growing up among all this precise splendor.

I saw plenty of the rich and famous on vacation filter through my hometown while I was growing up. For the most part, they're just like everyone else; some are perfectly normal and some act like jerks. My parents treated all their patrons the same, regardless of whether they wore designer labels or not, and most respected them for it. Those that didn't . . . well, they were good examples of my dad's maxim about money not being able to buy someone class. While it all taught me not to fear others' wealth, it also gave me a healthy appreciation for how the rich can use their influence—and not to be on the bad side of it.

Cam lifts Hannah as if she weighs nothing and props her against his hip so she's more on their level. "Hannah, meet Merry and Pippin," he says, indicating each horse. "My sister named them." Pippin snorts and Merry tosses his head, drawing a startled giggle from my little girl. With patience that warms my heart, Cameron shows her how to hold the carrots so the horses can take them without biting her fingers in the process. It's adorable; I can't take my eyes off them. Hannah pays rapt attention to his instructions, all business. When her offerings are accepted with more snorts and loud crunching, her joy could light up all Boston.

I'm pulling on my own hat when I hear a throat clearing behind me. "Excuse me, Miss. Can I help you?" I turn to see an iron-haired man with an impeccable black suit looking at me expectantly. His proper English accent prompts images of afternoon tea and crumpets. But before I can say anything, Cameron laughs and rejoins me, Hannah now walking beside him, hand in hand.

"Good morning, Henry!" Cameron gives him a friendly wave. "May I introduce you to my guests today? Samantha, this is Henry, the man who keeps this whole place running."

Henry's lips twist in amusement before turning a warm smile on my daughter. "It's a pleasure, miss. And who might this be?"

"I'm Hannah! You have very nice horses," she says politely. We've been working on her manners more lately.

"They're not mine, dear, but I'll pass your kind words along." He gives her a wink, eliciting another giggle.

"Are we ready to go, Henry?"

"We are, sir. The Norway spruce is the final choice." He motions to the wagon. "Please get comfortable. There are carriage blankets waiting for you. I'll have some hot chocolate and hand warmers brought out for the ride." With a final glance at Cameron that makes him huff out a chuckle and rub the back of his neck, Henry turns and disappears through the double doors.

"Wow. A real, honest-to-goodness English butler." I shake my head in amusement. "Why do I feel like I've walked into a Disney movie?"

Cameron barks out a laugh. "I feel like that sometimes myself when I come back here." He claps his hands together and grins at my daughter. "Ready to get a tree?" She cheers and runs to the wagon, the pom-pom on her knit cap bouncing madly. He leans in, his warm, spicy scent swirling around me. "Ready?"

"As I'll ever be." He gives me a devilish smirk in reply that makes my knees weak and leads me by the hand to the wagon, where my daughter is bouncing in place, hands behind her back and a mischievous grin on her face. I instantly know something's up, but Cameron doesn't seem to catch on until her hidden snowball explodes against his chest.

"Oh, so that's how it is?" he exclaims in mock outrage. Hannah squeals with glee, darts out of his grasp, and the chase is on. Around and around they go, stopping to scoop up snow in hastily thrown snowballs. Cam is obviously letting her get the best of him, his own projectiles purposefully missing either high or wide.

Hannah ducks one of his fat snowballs and scrambles in the snow for another handful. Her laughter rings in the clearing, making my heart swell with love. How could I have thought that this wasn't a good idea—

Splat!

My outraged yelp blends with my daughter's howl of delight as I swipe away the freezing remnants of Cameron's surprise attack from the side of my face. A shiver rips through me as icy water drips down my chin and the corner of my mouth curls in calculation. So that's how he wants to play it, huh?

I charge.

His impudent grin morphs into shocked alarm as I launch myself at him, planting my shoulder solidly in his midsection. The air whooshes out of him in a muffled curse and we hit the ground. Snow flies as we tumble and roll, laughing and struggling. We finally come to a halt, the weight of his firm body resting deliciously on mine, and I stare breathlessly into his eyes. In an instant, the playfulness in his gaze turns to an intense desire that sets my blood on fire.

"Samantha," he breathes, and I stop thinking; I loop my arms around his neck to pull his lips to mine . . . until quick footsteps jerk us back just in time.

"Me too!" We both grunt when a small body jumps on us.

Cameron laughs, letting Hannah roll us back over until she and I are lying on him. "You want in on this too, eh?" Her shrieks echo as he dumps a handful of snow over her head. All three of us are scrabbling on our hands and knees, flinging snow and laughing like crazy. My heart is bursting, and my face aches from smiling back at the faces beaming at me.

This is happiness. It's been so long, I forgot what it feels like.

"Cameron? Stop roughhousing with the help and grow up. We have guests." His head snaps around so hard I'm surprised it doesn't fly off his neck. I follow his gaze to see an imperious woman I recognize as Mrs. Chapman, dressed impeccably with a cashmere pashmina and her face like a thundercloud. She gestures vaguely toward the solarium, where I can see a stunning blond woman staring at us through the glass with her arms folded. She doesn't look happy.

"Why, hello, Mother," he responds, his words clipped. He helps me up and stares his mother down as I nervously brush snow off Hannah and the front of my peacoat. I feel Hannah clinging to my jeans, and I place a calming hand behind her head. I'm acutely aware of our secondhand clothing and cold-reddened cheeks, but I lift my chin and smile politely, ignoring my hammering heart.

Cameron stands close, his hand on my lower back. "Mother, please meet *my* guests for the day." He graces me with a soft smile that eases my nerves. "Samantha McKenzie and her daughter, Hannah." Her eyes widen as he makes introductions, but she shakes my proffered hand in a delicate grip, her ingrained manners obviously taking over. "Samantha is a violinist with the symphony."

My cheeks heat as I look up at him through my eyelashes. The look in his eyes makes my knees weak. His mother clears her throat.

"Really?" She purses her lips. "The Chapman Center symphony? I don't think I've heard Maestro Hoffmann mention you before. How long have you been with—"

"We were just going with Henry's group to get the tree before the party. I promised *someone*"—he tweaks the pom-pom on Hannah's hat, making her grin up at him—"a wagon ride and hot cocoa."

His interruption saves me from further interrogation and diverts her attention. She's staring at him like he's lost his mind. "I see." She startles when the delivery truck, now empty and closed up again, starts its engine and begins to pull away. Smoothing a manicured hand over her perfectly coifed hair, she gives me a once-over. The vague distaste in her eyes tells me she finds me lacking. "Will you *all* be joining us later? The Beechams are here, as well as the Hamiltons—including Darcy."

"Of course she is," he mutters, shaking his head. But then he notices Henry and several other men in stout coats, boots, and gloves converging on the wagon. "Yes, we'll *all* be back, Mother. But now, we have a date with a tree." He reaches down and easily lifts Hannah again, who snuggles happily in his arms. His mother, however, looks like she just ate something unpleasant as she watches them, her eyes wide.

"Is she *your* momma?" Hannah whispers to him, shooting glances at the elder Chapman, who stiffens in surprise.

"That she is," he whispers back with a mischievous grin. "I don't look much like her, do I?" Hannah shakes her head gravely, and I bite my lip to keep from laughing at his mother's shocked expression. I have a feeling she isn't struck speechless very often.

We all stand awkwardly for a beat, until his mother straightens her shoulders and adjusts the soft-looking swath of fabric around her shoulders. "Well, try not to cut down the wrong tree. We'll see you in about an hour, yes? You and . . . Samantha." Her penetrating stare seems to burn right through me, and then she turns on her heel and strides off.

Once she's gone, I see the tenseness leave his body. "Well, that went well," he says, hitching Hannah higher on his hip. "No, really. I think she likes you."

I huff in disbelief, and let him steer me toward the wagon. He greets a couple of the men lugging a chainsaw, and then swings Hannah into the back of the wagon. He helps me up and hands me one of the blankets stacked in the back so I can wrap it around my daughter. "So, who's Darcy?"

He grimaces. "She's no one, believe me. Despite my mother's best efforts." He sits and leans against a side of the wagon and arranges his long legs out in front of him. He pats the space next to him, so I sit and gather Hannah on my lap. I hold my breath as he casually rests his arm on the edge of the wagon behind my shoulders. "Don't think about her. I don't."

I wish I could.

# chapter seven

## cameron

SAM'S HAND TIGHTENS AGAINST MINE as we stop in the hallway, warming up from our tree-cutting adventure and the sleigh ride. Hannah lets out a little squeal.

"You live here?" Hannah asks excitedly. "It's like a castle," she yells.

"Well, I don't live here anymore. My parents do." Henry appears, his cheeks red from the cold, offering his arm for our coats. "I'll hang them up in the private closet, sir." Sam crouches down to help Hannah with her zipper and boots, passing them tentatively to Henry.

"You have lights everywhere!" Hannah looks up the wide staircase, the sounds of music and hushed conversations floating through the air from the ballroom down the hall.

Sam shakes her head, her lips turned up in amusement as I

take her coat from her. "Private closet?"

Tilting my neck, I whisper next to her ear, "It's easier when we're ready to leave. Trust me."

"I'll take your word for it," Sam says, her lips so close, so tempting.

"Is that Cameron Chapman?" I smile at the sound of Maggie's voice and turn to see her eyes widen as she spots Sam and Hannah. "Twice in one week. It's a Christmas miracle." She stops, giving us a curious smile.

"Maggie, this is Sam and her daughter, Hannah. Maggie's worked with my father for . . ." I smirk at Maggie. "How many decades now?"

She swats my arm playfully. "Hush, you. And the answer is forever."

"He'd be lost without you, Maggie May."

"Tell me something I don't know. It's nice to meet you both."

"You too," Sam says.

"I like your jacket," Hannah says quietly.

"Thank you, Hannah." Maggie runs her hand over her velvet blazer. "Would you like to come with me? There's a room full of crafts just waiting to be put together."

"Can I, Momma?" Hannah blinks those blue eyes up at Sam, who hesitates, her eyes darting to mine. I hate that she questions everything.

"Kat will be back there with the other kids. It'll be fine."

"Of course it will be." Maggie smiles down at Hannah. "What can possibly happen with a room full of children and glitter glue?"

Sam laughs. "You'd be surprised what can happen when glitter is involved."

Maggie doesn't give Sam more of a chance to argue. "Let's see what we can get into, Hannah." Maggie holds her hand out and Hannah takes it, waving over her shoulder while Maggie leads her to one of the open rooms down the hall.

"She's in good hands. Don't worry." I brush my fingers across her cheek.

"It scares me how easily she goes with people," Sam says, her eyes lingering on Hannah's retreating form while she skips beside Maggie.

"Maggie's not *people*. She's more like your sweet aunt with a hidden rebel side who will ply you with cookies all night."

She laughs. "That must be why you like her so much."

"Must be. Seriously though, I've known Maggie my whole life. She's one of the sweetest people in the world." Sam lets out a sigh, relaxing slightly.

"You never said we had to dress up."

"Because you don't."

"She was wearing velvet! I'm totally underdressed." Sam wraps her arms around her waist, glancing nervously toward the muted sounds of the party. I follow her gaze, frowning when I finally realize what she's seeing; a roomful of strangers dressed in designer labels—casual, but still designer—looking like they've just stepped out of an issue of *Travel and Leisure*. But she has nothing to worry about; Sam is beautiful no matter what she's wearing.

"They're just people; no better than anyone else, no matter what they're wearing. You're perfect. Don't ever think otherwise, Sam." In her jeans and simple sweater that hug her curves, her auburn hair curling deliciously around her face and long neck, she has no idea just how striking she is . . . which makes her even more tempting.

She glances down at the marbled floor, hiding her face from me. "Hey." Tracing my fingers against her cheek, I lift her chin so her eyes meet mine. "I mean it. You're perfect. In every way. Please don't doubt that."

"I'll try not to." She leans forward as I hear applause from the ballroom.

"Tree must be up. Did you want to take a look? Maybe have a dance?" I take her hand, leading her down the hallway.

"There's dancing?"

"There's a ballroom. It's good for something at least a couple of times a year."

"You have a ballroom."

"No. My parents have a ballroom."

"Semantics. Holy . . ." Sam's voice trails as I step into the room that easily holds five hundred people. Right now, it's full of the socially influential, mingling and trading secrets. "This is just . . ." She glances up at the high ornate ceiling with crystal chandeliers, her eyes darting around the elegantly decorated room of black and gold until she finds the tree we helped cut down. It's already lit with white lights, just waiting to be decorated. It fills the center of the room in all its grandeur.

"This is crazy, Cameron." She squeezes my hand.

"It's just a room."

"It's stunning. It could be in a magazine."

I don't tell her it frequently is. That there are photographers here hired to snap strategic pictures of Boston's elite at one of the premier social events of the season. I don't tell her that people are starting to stare at us, murmuring, whispering behind their glasses of expensive champagne, wondering who the rebel Chapman brought to the party.

Instead, I sway us away from the gathering crowd around the tree. "We don't want Tony singing all alone and no one dancing. That would be a crime."

She laughs, pure and sweet, resting her hand over my heart.

"Wait. Tony Bennett is here?" She pushes up on her toes, looking over my shoulder as the familiar raspy croon of his voice fills the room.

"Nah, it's just a recording. He couldn't make it this year."

She blinks at me. "You mean he's sung here before?"

"Many times. My mother is a big fan."

She's quiet for a few beats, and it's perfect. Just us and Tony starting to sing about the way she looks tonight. I can feel her soft, gentle curves against my palm, and it takes everything in me not to grip her tighter and haul her against me. "Will we hear some Redfall too?" She glances up at me.

"Only if hell has officially frozen over." She frowns as I turn us beside one of the bars set up along the side of the ballroom. It's less busy over here. Away from the gossips and photographers. Safer. "My mom is not a big fan of our music."

"Well, I am." She glides her free hand up my shoulder, her fingers gently resting against my neck. It's the lightest of touches, but I feel it bone deep.

"You didn't even know who I was." I give her a fake pout.

She rolls her eyes. "Did that hurt your ego?" she teases, her body pressed against me.

"No. It's one of the things that drew me to you, actually."

"To be fair, not everyone knows who's who in every band."

I try to hold back my laugh. "Sure they don't."

"Okay, smarty-pants. Who's the guitar player for U2?" She juts her chin out, but I ignore her little display, spinning her away from me before easing her back to my chest.

"Please. Give me a challenge at least. The Edge. We've had dinner." Tilting my neck, I mutter against her ear. "Many times."

She shivers as we find our rhythm once more, her body flush to mine. "No. The bass player," she clarifies, her voice lighter.

"Adam Clayton."

She lets out a frustrated huff. "Damn. What about the Vandals?"

I narrow my eyes. "Landon Ravine. The guy's an idiot."

"A talented idiot. What about the others?" Her green eyes seem to shine in the path of light from the tree, and I think it's the most relaxed I've ever seen her. To know I had something to do with putting that look on her face is everything.

"Malcom Stevens and Rob Felix. You want to know the former members too?" She gives me a fake scowl, but I can tell she's enjoying herself. "Sam, trust me, we can play this all night, but you're never going to win."

"Fine. *You* may know, but ask the average person on the street, and they probably wouldn't be able to pick them out of a lineup much less know their names."

"I only care about you picking me out." My hand skims a circuit against her side, and I feel her relax further.

"Will you sing to me?"

"Anytime." And I press her closer, lowering my voice so only she can hear. *"Lovely, never, never change . . ."*

WATCHING SAM AND HANNAH DECORATE the tree with some of the other kids does things to my heart I wasn't expecting. It's pure joy for Hannah. You can see it with every squeal of delight she has when she picks an ornament from one of the boxes to hang.

And Sam, she's right there, helping Hannah and the other kids with a kind of patience and caring that you can't fake. She gently tries to steer the excited group around the massive tree in the ballroom so the decorations aren't all clumped together in one spot.

It's such a simple thing, decorating the tree. I've done it for my entire life, and I realize I took it for granted. My chest hurts thinking about Sam and Hannah spending time in a shelter, never really having that sense of home.

I've never been more aware of just how good I had it growing up. How good I have it now. How much I can give to Sam and Hannah if she'd let me.

Christmas music pipes through the ballroom, the kids still running high on the thrill of Santa's arrival an hour or so ago. I'd do just about anything to see that look of sheer wonder on Hannah's face again when she saw him.

Glancing across the ballroom, I catch Darcy and my mother whispering to each other. Darcy is dressed like she's just come off the runway. Not a hair out of place, designer outfit that probably cost a couple of grand, stiletto boots even though there's snow on the ground. She gives me a wave when she catches me looking at her before snagging a flute of champagne from a passing waiter.

"Looks like your number's up, little brother," Brooks mumbles, nudging me in the side as he joins me. At least his suit is gone and he looks less stressed than he did at the office. Part of me hates that Brooks and Nathan have chosen to follow my father in the family business. I know the path is a nasty route to a heart attack waiting to happen. As much as we all get on each other's nerves, I'm not sure how I'd handle something happening to either one of them.

"In what way is my number up?"

Brooks lifts his chin in the direction of Darcy. "In the way that says I'd bang that all night long." He takes a lazy perusal of Darcy as he sips his beer. It's one of our own Chapman IPA brands. It was Nathan's brainchild to start a microbrewery a few years ago when they started exploding across the country.

We spent a few drunken nights a couple of Decembers ago, back when I was home for the holidays, sampling what would turn out to be a best seller. Another jewel in the diverging Chapman empire. Nathan may be a womanizing idiot, but when it comes to business, he's a genius.

Never satisfied, Brooks started talks a few months back with a whiskey distillery in Ireland. He's mentioned wanting us to head over once the deal is inked. It's been a while since I've been to Ireland. Our tour has skipped it the last couple of years. I wonder if Sam has ever been. Hell, I wonder where she's been in general. There's so much I want to know. So much mystery there hiding away that I feel the need to uncover.

"Did you forget that you're married? I mean, I kind of expect that kind of crap from Nathan after what I heard at the office, but not from you."

"Relax. There's nothing wrong with appreciating a beautiful woman. And I'm not Nathan. I actually like my wife." Brooks nods toward the tree where his wife, Paige, is trying to tame the terror that is my four-year-old nephew, Ethan. I'd like to bottle the energy he has. "Heard you were out pretending to be a lumberjack with Henry this afternoon. That's a first."

"It was actually a lot of fun."

Brooks puts the back of his hand on my forehead, and I swipe it away.

"Just checking. You and manual labor don't exactly go hand in hand."

"Shut it."

"Who's the girl?" he asks, and we watch Sam laugh as she lifts Hannah up to hang a glittery gold angel on one of the branches.

"You noticed that, huh?"

"I noticed *you*. Typically, you'd be all over someone like Darcy Hamilton, but you can't seem to tear yourself away from this one. First, you're dancing with this mystery woman, now you're watching her like a hawk." He touches his beer to my bottle of water. "And you're drinking sparkling water? Please. Who is she?"

"She plays in the orchestra." I'm being deliberately vague. The less he knows, the better.

He shoots me a look. "Mhmm. And?"

"And nothing, Brooks. I invited her. We're friends." I shrug, giving Sam a smile when her gaze meets mine.

"Is that what you're calling it? You know that never works, right? Friends with benefits? I thought I taught you better than that."

I laugh, shaking my head. "If you're my teacher, then we're in serious trouble."

"Aren't we always?"

Paige looks over at us, throwing her arms up in frustration as Ethan starts to scramble under the tree, and I clap Brooks on the shoulder. "I got this."

"Sure you do." Brooks laughs as I retrieve my nephew, hoisting him up onto my shoulders. Ethan's shriek of laughter pierces through the ballroom as his little hands tug at my hair.

"Let's see if we can't tire you out. Wave to Daddy." I turn back so Ethan can wave to Brooks, before taking off with him to the kitchen.

A couple of hours later, I'm elbow deep in sprinkles, gingerbread, and sticky icing. Yep, I've officially crossed into some alternate universe. Screaming fans at one of our after-parties have nothing on a room full of kids hyped up on sugar.

The staff has pulled out all the stops this year. We even have Mrs. Claus helping us in the kitchen. Whatever my parents are paying these people, it's not enough. I'm one more high-pitched squeal away from actually offering these kids money if they will just be quiet for five minutes.

"Look, Mommy! Cam got the woof to stay on!" Hannah's sweet, excited voice reaches into my heart, making me smile.

"He did?" Sam glances across the table at me, light shining

in her green eyes. She's happy, more relaxed than I think I've ever seen her, and all we're doing is building gingerbread houses. "Make sure you thank him, sweetie."

"She did. Even said I could have a gumdrop." I pop a red one into my mouth, holding Sam's gaze as I chew slowly. Her eyes fall to my lips, and I see the heat rise in her cheeks. "The red ones are the best."

"If she's letting you have her gumdrops, you're doing something right." She turns quickly back to the gingerbread mess on the table, hiding her face again. I reach across to brush a strand of her soft hair back, and she peeks up at me.

"I sure hope so."

"Cam!" Hannah pulls on my sleeve, and I squint down at her. "Yes, Hannah?"

"Henry said there's a new baby horsie. Can we see her? Please?" Those big blue eyes of hers are going to break a lot of hearts one day.

"I don't know, Hannah," Sam says. "It's getting really late and Mommy has to work tonight."

"Please? Please, Cam." Seeing tears brim in Hannah's eyes is more than I can take. I'll give her whatever she wants.

Glancing back at Sam, I cave. "It won't take too long." Sam shakes her head, but I see that small smile playing on her lips, like she knows I've been played by a four-year-old. "I'll have you home before you turn into a pumpkin."

Hannah giggles and jumps down from the chair. "Mommy's not a princess, silly."

Leaning down, I whisper next to Hannah's ear, "She is to me."

"THIS IS UNREAL," SAM SAYS as I lead her and Hannah down the snow-covered path to the sprawling stables. Like the rest of the property, the stables have been decked out with blue spruce trees lit and decorated on either side of the large doors.

"How does Santa know where to leave the presents here?" Hannah asks, still holding her beat-up doll and her bag of carrots they brought with them. I look back at Sam in panic. I'm totally unprepared to answer questions about Santa. Actually, questions about anything a four-year-old could ask are probably dangerous for me to answer.

"Um . . ."

"You have a lot of twees. How does he know where to put the presents?"

"Twees?"

"*Trees*, sweetie." Sam gently corrects Hannah. "We're working on Rs. They can be tricky when she's excited," Sam whispers.

Grinning, I step into the stable, making my way to the nursery stall at the back. It's quieter here, and the heat has been turned up, making the horses more comfortable. The new foal was born yesterday. Quite the ordeal, so I'm told. My mother is in crisis mode trying to come up with a name. My suggestion of calling her Redfall was ignored completely.

"Santa leaves them at the one you helped decorate at the house," I explain to Hannah.

Hannah's eyes widen. "But it's so big!"

"Santa doesn't worry about how big the tree is, honey," Sam says as I stop at the stall. "Or if you have a tree at all."

Concern stabs at me and I mouth over the top of Hannah's head. "You don't have a tree?"

Sam shakes her head quickly, crouching down with Hannah as she peers into the stall. "Tell me what you see in there." It's amazing how Sam doesn't miss a beat, while I'm speechless and floored that they don't have a Christmas tree. I should've fucking thought of that. I gave them that entire box of decorations without even thinking. How much of an idiot am I?

I watch Hannah drop her doll, and her mitten-clad hands come up to cover her mouth as she practically vibrates at the wrought-iron gate. "It's the baby horsie!"

"Shhhh!" Sam whisper-yells. "The horsie looks like she's sleeping." Sam looks up at me. "Is it a she?"

Nodding, I crouch down with them both. "It is. She was born yesterday."

"She's beautiful," Sam says quietly, her eyes fixed to the jet-black foal surrounded by a bed of hay. Northern Star stands on guard beside the foal, giving us a huff.

I stand up with the bag of remaining carrots Hannah brought, pulling a few out. Clicking my tongue, Northern Star turns her head to me as I gently open the latch on the gate. "Hey, Momma." I keep my voice low, letting her get comfortable with me. Slowly, I take a step into the stall, running my palm along her neck and down her muzzle just like I've done tons of times over the years with other mares when they've had new foals.

"There you go. You must be exhausted." The mare nudges my palm, closing her eyes for a moment as I softly stroke between her ears. "I know." I shake my head. "Well, I don't, but I wouldn't want to push out a hundred-pound pony."

"The horsie weighs a hundred pounds?" Hannah tries to whisper, but doesn't really succeed. She's too excited.

I turn back to see Sam, standing behind Hannah, her arm around her waist holding her in place. "Just about."

"But she looks so little." Hannah pushes up in her little boots onto her toes to try to get a better look.

"Mr. Chapman." I turn to the sound of David Adams's voice, the man in charge of the stables. "Come to see our little no-name?"

"We did. David, this is Samantha and Hannah. Hannah, David is in charge of the horses here."

"All of them?" Hannah asks.

David laughs. "I do have help. We have sixty horses here, Hannah. I can't handle that all by myself, you know." He leans against the stall.

"Sixty?" Hannah's voice gets higher as she looks down the row of stalls. Her hands flap at her sides in delight.

"Sixty-one now with no-name here."

"How's she doing?" I ask, offering Northern Star one of the carrots. She takes it gently, crunching away.

"If I said healthy as a horse, you'd just laugh at me. But they both are."

"Mommy, the horsie needs a name," Hannah says firmly.

"I'm sure they'll name her soon, sweetie."

"Why don't you name her?" Hannah giggles at me, but I press on. "What do you think?"

Hannah bounces in place, vibrating with energy. "Really?"

"Really. Come here." Hannah takes a small step over to me, and I lift her into my arms, so she can get a better look at the foal. She squirms a bit, leaning forward, a little crease in her brow.

"Midnight," she finally says, flashing me a full smile.

I turn to David. "There you go. Midnight it is."

David smiles in amusement. "That's a great name, Hannah. Would you like to help make up her name tag? We do up one on a chalkboard until her name plate arrives." I let the wriggling Hannah down to the ground, and she runs the few steps back to Sam, picking up her doll again.

"Can I help, Mommy?"

"I don't know." Sam hesitates, worry marring her features as she sizes up David.

"Please, please, please!" How the hell does Sam do this all day long and not give in every single time?

"Office is right over here." David nods in the direction of his small office, housed just down from the nursery stall. "It'll only take a few minutes and then Hannah can help fill up the carrot bins. You good with that?" David asks Sam, and I want to fall to my knees and worship at his feet. Alone time with Sam. Fucking finally.

Sam looks at me hesitantly, trying to ignore Hannah, who's tugging at the sleeve of her coat. "For a few minutes, I guess it's okay." She crouches down to get eye-level with Hannah. "You listen to everything David says, okay? I'll be right here."

"She's in good hands, Samantha," David vows with a reassuring smile. He holds out a hand and Hannah takes it, grinning up at him. Sam rises and shoves her hands in the pockets of her coat.

"You know, I have a daughter just a couple of years older than you," David says, leading Hannah away from the stall. "She's at the party, too." I hear Hannah's excited voice rambling away to David as they move into his office.

"So, sixty horses, huh?" Sam grins up at me.

"Well, sixty-one with Midnight." Letting Northern Star take the last carrot, I back out of the stall, closing the latch.

"You're going to actually name her that?"

"It's a done deal." Slowly, Sam starts walking through the stable, peeking in at each one of the horses as we pass.

"I'm pretty sure you've made Hannah's day, probably her entire year." I can hear the sincerity in her words. I don't think Hannah or Sam get to do things like this often, and it makes me want to do more.

"I'm glad she's having fun." The impulse to touch her, to keep her close, fires through me. I stuff my hands into the pockets of my jacket. As much as I want to take the lead, I want her to make the next move. I want her to feel in control.

"So am I."

"You're glad or you're having fun too?"

"Would it be bad if I said both?"

"It would be bad if you didn't."

"Seriously, this day has been amazing. The wagon ride, chopping the tree down, the dancing, Santa." She stops herself, shaking her head like she's said too much.

Sam pauses at one of the curious horses leaning out of the stall near the front of the stable. Her smile is everything. The fact that I had something to do with putting it there makes me feel like I can take on the world. "Yeah. The big guy in red is always a hit with the ladies."

Her face falls. "So, you do this a lot then, I'm guessing?" She props a hand on her hip, her chin jutting out in defiance. "Bringing women here?"

My eyes widen, an odd sense of pleasure flowing through me at her surprising show of jealousy. But I don't ever want her to question my feelings for her. "I've never brought anyone to the Christmas party."

"Never?"

"No. Never."

Her freckled cheeks flush again with that blush that serves to disarm me. Her shyness is just something else I can't get enough of. Typically, women aren't shy around me. Bold and demanding, yes. Shy? Not very often. "Oh . . ."

"Yeah. Oh."

She turns away, reaching her palm out to stroke over the neck of the horse that's demanding her attention.

"It must have been incredible to grow up here," she says, her eyes moving over the horse.

"Never a dull moment. Tell me about where you grew up." Her expression hardens as she stares back at me. "You said you're from the Midwest? What was it like?"

More silence that feels like a stake in my heart. I've let her in, let her see my family, a tradition I've not even shared with the guys in the band, and it hurts she won't give me a single thing. "Come on. Give me something. *Anything*. Please, Sam."

"It wasn't exactly the Midwest," she says quietly. "I lied about that."

"Why would you lie about that?"

"It was Colorado." She ignores my question, and I let it slide because she's giving me something. "We spent a lot of time outdoors."

"Hiking? Camping? That sort thing?" She moves over to study the lit display case on the wall, examining the blue ribbons and trophies inside.

"Yes, and skiing and riding. All that kind of outdoorsy stuff." Her hand covers her mouth on a laugh as she leans closer to the trophy case. "Is that you?"

I groan at the framed picture of me when I was sixteen and captain of the polo team. I think it's the last time I played. I'm decked out in leather riding boots and white pants with the navy-blue team polo shirt. If the skinny, awkward version of me at sixteen isn't enough, I'm standing proudly with a huge-ass trophy beside Panda, the white-and-black spotted mare I used to ride, named by Kat because she reminded her of a panda bear. I look ridiculous.

"You played polo?" Sam asks, trying to contain her laugh.

"Sure did. Was pretty good at it. I was number three." She

squints at me. "I was the captain. I had a high handicap, and a powerful hit." There's a playful glint to her eyes. "There's four positions based on what your skills are in polo."

"The captain. Why am I not surprised?" She laughs and it lights me up inside.

"That's Panda." I nod at the hilarious photo. "She was amazing. Could turn on a dime. We won a lot of championships together. I even went to London one summer to play. It was intense there for a few years. Mom would have loved it if I decided to pursue it further." I glance at the rows of trophies behind the glass case. I was good enough to play professionally. If I had chosen that path, my life would be entirely different, and I may not have even met Sam.

"It sounds like you really loved it."

"I did. I mean, I grew up around horses. I started riding when I was two. We all did. But, I guess I just took to polo more than my brothers and my sister."

"So why did you stop?" I love that she's interested enough to ask and want to know the answer.

"I found out I could play the guitar." I shrug as she tilts her head, studying me.

"Couldn't you do both?"

"I wanted something that wasn't related to all this." I spread my arms wide, and her gaze sweeps over the stable. "I wanted to do something on my own. When I first met Kennedy, it was at some seedy bar in LA. He had no idea that I came from money, and I tried to keep it that way for as long as I could. I just wanted him to accept me for what I could do with a guitar, not because of my last name." Gently, she reaches over to touch my arm through the leather of my jacket. I take it as a silent encouragement. Plus, I think the more I talk, the more likely she'll be to open up a bit.

"I wanted to have something just for me, you know? My whole

life people had done things for me because of who my parents were. And I'm not complaining, although I know it might sound like I am. I got whatever I wanted whenever I wanted it. But it also kind of felt hollow. Like it wasn't sincere. It felt like I didn't really deserve it or earn it." I shake my head. "I'm not making any sense."

"No. I understand that. Wanting to make it on your own terms." She swallows thickly, her eyes searching my face.

"Exactly. Anyway, I kept who I was from Kennedy for months. Long enough for my parents to send a crew out to LA to collect me. By then we had found Matty and Sean, and were just starting to play a few gigs." I laugh at the memory of some of those first "concerts." "I had to come clean and tell them. But, they got it. They didn't want to use any of my money, and we never did. We made it just by being us. And that's the best feeling. Playing for the crowd. Knowing they appreciate you regardless of what your last name is."

"I know. I feel the same way when I play," Sam says quietly. "You can just let go and be *you* for a while. Everything else, the stress, the worries, it all just kind of fades away."

I take a step forward, closing the distance between us, scanning the mistletoe hanging throughout the stable from the wooden rafters. Fuck, I need to kiss her like I need my next breath. It's been taunting me for days. "You know, there's a tradition about mistletoe . . ."

She lets out a little laugh. "You don't strike me as a traditional person."

"You'd be surprised. There are some traditions I take very, very seriously. It's bad luck or something if you ignore mistletoe."

"I don't think that's how it works." Her voice softens, but she's playing along.

"But why risk it?"

"That's a good point."

I brush her hair behind her shoulder, feeling the thick strands move between my fingers. "I've been known to have one from time to time."

"And this is one of those times?" She's letting her guard down with me, but I know I have to be patient. Sam is vulnerable and still stuck in whatever nightmare she escaped from.

"This is the best point I've ever had."

"We really shouldn't," she says, her eyes fixed to mine.

"Mess with tradition? No. We really shouldn't."

Her hand drifts up my jacket, fisting the leather firmly, and with a small tug, my lips press to hers. It's a struggle to hold back a groan at the fact that she made the first move, that her velvet tongue is sweeping over my lips, that she tastes like melted chocolate and frosting.

Sliding my arms around her is as natural as breathing, and I let her lead me. I know I have to, given her past and that I still think it directs every single move she makes. The softness of her lips makes my head spin. When she presses against me, her kiss becomes less tentative, and her hand releases the death grip on my jacket, stroking up across the back of my neck.

I can feel her lift up to her toes, trying to close the height difference, and my arms tighten around her, while I struggle to keep us in the PG-rated zone. Now that I know what she tastes like, what it feels like to have her in my arms, I only want more. More of the faint little sound she just made, more of her touch—not just teasing the back of my neck, but everywhere, more of her lips, her tongue, her taste. Just more.

Taking her face in my hands, the kiss deepens, becoming urgent, and I savor every mind-blowing second until the shrillness of Darcy's voice breaks us apart.

"Cameron?"

♪ ♩ ♪ ♩

## samantha

MY HEART IS POUNDING A mile a minute as I try to disentangle my arms from around his neck. The expression of simmering disgust he shoots in the direction of that voice is 180 degrees from the tender passion he had just shown me. Passion I haven't felt in years, if ever.

Passion I want more of.

He looks back at me in resignation and lets out a slow breath. "To be continued," he murmurs. He seems to release my face reluctantly, his rough fingertips leaving a trail of fire across my skin. The click of footsteps comes closer, and I step back from him, pressing my cold hands to my cheeks in a vain effort to calm the blush that's raging. I feel like I've been struck by lightning; my entire body's tingling. And all he did was kiss me.

"Cam, are you out here—oh, there you are!" The blonde beauty who's been stalking him from afar all day comes around the corner of the stall and saunters right up to him like she owns the place. Based on what Cam has said, she probably hopes she will someday. "I thought I saw you come this way."

Her society smile falters when he deftly sidesteps her attempt to link her arm with his. Instead, he folds his arms and steps closer to me. "The stable isn't really the best place for stilettos, Darcy. I'm surprised you'd risk 'em."

"Your mother wanted you to know that some of your guests are preparing to leave. I volunteered to come find you." She keeps her eyes and her smile on him, as if I'm not even there. Cam's jaw tightens.

"She can see them off just fine without me." His smile becomes brittle. "In any case, they're her guests, not mine."

"Oh, Cameron." She shakes her head a little in fond familiarity, as if his statement was expected. And maybe it was, I realize with chagrin; she probably knows him better than I do. She extends a finely manicured hand and smooths the leather over one of his biceps. "Come on—let's go back inside and have some champagne."

"I'm fine where I am. But you go ahead—don't let me stop you." He moves toward me again, and out from under her hand. He's so close that it's impossible for her to ignore me. But she pretends to be surprised to find Cam isn't alone.

"Oh! Mrs. Chapman was wondering where you'd gone. Your charges are running wild in the ballroom," she says with a patronizing little smirk. She adjusts her fur lapel and casts a baleful eye over my wool peacoat. "If you want to get paid today, you'll get back to your job."

My eyes widen as Cam's narrow. "Darcy," he growls in warning.

"What?" She blinks at me in mock innocence. "You *are* the nanny Victoria hired, aren't you?"

Her act is so transparent, I have to stifle a laugh. She's like a character on a bad sitcom. "I beg your pardon?"

"She's not a nanny," Cameron says flatly. His jaw is clenched so tight the veins in his neck stand out. He slips his hand in mine and my breath catches. "Samantha, this is Darcy Hamilton, a friend of my mother's."

Her eyes dart to his, but she manages a little laugh. "One of your friends too, I hope, Cam." Her hand flutters at her throat, the huge diamonds on her ears winking at me. "And you can't blame me for mistaking you, Samantha. I mean, you seemed so . . . ah, *well-suited* to childcare."

I refrain from rolling my eyes. She obviously doesn't think much of children. Cameron opens his mouth to retort, but clamps it shut again as the thundering of little feet approaches. "Momma!" Hannah flies around the corner and crashes into Cam's long legs, making him laugh.

"Whoa, there, little missy." He reaches down to steady her. "You don't want to run around too fast near the horses, even if they're in their stalls. Now, what's so exciting?"

"David put the name tag I made on Midnight's stall." She beams up at us. "He said I'm one of the bestest horsie namers you've ever had!"

"I think he's right." Cam's fingers return to the back of my collar, and I feel them burrowing in my hair. Electricity jolts through me when his fingertips connect with my skin. How can he cause that kind of reaction in me from such slight contact? I shoot Darcy a look, hoping that she isn't noticing, but my concern is unfounded. She's staring at Hannah with a mixture of horror and distaste that I'd normally expect if someone had stepped in something foul.

Hannah is oblivious, staring with fascination at the sleeve of Darcy's designer leather coat. "That's so pretty! Is it soft?" She reaches for the fur trim, causing the blonde to rear back and snatch her cuffs out of reach.

"Keep your grubby hands to yourself!" She strokes the fur absently, glaring at Hannah. "This is fox."

Hannah jerks her hand back in fear, as if she touched a hot stove. I shoot Darcy a scathing look and crouch down in front of my abashed little girl, whose bottom lip is quivering. "It's all right, sweetie. Don't worry. She's not a very happy person."

"*What* did you say?" Darcy's irritation directs at me, which is preferable. I can handle her.

But Cameron isn't as pleased. The scowl he levels at her makes her blanch. Then he kneels and joins me next to Hannah with a reassuring smile. "No worries, pretty girl. I think I need to get you and your momma home. Let's go say good-bye to Midnight, okay? She'll be sad if you leave without saying good-bye."

Hannah gives him an uncertain smile, but nods and lets me tug her knit cap on. "I don't want Midnight to be sad. It's not nice." She giggles as he swings her up into his arms, her good humor restored. Darcy stares in confusion as he carries my daughter past her.

"Cameron?" He ignores Darcy and continues without a word, leaving her reddening face in his wake. I toss her a withering glance.

"Perhaps you should pick on someone your own size next time."

"SORRY ABOUT DARCY."

Cameron is gripping the steering wheel as if he wished it was somebody's neck. I shrug, trying to make light of it. "It wasn't your fault. She's responsible for her own bitchi—er, behavior," I add. His lips twist in amusement.

"She certainly is," he says. "Not that she'll ever admit it."

As long as Hannah's okay, I can take whatever words that spoiled bitch chooses to spew. I snort to myself, remembering her "insult." She'll probably never know what joy children can be. I glance in the back seat; Hannah is still out like a light. She crashed about five minutes after we got back on the road. Mrs. Finnegan's going to have it easy tonight.

"You said she was a Miss Massachusetts?" I say, trying to distract him. "What was her talent? Let me guess—ballet?" I can totally picture her in a pristine tutu, pirouetting on a stage.

He grins and takes the next corner. "According to Kat, she did a dramatic reading from *War and Peace*."

The words are out before I can stop them. "The whole thing?"

He snorts out a laugh, checking quickly in the rearview to ensure he didn't wake Hannah. "It would've been fitting, considering how much she seems to enjoy hearing herself talk."

We stop at a light, the deep purr of the engine changing to a restrained growl. "Aside from Darcy's unwelcome interruption, did Hannah have fun today?"

I chuckle. "Are you kidding? It's all she's going to talk about for weeks—months, probably. Thank you, Cameron. Really. It was a magical day . . . for both of us."

"I'm glad. I never knew I had such a talent for gingerbread houses," he quips, tapping the wheel with his index finger. Then he pauses and gives me a look that sets the butterflies loose in my belly. "I enjoyed our time in the stables, too. I've never been sorrier for an interruption as I was when Darcy showed up."

The pulse in my throat thrums as I remember how his lips felt against mine. I tear my eyes away from him and focus on a loose buttonhole thread. "She's very beautiful."

"She is." He reaches over to thread his fingers with mine. "But she's like those diamonds she was wearing. Beautiful to look at, but cold to touch." He gives my hand a squeeze. "I prefer fire to ice."

My breath catches, and I glance at him, enjoying the way his hand feels. "I do, too. What if we get burned?" I whisper, wishing I didn't want to feel his arms around me again. And his lips. Oh, his lips . . .

"I'm willing to risk it if you are." He pulls our joined hands to his mouth and presses a soft kiss to my knuckles. I give him a soft smile in response, the sudden lump in my throat making words impossible.

I just wish I didn't have so much to lose.

I'M NOT SURE IF IT'S wise to let Cam walk me to our apartment, but one look in those sparkling hazel eyes and I can't say no. Besides, it's only fair, since he welcomed us into his own life today. But his silence when he ducks under the doorframe and enters my haven makes me second-guess my decision.

He sets a sleepy Hannah on her feet, and I steer her into our shared bedroom to change into pajamas before I leave her with Mrs. Finnegan downstairs. When I come back into the main room, I see him staring at some of the ornaments he'd given Hannah. She'd hung them along the single strand of Christmas lights I'd mounted around our window. The place seems even smaller with his huge frame in it; the ceiling is scant inches above his head.

"It'll just take her a minute, and then we can go," I comment and move to change out of my boots and into my sneakers by the door. "You don't really need to walk me to work, Cameron. It's just a couple blocks away." Sneakers on, I brush the tangles out of my hair quickly and braid it. All the snow today has made it a frizzy mess.

"Of course I'm going to walk you." He turns away from the pitiful strand of lights and takes in the rest of the room and small kitchenette before facing me with a helpless expression. "Sam . . ." He gestures around the sparse room, palms spread.

My heart twinges. I know what he's thinking. "Don't. I don't want your pity. I know it's not much, especially compared with everything you shared with us today, but it's the best I can do right now." I stand, brandishing the hairbrush, chin raised. He doesn't know how much better we have it this Christmas than we did last year. My aunt in Chicago is a wonderful woman, but she lives on my deceased uncle's tiny policeman's pension, and can't help much. I've come this far mostly on my own, and I'm proud of it. "Don't judge me."

"I'm not. I'm not like my mother or Darcy." The hurt in his eyes wounds me. I let go of some of my defensiveness with a sigh and walk over to touch his arm in apology.

"I know you're not. I saw that today." I look around the clean but meagre apartment. "It's been a good place for us, all things considered. It's really not a bad neighborhood and the Finnegans have been a godsend. But I need to think about moving during the summer. Hannah begins kindergarten next fall, and I'm not thrilled with the schools in this district." I dread the thought of relocating. A better school district means higher rent; it'll be tough finding an apartment I can afford.

"Let me help, when the time comes." My eyes flare and he quickly adds, "I know you don't need it. I'm not offering out of pity or charity. But please accept it, for Hannah's sake."

He presses a soft kiss to my forehead, and I relax against him. His soothing touch makes it so easy to forget my fears and worries about Ray, Hannah's schooling, and the fact that I'll need to find money for a new coat for her soon. But as tempting as it is, I can't let myself get too comfortable. Considering all the baggage that comes with Hannah and me, I'll be surprised if he's still interested next month, much less next summer. Darcy—even with all her expensive coldness—would probably be a much easier and acceptable alternative for him.

Raising my face, I give him a soft smile. "I promise I'll think about it. When the time comes."

"SHE'S QUITE THE WATCHDOG," CAM mumbles, keeping pace beside me. His breath billows in puffs around his head in the cold.

I cock an eye at him. "Mrs. Finnegan? She's the sweetest woman alive. I'm lucky she's always so willing to look after Hannah for me." She had accepted Hannah with open arms tonight, but she cast a fishy eye at Cam that made me chuckle. God bless that woman. With a few charming smiles and assurances he was just walking me to work, he was able to make her smile—a bit. "It's Mr. Finnegan you have to worry about. He has a shotgun hidden beneath his cash register."

Cam chuckles. "Good to know." But his amusement evaporates when I stop in front of the Black Arrow. "This is where you work?"

"For now. The schedule works well around rehearsals and performances." And until I can safely take a first string or principal position that pays more, I need the income. I can hear the night's band warming up inside, and a small crowd of people brush past us to enter. The buzz of conversation and scent of beer and sweat hit us as the door swings open. "Thanks for walking me, but I really need to get busy. My boss is going to be looking for me."

He's eyeing the bar with alarm and suspicion. "Oh, come on," I say, trying to reassure him. "It's not that bad. And my boss is a great guy."

He grunts. "I used to play in places like this—I know what they can be like."

I roll my eyes and stretch up on tiptoes to try to kiss his cheek, but he wraps an arm around me and turns his head, planting his lips on mine. Just like in the stables, my body ignites and blood surges in my veins. His lips are an amazing combination of firmness and softness that drives me crazy and makes me want more . . . so much more.

"Cam . . ." I'm panting and have never wanted to skip work

more than now. "I have to go." A huge biker grumbling about someone getting a room steps past us and enters the bar. I pull away from Cam and try to calm my breathing. "I'll see you later."

"When?" He brushes my cheek with his fingertips. "What are you doing tomorrow?"

I wrack my brain, unable to think of a single thing while I'm looking at his lips. "Um . . . I'm not sure. Oh, wait—I was going to play in the park."

"In this weather?" He frowns. "Come on, let me take you to Sunday brunch. Or, do you take Hannah to church?"

His nose wrinkles adorably, and I giggle. "I'm a lapsed Catholic. The Finnegans take her to Mass sometimes, but I usually don't go. How about I call you in the morning and let you know."

"Will you really call me this time?"

"I promise." I back away and hold onto the door handle to anchor myself.

His soft smile melts my heart. "I hope so, friend." With a last skeptical look in the window of the bar, he heads back down the street to his car. I watch until he rounds the corner and then race inside. Grabbing an apron off a hook in the back, I pull it over my head and hastily tie it around my waist. Ned, the bartender, grunts as I scan the chalkboard to find out what section I have for the night.

"What put that smile on your face?" he asks as he pulls another pint.

*Friend,* Cam had said. I doubt he kisses his friends like that. I run a finger over my lips and smile. "I had a good day."

# chapter eight

## cameron

MY FINGERS HURT FROM PLAYING, but it's the only thing keeping me from going back to that bar. This whole afternoon didn't end the way I wanted it to. I hate the thought of Sam working at that dive. It screams of a bad idea. And seeing where she lives? Above that grocery store with threadbare carpet in a place so tiny, if you breathe, you hit a wall? My mind spins thinking about it. The Finnegans seem like nice people, and they obviously adore Sam and Hannah, but they can only offer her so much.

Sam deserves more than that. She deserves everything. And it pisses me off that some jackass has made her feel like she needs to hide away. Like some cheap apartment in a sketchy neighborhood is her only option.

It's tempting to go back to check on her, make sure she gets home safely, maybe leave her an anonymous tip, but I can't. Sam's fiercely independent, and she already has one protection order. The last thing I want is for her to see me as another man who takes whatever he wants.

The doorbell chimes, and I frown, setting the guitar into the stand. Maybe the neighbors are actually going to complain this time. I wouldn't blame them. I've been at it for hours.

Unfortunately, it's not little old Mr. Sampson I see through the peephole. No. It's someone much worse.

Opening the door, I lean against it, feeling a gust of cold air swirl inside. "How did you find out where I live?" I cross my arms, not budging an inch.

"Your mother, and is that how you greet all your guests?" Darcy blinks up at me from the snowy doorstep, a coy smile on her lips. My eyes fall over her fox-cuffed jacket, and I remember her scathing reaction to Hannah. Something tells me Darcy would rather walk across hot coals than spend any time with children. I'm also going to need to have a discussion with dear old Queen V. Trying to play match-maker is one thing. Giving women I barely know my address is stepping over the line, even for her.

"I don't typically get uninvited guests." The wind blows her blond hair, making it tangle around her face. She gasps a little, preening it back from her eyes. God forbid she should have a single hair out of place. But no matter how cold it is, there's no fucking way I'm letting Darcy into my house.

"Aren't you going to invite me in?" She pouts—a move I'm sure would work on a lot of men.

"No." Her eyes widen and she lifts up on those ridiculous high-heeled boots and tries to peer around me into the living room.

"I wanted to make sure you were okay. You left the party so quickly, I didn't have a chance to give you a proper good-bye." She tries on a sweet tone. Unfortunately, it's fake. There's no mistaking who Darcy really is. All the designer clothes and the expensive jewelry in the world can't hide the fact the only person Darcy cares about is herself. If I didn't know within the first few minutes of meeting her at the symphony, I sure as hell knew when she showed her true colors in the stables.

"I'm not alone, Darcy."

"Oh. I see." She tilts her chin up, an air of privilege and entitlement I recognize radiating off her. "I heard you playing. Is the rest of the band here?"

"No."

Darcy blanches, her lips pinching together in annoyance. Poor thing is obviously used to getting her own way.

"Don't tell me it's that woman from the stables?" Her voice drips venom, and I shake my head. The way her entire demeanor changes so quickly is disturbing. My initial assessment of bat-shit crazy is bang on.

"Okay. I won't. She saw right through your pathetic act today, you know."

She glares at me. "She has a child, Cameron," she hisses as if Hannah is some dirty little secret she doesn't want anyone to hear her talking about. My grip tightens on the door. She needs to leave. Darcy is the picture of everything I can't stand. Shallow, vindictive, and elitist.

"I'm aware of that."

She squares her shoulders, her eyes hard as they hold mine. "I never really had a chance, did I?"

"Even without Sam, you never had a chance, Darcy. And I hardly know you."

"And you think you know Sam better?" she fires back. She does have a point there. I do hardly know Sam, but the scary thing is that I want to.

"You're making a big mistake here, Cameron." There's something in her tone I don't like. Darcy is clearly pissed, but pulling a stunt like this is never going to change my mind.

"It's my mistake to make if that's the case. I trust that you can find your way home." Closing the door on her is easy. The call I need to make now may not be.

"DARLING, I'D ALMOST SAY IT'S becoming a habit, you reaching out to me. To what do I owe the pleasure?"

My mother's condescending tone only serves to amp up my anger. "Cut the crap, Mother. You sent Darcy to my house."

"Yes, well, dear, she was concerned that you disappeared."

I pace in front of the window. "Bullshit. You know how hard I work to keep my private life private."

"You didn't seem worried about privacy earlier this evening, Cameron, when you were dancing around the tree and trailing after that girl like a lost puppy dog with photographers everywhere, not to mention anyone with a smartphone."

"What I do with my personal life is none of your business." My voice rises as I clench a fist. My mother has always pushed my buttons. She seems to savor it, but this is crossing the fucking line.

"I'm afraid to burst your bubble, Cameron, but it's exactly my business. What you do reflects on this family. Reflects on me. I'm simply trying—"

"You're meddling is what you're doing." She lets out a long sigh, as if I'm the one trying *her* patience.

"Cameron—"

"No. You don't get to 'Cameron' me. I'm not letting you do this. Sam is the best thing that's happened to me in a long time, and

I'm not going to let you or anyone else ruin it." The truth of my words hits me square in my face. It's more than just an attraction; I want this woman.

I'm greeted with silence, and I let her sit there and stew. I can't remember the last time I spoke to my mother this way—if I ever have. It was engrained in us as kids to speak with respect, to never question, and for the most part, that's exactly what we did when we were growing up. My mother views me branching out and joining Redfall as one huge slap in the face. It goes against all of the plans she had for me . . . as a premier polo player, or following dad into business, or whatever else she deemed 'acceptable.' Plans I know I would never have been satisfied with.

"I didn't realize this girl meant this much to you." My mother's voice barely registers through the phone.

"Yeah? Well, she does. So back the fuck off Darcy or anyone else you may be planning on springing on me, because it's not going to happen. Not now. Not ever. And her name is Samantha. Please remember it the next time you see her."

"I see." There's that elitist tone I grew up with. I know it well. It's the one that says, I'm disappointed in you without actually having to say the words. Fuck if it doesn't still sting. "If that's truly the case, I apologize, Cameron. It won't happen again."

I'm momentarily stunned. An apology from Queen V. This has got to be a first. Still, I can't resist firing back at her, "You're goddamn right it won't."

"Watch your tone with me. I'm still your mother."

I rub my hand across the back of my neck. "I'm sorry, Mom. I didn't mean to snap at you. It's just—Sam's been through a lot, and I really want to try, you know? See where this goes."

"How much do you know about this girl?"

"Samantha, Mother. Her name is Samantha," I grind out in

a growl.

"*Samantha.* Well? What do you know about her? I don't think I need to tell you that another scandal would not be well received."

Looking up at the ceiling, I blow out an exasperated breath. "I'm not going to have this conversation with you. You want a scandal? Go talk to Nathan. He's got one brewing as we speak." I almost feel guilty about throwing my brother and his office quickie under the bus—almost.

"What? What's going on with Nathan?"

"You should really talk to him about that. Or better yet, ask Dad. He's well versed on the subject."

"You boys." She pauses and I can picture her frown of disapproval. "Just be careful, Cameron. I don't want to see you getting hurt."

"Always am, Mother." Hanging up, I'm still rattled. I know the pent-up energy and free time aren't a good combination for me. Thankfully, I have a gym and heavy bag, and right now, they're calling my name.

"IT'S MY TREAT, REMEMBER?" SAM'S eyes flash in warning as I pass over my credit card to the waiter.

"I know, it's just . . . I can pay for our half," Sam whispers. "I had a good night in tips." I try to tamp down the annoying sting of jealousy. I don't want to think about how many men she must have served at that bar last night. How they probably watched her, hell, probably flirted with her. At least she called me when she got home, accepting my invitation to brunch. To know she was okay, that she wanted to spend time with me despite her initial objections, was as much a surprise as it was a relief.

"And you should use that for other, more important things." I tilt my head in the direction of Hannah, who's oblivious, playing with her beat-up doll.

Hannah has been an angel at brunch and charming everyone in her path. I'm pretty sure they don't go out for meals often judging by the look of awe on Hannah's face when we walked into the restaurant.

It's a newer place on the waterfront with a view of the city skyline and Boston Harbor. The menu is heavy on seafood, but there were more than enough choices for Hannah. She's probably eaten her weight in waffles alone.

Sam sighs, studying her coffee cup. "Do you always get your way?"

"Usually. It's just brunch, Sam. Don't worry about it, okay?"

"Thank you," she says quietly, reaching across the table to touch my arm. "We haven't been out to a place like this in a long time."

"I'll take you every damn day if you want."

She laughs and the sound sinks into my heart. I'd give anything to see her like this all the time. Open and full of life. Most importantly, not afraid. That's what I want more than anything. For Sam to see she doesn't have to hide any more. That she's got options that go well beyond a dingy apartment. I want to be one of those options. Hell, I want to be at the top of the list.

"Every day?"

"Yes, ma'am. That's what friends do, right?" I add a tip to the bill when the waiter passes over the credit card machine to me.

"Are you like this with all your *friends*?" She twists a strand of her hair behind her shoulder. I want to do that. I want to feel how soft it is against my fingers, sweep it away from her neck, and kiss the freckles I imagine are hiding on her smooth skin.

Handing the machine back to the waiter, I keep my eyes locked to hers. "I have you in a special category."

"Is that right?"

"I only speak the truth."

She leans back in the chair, crossing her arms, causing her breasts to rise, the gray sweater she has on stretching slightly. She doesn't have a clue how tempting she is. "And are you going to tell me what category that is?"

"I think I'll borrow from our drummer's advice and keep you guessing."

Her smile widens. "Your drummer sounds like he might be a little dangerous."

I shake my head, laughing. "Sean is a lot of things, but dangerous isn't one of them."

"It is you!"

Breaking my gaze from Sam, I look up to a group of twentysomethings—three guys with that starstruck look I've come to know. Sam pushes away from the table as if it's on fire, turning away from the group and muttering to Hannah.

"Guilty."

"Oh my God. Your *Crash* album is awesome," one of them blurts out.

"I'm glad you liked it."

"Can we get a picture?" another one asks.

"Ah, sure." I glance over at Sam, watching as she shoves her hat on, tucking in those amazing curls. She's back to being nervous and guarded. She's focused on Hannah, crouching down to help her with her coat, and doing anything and everything to stay out of view. It stabs at my heart, and I wonder if there's ever going to be a time when she actually feels safe.

I push up from the chair as the group gathers around, and one by one, I take their phones, holding them out to snap off a few pictures. They're rambling on about a concert they saw, but for once, I couldn't give a shit. Typically, I'd take my time, ask them a few questions before I sent them on their way. But I need to get Sam and Hannah out of here before she shuts down on me completely.

I hand the last cell phone back. "Thanks, man. My girlfriend is never going to believe this," he says.

I shake the guy's hand again. "If you could just hold off on posting those for a while, I'd appreciate it."

"Oh, yeah. Sure, no problem. Keeping it on the DL. I got you," one of the guys says nervously, giving me the sign of the horns.

"Thanks." One of them practically trips over the chair as they back away and return to their table.

Sam finally looks at me, all the light gone from her eyes, replaced with something darker, something I don't like. Her voice is hard, clipped when she finally does say, "We need to go."

Outside the restaurant, Sam plants one hand on her hip, the other holding Hannah's hand as she bounces in place. "Please! Please, Mommy! I want to go to the museum!"

"Maybe another time, sweetie." It's been like this for a few minutes now, since I suggested we spend the afternoon at the children's museum. It's free admission today, ending any argument that I not spend money on her, and there's a dinosaur exhibit. A win-win in my books, but apparently not in Sam's.

Hannah's little bottom lip quivers, tugging at my heart again. How the hell Sam denies her anything, I'll never know. Sam leans closer to me, her voice lowered so Hannah can't hear. "We got lucky today in the restaurant, but I don't want to risk it."

So many things I want to say and need to know. I said at the café that first day that we would get it all out and leave it in the past, but I know we can't. What this asshole has done to Sam has left permanent scars. No afternoon at a children's museum is going to take them away. I'm not sure if there's anything that will. I'm also not willing to give up that easily.

"I'm sorry. I should've run it by you before I opened my mouth."

Shaking her head, she gives me a soft smile. "No. You shouldn't have. You should be able to go wherever you want without worrying about me." Hannah tugs on the sleeve of Sam's coat.

"But I want to worry about you. I want—" She silences me, reaching up to place her fingers over my lips. They're cool and shaking slightly, reminding me of how careful I need to be with her. How much I want to find the animal who made her afraid to have her picture taken and rip his fucking arms off. This isn't who she is. I've seen her play with a fire that can't be faked. I've seen her fiercely defend Hannah, not backing down to Darcy. I've seen the love and devotion she has despite the hell she's been through. I just wish she could see how strong she is.

"Don't, okay? Don't say anything. We really enjoyed today, isn't that right, sweetie?" Sam lifts Hannah into her arms, kissing her cheek when she sniffles. Hannah nods and buries her face into Sam's shoulder.

I can't stop myself. It feels like she's trying to tell me good-bye, and I can't let her. "What about visiting the horses at my parents' place? I can guarantee you there'll be no one there taking pictures." I try not to sound desperate. Sean would never let me hear the end of this—practically begging to spend time with a woman.

Sam's eyes search mine. So much uncertainty and doubt that I want to erase. I know I've probably already pushed her as far as I can. I never want her to feel like I'm telling her what to do, so I just wait, leaving the decision to her, and she surprises the hell out of me again.

"We'd like that, wouldn't we, Hannah?" Hannah lifts her head from Sam's shoulder. "Would you like to go check on Midnight?"

Hannah beams a smile that could light the city.

SAM LETS OUT A GASP as I snap a quick picture with my phone of Hannah with one of Kat's old riding helmets on at the stables. The kid is adorable. "Delete that. Right now, Cameron. I mean it." There's no mistaking the warning in Sam's voice. I glance over at her as she glares at me from beside Galaxy, the gray mare she'll be riding this afternoon. Hannah takes off, skipping through the barn.

"I'll print a copy for you and then I'll delete it. You can even watch me. How does that sound?"

She grips the reins tighter. "No. What if your phone gets stolen or you accidentally post it or something?" I stuff the phone into the pocket of my jacket.

"That's not going to happen. I promise." I move beside her, and she blows out a breath.

"You can't know that."

"You can't keep thinking about all the things that could possibly happen. You'll drive yourself crazy."

"I have to. I always have to." Her voice is quiet, resigned.

"It's just a picture, Sam. I didn't see any at your place." Leaning down, I run my hand along her thigh, down to tap on her boot. "Up you go. Foot in the stirrup. There's a trail calling your name."

## samantha

LEANING BACK IN THE SADDLE, I raise my face to the winter sunshine filtering through the trees. I haven't been this relaxed in ages. I'd forgotten how much I enjoy riding.

Cameron's back is a solid block of worn black leather in front of me as he leads us confidently through a narrow spot in the trail on the way back to the stables. Although the sun is shining, there's still a lot of snow on the ground and a chill in the air. We cut our excursion short because the last thing I need is Hannah getting a cold.

I can hear him murmuring to her, the soothing sound drifting back to me. She had been excited at the thought of going horseback riding for the first time, but when she looked up at me on my perch on Galaxy, the excitement in her eyes turned to anxiety. I mentally chide myself, remembering how intimidating horses can seem when you're only three feet tall. She allowed David to hand her up and place her firmly in front of me, but had remained uncharacteristically quiet. After about twenty minutes of watching her clutch at me with a death grip, Cam asked if she wanted to ride with him. I've never seen her agree to anything faster in her life. Since then, she's been looking around with interest and smiling more, her little hands clinging to his arm holding her securely against him. I'm trying not to feel snubbed that my daughter feels more comfortable with a stranger than with her mother.

Except . . . Cameron isn't a stranger. Not anymore. He's become a good friend, fast becoming more. I frown and duck my head a little to avoid a drooping tree branch. How much more he becomes is something I'm going to have to decide soon, before my heart decides for me.

Because, look how well that turned out in the past.

"Momma?" I look up to see Hannah peering back around Cameron at me, and I wave. A few strands of strawberry blond have escaped from the old riding helmet Cam let her borrow, and she swipes at them impatiently.

"I'm right here, sweetie," I call and urge my horse into a trot to catch up as the trail widens again. When I pull alongside, she nods in satisfaction and resumes humming softly to herself as she takes in our snowy surroundings.

"So . . ." Cam pauses and steers his horse, Whiskey, around a fallen log. "Are you going to tell me where you learned to ride?" He shoots me an amused glance. "Because, I have to say, I was looking forward to some close contact while I taught you a few basics, and now I feel cheated."

I laugh. "Oh? Exactly what kind of contact did you think you'd get away with, *friend?*"

He smiles and grips his reins a little tighter. "Oh, you know. Just a little friendly, friend-like contact." The smoldering glint in his hazel eyes makes my breath catch and my heart beat faster.

I swallow down my sudden emotion. "I told you I grew up in Colorado, yes? I learned there." Taking a big breath, I pray I'm not making a mistake. "In Telluride."

"Really?" He smiles over at me. "I love Telluride. Haven't been there in years though. The band stopped there between shows one summer for a little R and R." He chuckles. "It seems like such a migratory place. I guess I never thought that people must live there year-round."

"Oh, they do," I retort, my sarcasm thick. "We're the fixtures who keep everything running so the winter ski set and the summer jet set can just come and go as they please, leaving their money behind."

He has the grace to look sheepish and clears his throat. "It's a beautiful place to grow up. Do your parents still live there?"

"No." A sudden chill falls over my heart, and I close my eyes briefly, willing away unwelcome memories. I shift in my saddle and tug my coat closer around my throat. "They ran a pub on Pine

Street that featured live music. It was especially popular with the tourists from LA. We lived in an apartment above it. Mom and Dad tended bar, and I waited tables once I was old enough." It feels weird and a little risky to talk so much about myself, but it also feels like a weight I wasn't aware of is lifting from my shoulders. It feels . . . normal. Blessedly normal.

I miss that feeling.

He squints and looks heavenward for a moment, before his eyes pop open in recognition. "I think I've been there. Did it have a huge wagon wheel mounted above the bar?"

"Yep," I affirm, surprised he knows that. "It didn't really go with the décor, but Dad loved it. Said it was in honor of our ancestors who came west in wagons or something like that. It was called Murphy's."

Cam slaps his thigh, his eyes lighting up. "I *have* been there. Shit. Murphy is our drummer's last name, so of course he thought it was in his honor. Made us drink there almost every night."

I smirk. "Sorry to break it to him, but Murphy was my goldfish."

Cameron's booming laugh echoes through the trees, startling my daughter and Whiskey. Hannah scrambles to grip the saddle pommel as the horse prances to the side. Cam quickly settles them both with soothing words, but I have to stifle my own laugh at the stink eye my feisty daughter shoots him over her shoulder. I wonder if he recognizes his peril.

"I can't wait to tell Sean. His ego could stand being taken down a peg or two." He reaches forward to pat the horse's neck, and then looks at me quickly as another thought occurs to him. "I might have been there when you were working. We could've met then." He runs a hand through his hair, his eyes looking slightly dazed at that revelation.

I huff a laugh. "Maybe so. We had a ton of famous people filtering through, all year 'round. Movie stars, athletes, politicians. I suppose it's only natural there'd be some itinerant singers thrown in." I shake my head, remembering how starstruck I was when I waited on my first celebrity. The novelty wore off fast. They're just like everyone else; they can be kind or complete assholes. Some tip well. Some don't. Just because they make a lot of money and a million people know their names doesn't make them any better than anyone else.

The stables come into view and the horses automatically break into a trot, eager to get out of the cold. I can't blame them. David comes outside to greet us and takes Hannah as Cam hands her off. By the time I swing off Galaxy, he's already dismounted and takes my elbow to steady me. A couple stable hands take our horses and lead them inside as we trail behind. I unbutton my coat; in the warmth of the stables, I feel overheated. Craning my neck to see where Hannah went, I'm surprised when Cam suddenly grabs my hand and swings me into an empty stall.

His hand cups my jaw, drawing my face up to his. The intensity in his dark eyes takes my breath away. "I know we never met back then," he breathes. "If we had, I definitely would've remembered *you*."

Warm, soft lips cover mine, tentatively at first, and then with rising intensity as I respond in kind. A tiny voice in the back of my mind yells at me to slow down, but it's an annoying distraction—like the flies buzzing about the stables—compared with the suddenly blazing desire burning in my belly. An appreciative groan escapes him when I glide my hands up his chest and around his neck to hold him to me. The masculine smell of warm leather somehow goes perfectly with the faint taste of cinnamon toothpaste. His other hand dives in my coat, pulling me tight against his firm body. My pulse thrums in my throat; I feel like I could fly.

"Samantha," he breathes in my ear, his voice low and urgent. "I can't . . . I need *more*."

"Me too," I gasp, and his hips buck against me. The feel of him, hard and ready, makes my blood race. Releasing my jaw, he plucks my beanie off and buries his hand in my hair. He holds my head in place while our kisses grow more frantic.

Shrill giggling from somewhere nearby breaks through my lusty haze, and I wrench my face away from his. Cam's cheeks are flushed, and he's panting like he's run the Boston Marathon—we both are. It takes a second for me to regain my senses. My legs are shaky. He pulls away so our bodies aren't glued together any-more, but doesn't release his hold. He blows out a sharp breath and chuckles.

"Um, I suppose we should go find Hannah," he whispers, his eyes searching mine. I give him a shaky nod and try to disengage, but he holds me fast. "But I want you to know I don't regret this, Sam. And I meant what I said; I want more . . . more of that. With you."

I feel like I could drown in the dazzling golds and greens of his eyes. Despite the risks and the sheer train wreck my life has become, I can't help it. A shiver runs through me at the realization. I want more too.

"Yes." The word tumbles out before I can second-guess it. His face lights up and he leans down for another kiss, but this time I manage to pull away. "But, Cameron, there are things, things I need to tell you first before we . . ." I take a ragged breath. Can I really risk telling him? Maybe not *everything*, but I have to tell him *something*. It's not fair to keep him completely in the dark. "You may change your mind. I have a lot of . . . baggage."

He straightens and I realize how much he must have leaned

over to kiss me. Jeez, he's tall. I'm going to need a step stool next time to make things easier for him.

"You mean about Hannah's father?" At my nod, he runs a hand through his hair and a pensive look flickers across his face. He takes my hand and gives it a squeeze. "I'll listen to whatever you want to tell me. Whatever it is, it's going to be all right, Sam. We all have baggage. Let me in. I promise, you won't regret it."

God, I hope he's right. He smooths a stray hair from my face, and I lean into his hand, savoring the contact. As I look up into his warm, mossy brown eyes full of hope and longing, my heart squeezes. What is it about this man that affects me so?

"Momma!" Hannah calls, the sound of her scampering feet coming closer. "Midnight wants to come home to live with us! Is that okay?"

Cam and I both break out in a laugh, and I sweep a hand over my mussed hair. I'm a mess. Still chuckling, he bends down and retrieves my beanie from the floor, shaking some straw off so I can cram it back on my head.

"Let's go give her the bad news," he jokes, holding out this hand for me to take. I don't even hesitate; I place my hand in his, enjoying the feeling of hope for the future that bubbles up inside me.

"OKAY, DELETE IT NOW." I point at his phone. He rolls his eyes and pokes at the glassy surface. He thinks I'm being ridiculous, I know.

"Done." Then he pulls the paper from the printer and hands it to me. "See? Aren't you glad I took it? She's adorable."

We're standing in his father's home office in the main house, where he printed the photo of Hannah he'd taken earlier. I may have decided to open up a little more with him, but there's still no way I'm going to risk a photo of my daughter getting out there on the Net.

Looking at the photo, I smile. Hannah is grinning like a loon, the riding helmet slightly askew and allowing some of her red-gold ringlets to escape. He's right—she is adorable. I roll it up carefully and tuck it in an inside pocket of my coat. "That she is. Thank you for this. And thank you for today, too, Cam. She had so much fun. I've never thought about taking her riding anywhere." *Not that I'd be able to afford it if I had thought about it*, I think wryly. I can't even pay for the American Girl doll she's dreaming of, much less luxuries like horseback riding.

He smiles and steers me out of the office and back toward the grand staircase that leads to the foyer. When we came inside, the ever-present Henry took Hannah to get a cup of hot chocolate while Cam and I dealt with the photo upstairs. "She really seemed to enjoy it, once she relaxed a little. I'm not sure she'll ever forgive me for not letting her take Midnight home though," he says with a chuckle, letting me descend the stairs ahead of him.

"Oh, I'm sure you don't have to worry about that." I shake my head, remembering how happy Hannah was riding with him. "After the waffles this morning and horses this afternoon, I think you're fast becoming one of her favorite people."

He stops me on the second-to-last stair and skips down to the floor to face me; we're at the same height now. "Am I just one of Hannah's favorite people?" he asks, his eyes wide in fake innocence. My lips quirk in amusement.

"Fishing, are we, Mr. Chapman?" I tilt my head at him, my hand resting lightly on the curving, wrought-iron balustrade. "I would've thought that with your legions of fangirls you'd be more confident in your abilities."

His lips unfurl in a lazy smile. "Oh, I'm plenty confident in my abilities." He leans forward, our lips mere inches apart. "And there's only one girl I'm interested in." This time, I'm the one to close the gap, my lips melding effortlessly with his. I sigh into his mouth when his hands come up to cup my face as if I'm the most delicate china. Even when I can feel that he's restraining himself, like in the stables, there's always so much care in his touch, as if he's afraid of breaking me. It's so not what I'm used to, but I like it.

He nibbles lightly on my bottom lip, and then pulls back with a regretful smile. "As much as I'd like to show you more of what I'm capable of—and believe me, I do—I suppose we'd better table this for now. Queen V is off with her charity group for the day, but we'd give some of the older staff heart attacks if they stumbled on us." After one last soft kiss that sets my blood racing, he steps back and takes my hand with a smile. "Come on; let's go find Hannah before all the cookies are gone."

"Cookies?" I giggle. "I thought Henry took her for cocoa?"

He leads me across the expansive foyer, past the sweeping living room archway and, with a flourish, opens a door that I now know leads to the back of the house and the kitchen. "I think Henry would resign his post before allowing someone to serve cocoa without cookies. After you, m'lady."

AFTER THE LOVELY WEEKEND CAMERON gave us, I've tried to get back into my usual routine, but I feel off. Our small apartment feels stifling. The lovely decorations he gave Hannah have made it feel more Christmassy, but I'm still agitated, chafing against something I can't define.

Today's rehearsal will be the first time I've seen Cam since we went riding a few days ago. It's unsettling how much I want to see him again. Thoughts of him have filled all the empty spaces in my life that I've been ignoring. Although I've talked to him a few times over the phone, we haven't discussed any of the things I know I should talk to him about. Instead, we've done the twenty-question thing, learning more about each other's likes and dislikes, always keeping our banter light and away from the elephant in the room. And we talk about Hannah. He never fails to ask about her and seems genuinely interested in the little things she does. I get the feeling that he's letting me move at my own pace, which I appreciate. I should be worried about how attached I'm becoming to him, but I just want to pretend a little longer that everything will be all right and that he won't disappear once he learns the truth.

The ground I stand on is shaky; it's not fair to expect someone to join me until I can stop running.

I put all my anxiety aside when I get to the arts center. I greet Olivia and half-listen to her chatter as I hang my coat in my locker, wondering if Cam here yet. I want to try to say hello before everyone gets here. I snicker to myself—would he think it too much if I dragged him into a practice room and gave him a proper hello? *Get a grip, Sam; your fangirl is showing.*

When I grab my violin case off the shelf, a note flutters to the floor. I stoop to pick it up and turn to see Olivia staring at me, her eyes narrowed. "What?" I look myself over and smooth down my blue sweater. "I haven't spilled something on myself, have I?"

"What's with the dreamy look?" She has an inquisitive smirk on her lips. "You haven't heard a word I've said, have you?"

My cheeks heat. "Of course I have. You went out with Dean, the trumpet player, and enjoyed his tonguing technique up close and personal."

"Sam!" She slaps my arm lightly with a laugh. "I didn't say it like that!"

"Well, that's what you meant." I smile at her huff and open the note. "Hmm. Well, I'll see you in there in a few. Wendy from HR wants me to stop by first."

She hoists her cello case on her back. "You'd better hurry before Maestro gets here then." I nod and head toward the front offices, hearing her call behind me, "Don't think you're not going to tell me later why you're so swoony today!"

"Wouldn't dream of it," I mutter, my steps quickening. Wendy, the symphony HR manager, is one of the few people I've confided in regarding Ray. I had to—it's the only way she'd agree to arrange that I get paid in cash instead of a check or electronic transfer. She also ensures that I don't need to participate in any publicity photos for the symphony. I jog down the hall, passing the occasional player and dodging instruments, and knock once when I reach the correct office before entering. Wendy sighs in relief when she sees me.

"Samantha!" She stands and tucks her gleaming chestnut hair behind her ear. "Thanks for coming so quickly. Listen, I need to give you a heads-up."

*Holy fuck—he's found me.* My blood freezes. Knuckles white, I cling to a chair back to stop swaying. At my terrified expression, Wendy waves her hands in front of her and quickly comes around her desk.

"No—not that," she says soothingly. "I'm sorry. I should've worded that differently." Taking my elbow, she guides me to sit before my knees give out.

"Sorry," I choke out, but she waves my apology away.

"I didn't mean to scare you. But I want to let you know that I have had an inquiry about you. From Mrs. Chapman—Victoria Chapman."

I blink, not sure I'm hearing her right. "Are you kidding? What did she want to know? What did she say?"

Wendy taps her fingers on the arm of the chair. "She stopped by yesterday. She wanted your address and a copy of your file. I replied that all personnel files are confidential. She seemed to accept that, but I could tell she wasn't happy about it."

"Somehow that doesn't surprise me," I mutter, pressing a hand to my forehead. "She's used to getting what she wants, I think."

Wendy snorts. "That's one way of putting it." She leans back in her chair, studying me with concern. "I thought you should know what happened, considering your need for privacy. Do you know what's going on? I mean, I can count on one hand the number of times I've talked to Victoria Chapman. She doesn't mingle with the staff, so for her to seek me out is rather extraordinary. Have you applied for a scholarship or something?"

Unfortunately, I have a good idea what the infamous Mrs. Chapman is after. I stand and give Wendy a smile that's more confident than I feel. "No, I haven't. But I have to get to rehearsal now, so I'll worry about her later. Thanks, Wendy."

"Anytime, Sam. See you later."

MY HEAD IS SPINNING AS I navigate past people preparing their instruments and take my seat in my row. The situation seems clear. Cameron's mother has been trying to hook him up with that Darcy snob. Even if Cam isn't going to go along with that little scheme, I'm sure the last thing his mother wants is for him to turn around and become involved with a nondescript little nobody with no family name or fortune to commingle and make new little baby fortunes.

I remove my violin and push the case under my chair, trying to fight off the panic bubbling just beneath the surface. What if she finds out the truth before I have a chance to tell Cam? Or worse, what if she finds out about Ray and contacts him? I swallow a sob, knowing I'd have to run again, for Hannah's sake.

Just when I may have found something worth standing and fighting for.

An excited buzz rises among my compatriots, and I look around quickly for Cameron. Despite my churning emotions, the sight of him standing tall and handsome down in the audience seating brings a smile to my lips. But, who's he talking to? Based on Cam's hand gestures, he doesn't look happy. The other man runs his hand through his dark hair, and my eyes widen in shock when he glances up at the orchestra. Kennedy Lane. Redfall lead singer and part of Cam's inner circle. He looks just like he did in that *Extra* interview I saw a couple years ago. What's *he* doing here? No wonder everyone is extra twitterpated today.

Cam looks up at me, a warm smile spreading across his face, and Kennedy follows his gaze. But when his eyes land on me, they narrow; in fact, his steely regard takes me aback. He motions and says something to Cam, and then they turn and make their way up the aisle toward the back of the hall and out the doors, disappearing from sight. When Ivan announces that Mr. Chapman won't be participating until tomorrow's rehearsal, my unease increases.

Why does it feel like another shoe is about to drop?

# chapter nine

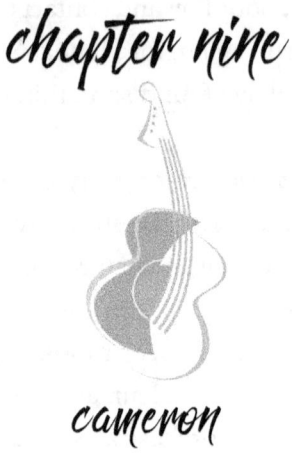

## cameron

"THIS BETTER BE FUCKING GOOD." Tossing my keys to the table near the door, I head into the living room with Kennedy and Tucker following along. I'm stuck somewhere between annoyed and comforted at their sudden appearance. They're not supposed to be here until the weekend when we head to Vermont. I'm working my way up to inviting Sam.

Alarm bells went off the second I laid eyes on Tucker at the concert hall, and they've stayed with me the entire drive back to my place. Something is wrong.

"Remember how much you love practicing the next time we have a rehearsal at six a.m." Kennedy's trying for sarcasm, but he's tense as he moves in front of the window, hands stuffed into the pockets of his leather jacket as he glances out to the light dusting of snow in my yard.

I lay my jacket on the back of the couch. "I'll never complain about playing. You know that. But the maestro isn't used to his guest artists bailing on rehearsal. I'm lucky he let me go." Although I wish I'd had a chance to tell Sam I was leaving. God knows what she's thinking about my sudden departure.

"Please. You can play Bach in your sleep. You don't need to practice. Something tells me your piqued interest has more to do with a certain redhead than your appreciation of the classics." I frown at Kennedy as he turns to face me.

"You told him?" My eyes cut to Tucker, but he doesn't flinch. He's fucking impossible to read.

"It's my job to protect you guys." It's that simple for Tucker. Never mind whatever invasion of privacy he's done, or how pissed off I'm rapidly becoming. Tucker's one and only focus has always been our safety. There have been plenty of times I've been grateful for it, but now not so much.

"I told you to drop it weeks ago!" I explode. "And I don't need protection from Sam."

"Sandra," Tucker says. "Or Sandy. Sandy Mitchell. That's her real name."

My heart stops, white noise buzzing in my ears. "What the hell are you talking about?"

"How much do you know about her?" Tucker asks, dropping a file onto the coffee table. It lands with a thud, and my eyes dart down to the thick file. I have to clench my fists to keep from picking it up.

The adrenaline fires through me, and I take a step toward Tucker. "I told you to leave it alone."

"I'd apologize, but I'm not sorry, Cam. I did the same thing for Kennedy and Matty," Tucker says calmly. "And when the Brit decides to spend more than ten minutes with someone, I'll do the same thing for him, too."

"Fuck's sake." I push against the solid wall of his chest, stalking away from him and sinking into a chair before I do something I'm going to regret. My leg bounces with nervous energy as I stare at the file. It looks so innocent sitting there.

"What did she tell you?" Kennedy settles in on the couch.

I rake my hand through my hair. There's no point lying to either one of them. Clearly, they know more than I do at this point. "She's got a restraining order against Hannah's father." Shaking my head, I shift forward on the chair. "The guy's an asshole abuser. I don't know all the details, just enough to know she's been hiding from him."

Kennedy shoots a glance at Tucker before focusing back on me. "That's it? That's all she's told you?"

"Fuck, it's not like she wants to talk about it. I didn't want to push her. All I know is that she's from Telluride and her parents owned that bar we drank at almost every night when we were there." That saying about silence being deafening really is true. I can almost hear that file calling out to me to pick it up. I push up from the chair, needing some space from the temptation. "Just fucking tell me, all right. Because I can't—I can't look at that." I wave my hand at the table.

"I think you need to, man," Kennedy says.

"I don't give a fuck what you think. It's bad enough you two know anything. She'd lose her shit if she knew about this." The urge to scream, to beat the living hell out of someone or something, fires through me. "Just fucking tell me."

Tucker doesn't hesitate. He launches right in, his words short and to the point as he keeps a close watch on me. "The guy she's got a restraining order against is her ex-husband. Ray Mitchell."

*Ex-husband?* I should've guessed she'd been married before. I didn't want to think about it.

I swallow past the lump in my throat. I almost tell him to stop, that this is too much, but I can't. "He spent some time when he was younger with a petty gang of thugs and general all-around assholes. Your break and enter, minor drug dealer types. They were married for about half a year when the first incident shows up. The official report is that she fell from a ladder." He pauses, and it's the first break I see in Tucker's typical stone-faced exterior. "She did a lot of falling it seems over the next couple of months. Then there's nothing for about another year when Hannah was born."

It's like I've been hit in the chest with a hammer. It hurts to take a breath. Given the little Sam's told me, I knew it was bad, but just the thought of anyone hurting her or Hannah, let alone someone who's supposed to love and protect them, slices me raw.

"Just before Hannah's first birthday, there's another incident." Tucker scowls, his eyes darting to the file. "He threw Sam down a flight of stairs. Landed her in the hospital with a concussion. He spent a year or so in prison for domestic assault until the good people at the Department of Corrections deemed him fit to be put back into society."

I grip the back of the chair, my fingers digging into the supple leather. "She divorced him while he was doing his time, got full custody of Hannah, and the protection order that she told you about, and moved to Chicago. Stayed with an aunt there. Ray tracked her down and broke into the house, but they got out before he could hurt the aunt or them. He went back to prison for another ten months. Then, Sandy Mitchell disappears. There's nothing for months until Samantha McKenzie hits the radar in Boston."

"Where is he now?" The words almost get caught in my throat.

"He's out of prison. He made his way through Upper New York and was here at the end of the summer." A chill rolls through me. "Kind of like he followed her. Worked as a deckhand on a fishing boat. He's in Florida now. But he's not laying down any roots. He's been catching odd jobs here and there, mostly working construction, but he's got no legit place to live, no possessions to speak of. Seems he likes to be able to move around if he needs to."

I blow out a breath, glad to still be gripping the chair. I need something to ground me. "You mean if he finds her."

Tucker's stoic stance doesn't waiver as he holds my gaze. "I'm putting someone on Sam and Hannah."

I rub a hand over the scruff on my jaw. "Fucking hell."

"She won't even know."

"Bullshit." My voice raises, but Tucker plows on.

"You haven't noticed Brent and Lincoln, have you?" Tucker crosses his arms, assessing me in that scrutinizing way he has. "I've had them keeping an eye on her for the last three days."

"You've known this for three goddamn days, and you're just telling me now?"

Tucker frowns, obviously not used to the hard tone of my voice. "I wanted to have all the facts before I told you. Listen, this guy is bad news. Now, I'm the last person to give advice on women, but if this isn't serious, you might want to think about cutting your losses now."

"I think it's too late for that, Tuck," Kennedy says, sizing me up.

"You know there'll be pictures of you and Sam sooner or later, and if Ray finds out who you are, he could be a threat. Not just to Samantha, to all of you." Tucker pauses, sharing a look with Kennedy. "Maybe I'm wrong, and the guy's completely rehabilitated. He had to take a mandated domestic violence treatment program in jail, but experience tells me assholes like this don't change."

"Do Matty and Sean know?"

"No. But we'll have to tell them something if you think Sam's sticking around," Kennedy answers. "We can't keep something like this from them."

Leaning against the chair, I hang my head in my hands. "What am I supposed to do now? Just pretend that I don't know any of this?"

"I don't know, man," Kennedy says, leaning forward and spreading his hands. Helpful as always.

I shoot him a glance. "If this was Abby, what would you do?"

"I'd do anything to protect her the best way I can. You know Tucker's guys are good. She's safe." Kennedy's right. Tucker is always looking for new members of the team, and finding Brent and Lincoln a few months ago was like hitting the jackpot. They joined us on the last leg of the latest Redfall tour, took over backstage security and ran it like a well-oiled machine.

Brent is a beast of a man, an ex–Navy SEAL and pushing two fifty of solid muscle. Lincoln played pro football for a while until an injury sidelined him, and he took up security. The guys are good, but that doesn't mean I have to like the fact that he went behind my back.

"And then what? What about when this asshole decides to come for her?" Fuck, I hate this feeling of helplessness. It's not something I'm used to. My instincts are to go to Sam, protect her, and take her away from the things that threaten to tear us apart before we even have a chance. Rationally, I know that's not the answer. Caveman behavior, no matter how engrained and tempting, is the exact opposite of what Sam needs or wants.

"*If* that happens, we'll know, and we'll deal with it," Tucker says. So calm, so fucking composed in the face of uncertainty.

Crossing the room, I plant myself in front of Tucker. "You went behind my back. Don't fucking keep things from me again." Tucker gives me a tight nod. "All right. Show me this prick so I know who I'm dealing with."

Tucker reaches down for the file, opening it up to slide out a photo, passing it to me. "It's his prison photo. We've got shots of him from the last few days if you want . . ." Whatever else Tucker is saying fades to a dull roar as I look at the photo of the monster who made Sam afraid of everything.

Vacant, dark eyes, shaved head, angry tattoo inching up his thick neck. The guy is obviously in love with the gym. My hand tightens on the picture, but there's something strangely calming about putting a face to the name of the fucker whom I'll destroy if he ever sets foot near Sam again.

"YOU KNOW, YOU MIGHT ACTUALLY hit the dartboard if you didn't lean so much to the left." The sound of Sam's voice has me fumbling my shot, and the dart just misses Kennedy as he ducks out of the way.

"Jesus, man. Watch it!" Kennedy complains. We're at the Black Arrow where Sam works in a job she shouldn't need. For the last half hour, I've watched as she rushes around, waiting on the tables in her section. She's attentive, always polite, and has earned a few leering glances from a couple of guys I'd like to beat the hell out of.

"You think you can hit the board?" I ask, ignoring Kennedy's glare from the corner.

"I don't think I can. I know I can," Sam replies, balancing a tray of empty drinks. Fuck she looks good. Even with a greasy stain on her shirt, and her hair pulled back, she's beautiful. Her feisty comeback only adds to the temptation I always feel when I'm around her.

"Is that right? I didn't think you noticed us over here, let alone what shots we're taking," I say, shooting her a teasing grin.

"You're kind of hard to miss," Sam says and quickly glances over her shoulder, like she's afraid to be caught talking to us.

I feel the weight of Tucker's punch in my arm. "Nice manners on you, Chapman." Tucker moves beside me. "Tucker Pearson. It's nice to meet you."

"Right. Sorry." I shove him out of the way. "Samantha McKenzie, Tucker is our head of security, and this one trying to blend into the corner is designated leader of the pack, Kennedy—"

"Kennedy Lane. I know." She gives him a wry smile as she plucks an empty glass from our table and sets it on her tray.

I slap a palm over my chest. "Twist the knife a bit harder. You recognize him but not me." Sam just shrugs.

"Don't you have your picture up all over this city?" Kennedy teases, pushing off the wall and out of the shadows.

"Hey, I work hard to not have that happen," I fire back at him.

Kennedy shakes his head and looks at Sam from under his Boston baseball cap. A lame disguise, but so far no one has noticed him. "It's nice to meet you, Samantha."

"You too. I didn't know you lived here."

"I don't. Just visiting our man here." Kennedy glances at me before turning back to Sam. "Actually, we're going to be heading up to Vermont with the rest of the group for a little R and R this weekend. You should come."

Sam's eyes widen as she looks at me. "I couldn't. I need to work on Sunday."

"I could make sure you're back for your shift." I try to not sound like I'm pleading, but I'm not sure it's working.

"I don't—"

"You can bring Hannah," I blurt out before she has a chance to use her daughter as an excuse.

"Are there going to be other children there?"

"Well, our drummer Sean is like a child, so yes," I answer, earning a laugh from Kennedy.

"I wouldn't want to intrude." She's hedging, but I can see that she's at least considering it. I'll take whatever small victory I can get.

"You wouldn't be. Abby, my girlfriend, is coming up, and Matty is bringing Tess. You'll have fun." Sam shakes her head. "It's in the middle of nowhere," Kennedy continues. "Ski hill, sledding, and best of all, away from the paparazzi. You need that sometimes, you know?" Sam glances down at the floor. "At least we do."

"I really can't afford to—" Sam starts to protest, but I interrupt her.

"No cost. It's at my place up there."

"You have a place in Vermont?" Sam asks, a slow smile breaking across her face.

"You name it, he's got a place there. A real estate tycoon this one here is." Kennedy slaps me on the back. "You can really hit the bull's-eye?"

Sam flashes a smile. "I can. My parents owned a bar back in the day. I played a lot of darts."

Kennedy holds out the dart that just missed his head. "Let's see it then. I bet you a grand you can't hit the bull's-eye."

Sam's mouth drops open as she looks at the dart before shoving the tray in my direction. Tucker laughs as I take it from her, the glasses clinking together. "I don't have a thousand dollars," Sam says, plucking the dart from Kennedy's open palm.

"Then you better not miss," Kennedy says, his lips twitching in amusement.

She lifts her chin, squaring her shoulders. "I'll hit the bull's-eye, but I won't take your money. That wouldn't be fair."

"Course it's fair. It's a bet," Kennedy argues, crossing his arms.

If she only knew the bets we've had in the band over the years, like the recent one I made with Matty that I'm currently regretting about no sex for the entire month of December.

"Not if I know I'm going to win," she counters.

"You seem pretty sure of yourself." Kennedy sweeps his hand toward the dartboard. "Be my guest."

Sam squints at the board. "One shot. I hit the bull's-eye. No money."

"Whatever you say," Kennedy murmurs, grinning at me.

Sam studies the board and I study her. The gentle curve of her neck, and her perfect ass. That look of determination as she confidently pulls her arm back and lets the dart fly is something I need to see more of.

Tucker's loud clap and Kennedy's exaggerated whistle tell me everything I need to know. Of course she hit the shot. Unlike me, who almost impaled our lead singer.

"Remind me not to bet against you," Kennedy says with a laugh.

A crash from the bar has us all turning in the direction of the sound. The bartender waves a hand in Sam's direction. "A little help here?" he hollers.

"I really have to get back to work." Sam reaches for the tray. "It was nice to meet both of you."

"What time do you get off?" I ask, blocking her path and holding the tray steady.

Those green eyes slay me as she looks up. "In a couple of hours."

"I'll walk you home."

She gives me a hint of a smile. "You don't have to."

"I know. I want to." My eyes dart down to her lips. The things I want to do with her, to her, for her. *Fuck.* She ducks her head, giving it a shake before I release the tray, and she darts around me, scurrying to the bar.

"You're royally fucked, my friend." Kennedy nudges me in the shoulder as I watch Sam help clean up the broken glass at the bar.

"I know, man. I know."

THE FEEL OF SAM'S HAND in mine spreads an unfamiliar warmth through me despite the plunging temperature. Kennedy and Tucker called it a night about an hour ago. Sam seemed surprised I stayed to wait for her shift to be done. I wonder when the last time it was that someone did anything nice for her. I wonder how many times that asshole of an ex-husband met her after work. I shouldn't be thinking about the sorry excuse for a man. He doesn't deserve to take breath, and he sure as fuck doesn't deserve any of my time, but I can't stop. That picture of him is permanently planted in my brain.

I'm on edge, glancing into the shadows of alleys we pass on the way to Sam's apartment, aware of Brent and Linc, who are damn good as they track us on the other side of the street. Fuck, I wish we didn't need them. I'm keyed up to every sound of a car and every door closing. Every single person who moves around us I see as a potential threat.

How the hell does Sam live this way, in this constant state of worry?

"I had a good night in tips," she says after way too much silence.

I try not to grin. I know what she's talking about. Kennedy left the thousand dollars he bet her as a tip with our waiter once he found out it's the restaurant's policy to pool and share the tips between the staff. "That's great. It was pretty busy in there tonight."

She squeezes my hand, looking up at me. "It wasn't *that* busy. I know it was Kennedy, and you."

"I don't know what you're talking about." I try for innocence, but she sees right through me.

"You can't keep doing that, you know."

"Doing what?" I steer her around a slush puddle on the sidewalk.

"Dropping money on me like that."

"I didn't do anything. It's Kennedy's money, and trust me, the guy has enough. A grand is nothing." I regret the words as soon as they're out of my mouth. I feel her tug her hand from mine, her body going stiff as she stops at the corner of her street.

"Not everyone can live like a rock star, you know."

"I know, Sam. I'm sorry." I can't resist reaching to brush a few windblown strands of her hair behind her shoulder, my hand sweeping over the back of her neck. She leans slightly into my touch. "I didn't mean—"

"Oh my God." Sam's face is white as a ghost as she looks over my shoulder in the direction of her apartment. "No!" She sprints forward, toward the flashing blue and red lights of the police cars and yellow caution tape. "Hannah!"

*Shit.* I take off after her, easily making up the distance. My arm catches her waist, lifting her up from the ground as we reach the first squad car, her legs flailing, her feet kicking at my shins. "Let me go!"

"Calm down, Sam."

"Don't tell me to calm down. That's the store, our apartment . . ." I hold her tighter, seeing tears stain her cheeks. "Please, please, let me go. I have to—"

"Momma!" Hannah's voice pierces the air, and I let Sam down, releasing her as Hannah waves from beside a police officer and Mr. and Mrs. Finnegan. Sam races to her, dropping to her knees, and practically crushes her to her chest.

Fucking hell. She's safe. Hannah's safe, and I can breathe again. My heart pounds like I've just run a goddamn race. The whole thing took less than minute. I've probably aged a decade in those sixty seconds.

I glance over at Brent and Linc, who are already crossing the street, moving to one of the police cars. Finally reaching Sam and Hannah, I help Sam up, keeping my arm around her. "What happened?" I ask Mr. Finnegan.

"The store was robbed while we were out looking at lights," he says, his voice shaking.

"Looking at lights?"

He nods, tightening his arm around his wife. "We took Hannah to see the Christmas lights at the crossing, and the windows at Macy's. When we came back, I saw the glass on the sidewalk." He nods to a jagged hole in the glass door of the store. "And we called the police. We tried to call you, but—"

Sam frowns, leaning against my side. "I must not have heard it at the bar."

I glance up at the shattered glass, my heart hammering. Sam and Hannah could have been here when this happened. "Jesus Christ."

"He swore, Momma." Hannah's small voice is enough to break the tension only slightly.

"Yes he did, sweetie." Sam presses a gentle kiss to her cheek.

"Sorry about that." I give the tassel on Hannah's hat a tug, and she cuddles in closer to Sam. "I'm going to see what the story is, and then I'm taking you my place. You can stay with me tonight."

"But—" I ignore Sam as she starts to protest.

"Can we, Momma?" Hannah glances at the police car before turning back to Sam. "I don't want to stay here." My heart breaks a little, hearing the worry in Hannah's voice, but I also know there's no way Sam's going to deny her daughter. She's staying with me tonight, and if I have anything to say about it, for much longer.

Sam nods at Hannah, and then looks up at me. "Okay."

"And if you'd like to stay in a hotel tonight while the police do what they need to here, I'll arrange it for you, Mr. and Mrs. Finnegan."

Mr. Finnegan glances down at his wife, and she manages a weak smile at him. "I think that would be a good idea. Thank you, Cameron."

Looking at the jagged edges of the broken window, I rub my neck. "Think you might have gotten a video of whoever did this?"

The shop owner grimaces and shoots a guilty look at his wife. "Our camera went on the fritz about six months ago. I've been meaning to get it fixed, but—"

"I'll get a new security system installed in the morning too and fix your door."

"You don't have to do that, son," Mr. Finnegan answers. "Insurance will take care of it."

"If it doesn't, I have it covered. Okay?"

"Thank you, dear," Mrs. Finnegan says, looking between Sam and me with a tired but sincere smile. "You're one of the good ones."

# samantha

"BEDROOMS ARE UPSTAIRS." CAMERON'S DEEP voice seems

loud in the hushed, dark brownstone, even though he's speaking quietly. I nod and he follows me as I carry my dozing daughter up the long, narrow stairs.

The ride from the Finnegans' was mostly quiet. I distracted Hannah with a few questions about the Christmas lights she saw, until I felt her finally relax and start nodding in my arms. I was so wrapped up in her, I barely noticed where we were, until I saw the row of stately homes. It's the type of historic, affluent neighborhood in Beacon Hill that you'd see featured in a magazine. Christmas wreaths hang from the streetlamps and it's started snowing again, creating a scene worthy of a greeting card.

He opens a door near the top of the stairs, and I carry Hannah inside, depositing her on the bed. It's a lovely room, with soothing sage-green walls and dark furnishings.

"Do you need this?" he whispers, holding out the small bag I'd brought with us.

A policewoman had escorted us upstairs at Finnegan's so I could retrieve a few things we needed. The store was littered with broken items, and my heart went out to the Finnegans. They didn't deserve this. Our apartment was still locked, although I pointed out to her a few marks on the door that hadn't been there before. The possibility someone had tried to get in our apartment sent chills down my spine and made my decision to stay with Cam easier. My thoughts went immediately to Ray. A botched break and enter screams of something that he'd do. What if he's here? I take a deep breath, needing to focus on getting Hannah to bed.

"No. I think I'm just going to tuck her in." I quickly remove her shoes, coat, and hat, and ease her under the covers. I kiss her forehead and start to rise, but Hannah's little hand shoots out and grabs mine.

"Will the scary man find us here, Momma?" My heart is in my

throat as I look down at my sweet girl, her red-gold hair spilling over the creamy sheets, and her eyes full of worry.

"No, sweetie. You don't need to worry about the scary man, ever again." I pray that I'm right. I smooth her hair back from her face, and she nods, apparently satisfied for now. She snuggles down into the plush bedding with her doll. I really hope I can afford to get her that new one—this one is on its last legs.

I give her another kiss and stand. "I'll be back in a few minutes to sleep with you tonight, all right? I need to talk to Cameron first."

"Okay, Momma," she mumbles, her eyes already closed. I join Cameron where he's waiting at the doorway, looking over my shoulder for one last check on my daughter. She looks so tiny in the big king bed. But she's safe, and that's all that matters.

Back downstairs, I finally have time to take in the surroundings. A light lemony fragrance of whatever cleaning products he uses floats on the air, mixed with his own spicy scent. Although it's obviously been updated, there are plenty of touches in keeping with the colonial roots of the building. Elegant, wood-lined archways graced with carved medallions. A magnificent mahogany mantelpiece adorns a gas fireplace. It's warm, masculine, and classic. Very apropos, considering the owner.

He shrugs out of his leather jacket and helps me out of mine with one hand. After he hangs them on a row of brass hooks at the base of the stairs, we stand facing each other, a sudden awkwardness descending between us. I hope he's not regretting his offer. He shuffles his feet on the dark wood floor and rubs his neck. "Would you like something to drink? Eat?"

"I'd love a glass of whiskey. Irish, if you've got it." His eyes pop open in surprise, and then he gives me a wry smile.

"Um, I don't have any liquor in the house at the moment. Booze was never my problem, but I figured it wouldn't hurt to go without for a while. I was thinking more like water or tea?"

I squeeze my eyes shut for a second, embarrassed. "I'm sorry—water is fine. And thank you," I babble. "Thank you for everything tonight." I run my hand through my hair, hoping I haven't offended him.

"Don't worry about it," he says, his eyes understanding. He turns and waves his hand toward a pair of leather couches near the fireplace. Stooping, he plucks a remote sitting on a side table and instantly flames appear behind the hearth glass. "Make yourself at home. I'll be right back."

He walks under another archway in the long room, passes a dining table, and disappears through a door at the rear into what I presume is the kitchen. I follow the sounds of him closing cabinets and such filtering out to me. In a room off to the left, I can see a row of guitars sitting in their stands, moonlight glinting off their faces. I would dearly love to hear him play again.

This place is far more comfortable than the formal majesty of his family home. I love it. Sinking into one of the sofas, I soak up the heat of the fire and sigh in relief as my tense shoulders begin to relax. I tug my shoes off and look around with interest, seeking more insight into the man who came to our rescue this evening. But when I spy a folder sitting on the edge of the coffee table in front of me, my blood freezes in my veins. It has my name on it.

My *real* name.

He knows. He knows the whole fucking story. His mother must have found the answers she's been looking for and wrapped it all up in a neat little presentation. Anger over her interference, shame that I hadn't plucked up the courage to tell him myself, and embarrassment from having to hide in the first place war within me.

Anger is winning.

"I hope you don't mind mineral water. I'm out of . . ." He

trails off as he approaches, two green bottles in his hand, and an expression of growing alarm on his face. "Oh, shit! Sam, it's not what you think."

"Really?" I think my voice could freeze lava. "What exactly do you suppose I'm thinking?"

"Look, it wasn't me," he blurts, his eyes wide. "I was going to—"

I spring to my feet and stalk toward him, my wrath building; he takes a few hasty steps backward. "Oh, I know exactly who it was. Nobody says no to Victoria Chapman! Even if it involves invading a person's privacy."

"Wait—what's my mother got to do with this?" He plants his feet. I glare up at him.

"Oh, please. I know she's been snooping around about me. The HR manager told me."

He blinks, confusion mixing with his frustration. "Fuck. I didn't know that." His mouth presses into a grim line when I scoff in disbelief. "I didn't! It was Tucker who told me. It's his job . . . *and* he was worried about me." Holding the bottles in his fists, he glowers down at me. "Besides, it's not like you were exactly forthcoming with the information."

I rear back as if he slapped me. Remorse tempers my outrage and embarrassment. "I . . . I was trying! I told you what you needed to know! I wanted to tell you more, but . . ."

"But what, Sam?" He scowls down at his feet and then looks at me, his frustration evident. "I don't even know what I should call you. Sam? Or Sandy?"

"My name is Samantha!" I cast a wary glance upstairs, hoping Hannah didn't hear me, and lower my voice to a hiss when I look back at him. "I didn't know if I could trust you! I wanted to, and also I wanted to tell you more. About me. But I needed to ensure that

Hannah was safe, because my daughter is *everything* to me, Cameron. I tried to tell you my life was complicated, but you, you . . ." I pause to angrily swipe at my eyes, my voice beginning to crack. "You just kept being your . . . being your wonderful, generous self. I told you what I could. I wanted to let you in, but I was afraid."

He takes a deep breath, his eyes full of sorrow and empathy. "Sam—" He takes a step toward me, but I back away.

"So now you know. You know it all." I wave a hand at the damned folder sitting there like a poisoned pill. "Thank you for letting us stay tonight. It's very kind of you." Swallowing thickly, I force my voice to remain steady. My face is hot. "We'll be on our way tomorrow. All I ask is that you keep it to yourself."

As my stupid tears finally let loose, I hear two muted thumps as the plastic bottles hit the floor, and then his arms are enfolding me, holding me tightly. He's so much taller when I don't have shoes on. "You don't have to go anywhere. Please, stay. Stay as long as you want. You're safe here." I cling to his shirt, suddenly exhausted and needing the comfort he's offering. "And I *don't* know it all, but I want to . . . and I want to hear it from you. You *can* trust me, Sam. *Let me in.* Please."

Looking up into his beautiful eyes, so full of concern and longing, I realize I don't want to run anymore. I'm so damn tired of hiding. I need to tell him, even if it means I never get to see him again. Warmth floods my veins when his lips press to my forehead.

"Okay."

# chapter ten

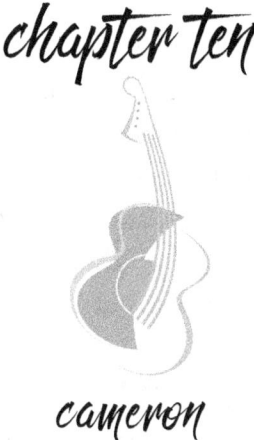

## cameron

THOSE GREEN EYES OF HERS slay me. I'm already on edge with what's happened tonight, but now, to have her between my arms, her soft curves pressed against my chest, my resolve is slipping. It feels like this is where she's supposed to be. It's like some piece of the puzzle clicking into place. Kennedy was right this afternoon when he said it was too late for me to walk away. It's not an option for me. I'm not sure it ever was.

Brushing her hair away from her face, my fingers lightly trace over her cheek, ghosting over her freckles. She closes her eyes, leaning into my touch, but I can feel that live wire of tension running through her. A battle raging between wanting to move closer and running as far away from me as she can get.

Given what I know about her bastard of an ex, I can understand her reluctance. I wonder if there's ever been a man she's trusted since she left him. Can she make room for someone now that he's gone? So many fucking questions, but I don't think I have the right to ask any of them. Instead, I keep my arms around her, letting her make the next move.

I feel her shake her head against my chest before she leans back. "I'm sorry. You're being so nice, and I'm just—"

"You don't have to apologize, Sam. Not to me. Not ever. I've got no idea what you've been through. The fact that you're still here, playing in the symphony, making sure Hannah's safe." Her silky hair brushes over my fingers, and I resist the overwhelming urge to tighten my arms around her. "You're the strongest person I know."

She takes a step away from me, shaking her head. "I don't feel strong. Most days, I'm just hoping I don't break apart."

"I'll hold you together."

She glares, that protective wall she's built up slamming firmly into place. "You don't get it. I don't want someone to hold me together. I want to do this by myself. I need to. Can you understand that?"

"You have been. Look what you've done so far by yourself. That doesn't mean there aren't people who want to help you, and it's okay to accept it. It doesn't mean you're not strong."

Her shoulders slump. "When is this going to stop?" Sam asks, her voice soft, her eyes searching for answers in mine. "When am I going to stop thinking the worst?"

"I don't—"

"I'm so tired, Cameron." She wraps her arms around herself. "Always looking over your shoulder, it's a horrible way to live your life. I'm tired of running all the time. Tired of hearing some random noise and jumping out of my skin. Tired of thinking everything and everyone is a threat. I shouldn't be afraid of you. Rationally, I know that, but I am. Even though you've only been sweet and kind, and a perfect gentleman." She moves to the French doors that lead to the backyard, looking out to the patio. "He was like that too, at first." She glances over at me. "They tell you that, you know? At the shelters, in counseling. They charm you, work their way in, and earn your trust, your love, before they slowly chip away at it until there's nothing left of it or of you."

"Sam." She's killing me. I want to go to her, pull her into my arms, and tell her it's going to be all right. I want her to know I'm not *him*. That it destroys me to hear her compare me to that useless waste of space.

"He wasn't like that all the time. In between, it was . . ." Sam pauses, squeezing her small waist. "Normal. We were normal. It was a relief when he wasn't hitting me or blaming me for something. And every time, I thought it was going to be the last. The last time he punched me, the last time he screamed at me." She closes her eyes, shaking her head. My stomach rolls, pain slicing through me. I want to take her pain away, protect her and Hannah from everyone and everything.

"I wake up every day and think, is this the day he's going to find us? Sometimes it's hard to believe we got away. And I still ask myself what I did wrong. Why I didn't see who he really was. How he was in control of my entire life." She twists her fingers together, glancing down at them.

"But he's not anymore."

"Isn't he?" Tears stain her cheeks as she lifts her face, and I can't bear to see her this way. I move to her because there's no other place I should be. She puts her palm on my chest before I can pull her into my arms. "Look at me. You've seen where we live, what I have to do. He may not be physically here, but he's still in control. He's still manipulating me. I'm afraid he's always going to be." She fists my shirt in her hand, but I don't move. I can't. I know I've got to let her come to me on her terms, in her own time.

"He's not right now. You're here and you're safe. You always will be with me, Sam. I promise."

"You can't promise me that. No one can," she whispers.

"Tonight, I can." I nod over to the door. "Look, I've got a security system that rivals Fort Knox. Nobody's getting in here." She looks at the keypad beside the door, letting out a shaky breath, and nods. "There're five bedrooms upstairs. Pick one and sleep. Really sleep for once. And in the morning, we can talk some more if you want."

"I'll sleep with Hannah. I always have. She'll be scared if she wakes up and I'm not there." My chest hurts listening to her. My arms feel empty without her in them, and this whole situation is about as fucked up as it can be. No one should live this way, and I'm making it my mission to see that Sam understands she deserves more.

♪ ♩ ♪ ♩

"ARE YOU IN JAIL OR has someone died?" Matt's annoyed voice growls through the speaker on my phone.

I answer with a laugh. "No. Nothing like that."

"Fuck's sake. Then why are you calling me at . . ." I hear another muffled groan before he's back. "Four fucking thirty in the morning?"

Damn it—I didn't think about the time difference between Boston and San Francisco. "It's not four thirty here, and I'm making your famous pancakes."

Silence followed by a huff. "I'm on some show where they're going to jump out from behind the furniture and tell me I'm on live TV, aren't I?"

"No. But that does give me a great idea." I frown at the pathetic-looking thin pancake in the pan. What a joke. I wanted to make breakfast for Sam and Hannah, and I thought Matt's pancakes he's been making us forever were easy to do. Hell knows how many times he's made them for us over the years. If he can do it, how hard can it be?

"Start making sense, Chapman."

"I'm trying to make pancakes, and they won't fluff up like yours do."

"Are you fucking serious right now?" A faint female voice drifts through the phone, and I almost feel bad about waking Tess up. "Go back to sleep, Cardinal . . . No, everything's okay. It's just dickface Cameron with a pancake crisis." I hear rustling, and then his voice is back. "Is the pan hot?"

"Well yeah. I turned the element on. I'm not that much of an idiot."

He huffs. "Jury is out on that. Did you let the pan heat up before you just dumped the batter in?"

"Um . . ."

"Amateur. It needs to be hot before you start. And make sure you're using melted butter and whole milk. Oh, and add some cinnamon if you have it." Pulling open one of the cupboards, I scan the barely used spices that line the shelves. Jesus, when was the last time I cooked anything?

"Thanks, Wolfgang Puck."

"Why the hell are you making pancakes, anyway?"

Chuckling, I toss the bowl into the sink, searching for another one to start over. "I wanted to make breakfast for someone."

"She better be important."

I glance to the staircase. Still no sign of life from Sam or

Hannah. "She is, man."

"Mhmm. Is she the reason Kennedy took the jet to Boston?"

I rinse off the spatula and set it down to dry on the tray. "Yeah. There's a story there."

"Always is, my friend. Always is." Matt pauses before continuing, "I'm here if you want to talk about it. You know that, right?"

"I do know that." Finding another pan, I set it on the element to warm it up.

"Good. I don't want you slipping into old habits, when the rest of us are right here to help."

His words sting a bit, but I know Matty's just worried about me. He'd jump in front of a truck if he thought it would help me. They all would. "No worries there. If anything, she's more of a reason to not do anything stupid."

"You mean like calling me at four thirty in the morning kind of stupid?"

"Hey, you're the one who answered." I shove another slab of butter into the microwave to heat it up.

"And I always will. Wait, does this mean I won the bet?" I can hear the amusement in his voice. Stupid bet of me not having sex for the month of December. Not that I think that's on the table at all when the one and only woman I want in my bed is walking around on eggshells.

"I haven't slept with her or anyone."

"Yet," Matt says. "All right, if you're done needing my pancake expertise, I have a woman in my bed I'd like to get back to. I'm not the one with ten grand on the line stopping me from enjoying her."

"And here I thought you two were sleeping, caveman."

"Shut it. I'll see you in a couple days."

Matt ends the call before I can even thank him, and I get to work on the next batch of pancakes. It's good to have something to keep me distracted. If I slept an hour last night, I'd be surprised. Despite telling Sam I have a kickass security system, I was unsettled. I'm sure I heard every creak and crack in my place. If this is what Sam's nights are like, I don't know how she functions.

So, unable to take my own tossing and turning, I got up around three. Operating on little sleep and researching on Google isn't a good combination. After a couple of vats of coffee and an hour in my basement gym, the only thing I want to do is find this asshole of an ex-husband and bury him. The more she tells me, and the more websites I find on domestic abuse, the more I want to destroy him—slowly, painfully, so he feels the kind of pain he's caused her.

I also know the last thing Sam needs in her life is more drama. And me, going fucking nuclear on this jackass, no matter how much I want to or how much he deserves it, isn't the answer. Scraps with my brothers aside, I'm not by nature a violent person, and I never want Sam to see me that way.

Satisfied with the batter, I spoon some into the pan, hearing it sizzle. Huh. Guess it does help if you heat up the pan first. Surprisingly, the first batch isn't the throwaway it usually is. They don't fluff up as much as Matt's, but they're better than the first two rounds I tried.

The sound of little feet hitting the floor on the landing has me turning to the staircase. Hannah peeks up at me with those big blue eyes, still clutching her well-loved doll that looks like it's been dragged through the mud.

"Good morning, Hannah. Did you sleep okay?"

She nods quickly, strands of her hair bouncing in a tangled mess, and she tries to brush them away. "Your bed is so big," she whisper-yells, breaking my heart just a little bit more. I know that Hannah's been sleeping in a matchbox-sized bed in the room she shares with Sam. It's another thing I want to change. Soon.

"It's pretty comfortable, right?"

"Shhh!" She puts her finger over her lips. "Mommy is still sweeping."

I cover my mouth, crouching down to her level. "Sorry," I whisper back. "We'll be quiet then. Are you hungry?"

She pushes up on her toes to try to peer around me into the kitchen. "Is there enough for me?" She blinks up at me, and my heart can't take it. Sam said they've spent time in a shelter when they had to. How many times has she gone hungry?

"There're tons." I feel her reach for my hand, and I guide her to the breakfast bar. "Would you like to sit on the counter?"

Hannah's eyes widen. "Momma says I shouldn't do that."

I grin, lifting her up to the countertop. "How about we have some pancakes here." I pat the counter, and she swings her legs. Moving over to the first stack of pancakes, I set the plate beside her. "And then we'll make mommy a plate of her own. I don't want her being mad at me."

Hannah giggles, covering her mouth. "Momma isn't mad at you. She likes you."

I could read a hell of a lot into that, even if Hannah is four and doesn't really understand what's going on. But it stirs up the hope inside me. I pour a generous amount of syrup onto the pancakes, leaning back against the counter beside her. "I hope so."

## *samantha*

MY EYES FLUTTER OPEN TO see a play of morning light on the ceiling, courtesy of the plantation shutters on the windows. A sense of calm envelops me, my fuzzy brain slow to wake, and

I stretch, luxuriating in the soft mattress and plush bedding. It's like sleeping on a cloud.

When my fingers come up empty as I reach for Hannah, I sit bolt upright in a panic. My head snaps this way and that, looking in vain, and I'm about to scream her name when a delighted squeal, followed by tinkling laughter and Cameron's rumbling chuckle, filters up from somewhere in the house.

"Oh, thank God." I press my hand to my chest. Jesus. I'm going to give myself a heart attack. My conversation last night with Cam comes back to me—this is what I was talking about. We have to stop living like this. *I* have to stop living in fear, for myself as well as Hannah.

Springing from the bed, I pull a hairbrush from our bag and detangle my mop as best I can. A ponytail will have to do for now. I pull on a pair of leggings to go with the tank top I slept in, and grab the oversized cardigan I wore last night. A shower can wait.

"NOW, DON'T . . . move . . ."

Stepping into the kitchen, I clap a hand over my mouth when I see Cameron, his face screwed up in mock concentration, stick a spoon on the end of Hannah's nose. My daughter looks like she's holding her breath, her eyes wide with excitement, until they cross as she tries to look at her own nose.

I can't hold my laughter anymore—the blast of noise draws their attention, and the spoon drops to the floor with a clatter as Hannah twists to look at me. "Momma! Did you see? Cam says it's a magic spoon!"

"A magic spoon? That sounds pretty special." I glance over to where he's leaning against the wall with a lazy smirk. "What else have you two been up to?"

"Pancakes!" She throws her hands up like a game-show hostess and titters when I lift her down off the countertop and set her on the floor. "Cam makes 'em really good. With syrup and everything."

"I can make you some, if you'd like." His husky voice in my ear startles me, and I jerk off balance, falling back into his arms. He holds me like I weigh nothing. Our faces are inches apart, and I feel like I'm drowning in his sparkling hazel gaze.

"Pancakes would be great," I whisper, unable to take my eyes off him. He hasn't shaved yet; thick, dark stubble highlights his strong jaw. He licks his full and oh-so-soft lips, and a part of me melts.

Little hands pat his arm. "Can I have another pancake too?"

We both laugh weakly, and he steadies me on my feet, his hands lingering at my hips. He addresses Hannah, but his eyes never leave mine. "Sweetheart, you can have anything you want."

"I'LL BE JUST DOWN THE hall with Cameron, sweetie. Okay?" Hannah waves back at me, her eyes glued to the ginormous flat-screen as I ease the door shut. Thank goodness for *Paw Patrol*. We don't have a television, but I know Mrs. Finnegan indulges her whenever she looks after Hannah. Considering how little I can give Hannah at the moment, I'm certainly not going to complain about a few mindless cartoons. I figure it's a good balance to all the educational games and activities Kat lavishes on the kids at the day care.

Cameron meets me in the living room and hands me my coffee cup. "Is she going to be okay for a while? I was hoping we could talk."

I nod and let out a deep breath. "She's good for about an hour or so." I know I need to have this conversation—I want to have it. But that doesn't make it easier. Taking a sip from the steaming mug, I walk over to the fireplace and draw a finger down the fine wood of the mantel. The lines in the wood are straight and clean. If only life could be like that.

Glancing over my shoulder, I see Cameron settle himself on the sofa with his own mug. A nervous chuckle escapes me. "I don't know where to begin," I confess.

He shakes his head. "Wherever is easiest. Or we can wait . . ." He looks up at me, uncertainty written on his face, and my heart squeezes. Turning, I join him on the opposite end of the sofa where the folder holding all my secrets lies on the coffee table. I flip the cover open.

"Sam—"

I hold up a hand to stop him, and then flip through the contents, my nose wrinkling in distaste when I lay eyes on the face I'd hoped never to see again.

"He finally shaved his head," I scoff. "He's wanted to since his bald spot became so apparent. He thought it would make him look tough. But he's the coward he's always been." Scooting back into the corner, I draw my knees up to my chest and take a sip to steady myself.

"My legal name is Sandra. Everyone called me Sandy. My mother was a huge fan of *Grease* when I was born," I begin with a small laugh. "After I graduated from UC-Boulder, I went home to Telluride for a couple months. One of my professors had an in with the Denver symphony, and I was planning to audition during the summer. I had a gig playing in a hotel lobby when I wasn't working in my parents' bar. Ray Mitchell was staying in the hotel. He played in a fifties cover band based in Vegas. He boasted of having all this experience in the entertainment business and said he was 'blown away by my talent.'"

"I'm sure he was," Cam grunts into his mug. His knuckles are white against the blue stoneware; if he grips it any harder, it may break.

I wrap an arm around my shins and balance my mug on a knee after taking another sip. "I hadn't really dated much before then. I ran around with my band geek friends, and we did everything in a group. Ray swept me off my feet. He sent me flowers every week and overwhelmed me with charm. He seemed so worldly; he'd traveled all over and had a devil-may-care roguishness about him. I'd never experienced anything like it before, and I was smitten."

Running a fingertip on the rim of my mug, I avoid Cameron's worried gaze. "We moved to Denver, I joined the symphony, and we got married. I loved my job and achieved second chair quickly. Ray quit the band because it was going nowhere and got a job in a local department store. He was a natural salesman," I say with a derisive snort, shaking my head. "Everything was going great . . . at least, that's what I thought then. I rationalized his need to know where I was all the time as his being 'protective.' I let him talk me into sex when I didn't feel like it because he 'needed' it. He had a knack of turning every subject to his benefit and I just . . . went along with it. Mom always said that cooperation—besides love, of course— was the basis for a good marriage, and I thought that's what I was doing. I failed to see that I was the only one cooperating."

My stomach churns as I replay the memories I've tried to bury. "I told you at the café about when it first started to happen. We had been married for about six months, and Ray started to chaff at how 'mundane' our life was. He said that we should move out of Denver, go to a bigger city with a more renowned orchestra so I could advance faster. But I was happy there; I liked the city and didn't want to move farther away from my parents. That's what our argument was about—him wanting to move. When he hit me, I was in shock. I just couldn't believe he would do that."

Cam sucks in a breath and sets his mug on the coffee table with a bang. Standing abruptly, he stomps to the fireplace and braces his hands on the mantelpiece. I can see his scowl reflected in the mirror hanging above, but he stays silent.

"He apologized, of course. Said he didn't know what he was doing. He seemed so sincere, and I believed him. I was so fucking naïve," I growl, remembering my idiocy with disgust. "I just couldn't conceive he'd done it on purpose, so I ignored it and things went back to normal. But it was just the beginning." I peek up at Cam's stiff back and shoulders, but he's hanging his head so I can't see his face. Shame burns hot within me—shame that I didn't recognize Ray's actions as abuse sooner. Shame that I let it go on for so long after I realized I was in trouble. Rationally, I know it's not my fault, but that doesn't stop the sting that I didn't have the strength to do what I needed to do until I had Hannah.

"I didn't see it happening at the time, but I know now we fell into a typical cycle. He'd provoke a fight so he'd have an excuse to lash out, and then he'd apologize. Usually his apologies included some grand gesture in public. Because even that was all about him. He'd do something or give me some extravagant gift when we were out with friends so everyone would think what a great guy he was. What they couldn't see were the bruises," I whispered, keeping my eyes on my cup, afraid to see Cam's reaction. "He knew where to hit me so no one would see. And I didn't know what to do. I was so embarrassed to be in that position. Half the time I thought it *was* my fault."

Cam snaps and whirls around to face me. "How can you think that? How can you ever think that anything you may have done warranted him using you as his punching bag?"

"I wasn't myself! I simply couldn't fathom why he would . . ." I sit forward and set my cup on the table, wrapping my arms around myself to keep from flying apart. "What rational person would *do* that?" Agitated, I rock back and forth, feeling angry tears hot on my cheeks. "Sometimes I figured I *must* have been doing something to trigger it because why else would he *do* that to me?"

Unable to sit still, I spring up and stride across the room, looking through the shutters at the snowy front street. A few cars drive by, life proceeding as normal. Keeping my back to Cameron, I hug my elbows, drawing in on myself. "It became worse when I made first violin. It was almost unheard of—me getting the post at twenty-six. I could hardly believe it, and I was so excited. Nervous about the responsibility, but so determined to prove myself. My parents were so proud of me." A bittersweet smile flickers on my lips, remembering my parents' excited voices on the phone. "But it made things worse with Ray. He missed the attention he'd gotten in the band. He became resentful and jealous of my success and used it against me."

"How?" Cam whispers from somewhere behind me, his voice thick with emotion.

"He convinced me that if people knew, it would damage *my* reputation. That I wouldn't keep my position for long if I created a public scandal." I sneer at the memory of my fearful former self. "Our conductor was a bit of a jerk and image was everything to him, so I *could* see how it might actually hurt my standing with the orchestra. I was embarrassed and ashamed; I didn't want anyone to find out. I just wanted it to *stop*."

I turn to see Cam, hanging onto the mantel with one hand as if to anchor himself. He shakes his head, his free hand scrubbing at his hair. "What about your parents?" He looks at me, his expression pained. "You were close to them. They must have suspected something wasn't right?"

Drawing a stuttered breath, I rub my chest, trying to ease the ache I feel at the mention of my parents. "They were still in Telluride and we were in Denver. Ray made sure we didn't see them very often, so they never saw my bruises. But I couldn't hide how upset I was over the phone. They kept asking questions, and I tried to put them off. I was stupidly afraid that they'd think less of me if they found out what I'd fallen into." I close my eyes, remorse washing over me. "They decided to fly in to see me and find out what was going on. But it was a particularly harsh winter and another car crashed into them on their way to the airport." I bite back a sob. "My parents died on impact."

"Jesus . . . Samantha." Cam crosses the space between us, and I let him pull me into his tight embrace. He lets me cry into his shirt until I can finally take a full breath.

"I didn't know what to do. All I had left was my aunt in Chicago, but she wasn't well, and I didn't want to drag her into my drama. I tried to suck it up and figure out a plan, but it just felt so . . . futile." Cam rubs my rigid back, but I can't relax. "Ray was like a ticking bomb. Sex could be a trigger, too." My whisper is muffled against his chest. "During the calm times, it would be okay. He was different, like the man I fell in love with, but I'd always be waiting for the switch to flip. Sometimes he'd go out with his friends and show up drunk." I gulp and squeeze my eyes shut. "After the first few times, I stopped fighting him. It wasn't worth it. I was more afraid of ending up in the ER again and people finding out."

"Sam, baby. You don't have to tell me anymore." Cam's tortured voice floats above my head, but I can't stop now.

"Eventually, I got pregnant. It wasn't planned, but . . . no birth control is a hundred percent effective, you know." I wave a hand weakly. "And it stopped. Everything stopped." I can hear the surprise in my voice, even now.

"Everything?"

I pull away and look up at his cautious expression. "He said I was 'too fat and bloated' to sleep with, so he started spending more time away from home. I'm pretty sure he had a mistress. Sometimes, I could smell perfume on him that wasn't mine. It was a relief, although I think he meant it as a punishment."

Cam's eyes flare, his jaw clenched so tight it must hurt. After several seconds, he swallows and asks, "What happened when Hannah was born?"

I can't stand the anguish in his eyes, so I turn and move to pace in front of the fireplace. "It was like there was a truce between us. He acted like nothing had ever happened." I wave my hand weakly. "I didn't know what to think. It was apparent he didn't want her, but I thought Hannah deserved a father, so I pretended everything was okay. I actually started doubting what had happened before, even doubting my perceptions. That maybe I'd blown things out of proportion. You do that. You lull yourself into believing it wasn't that bad, or that it won't happen again." I stop pacing and sit on the edge of one of his leather chairs, my fingers digging into the arms. "Then, just before Hannah's first birthday, I went to pick up a new violin case and my credit card was declined. I went online to check our accounts and discovered he'd maxed out that card without telling me, and I didn't recognize the charges. I found out our savings, my inheritance from my parents, was almost gone. There hadn't been much left after I'd settled their debts with the bar, but still, it was mine. I was livid. I confronted him when he got home. Hannah was already asleep, thank God."

His hand flies to his hair, gripping it hard. "Holy shit," he whispers, fear coloring his words.

"He said he'd quit his job and had gone into business with some of his idiot friends. And his brilliant business plan? They had a grow lab!" I look up at him, still incredulous after all this time. "Pot was still illegal then! I couldn't believe what I was hearing. And then I . . . lost my mind."

Cam stares at me, shocked. "What happened?"

I let out a weak laugh. "I was horrified. There were always stories in the news about shootings involving growers. It's a lucrative business and they fought all the time to protect their piece of it. I started screaming at him, asking what the fuck he was thinking. How he dared to spend my money on something so illegal and dangerous. I was saving that money for Hannah, for her schooling. It was the worst thing I could do, of course. He went ballistic."

I lean forward, my knees bouncing with nervous energy. I can picture Ray's savage grimace as he shoved me away from him. "It was worse than ever before. He threw me down the stairs, and I smacked my head against the wall. I'm lucky I didn't break my neck. All I could think of was Hannah napping in her crib upstairs; that I had to fight, for her. I couldn't leave her alone with him." I'm practically panting, fighting to get the words out. "So, I dragged myself up and tried to get to the door, but he shoved me down and started kicking. He threw a lamp at me, but it went out the window. That's what saved me actually. The neighbors saw it. When they came to investigate the screaming, they found me on my back as he tried to choke the life out of me."

Cam spits out a curse, and then he's pulling me into his arms. He breathes in my hair, his hands coaxing my taut shoulders into relaxing. I rest my head on his shoulder and let my breathing slowly match his. "He went to jail. When I got out of the hospital, I took Hannah and ran. We stayed with my aunt in Chicago for a while, but he found us." My eyes sting from the tears, and I lean back.

"He said he'd always find us. That next time, he'd kill us."

"Sam, no." Cameron's voice is strained, his gentle touch a reminder of what more I have to lose.

"After Chicago, we ran again, and I changed my name. I'll explain the rest later."

He presses a gentle kiss to my forehead, and I can feel a shudder roll through him. "That's more than enough for now."

"Now can you see why it's so hard for me to depend on anyone else? If I make a wrong move, he could find us again. We've already escaped him once. Who's to say we'd be lucky a second time?" I feel my tears escape down my cheeks again, my anxiety bubbling over. "I have to keep Hannah safe. I'm all she has left!"

He makes soothing noises, holding me safe while I shake, and then I feel his warm lips cover mine. All tension drains out of me, and I sag against him. I'm shattered.

"You've been so brave, Sam. You've done what you had to do, and your daughter is safe and happy," he says softly, his lip moving against my temple. "And I hope you believe that I want to help in any way that you'll let me. You don't have to do this alone anymore, Sam. I won't let you down."

Raising my head, I manage a tremulous smile as I look at his handsome face through watery eyes. I'm so damn tired of crying. Despite my emotional exhaustion, something tells me that this time, with *this* man, I can trust my instincts. "I believe you, Cam. And I'll try. I promise."

# chapter eleven

## cameron

I WANT TO SAVOR THE feel of her pressed against my chest. I don't know how long it will last. If it can last. If she'll let me in. She tries to hide a sniffle against my shirt. Sam is all things sweet and good, and to hear her talk, to see the pain that's still haunting her, hurts like an exposed nerve.

"Get it all out, and then we're leaving it." I can barely manage the words, and they sound raspy and raw.

She looks up at me, her chin on my chest, her eyes wary and untrusting, slicing me deep once more. "You've said that to me before at the café."

Slowly, I coax her with me so we're standing, and gently press a kiss to the top of her head. "Yeah, but I don't think you were ready to leave it before." Truth is, I'm not sure if she's ready now, or if she'll ever really be ready. I'm not stupid enough to think I can erase the nightmares of her past, but I want to create new ones, better ones, ones that don't make her cry.

I feel the loss of her as she takes a step back, that hardened, lost look in her eyes returning. "I've told you most of it. The rest is just us in survival mode." Her words are hollow. She's resigned herself to life on the run, convinced that's all there is. She nervously twists her fingers together, her eyes focused on her hands, afraid to look at me. So much pent-up worry and stress. I wonder when the last time was Sam did something without this cloud of anxiety hanging over her.

Reaching for her hands, I gently take them in mine. "It doesn't have to be that way, you know."

"Why do you want to help me? You hardly know me, and what you do know should send you running in the other direction."

"I've never really liked running." She gives me a half smile. "And I've found that it doesn't matter how long you've known someone." She either doesn't understand or doesn't trust me. Maybe it's both. Maybe explaining will help, or maybe I'm wasting my breath, but I have to try.

"I know that sometimes the people who are supposed to support you are the ones who can't or won't, and that perfect strangers can save you." With a gentle tug, I lead her back to the couch, sinking down, a little surprised when she does the same. "I'm not saying I understand what you've been through, Sam. There's no way I can. I do know what it's like to feel alone. Like you don't have anyone." She curls up in the corner of the couch, gripping one of the throw cushions to her chest. It feels like she's an ocean away, but I can sense she needs a little space. "No one knew who I was in rehab. They didn't know my last name or what I did for a living. If they recognized me, they kept it to themselves. But those people saved me. They listened without judging me, without being disappointed in what I had done because they'd been there too. They were fighting their own battles. Some of them a lot worse than mine. And even though I was surrounded by strangers, I didn't feel alone."

"It's not that I feel alone." I know that's a lie. Sam is alone. No friends outside of the few people in the orchestra I've barely seen her speak to. Hiding away in a dingy apartment, afraid of everything and everyone. "I just feel numb, and I'm tired. Tired of looking over my shoulder, wondering where he is."

"Florida. He's in Florida,"

Sam's eyes widen, her skin paling. "How do you know where he is?"

"Tucker found him." My eyes dart down to my feet; I know I should tell her Tucker's got a team watching her and Hannah, but I don't dare now. I don't think she'd deal well with that information right now.

She grips my shirt with a shaky hand and I meet her fearful gaze. "He can't find out, Cameron."

"He's not going to find out."

"He's not stupid. He notices things." Her eyes squeeze shut, a slight tremor rolling through her. "He notices everything."

"Hey." I move closer, tentatively touch her arm. "He's more than a thousand miles away. He's not going to get to you. I won't let him."

Her eyes snap open, flaring with heat. "I don't want a protector. I thought I made that clear. I just want normal."

"Then come with me this weekend to Vermont. You won't have to worry about a thing." Her fingers worry the edge of the pillow and I use her silence to my advantage. "You heard Kennedy. It's in the middle of nowhere. Lots of snow, fireplaces, hot tubs."

She gives me a half smile. "That doesn't sound normal at all."

Ignoring her protest, I continue, "You wouldn't even have to see me if you didn't want to."

"And what if I want to?"

My lips twist. "That can be arranged." She ducks her head, hiding her face. I brush her curls back. I can't resist even though I should. I don't want her to fear my touch. To not wonder if I'm going to be the one to explode. I never want her to compare me to *him*. I think that would kill me. "I want you to know that this, us, whatever we are and whatever we'll be is up to you. On your terms, in your own time."

"Friends, right?" she asks, lifting her chin, her green eyes shining. Fuck, she's killing me. I want her closer. I want her trust.

"Right. Our own definition of friends."

She leans closer, the scent of maple washing over me. "Do you think we can do that? Redefine things?"

Covering her hand against the cushion, I trail my fingers over her smooth skin. "I know we can." Her eyes drop to my lips. She's so close. Those lips of hers right there. "Come with us this weekend. It'll be fun."

"Momma?" Little feet pad into the room and Sam leans back, catching Hannah when she jumps up onto the couch. "*Paw Patrol's* over." Hannah wraps her little arms around Sam's neck.

"Is it? We better get you cleaned up. I think you're having a special guest at school today, and we don't want to be late." Hannah's eyes widen, and she practically bounces with excitement.

"We are? Who? Who?"

Sam laughs, shaking her head. "If I told you, it wouldn't be a surprise." Hannah pushes off Sam, landing on the floor, and tugging at her hand.

"Let's get ready!"

"There's a bathroom connected to your room. I'll drive you

when you're ready to go."

Sam glances back at me as Hannah tries to lead her away. "Thank you, Cameron. For everything."

Hannah takes off to the stairs, and I watch Sam follow, taking my heart with her when she goes.

"KEEP YOUR LEFT UP AFTER the jab. We wouldn't want to ruin that pretty face." Tucker smirks at me as he ducks out of the way.

After the stress of the last twenty-four hours, Sam toyed with the idea of keeping Hannah with her today. Seeing how excited Hannah was about the Christmas activities scheduled for the day changed her mind. Once we dropped Hannah off at the day care, Sam and I came back to my place. She's exhausted, and after hearing my suggestion of her spending the morning relaxing in the Jacuzzi, she disappeared behind the door.

It's torture imagining her naked, immersed in warm, inviting water. It's where I want to be. Instead, I'm in my home gym with Tucker and Kennedy, burning off the pent-up energy. Nosy bastards showed up with the excuse of needing a private place to work out, but I know better. Like they couldn't rent out a fucking gym somewhere else in town. If only I could land a punch on Tucker, I might actually feel better.

Kennedy laughs from the weight bench, sitting back up. "Good advice, Tuck."

"You shut it." I point my gloved hand at Kennedy. "Don't you have a girlfriend to pick up or something?" I'm panting like I've just ran a marathon, sweat dripping down my face. Tucker, on the other hand, shows no signs of tiring.

Kennedy takes a long sip from the energy drink before he gets back to the bench press. "She doesn't get here until later tonight. Matty and Tess, too. Sean's arriving in the morning. He'll be a nightmare with the time change."

"Tell me something I don't know." Tucker lands a punch against my shoulder. I wince, bouncing back away from him as he circles me like a dog. "That fucking hurt."

"It's supposed to. Pay attention. I'm trying to teach you something."

"Asshole," I mutter, trying to return a jab to his side. Tucker is too fast and too good. If he wasn't our head of security, I'm sure he could make a career out of boxing.

"FYI," Tucker says, angling his shoulder away from me. "There's a couple of grainy pictures making the rounds on Twitter of you and Sam."

I drop both hands, adrenaline kicking through me. This is Sam's worst nightmare. I don't want to think about her reaction when she finds out. "What? From when?"

"Relax. They look like quick snaps taken with a camera phone. You can't really make out her face, and both of the pictures are dark. It looks like you're dancing. There's a big-ass tree in one of them." He motions for me to come at him and I take a healthy swing.

"Fuck. That's from the party at my parents' place." I punch the air, missing Tucker again.

"You haven't seen them?" Kennedy asks from the bench.

I let out a huff, trying to take a normal breath. "I don't pay attention to any of that shit."

"I'm guessing she hasn't said anything about it?" Tucker asks while he adjusts my left. "Keep this up. You drop it too much." He shoves me back a bit on the mat.

"She doesn't have a computer." I shake out my shoulders, getting ready to go at Tucker again. "Or a phone from this decade."

"She may be onto something there," Kennedy says, sitting back up after he's done another set of reps. "I wish I didn't see half the crap I do." He leans forward, running a towel over his face. "Safe to say she doesn't know. Maybe best to keep it that way."

"Hi." My head turns to the direction of Sam's voice. She steps into the room, and I can breathe again. She's fucking stunning; that mass of red hair piled high on top of her head, cheeks pink from the heat of the Jacuzzi, dressed in leggings that make her legs look like they go on forever, and a simple T-shirt. My heart lurches at the same time as I feel Tucker's knee in the small of my back, and see Sam's alarmed expression. I land with a loud thump on the mat. He's managed to twist my arm behind me in the process, and I'm completely immobile, my face smashed against the mat. Fucking asshole.

I can hear Kennedy's laugh as Tucker hauls me back onto my feet. "Rookie," Tucker mumbles, clasping me on the shoulder.

"Are you okay?" Sam asks, a little breathlessly. She glances between Tucker and me, her eyes roaming over my bare chest before falling to the boxing gloves covering my hands. I shove them behind my back.

"Tucker's just putting us through his special kind of hell." I don't want her to see me this way, like an aggressor. Though getting taken down to the mat as if I'm a rag doll probably eliminates that possibility.

"I see that. Can you teach me?" Sam takes a few tentative steps into the workout room, looking at Tucker expectantly.

"Ah . . ." Tucker's eyes cut to me as he rubs his palm across the back of his neck. He glances over at the heavy bag hanging from the ceiling.

"The bag's not asking. I am," Sam says. A twinge of pride fires through me. "I want to learn how to defend myself."

My pride is replaced with annoyance. She shouldn't have to learn anything. She shouldn't need to. "Sam . . ." I want to protect her, to make it so she never has to worry again. I'm slowly learning it's not about me, and I need to keep my inner Neanderthal in fucking check. Maybe this is exactly what she needs. A boost to her confidence. To feel in control.

"Everyone should know, right?" A weighty silence fills the room. Even Kennedy has stopped his endless reps at the bench press.

Finally, Tucker nods, motioning for Sam to join us. "Yeah. You're right. Everyone should know."

"I'm not very strong," Sam says, almost apologetically.

"Strength doesn't matter. A shot in the right place at the right time can take down anybody. Trust me." Tucker speaks with a certainty no one would question. "It's all about knowing where the weaknesses are. The soft spots."

"The soft spots?" Sam steps onto the mat.

"Yeah. Where you're most vulnerable. The eyes, nose, throat, knee, groin."

Sam nods, enthralled like she's in a trance. "Avoid the thick areas. Chest, top of the head, arms. A swift open-hand strike with the heel of your hand upward to the nose will give you time to run." Tucker turns to me with a grin I don't like, and I lean back slightly. "Relax, princess. I won't hurt you. This time."

"Famous last words," I grumble. Tucker shifts his weight, and his arm flies out, the heel of his palm stopping just inches before making impact with my nose. "Like that. Pivot from your feet. It will drive the energy forward. Try it on your own first." I watch with a burning mix of mindless, blurring jealousy and pride as Tucker corrects her position, squares her shoulders with the gentlest of touches. "Good. That's right." I hear Kennedy set the bar down with an almighty clang as I watch Sam repeat the move over and over until Tucker's satisfied.

"Okay." Tucker turns to me, stepping over to remove my boxing gloves. He drops them to the mat, passing me a soft leather punch shield. "Now we'll try together. Come at her."

I lower my hands, the shield dangling, a lump stuck in my throat. "No fucking way."

Tucker shoves me in the shoulder. "Don't be a pussy. The best way to learn is with a partner. Are you okay with him taking a few steps toward you?" He looks at Sam. "He'll hold up the shield and you take a shot just like I showed you." She nods eagerly, looking up at me.

"No, Tuck. I can't." I can see the worry in Sam's eyes. "I don't want you to see me that way. I'd never hurt you."

Sam reaches over to touch my arm, the heat melding with my own. "I know that. That's why it's okay. I trust you." She trusts me. Those words mean a hell of a lot coming from her. No matter how much I hate this idea, I know I can't refuse. I'm so far gone, I'll do anything she wants.

♪ ♩ ♪ ♩

## samantha

THE TREPIDATION IN HIS EYES melts away, replaced by an elation that lights his whole face. Brushing my cheek with the back of his hand, he gives me a tender smile and speaks so only I can hear. "I wish I could tell you how much that means to me. I'll never make you regret it, Sam."

My heart flutters, and I swallow down the sudden lump in my throat. The things this man does to me . . . I love that he's so considerate, protective even, of both Hannah and me. He's been wonderful—generous and thoughtful—and has done nothing except prove himself to me. Plus, his attention and obvious desire have awakened emotions in me I didn't think I'd feel for years to come, if ever again.

Maybe it's not too late for me after all.

"I know you won't," I say simply and take a step back. "So, are you okay with this then?"

"If it will help you, sure." He nods and raises the shield. "Ready?"

Positioning my feet as Tucker showed me, I ready myself. But when I look up again, I no longer see Cameron's sweet, encouraging smile. The emotions of our earlier talk rush back, and it's suddenly Ray's ugly sneer I see in my mind—I launch myself without further thought.

I ram the heel of my hand into the shield, slamming it back into his face. But instead of stepping back, I follow through with a foot to the side of his knee. With a startled curse, he falls like a giant tree, and I don't stop. All I can see is Ray's enraged expression right before he shoved me down the stairs. I leap on him and start swinging—I rain blows on the soft shield, occasionally hitting a solid bicep, until a strong arm loops around me and hauls me upright. Still flailing, I fight against my unseen captor until a booming laugh echoes in my ear.

"Whoa, whoa! Down girl!" Tucker cries. "You got him, Sam."

The haze clears as I regain my feet. Kennedy is gaping with shock and amusement, while Cameron is smiling proudly at me from his twisted position on the floor.

The floor!

"Oh my God!" I drop to my knees next to him and lift the shield away. "I'm so sorry! Are you okay?" I frantically pat his chest and shoulders to see if he's hurt, and he starts chuckling and sits up, taking hold of my hands gently.

"I'm fine. It's okay." He raises my hands to his lips and kisses them. "Are *you* okay? What happened there?"

"I—I'm not quite sure. Suddenly, all I could see was *him* and I had all this rage." I shake my head to wipe the grimace off my face and look down at our hands. "Maybe it's because all that is fresh in my head after telling you about it this morning. I'm sorry."

He squeezes my hands to draw my attention. "Hey, you have nothing to be sorry for—you were awesome! At risk of sounding condescending, I'm proud of you. You rocked it, Sam."

I blink, trying to remember exactly what I did. That simple takedown seems to have removed a huge weight from my shoulders. It's amazing.

"I did, didn't I?" I beam at him and he laughs.

"Yes, you did." The honesty and enthusiasm in his voice strike a chord and a sudden longing consumes me. Surprising myself, I tug him closer and press my lips to his. His eyes widen for an instant, and then he's wrapping his arms around me and pulling me into his lap. I wrap my arms around his neck and bury my fingers in his soft hair. He smells deliciously of sweat and warm leather.

He parts his lips and I waste no time, my tongue tangling with his. A low growl vibrates in his chest and then we're rolling until I'm stretched out on top of him. With nothing but his sweats and my leggings between us, his desire is immediately obvious. And, uh, big.

Really big.

Instinctively, I buck my hips against his, and he groans as he reaches down to grope my ass. My hand drifts along his warm skin and glides over his firm stomach, sending a shiver through him. He shifts and brings his free hand up to cover my breast and I arch into him, craving the contact. He kisses his way down my neck, murmuring against my skin about how good I feel and taste, and the breath catches in my throat. God, it's been so long since I've been this attracted to a man, and felt so desired in return, if ever.

"Cam, I want, I want—" I don't really know what I'm saying. I just know I can't stop. I'm panting so hard I can barely get the words out. I kiss and nip at his bare shoulder, savoring the salty taste of his skin.

"Tell me," he gasps. "Tell me and you'll have it." He cups my cheek and brings my eager lips to his again for another devastating kiss. I scrabble with a hand to gain purchase on the mat below us, but I bang my knuckles against Kennedy's discarded barbell. Kennedy!

Shit!

I jerk my head up and frantically look around the room, but we're alone. "Did you hear them leave?"

He lets his breath out with a whoosh and shakes his head with a soft chuckle, looping his arms around me again. "No, I was a little preoccupied."

"Me too," I say with a laugh, and he grins.

He kisses me on the nose, and I press my forehead to his, my senses—and responsibilities—returning. "I'd . . . I'd like to continue this, but . . ." I sigh, trying to slow my racing heart. "I have to go pick up Hannah pretty soon."

"But you want to continue?" Hope sparkles in his eyes, and I smirk at the wary eagerness in his voice. I nod, smiling shyly.

"Yes."

He lets out another deep breath and moves us into a sitting position, his eyes boring into mine. "But not now."

I sigh, hearing the murmur of male voices nearby. "Your friends are in the next room." I let my fingers trace the flowing script of his one and only tattoo wrapped around his bicep, wondering which one of us I'm trying to convince. "Plus, I wanted to stop by the Finnegans' today to see if they've returned and started to clean up. They may need help."

"That's okay." His hands move smoothly up and down my back, and his lips brush my ear. "When we *do* continue, I'm going to need more time with you than just an afternoon quickie."

I gasp softly, unable to control my shiver at the promise in his voice. Feeling my resolve slipping, I'm about to say . . . I don't exactly know what . . . But . . .

"Hey, are you two done in there?" Kennedy's plaintive voice calls from somewhere, and I bury my face against Cam's firm chest. "Tucker's griping about all the processed crap you have in the fridge, Cam. He's scaring me."

We both chuckle and finally ease apart. "I guess I'd better get going," I suggest, but welcome one last soft kiss.

"*We'd* better get going," he murmurs against my lips. "I'm going with you, if that's okay. I don't think I can be apart from you now, Sam."

Music to my ears.

DRESSED IN MY CONCERT BLACK, I carry my instrument down the hall, ready to take the stage. My long black skirt and blouse were some of the additional items I picked up yesterday from our apartment. Although he accepted our help in cleaning up, Mr. Finnegan was insistent about our not moving back in until the window and door were repaired, and the new security system installed. He's working with his insurance company, but it's going to take a few more days to get the repairs done. That, plus Cam and

Hannah's hopeful looks, were what made me agree to continue to stay with Cam for the time being. I don't want to take advantage of his generosity for too long, but I'm relieved to have someplace safe for my daughter to stay. And I'm very glad it's with Cameron.

I can't seem to get rid of gnawing thoughts of Ray. Could he be somehow connected to the break-in? I hate that he's invading my thoughts even now. I've been on edge since the Finnegans' store was vandalized, and that, coupled with my conversation with Cameron, has all those raw feelings simmering to the surface. I feel exposed, vulnerable, at a time when I should feel safe.

"Come on, Sam. Here we go," Olivia whispers as she grins and moves past me to her section. I smile at the familiar butterflies in my stomach. It's like this before every performance. Tonight is even more thrilling though, thanks to our guest artist. Cam is amazing. He and Kennedy played for us last night at Cameron's place, and it was simply magical. Cam's deep bass voice is a smooth, warm counterpoint to Kennedy's brighter tone. They must have been something when they had been just starting out before Matt and Sean joined them.

It's going to be tough to move back to our apartment, but this thing between us is so new, I worry about progressing too fast. No longer worried about being *with* Cameron, I now worry about screwing it up. It's enough for now that I've agreed to join them in Vermont. Matt and his girlfriend, Tessa, had gone straight to their hotel when they arrived last night, but I met Kennedy's girlfriend, Abby. She's a lovely person, and I recognized the adoration with which she gazed at Kennedy while he played. It was difficult to keep the same expression from my own face while I watched Cam. Luckily, Hannah sitting in my lap gave me a distraction.

The drummer I've heard so much about, Sean, arrived this morning, and now they're all sitting out there in one of the loge boxes. Except Cam, of course. He's stalking around backstage, his guitar slung over his shoulder and looking lethal in a beautifully tailored black suit and tie, and brilliant white shirt. He's nervous, too. It will be the first time he's played in front of his parents since he made it big. I guess Kat and his brothers have been to a few of Redfall's shows, but his parents apparently wouldn't be caught dead there. The regretful look in his eyes as he talked about his parents made my heart ache. I shake my head. I can't imagine not being willing to openly support your son. I know I will always support Hannah, in whatever she decides to do in her life, as long as it makes her happy.

But all the Chapmans are here tonight. Sitting in another reserved loge box, dressed to the nines, and dripping in diamonds and distain, no doubt. Even I know that the annual Christmas concert is one of Victoria Chapman's principal events, and she pulls out all the stops at the reception being held in the mezzanine lobby afterward. I think Cam said something about making an appearance, for his mother's sake, but he wasn't going to stay. We, the orchestra, aren't invited, of course, and Cam said he wouldn't stay without me.

The thought warms my heart as I take my seat and sit at attention while we wait for the curtain to open. As much as I don't want to be an issue between him and his family, I secretly love his rebellious streak. He's his own man. Rare these days, in my limited experience.

Ivan, our concertmaster, taps his music stand and brings us to attention. My nerves are forgotten, and my focus immediate. We rise as one in silence, and the huge curtain sweeps aside to gratifying applause. Then we sit again so he can lead us in one final tuning before Hoffmann sweeps out to take the baton and finally introduce Cam.

I try not to hold my breath.

"MY GOD, SAM!" OLIVIA GUSHES as our compatriots swirl around us backstage after the show. I can barely hear her over the excited buzz of exultant musicians. "That was incredible. Did you see Hoffmann's face? I swear, I didn't think that man was capable of smiling that much. I think his face must be frozen by now."

I share her grin. My adrenaline is still flying after one of the best performances we've ever given. "Well, he's got a lot to smile about." I move out of the way of a rambunctious bassoonist. The last thing I need is to be beaned by a wayward woodwind.

"Where is the mysterious, but delicious, Mr. Chapman?" She peers around the room, disappointment on her pretty face. "I thought he'd at least come backstage for a few minutes."

"I heard someone say that he was going to the reception," I say smoothly, improvising. "We probably won't see him again back here." I don't add that I'll be definitely seeing him later.

She sniffs, raising her chin. "Humph. I guess I was wrong about him."

"Wrong?"

A devilish smirk appears. "Based on how he kept sneaking peaks at you between numbers, and all during rehearsal this after-noon, I figured there might be a reason for him to come backstage afterward."

"Olivia!" I feel my blush rise, but roll my eyes anyway. "Don't be ridiculous." I'm enough of a realist to know that eventually, assuming we stay on our present course, news of Cameron and I will get out. But that doesn't mean I'm in a hurry to rush that eventuality.

Secrets are good. Secrets are *safe*.

"I don't think I am." Her inquisitive blue eyes study me, her smirk still in force. Then she shrugs and flips her blond hair over her shoulder. "Oh well, let's go. We have our own party to get to."

We continue on to the locker room. "I'm sorry, but I can't tonight. I need to pick up Hannah. Mrs. Finnegan couldn't look after her tonight, so I had to bring her to the day care." Or evening-care in this case. One of the great things about Kat's children's center is that they stay open late to care for the musicians' children during concerts. It's also where Cam said he'd meet me after he escapes his mother.

Olivia pouts, but it doesn't last long. She knows my priorities. "All right. I'll just have to have an extra cosmo on your behalf." She laughs. "Give Hannah a good-night kiss from me."

"I will."

She gives me a hug and a cheery wave good-bye before following some of our other friends out to the musicians' gathering being held at a pub down the street. I lay my violin in its case, grab up my coat, and turn toward the door, only to almost run into Cameron in the doorway.

"What are you doing here?" I ask breathlessly, surprised but pleased. "I thought you were at the reception." He takes my hand and gives me a warm smile, oblivious to the looks directed at us from a few lingering musicians.

"I was." He gives me a wry smile. "I escaped before some of my mother's other guests—one in particular—arrived."

I stiffen and can't help my frown. "Ah. A certain blonde, I assume." I sigh. "She's not going to give up, is she?" I'm referring to Darcy, but the statement could refer to his mother as well. I haven't forgotten about her trying to snoop into my background.

"She'll get the hint eventually." He gives me a knowing look.

"*Both* of them will."

I'm not so sure, but I let it go for now. "So are you ready to leave then?"

He runs his other hand through his hair, making the dark brown strands stick up a little. "I want to introduce you to some people first—the rest of the band—before we take Hannah home. Do you mind?"

"Now?" My eyes shoot open. I didn't think I was going to meet them until we leave tomorrow. "Where?" It's hard to admit the thought of meeting the drummer is a little overwhelming, after the things Kennedy and Tucker said about him. He sounds a bit . . . mercurial.

"Come on." He takes my coat from me and then leads me back down the hall to a larger rehearsal room. My stomach quivers, but I square my shoulders and stand tall when Cam opens the door for me to enter.

"Ah, here she is!" Abby's musical voice stills all conversation in the room. She's beaming as she steps toward me, arms outstretched. "You were all wonderful tonight, Sam. Really exceptional."

"Thank you," I say, accepting her light hug. "I'm glad you had a good time. It's always fun when all our hard work comes together in a performance like that." I smile up at Cameron, who slips his hand into mine. "Cameron's addition really breathed some new life into the *Oratorio*."

"Bach can use some shaking up, the stuffy old bastard." Hearing an English accent behind me, I turn to see a man in black jeans and a suit jacket with positively electric blue hair. It's mesmerizing. "So you're the one who's got our boy all mixed up, eh?"

"Jesus, give it a rest," Cam mutters. "Sam, this is Sean Murphy, Matt Logan, and Tessa Baker. Everyone, Samantha McKenzie."

Matt's large hand envelopes mine and we shake as Tessa smiles warmly beside him. With her mass of black hair and lacy red cocktail dress, she looks like she belongs on the cover of a romance novel. "It's nice to finally meet you, Samantha," she says. "We've heard good things about you."

"Oh?" I wish I wasn't blushing so easily tonight. "That's nice to know."

"And she's coming with us tomorrow," Abby adds, stepping forward. The skirt of her dress rustles softly. "I can't wait to see Cam's place. It sounds like so much fun. Your daughter will love it."

Sean's eyebrows shoot up at the mention of Hannah, but he remains silent, pursing his lips in amusement as he looks at Cam. I'm afraid to imagine what's going on in that blue head.

"Um, yes, I think she will. We're both looking forward to it." I see Cam's affectionate smile out of the corner of my eye. I check my watch. "I'm sorry, but now I have to go—"

"Go?" Sean waves his hands as if that's the worst idea he's ever heard and steps around to my other side. Linking his arm with mine, he tries to pull me away from Cam. "You can't go anywhere now! The night is young. I have a VIP room booked down the street. You need to tell us all about how you managed to catch Three's eye here."

I look up at Cam, who's pulling me against his side and away from the pouting drummer. "Three?" I ask, and he rolls his eyes.

"Never mind." He glares at Sean, who merely grins back at him. "I'll explain later."

"He's Cameron Louis Chapman the Third," Sean announces matter-of-factly. "So, Three. See?"

"Ah, I see." I hide my smile behind my hand, as the tips of Cam's ears turn red. So cute. "And I'm sorry I can't come with you. I have to pick up my daughter and get her to bed," I say and look up at Cam. "Should I still wait for you at the day care?"

"No, I'll go with you now. You guys can take it from here, right?" Ignoring Sean, he looks at Kennedy for confirmation, who nods with a smirk.

"Sure. Abby and I are staying at the Fairmont tonight with everyone else. We'll try not to embarrass you in your hometown," he quips, smoothing a hand down the lapel of his dark blue suit. "Tucker has a straitjacket ready for Sean."

"Fuck off, the lot of you," Sean growls, rubbing his eyes. "It's not my fault the fucking jet lag plays havoc with my usually stellar personality."

We say our good-byes, and Cam turns us toward the door where Tucker is standing, a silent witness dressed in black. "Come on." Cam's warm whisper brushes my ear, making my skin tingle. "Let's get your girl and go home."

*Home.* I like the sound of that.

# chapter twelve

## cameron

CROUCHING DOWN AT THE FIRE, I watch as the flames flicker and grow. Something is going on with Sam. She was quiet in the car on the way home—more so than usual. Nervously twisting her fingers and looking out the window. I could chalk it up to meeting the rest of the guys. The Brit alone is enough to do anyone's head in. Something tells me that's not it.

There are times I can see Sam gaining confidence and getting stronger. Like the way she took me down in the gym, or the way she poured her soul into the performance tonight. But then, she shuts down on me and locks herself away with thoughts or memories she won't or can't share. It's frustrating as hell.

"A girl could get used to this." Grinning at the sound of her voice, I turn to see her cradling a coffee mug between her hands, giving me that shy smile that makes my heart ache. Just one look at her, and I'm completely lost. She's changed out of her concert black into simple leggings, and a T-shirt that stretches across her perfect breasts. "Hot chocolate, a roaring fire, company." Then my heart pangs for another reason. Sam has spent entirely too much time alone. Maybe going away this weekend isn't such a great idea. Maybe she needs to get used to me—to us, whatever we are—before I unleash the rest of the band on her.

"I hope you get used to it. I'm counting on it." She ducks her head, taking a long sip of the hot chocolate. "Hannah get to sleep okay?"

"Sleeping like an angel. I think the cloud bed helps." She sinks down to the corner of the couch, tucking her legs underneath her. "You could've gone out with the rest of the guys, you know. You didn't have to stay with us."

"There will be lots of time to go out with them." I move over to sit beside her. "Besides, I'd much rather spend time with you." I reach for the other mug of hot chocolate, needing something to hold on to so I don't completely overwhelm her. Already my fingers are itching to feel her again, her body pressed to mine where it's supposed to be.

"You were incredible tonight." Her voice is soft over the crackle of the fire.

"No. *We* were incredible." She shakes her head, glancing up at me. "I don't think I need to tell you how talented you are, Sam."

She ignores my praise. She's going to have to get used to taking compliments. "It just sounded so different. I think we shocked a few people."

"You mean the gaggle of society ladies in the front there? Probably. Waking people up and giving them something to think about is always a good thing."

She tilts her head, studying me. "Is that what you try to do?"

"I hope so. One of the things that I love about our band is it's never the same day twice."

"So, Sean's hair isn't always blue?" She laughs.

"He changes it all the time. I'm not even sure he knows what the real color is anymore."

"He's always been like that then?"

"Yeah." I shake my head, relaxing back against the leather cushions. "Sean's one of a kind, thank fuck. He's got a twin sister, but she's nothing like him."

I watch as Sam studies the fire, her cheeks coloring from the heat of the flames. "I can only imagine what the four of you have gotten into over the years."

"You probably can't imagine some of it, and trust me, it's better that way."

Her lips twist in amusement, tempting me to taste them again. "The quintessential bad boy band?"

"Not so much anymore."

"Why not?" she asks, her tongue flicking out to catch a dab of whipped cream lingering on the corner of her mouth. *I want to do that.*

"Because we've all grown up. We did go through a phase there where it was a bit of a blur for all of us, I think. But things change, you know? You realize what's important, and I wouldn't risk losing that."

Leaning back against the couch, she fixes those green eyes on me. "And what's important in your world, Cameron Louis Chapman the Third?"

"Relationships . . . Family." I rub the back of my neck, trying to ease my sudden nerves. "Speaking of family, I told my mother to keep her nose out of your business." Queen V hadn't liked it when I pulled her aside tonight and told her in no uncertain terms to stop her snooping, but she got the message.

"When?" Her lips part in surprise. "At the reception this evening?"

I nod, tamping down a flash of anger about my mother's intrusive nature. Going to the symphony's HR manager to get info about Sam? Abso-fucking-lutely unacceptable. "She forgets sometimes that I'm a grown man who's capable of living his own life. I reminded her. She doesn't have a right to meddle in my life, and she sure as hell doesn't have a right to meddle in yours. I told her she'll learn more about you if and when you see fit and not before."

A smile flits across her delectable lips, before she lets out a resigned sigh. "She's only looking out for you."

"Looking out for herself, more like," I mutter, brushing some dirt off my knee. If only it were as easy to brush away my mother's snobbery.

She takes another sip from the mug. "You said your family hadn't really been there for you when you needed them."

"I also said family isn't defined by blood. It's the people you care about, the ones you'd do anything for." I set my mug down, turning to face her on the couch. "The guys in the band, you, and Hannah." I want her to believe me, to trust me when I say she's important.

She swallows and the mug shakes slightly as she leans forward to set it on the coffee table. "You can't think that way, Cameron," she says, lifting her eyes to mine. "There's a good chance Hannah and I will have to disappear again." She picks up one of the pillows, hugging it to her chest, closing me out once more. This time, I'm not letting her.

I grip the edge of the pillow, pulling it from her death grip. Gently, I take her face between my hands. "You never have to run again. Do you understand me? Never." Her lip quivers, her eyes glossy as a few tears escape down the delicate lines of her face. "Hey, no crying."

She grips my wrists. "I just . . . I wish I had met you first," she whispers, pressing her forehead to mine. Her words skim like a warm caress over me, making me want things I know I can't have.

Shaking my head, I breathe her in, content that she's letting me this close. "But then you wouldn't have Hannah."

"I know. I shouldn't have said that. I didn't mean it that way."

"Just think about now. About possibilities. About staying." I can't resist brushing my thumb against her velvety, plump lips, and the soft sigh she answers with sends a surge of heat through me. God, that sound. I need to hear more of it.

Shocking the hell out of me, Sam launches forward into my lap; her hands coast around my neck as her lips meld to mine. I can feel her heat through her leggings, her hips rolling in a sweet, torturous rhythm that makes my cock throb with need.

On a groan, I sink my hands into her hair, drawing her closer. She takes her time exploring my lips, learning my mouth, and stroking the back of my neck with her fingers. Some raw and desperate noise escapes me, and my hips arch up from the couch to meet each mind-blowing grind of hers. I can taste the richness of the chocolate on her tongue, the lingering cream she licked off her lips, and it drives me out of my mind.

I skim my mouth along the curve of her neck, feeling her shiver as her breathing hitches. "God, you're so . . ." Any further thought I have is obliterated when I feel her still against my chest. She weighs next to nothing, but the weight of her flush to my torso grounds me.

Desperately, my lips skate back to hers, but this time, she doesn't respond. Sam seems frozen, those sweet, sexy breaths stopped completely. Panic fires through me as I study her beautiful face. She's zoned out, her eyes squeezed shut. "Sam." I take her face between my hands again, trying to draw her attention. "Sam. Come back to me."

I can feel her take a shaky breath, the color drained from her cheeks. "Open your eyes, Sam. It's me. It's Cameron. You're safe."

She opens her eyes, and they're wide and haunted. She looks like she's been woken up from a trance as she blinks into awareness. "What happened there? You were right there with me for a minute, and then you just tensed up."

She shakes her head, burying her face in her hands. "I'm so sorry," she croaks. "He used to . . ."

My hand stops on her back, my heart hammering. She's thinking about him. The one thing I never want her to do is to compare me to that worthless piece of shit. "He used to what?" My words are clipped and raw. I shouldn't be asking. I'm sure the answer is something I don't want to hear, and Sam needs to move forward. Away from the nightmare of her ex-husband.

"You're so stupid. You're so pathetic. You're so . . ." Her words die on a sob, and I press her tense body to mine. Wrapping my arms around her, I let her cry, her tears soaking my shirt. I'll take every single tear for her if it means she can move on. "He used to say all kinds of things when he was—"

"Shhh," I murmur as she buries her face in my shoulder. "No more. I'm sorry. I'm so sorry. I shouldn't have pushed." She melts against my chest, and I just hold her. I hate this feeling of helplessness. I want to fix this, to take her pain away. No matter what I do or say, there's nothing that can take away the years of damage that waste of space has done to her.

I draw the blanket from the back of the couch around us, cocooning her against me, rocking her while her tears continue to fall. The pain in my chest burns and grows with each agonizing minute. This kind of pain is new. Nothing comes close. Not when I fell off Panda during a polo match and was nearly trampled to death at fourteen, not even going through rehab, which was its own special kind of hell.

Sam leans back, her eyes swimming with tears. "I don't know why you're doing this," she says, playing with the fabric of my shirt. "I'm such a mess, and you?" She studies my face before wiping the tears from her cheeks. "You could have anyone." It kills me to hear the doubt in her voice. The fact that she thinks she's not worthy, that she's questioning why I care stings as much as it frustrates me.

She doesn't meet my eyes, instead focusing on the fire. I skim my palm across the back of her neck, feeling her shiver. "Hey, look at me." When her big, green eyes finally find mine, she looks defeated, and my chest tightens in response. "I don't want *anyone*. I want you. Right now, I'm exactly where I want be, with the woman I want to be with." I cup her cheek and she leans into my touch, her eyes closing. "I'm not going anywhere, so you're just going to have to learn to put up with me."

Keeping her eyes closed, her lips twitch into a smile. "That sounds like a lot of work." Her words are a welcome break in the tension that sits heavy between us.

"I'm a lot of work. A full-time job, if you want to know the truth." I press her to my chest, shifting us so we're lying down on the couch. Sam relaxes against me, bone-tired, and fitting perfectly against my side. I tighten my arms around her in the hopes it will hold her together.

"Is it okay if we just lie here for a while?" Her exhausted voice drifts up to me, muffled a bit as she buries her face against my chest. I pull my fingers through her riot of hair, feeling her warm breaths through my shirt.

"Of course we can. We can do whatever you want." Pressing a gentle kiss to the top of her head, I breathe her in, and a sinking realization hits me hard and fast. The scars Sam has run deep, and there's a good chance she may never actually be mine. Her grip tightens around me as mine does the same. If this is all I get with her, I'm going to savor every minute of it.

THE SMELL OF PANCAKES AND the muted sound of giggling wake me. Running a hand through my hair, I push up from my awkward position on the couch, my back complaining. Morning light filters through the slats on the blinds, and the fire is out. I've obviously overslept, and Sam is nowhere to be found, but I can hear her in the kitchen, her soft voice asking Hannah to try to be quiet. It brings a smile to my face to hear them both carrying on in my place. It's where they belong.

*Home.*

She's a welcome sight in the kitchen, laughing with Hannah as she tends to what looks like a waffle maker. "I thought I smelled pancakes."

Sam jumps at the sound of my voice, holding the spatula to her chest as she turns around. "You scared me!" Her cheeks flush with heat. "And they're waffles. I found this still in the packaging." She points the spatula to the shiny waffle maker on the counter. "I hope it's okay." She gives me a wary look that makes my throat tighten. She's worried that she's done something wrong by making breakfast.

"It's perfect." I move to the counter beside Hannah, swiping a grape from her small bowl of fruit, and popping it into my mouth.

"Cam!" Hannah squeals with delight as I bite into the grape.

"We have more grapes, don't you worry. And I didn't even know I had a waffle maker." I take a seat on the stool beside Hannah.

Sam shakes her head, plating up a perfectly cooked waffle with syrup, and pushing it my way. "How often do you use your kitchen?" She leans against the counter across from me.

"Not enough," I mumble around a forkful of fluffy goodness. "Amazing. You can cook breakfast every day."

"Momma?" Hannah tries to whisper, but I can hear her perfectly. "Can I ask now?"

There's a lightness in Sam's voice I want to hear more of. "Yes you can, sweetie. Remember your manners."

I feel Hannah's little hand on my arm, patting it gently. "Cam?"

"Yes, Hannah?" I pour some more syrup onto the waffle, turning to smile at her.

"Are we leaving for the sleepover soon?" Her eyes widen in excitement, and she squirms in her chair.

"Very soon. My friends are picking us up. Is that okay?"

Hannah glances at Sam before she looks back at me. "Is there room for Josie?" she asks quietly.

"There's room for whatever you want to bring, Hannah."

She bounces in the chair as the unmistakable sound of Sean banging on the front door drifts through to us. Sam nervously looks back at me.

"It's our ride. Don't worry." Shoving the last forkful into my mouth, I push off the stool and head to the door, opening it up to the cool morning.

"What in the hell is that?" I scowl at the bright pink retro VW van parked outside my house. Sean spreads his arms wide, proud as a peacock.

"Isn't it brilliant?"

"Way to keep a low profile, idiot."

Sean drops his arms. "Hey! I went to a lot of trouble to find this," he fires back at me. "I thought you'd love it."

"If it was 1969 and we were going to Woodstock, I might." He scoffs as the rest of the crew piles out of the back of the van. "Seriously. Is it even going to make it up the mountain?"

"Live a little, Three. It's been forever since we took a van anywhere. Remember the old days?" Sean slings his arm around my shoulder, looking back at the ridiculous VW.

"When we broke down almost every day on the side of the road in a beat-up Astro van with no seats in the back?" Matt steps up to join us. "Good times there."

I turn to Tucker. "And you let him get this why?"

"I didn't know he was doing it, or I would've stopped him. It's tricked out inside. It's pretty sweet, actually," Tucker replies, casting his gaze down the street. I see Tucker's security detail parked a few houses down, and it does nothing to set my mind at ease. According to his earlier texted report, we think Ray is still in Florida, but that doesn't mean we need to attract attention with that pink monstrosity.

"See? I get the seal of approval from the King of the black SUV himself," Sean says, heading into the house like he owns the place. "Let's get your bags all loaded up then. Ah, the lovely Samantha." Sean grins at the sight of Sam in the entryway, Hannah hiding behind her leg. Sam coaxes Hannah in front of her. "And who is this little poppet?" Sean crouches down in front of Hannah, and her eyes widen.

"Are you a Troll?" Hannah asks, causing us all to crack up with laughter. Sean ruffles Hannah's hair.

"Hannah! That's not nice," Sam says, trying to hold back her own laugh.

Hannah turns, blinking up at Sam. "But he has blue hair,

Momma. Just like one of the Trolls."

Sean smirks at me as I clamp my hand on his shoulder. "That's exactly what he is, Hannah. A Troll doll. A Troll named Sean."

Hannah giggles, swaying from side to side. "Can I have blue hair too?"

"Of course you can!" Sean gushes as Hannah tentatively reaches her little hand out to touch his hair.

"No!" Sam and I both counter at the same time.

"Why not?" Sean practically whines, standing back up.

"Because she's four and a little young for hair dye, genius." Sean rolls his eyes at me before winking at Hannah.

"You just stick with me, Poppet, and I'll set you up. Come and see what we'll be driving in." Sean holds his hand out, and Hannah happily places her tiny one in his, moving to look out the door.

Sam smiles tentatively at me until we hear Hannah squeal. "Momma! Come see! It's the same color as the American Girl truck!" Sam laughs, moving to the open door to glance out at the van. "Can I go see it, Momma?"

Sean glances over his shoulder at me, as he mouths, "American Girl?"

"I'll tell you later." I pass him Sam and Hannah's bag. "Make yourself useful, Troll-man, and load these up."

Sean snorts a laugh, lifting the bags and heading out the door. "Coat and boots, sweetie, before you go outside," Sam says, holding open Hannah's little winter jacket.

"This must be Hannah!" I hear Tess's excited voice as she appears in the doorway with the remaining Redfall crew. "I'm Tess and this is Matt, Abby, and Kennedy."

Hannah squirms as Sam tries to put her knit hat on. "We have the same jacket!" Hannah yells as Tess smiles down at her. "Yours is red too!"

Tess laughs, passing a large gift bag over to Sam. "Abby and I got a few things for Hannah for the drive. Some coloring books, crayons, a little puzzle."

Sam takes the bag, shaking her head slightly. "Thank you so much. That's very sweet, but you didn't have to do that."

Abby waves her off. "It was fun. And you'll get sick of singing *Wheels on the Bus* after a few miles."

"We can sing?" Hannah asks, jumping up and down, making it hard for Sam to put her boots on.

"These boys sing a lot, Hannah," Abby says. "There will definitely be singing."

"You bringing your guitar?" Matt asks, glancing down the hallway.

"Yeah. You want to pack it up? I just need to clean up and throw some stuff in a bag."

Kennedy chuckles, leaning against the doorframe in amusement. "Always waiting on you, aren't we? Hurry up. Who knows how long Sean will last before he's horning you from the clown car, and waking up half of Boston."

Glancing down at Sam, she gives me a hesitant smile. "I won't be long." I cut my eyes to Kennedy. "You, behave."

"When have I ever not behaved?" Kennedy throws his hands up in mock surrender.

## samantha

"COME TAKE YOUR BACKPACK, HANNAH. Please."

My bouncy daughter scampers over and takes her bag from me, and then runs back to where Sean is attempting to make a snow angel while the rest of us unpack. I step back out of the way to let Matt and Tucker start working on the straps holding a few duffel bags on the roof rack. After driving and singing three-plus hours in a refurbished VW van with an energized four-year-old and a man who—for some unknown reason—periodically howled out the window, it's a relief to stand and stretch my legs.

"This is a beautiful house, Cam," Abby says, gazing at the impressive building. "Where are we again?"

Cameron pauses, two guitar cases in his hands. "Ludlow, Vermont. I bought it as a getaway, but my whole family uses it from time to time. The Okemo Mountain ski resort is just over that hill." He nods toward a tree-covered peak. "That's where we'll go to ski later."

He called it a cabin, but I should've known better. It's more of a luxury lodge. A large A-frame structure dominates the center, with a pair of two-story wings angled off each side. It's gorgeous.

"It looks like it could be part of the resort. How many bedrooms does it have?" I shade my eyes from the sun as I study the balconies that line each wing.

"A lot. Plenty of room so that none of us will be subjected to Sean's antics at night." He grins at us and continues past me on the path leading up to the house, the cases swinging in his hands. I grip Hannah's and my bags and look over my shoulder. She's giggling and jumping in a circle around Sean, who's kneeling in the snow and looking like a gnome.

"Come on, Hannah. Let's get inside and warmed up," I call, and her head snaps toward me, a huge grin on her face. Sean rises and shakes the snow off like a dog, making Hannah squeal.

"Let's go, Poppet." He scoops her up and settles her on his shoulders. "Let's see what kind of trouble we can get into inside."

Cam's home is a beautiful blend of raw cedar panels, warm

cream walls, and plush carpet. Soaring windows fill the great room with soft natural light and provide a sweeping view of the surrounding mountains. I can see a portion of what looks like a kitchen around a corner. It's modern and spare, but not pretentious.

"Wow." Hannah takes the word out of my mouth as she stares at the wooden beams of the high ceiling. "It's so pretty!"

"Why, thank you, ma'am," Cam says with a grin and a nod to her. He sets the guitar cases down next to a couch. "Do you want to see your room? I can give you the grand tour later."

"Yeah!"

Cam takes her hand and beckons to me. He takes one of my bags from my hand and looks over his shoulder at Kennedy. "You guys okay for a minute?"

Kennedy waves a hand at us. "Don't worry about us. I remember my way around."

Cam leads us down the left hallway to a small foyer with a curved staircase leading up to the next floor. "Two bedrooms are down here." He gestures to two doors facing each other across the foyer. "But we're staying upstairs." He helps Hannah ascend the staircase to a matching foyer with two more doors.

"This will be your room. I'm across the hall." Hannah trots ahead of me into a huge room dominated by a king-sized bed. It's a magazine-worthy example of rustic chic, just like the rest of the house. My daughter gives a whoop and charges to jump on the bed, bouncing and laughing.

"Look where we're sleeping, Momma! It's bouncy!"

I laugh and open my mouth to reply, but startle when a large hand takes mine and a velvety voice whispers in my ear, "All the beds are *very* comfortable. Want to try one out?"

My cheeks heat and a shiver runs through me at his suggestion. Suddenly, I want to do just that. With him. To distract myself from my very nonmommy thoughts, I look out the French doors and spy a large, dark shape on the balcony. "What's that?"

"All the balconies are reinforced and equipped with a hot tub. There's nothing like soaking in a bubbling tub after skiing." He waggles his eyebrows, breaking the sexual tension between us, and I laugh. I give his hand a squeeze and release it just in time to catch my daughter, who's practically vibrating with eagerness.

"Are you going to teach me how to ski now, Momma? Are you? Are you?" She grabs my hands and I let her swing back and forth, grinning down at her.

"If you still want me to." She cheers and Cam chuckles.

"Let's go pick out your gear." He holds out his hand for her to take, which she does. "I keep some equipment and clothing in the garage for family. I think my nephew's gear should be about the right size for you."

"OKAY, KEEP YOUR FEET TURNED in so you make a V, but don't let the tips of your skis cross." I'm reliving weekends I spent in college as a ski instructor. You can't grow up in Colorado and not know how to ski. We've made it to the bunny hill at the nearby resort. Matt and Tess were still, um, *napping* in their room when we left, and Abby elected to curl up with a book at the lodge and wait for us. So it's just Kennedy, Cam, Tucker, and the blue-haired Sean. Who apparently doesn't like being told what to do.

"But how in the bloody hell do I keep them from crossing?" he whines, scowling at me and uncrossing his skis with difficulty. Hannah giggles.

"He said a bad word, Momma," she sings as she glides past him, illustrating a perfect snowplow. It took Hannah all of fifteen minutes to pick up my instruction, while Sean is a little bit . . . slower.

"Bend your knees more, and use your thighs to control them." I slide backward a few feet to give him room.

"Sweetheart, I could show you a better use of my thighs," he drawls, and then yelps as Cam swats him on the back of the head.

"Keep your thighs to yourself, idiot." He glares at the blue-haired man. "And that's another fifty in the swear jar." Abby set up the swear jar in the kitchen as soon as we got here and made the guys pony up for all the words they accidentally let fly on the trip from Boston. The jar has already boosted Hannah's college fund considerably and we've only been here three hours.

Sean shoots him a smug look. "I think I've had enough instruction. The mountain is ready for my fabulousness to be unleashed. Back up everybody."

I shake my head. This should be interesting. But I move out of the way and gesture for him to proceed. Instead of maintaining the snowplow, he straightens his skis and immediately starts gliding forward, picking up speed. The flailing starts after about ten feet and the yelling after about twenty, at which point he tips over, splayed out on the snow.

"That was an entertaining ten seconds." Cam's not hiding his smirk. "Maybe you should stick to the snow-tube park." A burst of snow from our right heralds the arrival of Kennedy and Tucker, back from a run.

"The snow is perfect," Kennedy says, raising his goggles and panting from his exertions. "Why don't you two go? We'll stay here with the children." Sean shoots him a dirty look, as he tries unsuccessfully to stand up.

"You don't have to tell us twice." Cam looks at me eagerly. "Let's go!" After assuring Hannah that I'll be right back, I let Cam lead me to the nearest ski lift.

"What level do you want?" Cam asks, gesturing toward the run signs when we reach the top. I adjust my goggles and point to the blue square.

"I think I'd better stay away from black diamonds for now. It's been five years since I've been on skis." My own excitement matches Hannah's. Although the ride on the quad lift was a little awkward—we were sharing with a newlywed couple who couldn't stop making out—it didn't dampen my enthusiasm.

Cam adjusts his own goggles and shoots me a grin. "I'll try not to leave you behind." I give him a playful shove and then grip my poles.

"Ha! Watch how it's done, Chapman. You might learn something." I push off; I've forgotten how much I love skiing. As the wind whips past me, my spirits rise. My body responds like it always used to, reminding me of the life I had before Ray. Digging my edges in, leaning into the turn, absorbing the shock as I take a mogul . . . it's exhilarating. Growing up in Telluride meant that you were practically born with boards on your feet. And knowing that I've now introduced my daughter to it is immensely satisfying.

The realization that this is still mine—that I am still *me* despite everything—overwhelms me. This, this sensation of speed and power and *control*, is something that he never touched. And if this is still uniquely mine, I know there is more out there for me to discover and make my own.

I just have to reach out and take it.

Cam's laughter floats back to me as he shoots past while I'm lost in my thoughts, and I grit my teeth and follow in hot pursuit. When I fly by him at the next curve, it's my turn to laugh. I keep the lead all the way to the bottom, feeling empowered and strangely cleansed. When we finally pull up, I whip off my hat and goggles, and smile up into Cam's beaming face.

"You're a maniac, McKenzie!" He laughs and slides his arm around me.

"Maybe, but you love it." I wink at him, my adrenaline still surging. The gleam in his eyes becomes more intense, and I feel his fingers flex as he leans down to kiss my upturned lips.

"I certainly do."

"WHERE'S HANNAH?" ABBY ASKS, CLOSING the fridge.

I chuckle as I rejoin her and Cam in the kitchen. "Out like a light on the sofa in the music room. Tess and Matt are down there with her. She'll be out for at least an hour." After we'd taken a few more runs, we'd packed it in. Hannah was running down and Sean was grumpy after not being as "fabulous" as he'd thought he was. He retreated to his room to soak away his aches and regain his dignity.

"Well, I was thinking of running into town with Kennedy and getting a few things for dinner. It won't take long. Do you want to come?" Abby asks. I perk up, despite being tired.

"A chance to shop without having to deal with a toddler? You bet." I pluck at my sweaty turtleneck and grimace. "Just let me change first. I'll be right back."

I swiftly make my way down the hall and take the stairs to our room. Cam catches up to me when I reach the top.

"I'm coming, too," he says, giving me a lopsided smile. "I'll meet you back here and we'll go down."

I nod and watch him disappear into his room. Knowing that he's so close makes me nervous in a good way. But I can't think about that now.

I quickly locate a black sweater and strip off my damp shirt.

Pulling the sweater over my head, I catch a glimpse of myself in the dresser mirror. Tousled hair, hardly any makeup, cheeks still red from the cold, and an old lace bra I got at Goodwill. Hardly a prize. But . . . I know it doesn't matter. I look toward the door and think about the man in the next room. About the desire I saw in his eyes on the slopes. He could have any woman he wants, but he wants me. And I want him.

I'm not going to waste time questioning it.

Smoothing the sweater down, I run a quick brush through my hair, and walk across the landing to his room to see if he's ready. But I stop cold at the doorway, eyes wide.

Cam is standing next to his bed, shirtless, muttering to himself and staring down at a crumpled ball of fabric in his hands. Desire, hot and strong, surges through my veins. I can't stop staring. A light smattering of hair across a firm chest, flat stomach, and a hint of a V disappearing into the jeans hanging low on his hips . . . He's perfect.

I suck in a loud breath, and he startles, his head snapping toward me. "Oh, uh, I'm just, uh," he stammers, his cheeks turning rosy. He quickly shakes out his shirt and fumbles for the opening, but I walk straight up to him and still his hands. Like magnets, my hands are drawn to his chest. His skin is warm and smooth, and he trembles slightly under my touch. His breathing is rough, but he stands like a statue and lets me explore. A graceful line of script spirals around his left bicep; it's his only tattoo. I trail my fingertips along the words. It looks like it's in French.

"What does it say?" I'm speaking softly, but my voice sounds loud in the room. His hands rest on my hips, twitching like he's holding back.

Suddenly, I don't want him to.

"It's about freedom." He clears his throat, and I look up. His eyes are burning with an intensity that strikes my heart. "God, Sam," he groans, and then his mouth descends to mine. I instantly loop my arms around his neck as he crushes me against him. The feel of his long, hard body against me makes my heart pound, and I can't get close enough. Finally, *finally*, everything else, all the bullshit in my past, falls away and it's just me and him.

My fingers tug at his hair—it's just as silky as it looks. I draw him closer and he moans; a sound of desperate need rumbles in his chest. He leans away and releases me, only to gently pull my hands from his hair and hold them between us. Before I can feel a sting of rejection, he sits on the bed behind him and looks up at me with a longing that steals my breath.

"Sam, I want you like I've never wanted anything in my life," he says quietly. "And before we go any farther, so there's no misunderstanding despite whatever I may blurt out, you need to know that I think you're amazing. You're incredibly talented, a fantastic mom, and so damn beautiful . . ." He swallows. "But I don't know your triggers. So to keep me from doing something stupid, I'm putting you in charge." A smirk tugs at his lips. "At least for now."

With a squeeze of my hands, he lets go and scoots backward, keeping his gaze on mine, before lying on the mattress. "Come and get me, Sam." His smile is in place, but his eyes hold a hint of doubt that tears at my heart. "If you want me."

Blinking away my sudden tears, I press my hands to my cheeks. I'm both embarrassed again that I freaked out last night and overwhelmed by his selfless act. Instead of becoming frustrated with my hesitancy, he's sought a way for us to be together while allowing me to feel safe. No one has ever given me such a gift.

And I know what to do with it.

I step back, holding up a finger when I see the flash of disappointment in his eyes. Then I quickly move to the door and close it with a quiet snick.

His eyes light up as I approach the bed. "We don't want to be interrupted, after all."

# chapter thirteen

## cameron

I LIKE TO THINK I'M a man in control of my emotions most of the time. Sex has always just been sex for me. I've never gotten attached or never wanted more than the satisfaction of a good, hard fuck. I already know this is different because it's Sam. She's gotten under my skin, taken up all the spaces I didn't even know were empty. She's been through so much, and I want to erase every single bad memory she has.

My chest tightens as I watch her watching me, the blood already hot and thrumming through my veins. Her bright green eyes track my movements as I reach for the phone on the nightstand and make a call to Kennedy.

As I wait for him to pick up, my eyes fix on hers, wide and excited. I'm caught in some magical moment I want to last forever. I'm fighting between holding back this live wire of tension that runs between us, and wanting to snap it just to get my hands on her. "Hey." I clear my throat when Kennedy picks up. "Sam's going to take a pass on the grocery run." Sam's pretty mouth curves up into a smile, her cheeks heating. I love that this is her reaction. That she's a little shy about it. It's a far cry from the women who typically orbit around us. There's nothing shy about them. They're as ready to post their conquests on social media as they are to get on their knees. Hell, they'd probably ask for Kennedy to join us.

"Everything okay?" Kennedy's voice registers through the phone.

"Yeah, man. Everything's fine. Sam's just going to lie down for a while." Sam covers her eyes, a quiet laugh escaping before she peeks back at me.

"Got it. We'll probably be an hour or so. That give you enough time?"

"Not even remotely. Make sure Matty and Tess stay with Hannah. And keep the Brit occupied."

I ignore Kennedy's chuckle, watching as Sam waits at the foot of the bed. She's so tiny, but her presence takes up the entire room. "Consider it done."

"I can't believe you did that," Sam says when I toss the phone back to the nightstand.

"You wanted to be interrupted?" I drop my hands to the plush comforter on the bed, fisting it to keep from lunging at her. The air seems thicker with anticipation. She breathes, I breathe. She stalls. I'll wait for as long as it takes.

"No. Not even a little." Her voice comes out in a whisper, her eyes glazing over as they roam across my chest. She's not even touching me, but my skin heats anyway, my breaths spike, muscles primed and ready.

"Can I?" It's a ridiculous question. The only thing I want is her hands on me. But when her eyes meet mine again, I know there's something else going on. She looks genuinely worried, that shy smile gone, replaced with a thin line that makes my heart ache.

"You never have to ask." Her eyes dart back to my chest as she hesitates. It's just enough to make me question whether she's ready for this. "Sam, please don't bring him into this. We don't have to do anything you don't want to do. I'd never—"

My words are cut off as she crawls up the bed and straddles my hips, the heat of her palms searing into my chest until her fingers come to rest on my lips. "I swear I'm not thinking about him. It's just that it's been a while and I'm nervous. I don't want to disappoint you."

I slowly shake my head, barely able to think with her this close, beyond relieved that she's not thinking about him. "Impossible. Nothing you could do would ever disappoint me." I don't know how I manage to get the words out with her fingers lightly tracing over my shoulder and down across the tat on my bicep. My fingers complain as I clench them harder into the covers.

"Touch me," she whispers, leaning back as she tugs her black sweater up and over her head. So much creamy skin for me to explore. A sweeping of freckles caresses her neck, her shoulders, highlighted by the black lace of her bra. She's fucking perfect.

"I'm not perfect," she whispers, continuing to walk her fingertips across my heated skin. I didn't think I said that out loud.

"You are to me." My voice is messed up, raspy and raw as if I've just finished one of our marathon concerts.

I feel her fingers on mine on the sheets, uncurling them with a leisurely pace until she lifts my hand over her breast. Keeping her bright eyes on mine, she takes a shaky breath, and then I can feel her heart hammering under my palm, the delicate lace of her bra seems to burn against my hand.

I guide her free hand that's taken up shop on my arm over my chest so she can feel my wildly racing heart. "You feel that?"

Sam catches her bottom lip between her teeth, and she just nods. "It's for you. All of me. I'm all yours." I brush the pad of my thumb across her bra, feeling her hardened nipple straining against the fabric. I could get addicted to the feel of her arching into my touch, silently begging me for more. And I give it to her, so painfully slow that my dick complains, struggling to push its way through my jeans. She answers with a plaintive sound, a half sigh, half whimper. I lean forward, letting my lips hover against the curve of her neck while I breathe her in. Sam is fucking intoxicating. Some sweet, pure scent that's meant only for me. "Now, what are you going to do with me?"

I don't wait for an answer; I'm too busy releasing one of her perfect rosy breasts from her bra, pulling her tight nipple into the warmth of my mouth. Her fingers dive into my hair as she presses forward on a panted breath. I could spend a long time right fucking here, worshipping these. I'd happily die at the altar of Sam's breasts. Flattening my tongue against a perfect peak earns me another desperate groan, until I release it with a pop.

She pouts a little as I lean back, reaching around to release the clasp on her bra, tugging it away. Sam immediately covers those delicious breasts, dropping her chin like she's embarrassed.

Cupping her cheek, I run my thumb across her smooth skin. "Hey, you're gorgeous. Don't hide from me. Unless you want to stop?"

She shakes her head, her eyes fluttering shut as she leans into my touch. "I don't want to stop. Unless you do."

"Fuck no." It's a growl of an answer. "But—"

Then Sam's mouth is on mine, claiming, devouring, taking what she wants. Her arms find their way around my neck; she tugs at my hair as she grinds forward, her breasts pressed against my bare chest, driving me out of my mind. It tears a groan from me, some raw and needy sound I've never heard before, and my palms skate across her curves, feeling her tremble as I fill my hands with her ass.

It's sweet, sweet torture when she rolls her hips against my lap, and my lips drop over her shoulder to cover a tempting smattering of freckles. This is what heaven tastes like. I feel her hands drift between us, and the muscles in my stomach tense while her fingers fumble with my belt. She growls in frustration, a sexy sound that goes straight to my cock.

Leaning back with a chuckle, I dip my head to tease her nipple. "I want these off," she murmurs through a groan while I trail a path to her other breast, lavishing attention on her aching nipple. I drag one hand from her ass and up the curve of her spine as she throws her head back. My fingers thread through her hair, and I pull her stiff bud back into my mouth.

"God, that feels amazing," Sam mumbles, her fingers stilling just over the zipper on my jeans. "Please, please." She squirms on top of me as I take a healthy squeeze of her ass, my fingers sweeping over the band of her tights. Her skin is silky smooth there, and I can't stop touching her.

"If mine come off so do yours," I whisper, glancing up at her before leaning back on my elbows. "Take them off." I run my fingers up her inner thighs, across the top of her leggings, watching as her body tightens in response. I don't go further even though I want to. I want her to bare herself to me. To do it because she wants to—no—because she *needs* to.

I'm letting her lead, as much I'm able to in my current amped-up state. There's a tremble in her fingers as she releases the belt and tugs my zipper down, the whole time keeping her eyes locked to mine. It's one of the most erotic things a woman has ever done to me. She's taking her time, exploring, feeling the dips and hard lines along the way.

Lifting my hips from the bed, I wait while she pushes my jeans down and away, watching as Sam's eyes widen when my cock slips out. "No boxers?" It's a breathless question from her, and I just shake my head in response. Her cheeks flush more so as she uses a featherlight touch to trace the length of my hard shaft. It's just enough to cause it to throb, to twitch, to ache even more.

"Jesus, you're fucking killing me." I don't mean for the words to spew out, honest to fuck I don't.

"Don't die. Please," she says in a hoarse whisper, tilting her head, her hair spilling over her breast. It's a tease designed to push me over the edge because she repeats the process, and then pulls her thumb along the wide head of my cock. Swallowing is a chore. I'm sucking in the air as if it's disappearing from the room. "Can I?"

"I just might die if you don't." My hips arch without thought, my cock seeking out her heat, needing to be buried inside her. "You wouldn't want that on your conscious now, would you?" She grins, a hint of a smug smile even as her hand closes around me, delivering a single long, firm stroke that makes my muscles draw tight.

My clenching jaw hurts from holding back. Restraint, I realize, is a little dose of heaven and hell mixed together. My hands trail up her back as she glides down my torso, her hair tickling along the path, making me shiver.

She glances up from the fascination of my cock, her eyes darker and laced with desire as they meet mine. Her lips part, her sweet tongue flicking out to wet them before she leans forward, trapping my cock between her breasts. On an achingly slow glide she pushes her breasts together, rocking forward and back just enough so I can feel the sweet softness engulfing me.

Jesus fucking Christ. I don't want to come all over her tits. Scratch that. Of course I do. Just not now. The first time that happens, I want to be inside her, but she's making it really hard. I almost laugh at my erratic internal thoughts, but then I feel her breath over my swollen crown, the warmth of her mouth as her lips stretch around me, and I'm fucking lost.

My hand finds its way to the back of her neck, my fingers tightening in her hair as she flattens her tongue along my length, her lashes fluttering down as her eyes close. It would be so easy to fuck her mouth, but I don't, even when she sucks me deep, her hand wrapping around my base, then dropping to cup my heavy balls.

I wish I was recording this. I'm almost tempted to reach for my phone because the sight of Sam lifting her gaze to mine, her mouth stuffed full of my cock is something I need to see many, many times over. Every day. Multiple times a day.

On a shuddered breath, I draw my fingers across her cheek, tracing the outline of her lips as I let my hips arch from the bed. My muscles tense and heat fires up my spine with each erotic tease of her tongue.

She repeats a teasing circuit, working my cock, alternating between deliberate licks of her tongue and maddening strokes of her hand along my shaft. She obliterates every thought in my head when she glances up, her mouth popping off me, and says, "Show me how you like it."

Jesus Christ. I like it however she'll give it to me. She flicks her tongue over my tip before sucking me deeper, and a groan tears from me. "Like that . . . that's good. Anything is good. Just don't stop."

I swear to fuck she smiles around me at that, but she doesn't stop. She doesn't want to. She's learning what I like, and I'll gladly be her willing teacher.

"Sam . . ." I'm a panting wreck with that warning, but it's all I can manage before I come, my hips flexing forward to push my length against the back of her throat, grinding harder with the intensity of my release.

I can feel her throat working to swallow, and then Sam's tongue tracks a leisurely path along my length, her eyes holding mine as my hips slow. She presses her lips to my hip and moves up to straddle me, her palm resting over my racing heart.

"Was that okay?" Fuck, is she serious? I'm decimated here, floating blindly back to earth.

I take her face between my hands and claim her lips. It's raw and needy, and I feel her melt against me, her hands gripping my shoulders as if she needs something to ground her. "So much better than okay."

"For me too," she says, her voice soft.

"Good. Then we'll do that again . . ." I brush my lips over her shoulder and she shivers. "And again . . ." She grinds her hips against me when my palm covers the sweet curve of her ass, giving it a squeeze. "And again."

She drops her forehead against my chest before she tilts back. Her green eyes seem darker in the muted light of the room. "It's scary how much I want you." Her whispered confession cuts me off at the knees because I feel the same way.

"You have me. I'm not going anywhere." She presses those sweet lips to mine, making my cock begin to twitch and throb to life again. "I'm yours for as long as you'll have me."

She studies my face, her fingers tracing over my forehead, along the line of jaw and across my lips. Each touch only makes me want her more, but I keep my hands fixed to her hips so she can take the next step.

It's sweet torture watching as she hooks her fingers into the band of her tights and drags them down with her panties. Trying to calm my speeding heart isn't working as she crawls back over me. The sight of Sam bare and wanting me is the stuff dreams are made of.

"Condom." I'm only able to break out one-word sentences at this point. My fingers skim along the crease of her soft thighs as she draws in a heavy breath.

"I'm clean but you're right. We shouldn't. Yet." She smoothes her palms up my chest, wrapping her arms around my neck, teasing her pretty pussy closer. She's got a trimmed, tiny patch of hair there, and I can't stop stroking, teasing, letting her feel the weight of my fingers against her clit. Her lips find my neck, her sweet breaths hitching with each pass of my thumb.

"I'm clean. I swear to fuck I am." My voice sounds gritty as I whisper against her ear. "Condoms are in the drawer." My hand sweeps along her back, her soft skin heating under my touch until my fingers find the ends of her hair, giving it a gentle tug. Her head tilts back so I can meet her eyes. "Take me, Sam. I'm all yours."

Her mouth is on mine then, and my tongue sweeps in, wanting more, wanting her to take what she needs from me. Her hands are everywhere, hot and urgent, clawing at my shoulders, and fisting into my hair.

My fingers tease into her, warm and wet and so fucking perfect I could come just from the sensation of feeling her snug and trembling. "Fuck, you're so ready for me." She groans at that, reaching across to the drawer on the cabinet beside the bed. I still my fingers, and she falters a little, letting out a frustrated huff. "Better hurry." She's angled so her breasts sway in my face while she fumbles for the condoms, and I can't resist pulling one pert nipple into my mouth.

Her eyes flutter shut, and she pushes her chest forward, pulling a condom free. "Cameron." Fuck if my name falling from her lips in a whimper like that doesn't make me harder. I tease my tongue over her hardened nipple and her hands grip behind my head, urging me closer. "You like that." I taunt her other nipple until her body shakes with want. My hands can't get enough of the warmth of her skin. It's like she's branding herself into my soul.

"I need . . ." She rises up a little as I take a handful of her ass.

"What do you need, Sam? Tell me." Her eyes are wide, searching out mine as she tears the condom package open. Then she's rolling it over my straining length in a move so erotic it makes my skin prickle with need.

"Is this what you want?" My fingers stroke into her once more, and she cries out, moving back over me. "Yeah it is. You're so beautiful. Show me, Sam. Show me how you like it." Her gaze flicks to mine, and then she takes control, guiding my cock where we both want it.

She's stretching around me, a strangled gasp falling from her lips as I let her lead me, let her set the erratic, raw pace. She throws her head back, her fingers digging into my shoulders as she rides me, her breasts bouncing as my hips churn to meet hers. I pull one of her hot nipples into my mouth and groan, trying to make it last for her. I can feel her shudder, her body drawing tight, clenching around my cock, milking me dry with each mind-blowing roll of her hips.

My name leaves her lips on a jumbled cry as she falls forward, her teeth grazing over my shoulder. I'm aching to be deeper, to press her closer so she's permanently part of me. I don't think I'll ever be close enough. Bracing my arm across her back, I pound into her, and both of my hands palm her ass, not wanting to let her go.

She answers each thrust of my hips with one of her own. Breathing becomes harder when her hands frame my face, and her forehead presses against mine. We exchange ragged breaths, and she takes everything I give her.

Sweet Christ, the feel of her tightening around me is too much. Her lips on mine, those hitched breaths of hers, the way she whispers my name when she comes, it's all too much, and my release surges through me on a ragged groan.

Our urgent kisses slowly melt into lingering, breathless whispers. Her hands are everywhere as are mine. I don't want to move. I don't want to break whatever spell she's cast over me. But, gradually, she does move, and the loss of her warm, wet heat almost causes me to sob.

She drops back onto the bed, her arm flung over her forehead. I can't resist pressing my lips between her breasts before I roll over and tie off the condom. I toss it into the trash and move back where I belong.

She doesn't hesitate burrowing against me as if she's seeking out my warmth. My arms wrap around her, and she lets out a soft sigh. Her fingers slowly trace across my chest until I hear her soft voice. "Cameron?" She peeks up at me from my chest. "Don't let me go."

My answer is as simple as breathing. "Never."

I don't know when we lost track of time. Somewhere after I started the fire and Sam spread herself out for me in front of it. Right now, I could do without the constant banging on the door from the one and only Sean.

"Three!" He's whisper-yelling as if that's going to make it better.

"Does he ever quit?" Sam mumbles from her prime location on my chest, her fingers drifting across my torso.

"No," I whisper against her temple. "He doesn't." Sam rests her chin on my chest, glancing up at me. She looks tired. Beautifully tired and gloriously fucked. "Ignore him. He'll go away eventually," I lie, palming over the curve of her back.

"I don't think that's actually true," she says, her voice sleepy. "He doesn't seem like the type that gives up easily."

I laugh, shaking my head. "You've got his number already, don't you?"

"He's not all that hard to figure out," she says with a smile.

"Three!" The banging gets louder, Sean's voice rising. "Don't make me come in there."

"There're five other people in this house. Go annoy one of them!" I holler at the door. Sam laughs against my chest, her warm breath fanning over my skin. I love that sound.

"We need you. Tuck says you can explain why there's extra security at the end of the road." My hand stills on Sam's back and I feel her tense. "I barely got past them. If there's something going on, don't you think we deserve to know about it?" Sam's eyes widen, her eyes flicking nervously from the door back to me. Just when I think we're distancing ourselves from her past, it sneaks right back in.

♪ ♩ ♪ ♩

## *samantha*

I STARE AT HIM, THE feeling of boneless bliss I've been luxuriating in quickly draining away. Cam heaves a sigh full of resignation and exasperation. "Fine!" he calls, scowling at the door. "We'll be down in fifteen."

The sound of muttering and scuffling feet from the hallway fades away. "Sorry about that," he mumbles. "We've tried muzzling him, but it never seems to do any good."

"What's he talking about, Cam?" The lovely bubble that surrounds us pops; I pull the blanket over my breasts and sit up, suddenly feeling vulnerable. A regretful look flits across his face, and he trails his fingers down my arm.

He takes a deep breath, as if steeling himself. "Tucker and I put security on you and Hannah."

"You did what?" I try to recall if I've seen any random faces hanging around, but come up blank. "Without telling me?"

"I know I should have," he says quickly. He runs a hand through his hair and squirms under my stern perusal. "But I didn't want to scare you. Tucker says Ray's in Florida, but I wanted to be on the safe side. I didn't want to burden you with it. You have enough on your plate—taking care of Hannah and holding down three jobs. You shouldn't have to worry about some asshole possibly stalking you."

My fingers clench the blanket as anger and alarm flash through me. I can't believe people have been following us and I didn't notice. And I can't believe he ordered it behind my back. I've had enough of men thinking they know what's best for me.

But . . . as I look into those beautiful hazel eyes, eyes imploring me to understand, my ire dims. He was only trying to help and keep me safe. Besides my aunt in Chicago, no one else has gone out of their way to do that.

He sits up and curls his long legs around me so we're facing each other. "Sam, I hope you know how important you are to me," he murmurs, taking my free hand tightly in his. "I should've discussed it with you first. But, I can't say that I wouldn't have arranged it even if you didn't want it. It would kill me if something happened to you or Hannah and I could've done something to prevent it."

Bringing my hand up to his lips, he presses a kiss to my

knuckles. Warmth bubbles up in my heart. This afternoon has been incredible—*he's* incredible. Never have I felt so desired by a man. Not as a possession or as a means of making himself look better, but desired as a *woman*, for my own merits. He was generous and patient, as well as passionate and determined. I never felt threatened or out of control. Even when he took me in front of the fire, I wasn't afraid of the strength in his hands or the force of his thrusts. I only wanted *more*.

I run my fingertips over his jaw and down his neck, relishing the feel of his scruff, before pressing my palm against his firm chest. His heart beats a steady, reassuring thump beneath my hand. This man has gotten under my skin—and into my heart—in the best of ways. I can't deny it. If the tables were turned, I honestly can't say that I wouldn't have done the same thing for him. The thought of something happening to him is unbearable.

"Okay. Thank you for taking care of us. But next time you're tempted to do something like that, I expect you to discuss it with me first. Hannah is my responsibility, and I need to know when something affects her."

His eyes pop open. "That's it? I thought you'd be more upset."

I smirk and pull away from him, kicking my legs over the edge of the bed to rise. "Oh, I'm mad. Furious, actually. But I've decided to give you a pass. *This* time. I do want to meet this security though. After a shower."

A deep groan echoes in the room when I bend to gather my clothes from the floor and head to the en suite. "I'm never going to understand women," he mutters, and I give him a wink before closing the door.

THE HEAVENLY SMELLS OF ROASTING chicken and something chocolate reaches us as we emerge from the hallway into the main living area. I feel a stab of guilt that I didn't help with dinner. But then, the warmth of Cam's hand in mine quickly squelches that.

"Momma! I helped Abby make dinner while you were napping!"Hannah rushes to me as we enter the kitchen, and I sweep her up in my arms. She smells of lemon and rosemary. Delicious.

"You did? That's my big girl." She beams at me, and I look over to where Abby is adding strawberries to a fruit plate on the black granite countertop. This place is a cook's dream—stainless steel, double ovens, industrial gas cooktop—the works.

"She stuffed the lemons in the chicken," she says with an amused wink. "She worked hard. While you were *napping*."

I feel my cheeks heat at Cam's soft chuckle behind me. "Sorry I wasn't here to help." I give her an apologetic smile and set my squirmy daughter on her feet. She promptly runs over to pop a grape into her mouth.

Abby waves a hand at me and turns toward a colander full of green beans. "Pssh. No worries. You can make dinner tomorrow." A burst of laughter from the great room draws her attention briefly. "I can keep her occupied in here while you guys talk, if you'd like. Dinner will be ready in about twenty—is that enough time?"

"Yeah, that should do it," Cam says, reaching across the counter to ruffle Hannah's hair, causing her to giggle. He exchanges a glance with me, his eyes pensive. "There's no need to belabor the point."

"Right." Abby turns to my daughter, a bright smile on her face. "Hey, Hannah, want to help me check on the brownies?"

"Yeah!"

We leave Abby and her enthusiastic helper and wander into the great room. The guys and Tessa are scattered around, talking and largely ignoring the droning of a newscaster on the big screen.

As soon as we walk in, all eyes swivel to us. Kennedy snaps the television off.

"So he's let you out of his clutches, eh, Sammy? Oh! Sammy and Cammy sitting in a tree," Sean sings, dodging a coaster that Matt throws at him. "Hey! What's that for? It's not like you weren't thinking it."

Matt scoffs. "I was not." Tess rolls her eyes.

"Ignore him. Sometimes it's for the best," she stage-whispers, and I laugh. Cam leads me to a sofa next to Kennedy, and we sink down.

Sean is sprawled sidewise in a plush chair, but sits up and swings his legs in front of him. "So, what's up? Why the extra sets of eyes out front?"

My stomach tingles with nerves, but I take comfort from the feel of Cam's arm around my shoulders. The shame I usually feel about the years I spent rationalizing Ray's behavior instead of calling it what it was—abuse—is tempered by the epiphany I had on the slopes. I'm still me. Yes, maybe I should've found the strength sooner to do something, fight back, but I didn't and I can't change it now.

As I look at the solemn faces before me, my stomach sinks. I hate that my messed-up past is affecting these wonderful people. I twist my hands together in my lap.

"I was married before, to Hannah's father. I divorced him about three years ago and I have full custody of Hannah, but . . ." I open my mouth to continue, but nothing comes out. Their faces are a mixture of encouragement, empathy, and worry. How much detail should I give them? Images of Ray's angry face, demeaning words, and visits to the ER flash before me. I owe them some kind of an explanation for adding extra hassle to their lives, but how do I explain without making me sound like an idiot or one of those awful stories you see on *Dateline*?

Blinking, I look up at Cam for inspiration. He presses a kiss to my forehead, and then faces his friends. "In a nutshell, Sam has been on the run from her abusive ex, and now she's in Boston. He's supposedly in Florida, but Tucker's got security on her just to be on the safe side," he says simply. He looks at me, his eyes determined. "And she doesn't have to run anymore."

Matt's eyebrows shoot up, and Tess presses a hand to her mouth, her eyes full of empathy. Sean's reaction is surprising. He looks murderous.

"Did he hit Hannah too?" He clenches his fists at his side.

"No. I left before he could take it that far." I take a deep breath. "I know I should've tried to get out sooner, but—"

"You don't have to explain now," Tess says quickly. "Or ever, really, unless you feel you want to. I can't even imagine what it must have been like. The important thing is that you're safe now." She looks between Cam and Tucker, who's leaning against the stone fireplace. "She is, isn't she?"

"She is." The bodyguard folds his arms.

Sean shoots him a glare before addressing Cam. "But you can't keep them on her indefinitely. That's no way to live. What are you doing to make sure this wanker stays away permanently?"

"Do we need to have someone pay him a visit?" Matt moves to the edge of his seat, as if ready to jump into action. He looks at Kennedy, who's nodding thoughtfully. "Maybe give him a little taste of his own medicine? Or at least encourage him to stay in his own fucking lane?"

"No!" I stiffen in alarm and clutch Cam's hand. "Please, don't—I don't want to provoke him. In addition to everything else, he was involved in some shady stuff back in Denver. It wouldn't surprise me if he still is, and I don't want you to be tainted by that."

Mortification hits hard; I can just see the headlines now.

Sean scoffs. "Like we care. Matty's right—let's go set him straight."

"Wait a minute." Tess holds up her hand, frowning at him. "Surely there's something else we can do. Something that doesn't involve you guys barreling down south to confront him in person like a pack of Neanderthals. What about a restraining order? Do you have one, Sam?"

I huff a weak chuckle. "I got one before I left Denver, but it didn't seem to matter to him when he broke into my aunt's house in Chicago and . . ." I trail off when I see her wince, and continue carefully, "A cop there said that restraining orders don't always do the job." I don't tell them what Ray said he'd do if he ever found me again. No protective order is going to stop him.

"Well, we have to do something," Kennedy states. "Cam, what do you think?"

"As satisfying as tuning the guy up would be, I think it's time to involve my lawyer. We need legal options we can apply at a distance." He purses his lips and glances at Tucker. "Do you have some ideas too?"

He rubs the back of his neck and nods. "Several, actually."

"Fine. Let's talk when we get back to town."

My gut is churning. This doesn't feel right, letting others into my crazy world. My ingrained inclination to hide is at odds with the glimmer of hope I now feel that maybe, just maybe it could all be over. It can't be that easy, can it? It never has been before. Ray always finds a way to hit me where it hurts the hardest, sometimes literally.

I try to swallow down my burgeoning panic as I look at Cam. "What if he finds out about us and tries to use my past against you somehow? Blackmail or something to start a scandal?" His eyes widen in surprise, and I shake my head, trying to make better sense. "You don't know what he's like. If he sees an in, he'll take it."

This is what I've been dreading. This is why it's better if I just take Hannah and run again. None of these people deserves the baggage that comes with me. My heart cracks at the thought of never seeing Cameron again. How can I leave him now? He's—he's everything. But I can't risk any harm coming to him. Ever.

"Hey, slow down." He leans down, his eyes full of concern as he scans my face. "Whatever you're thinking, it'll be okay, Sam. You aren't responsible for whatever he does. And whatever we decide to do, we'll decide together, okay? I promise. There isn't anything he can do to hurt us, unless we let him."

Tamping down my lingering worry, I place a soft kiss on his lips. "Okay."

Abby's voice sings out from the kitchen that dinner's ready, and we rise as one to head her way. As he walks past Cam and I, Sean pats me on the shoulder.

"Don't worry, lovey. We'll get things settled so you and Poppet will never be bothered again. We take care of our own."

Startled, I glance up at a grinning Cameron. He snugs me in a little closer to his side. "See? You're one of us now," he whispers in my ear, making me shiver. "And I take care of my own, too."

Feeling more settled, I soak up Cameron's warmth and the easy bonhomie that flows between all us. For the first time in a long time, I feel hopeful. When we reach the kitchen, I see something that banishes all thoughts of crazy ex-husbands instantly.

"Hannah Marie McKenzie!" My voice cracks across the room, stilling all other conversations. All eyes swivel to my guilty-looking daughter, who drops the paring knife she was holding onto the table next to the pan of brownies. "What have I said about you using sharp knives?" I stride quickly to her side.

She twists her hands in her lap and looks up at me through her eyelashes. I'm mostly immune to her excellently executed puppy-dog eyes, but I hear a couple of compassionate coos behind me.

Rookies.

"Never use a sharp knife unless you're here to help me," she recites softly, clearly embarrassed to be called out in front of our new friends. I hate having to do it; but I need to keep some order in the face of all this permissive decadence we've been surrounded with.

Hands on my hips, I stare down at her. "That's right. And what happens now?"

"I get a time-out," she says, resigned.

Behind her, Sean rubs a hand through his hair, distressed. "Now, Sammy, it was my fault. I asked her to—" I whip my hand up, cutting him off. He looks like he wants to protest, but clamps his mouth shut.

"That's right," I continue, looking at Hannah and thinking quickly. If I send her to our room, with all the road games and puzzles Abby and Tess brought her—not to mention the stuffed animals that have mysteriously appeared today—it wouldn't be a punishment. "The bathroom down the hall. Now."

She nods, but Sean blurts, "For how long?" He looks like I'm taking away his favorite toy. I turn on him.

"You, too. For aiding and abetting." I point to the balcony outside. "Go sit by the hot tub. I'll come get you when time's up."

"Are you kidding?" His eyes widen in horror.

I fold my arms across my chest. "Do I look like I'm kidding?" You can hear a pin drop in the room; the expressions surrounding us are a mixture of empathy and barely restrained laughter. Cameron is biting his lips so hard, I think he may draw blood.

Hannah pats Sean on the arm. "It'll be okay," she whispers. "It doesn't last too long." Then she trudges off down the hall. My gaze doesn't waver from the blue-haired man. After a beat, he turns on his heel and marches across the room, snatching his parka from a chair, and out the French doors to do his time in purgatory. The room erupts in laughter.

Justice is served.

# chapter fourteen

## cameron

I CAN FEEL HER ENTER the wine cellar before I see her. It's like I'm switched on to her, aware of every movement, a warmth spreading through me whenever she's near. Selecting the bottle of whiskey from the top shelf, I turn to see Sam tentatively looking at me.

"Everything okay? You disappeared," she says, moving under the exposed beams of the cellar.

"Yeah. Is Kennedy with Sean on the time-out?" I lift the bottle up. "I don't want him to see this."

Sam eyes the green bottle. "What is that exactly?"

"McGuire's Irish Whiskey. Chapman Reserve, batch number forty-one." I give the bottle a shake.

"Sounds impressive," she says with a smile.

"It's lethal. And Kennedy shouldn't be around it."

Her smile falters. "Then why are you getting it out?"

"Because I think the Brit needs a glass to calm the hell down. Just one though."

I open up the bottle, waving it under her nose. "Whoa, that smells strong!" She wrinkles her nose, making me laugh.

"Tastes really smooth though, from what I remember."

"Chapman Reserve?" She runs her fingers over the etched sailboat on the bottle.

"Yeah." I shrug. "My brothers are investing. Expanding the portfolio."

She tilts her head, taking the bottle from me. "Investing in Irish whiskey. You're full of surprises."

"I've got nothing to do with it. I was just the taste tester."

"They care about your opinion or you wouldn't be. And you're okay with this?" She nods to the rows of wine and liquor bottles stacked in the cellar. "It doesn't bother you?"

"I could care less what they decide to put our name on. Besides, they've been doing an 'enjoy in moderation' campaign, which I can appreciate." I pull her flush to my chest, brushing my fingers over her furrowed brow. "Don't worry, okay? Booze was never my issue, and if I ever feel the need, I have NA meetings I can go to."

My fingers press against her back trying to inch her closer. I don't think she'll ever be close enough. "Do you go to them often?" she asks quietly.

"Right after rehab I did. But now? I haven't needed to go in months." I rub the back of my neck, suddenly nervous, but the encouragement I see in her eyes helps me continue. "It's not so much about the drugs themselves. I know I don't *need* them. It's more about recognizing and managing potential triggers, like stress. I try to be more mindful now. Does that make sense?" She nods and hums softly, and I can see that she gets it; the relief that floods me is euphoric. I'm not used to women caring like this. It's been random, empty hookups for as long as I can remember. Sam makes everything feel whole, right. I reach for the bottle in her hand. "Did you want a taste?"

She nods, pushing up on her toes, and wraps her arms around my neck, her soft lips pressing to mine. It's a chaste, simple kiss that shouldn't rattle me, but it does. I want it all with Sam. All these light, easy moments, and more—a whole lot more of the intensity we had in my room before the Brit interrupted us.

Pulling away too soon for my liking, she steps backward to the door, a coy smile on her face. "Mmm. I'd invest."

"IS MY TIME-OUT OVER?" SEAN glances over at me as I join him on the deck. He's leaning against the thick cedar rail, huddling in his over-the-top parka as if it's minus forty.

I lift the glass of whiskey to him. "Almost over. This should help get you through the rest of it."

He takes the glass without question, draining back the contents in one gulp. "Christ." He lets out an exaggerated cough, a stream of his breath crystallizing in the air. "Warn a man, will you?"

Slapping him on the back, I take the glass from him. "You didn't give me time."

"What in the ever-loving fuck is that?"

"Batch number forty-one. Your thoughts?"

He shudders. "My thoughts are it should come with a damn warning label. Did it just get hot out here?" He unzips his jacket and pushes his hat off his head.

"Well, I'm out here, so maybe."

His laugh lacks its usual punch, and an uncharacteristic frown takes over. "You can't seriously be okay with all this. With everything you know about her ex."

"Of course I'm not."

"And yet you're doing nothing about it."

I glare at him. "I'm doing everything I can."

He waves his hat in my face. "Bullshit. You might be able to convince the rest of the lot of that, but not me, mate." My grip on the glass tightens as he takes a step toward me. "How are you letting this asshole continue to breathe?"

"Because Sam's had enough drama and stress to last more than a lifetime. Tucker's guys are watching her." I can hear the tension in my voice. Sparring in the gym aside, it's been a long time since any of us have gone a few rounds, but over this, I can see it happening.

"That's not a fucking solution. Is that what you honestly want? For someone to watch her twenty-four seven? What happens when we're out on tour?" His arms flail as he rants on. "I don't know, in the middle of Finland or something, and this asshole decides to show up again? How are you going to be able to live with yourself if something happens to her or, God forbid, to Poppet when you know you could've done something to stop it?"

I take a step toward him, closing the distance, shoving him in the chest. "You don't think I want to rip his fucking arms off? I think about it all the time. What good does that do us if I'm in fucking jail and Sam's name is plastered on every media outlet in the country? It's not what she wants." He scoffs, turning to scowl at the towering mountain in the distance. "Her opinion counts, dipshit. And you don't have a mean bone in your body. You wouldn't be able to live with yourself if you were involved in something like that."

He turns to face me. "What I couldn't live with is something happening to either one of them. Bastards like this don't change,

Cameron. This is a fucking time bomb waiting to go off. And when someone threatens my family, I take action. Because that's what you are. Whether you like it or not. We're family. She's with you, so she's family too. Just like Kennedy and Matty, just like Abby and Tess are."

"I'd never ask you to do something like that."

"You're not asking. I'm offering. Big difference."

"No, Sean. You have to promise me you won't do anything stupid." Just the thought of Sean getting involved in this is a nightmare. The press, the headlines, it would all send Sam running in the other direction just when she's starting to open up. As tempting as tuning up this son of a bitch is, I can't do that to her. I won't do that to us.

We stare at each other in a silent standoff. I've never seen Sean like this. This side of him goes against everything I know about him. But I also understand it. The fierce desire to protect the people you care about is something we all share. He rakes his hand through his hair. "I just hate the thought of some bastard hurting her." He swallows heavily. "Or the Poppet." He glances inside where Hannah is tucked up on one of the couches in front of the fire, watching as Matt and Kennedy play their guitars.

"We're on the same page there, believe me." I sigh and fold my arms, leaning a hip against the arm rail. "She's just starting to open up, to trust me, to trust all of us. She deserves some peace after all that violence."

"And you think she's going to get that while he's still stealing oxygen?"

"I think she's starting to." Sean paces the length of the deck. "And I don't want to screw that up. She deserves more than that. She deserves everything." I step in front of his path. "Just let this go."

Sean lets out a frustrated huff with a shake of his head.

"Fine. I'll let it go for now. But if we get wind that he's heading to Boston—"

"You'll be the one who has to hold me back."

LINGERING AT THE DOOR TO Sam and Hannah's room, I watch as Sam tucks Hannah under the covers with her Josie doll. She places a gentle kiss to her forehead before quietly crossing the room to join me.

"Out like a light," Sam whispers, stepping into the hallway.

"It's the fresh air. Brooks always says Ethan sleeps like a log after a day playing outside."

"You were really good with him at the Christmas party."

"I seem to do better with him than his father most of the time." She frowns, and I reach to cup her cheek. "No frowning. And no more talk of my brothers." I take her hands, walking backward away from their room, toward mine. "Let's talk about the big, warm, empty bed just over here."

She laughs, pulling me to a stop just in front of my door. "I need to sleep with Hannah. She'll be scared if she wakes and I'm not there."

Taking her face between my hands, I rest my forehead against hers. "I want to know what it's like to fall asleep with you. To wake up next to you. Tell me we can have that."

I hear her sharp intake of breath before her arms wrap around my torso. "We can. Soon."

Faint chords from the living room drift up, and I recognize Matty starting in on an acoustic version of *The Unforgiven Four*, one of the tracks off our last album. Played this way, it's got a relaxing vibe to it, which is in sharp contrast to the way we recorded it. Kennedy wrote it with one intention—to blow the roof off a stadium. Now, it sounds like a lullaby.

Sam smiles up at me, and I can see a slight windburn on her cheeks caused from our afternoon on the slopes. "Is that one of your songs?"

"Mhmm. Well, Kennedy wrote it, but yeah, it's ours." I brush her hair behind her shoulder and she leans into me.

"I'd love to see you play," she says, her palm inching up my chest.

I grin at her. "You have, or am I that forgettable?"

She gives my chest a playful smack. "No, with them, I mean."

"We can arrange that." I take her hand, leading her down the stairs to join the group around the stone fireplace.

"Hannah asleep?" Tess looks up from her spot on the couch.

"She's down for the count," Sam answers, eyeing my Gibson that's leaning against the wall.

"Do you want to play?" Kennedy crosses the room to pick my guitar up. He holds it out to Sam. Her eyes widen and she backs up slightly.

"I can't play guitar," she says, looking between Kennedy and me.

"Sure you can. If you can master the violin like you have, you can play a six string. It's easy." Kennedy nods to the guitar. "You can do it."

Sam shakes her head. "I can't. I wouldn't even know where to begin," she answers quietly, scanning the worn spruce of the body. I've got a lot of guitars, but I've had this one since before I met Kennedy. To say it's well-loved is an understatement.

"I've got this," Matt says, slinging his own guitar behind his back and lifting the Gibson from Kennedy.

"Hey! Why do you get to teach her?" I ask as he shoulders

me out of the way.

"Because I'm impartial." Sean snorts at Matt's answer. "Just give us a half hour, and she'll be back." I scowl, watching as he steers Sam into the kitchen.

"Easy there, Three," Sean says, taking a sip from his coffee mug. "Matty knows how to train women, isn't that right, Tess?"

A pillow hits Sean in the head, and I turn to see Tess glaring at him. "I could kick your ass if I wanted to, Sean. You'd do well to remember that."

Abby laughs as Kennedy sits on the armrest of the chair beside her. "It's too bad she didn't bring her violin. We could've worked on some songs with her," Kennedy pipes up. I hear a few faint disjointed chords from the kitchen, followed by Sam's soft laughter.

"What are you thinking?"

Kennedy shrugs but I know when he's got one of his ideas. He tries and fails to stop his leg from bouncing with nervous energy. "I'm just playing around with a few things, you know? Featured musicians, different instruments for the next album."

"We've done that already," Sean announces, stretching his legs out in front of the fire. "Did you forget the symphonies we played with this year?"

"Not symphonies, individual sounds. A single violin instead of, oh I don't know, say a drum solo for instance." Kennedy smirks at Sean.

Sean scowls. "You wouldn't dare deny the public of one of my drum solos." Kennedy's quiet for long enough to cause Sean to jump to his feet, spreading his arms wide. "You wouldn't, would you? Am I being replaced?"

Kennedy bursts out laughing. "Of course not, you idiot. Like we could ever do a song without you. It's good to see that you still give a shit though."

"Course I do. This is my bloody life. Don't ever kid about that. Ever!" Kennedy nudges Sean in the shoulder, and he shakes his head. "Damn lot of you. Why do I put up with you?" Sean stalks toward the door, lifting his parka from the hook at the door. "I'm going somewhere I'm wanted. I'll be at the lodge at the resort."

"We love you!" Abby calls out as Sean stuffs his boots on. "Remember, make good choices," Kennedy adds while Sean flips him off before slamming the door shut, a gust of cold air swirling in behind him.

"You think we'll see him again?" Tess wraps a blanket around her from the back of the couch.

"Probably not until morning now," Kennedy says, dropping a kiss to Abby's forehead. "I'm just going to make a couple calls, and then we'll play."

Less than a half hour passes, and Matt is leading Sam back to join us in the living room. "Did we lose the Brit?" He sinks down beside Tess.

"We did. He's gone over to the resort. There's no shortage of entertainment there." I smile at Sam as she looks up at me. "How did it go?"

"He's very good," she says, gently holding the guitar. "If this gig doesn't work out, I'm sure he could find work as an instructor."

Matt laughs. "I had a good student," he says, and I see that faint blush rise on Sam's cheeks. I hope someday she gets to the point where she believes the compliments she gets. Just another reason to hate her bastard ex. I'm realizing more and more how deep the damage he's done runs, and how long it's going to take me to reverse it—if I even can.

Kennedy's rejoined us and starts strumming beside Abby. "And what did Matt the Instructor teach you?"

"'*Perfect Hello*'?" Sam glances nervously at me. "The chorus."

"Nice, Matty. Just pick one of the most complicated riffs we have."

Matt gives me a salute. "Go big or go home, man. Besides, it's easy for Sam."

Sam lets out a huff, adjusting the strap on the guitar as Kennedy launches into the song. Her eyes widen as she watches him effortlessly morph the rock anthem into a stripped-back, emotionally charged masterpiece. As is often the case, Kennedy is lost in the song, but Matty meets him note for note in a display that can only come from logging countless hours of playing together.

When the chorus hits, Kennedy comes back to planet Earth, glancing at Sam and giving her a nod to join in. I watch as her brow knits together in concentration, her eyes focused on the strings while she plays. Kennedy and Matt deliberately slow down, and Sam only misses a few chords. It's impressive to hear, a massive turn-on to watch her control my guitar, breathing new life into the chorus. She needs to do more of this. More of letting go and trying new things. Every single time she does, I think it's another step on the road to regaining her confidence, to leaving her past behind for good.

Abby, Tess, and I give them a standing ovation when they're done, and Sam's smile lights up the room. "See? Easy," Matt says, holding his palm up. Sam gives him a high five and then quickly lifts the strap from her shoulder, passing me the guitar.

"I think I'll stick to my violin. Leave the guitar playing to the experts."

I lean forward, taking the guitar and placing a soft kiss on her lips. "You were incredible."

"Play for me, and I'll show you how incredible I can be," she whispers against my lips.

I can't resist claiming her lips once more. "Promises, promises."

♪ ♩ ♪ ♩

IN THE FOYER, TUCKER SQUEEZES the back of his neck, his eyes darting to Sam. It's so rare to see a break in his stern demeanor. The look on his face tonight when Sam asked—no, demanded—to meet Brent and Lincoln was priceless. He's used to calling the shots, but Sam made it clear the only answer she was going to accept on the matter was yes.

"Samantha McKenzie, this is Brent O'Neill. Ex–Navy SEAL, special reconnaissance." Brent is intimidating as hell, even standing at ease, his hands clasped behind his back. Tucker nods to Linc. Even though he hasn't played professional football in over a year, Linc still looks like he could block an entire roster of players. "Lincoln Davis. Used to play center for San Diego. They've been with our team for a while now."

"And you've both been following me and my daughter?" Sam asks, tilting her head up to meet Brent's serious gaze.

"We've been *guarding* you and your daughter. Yes, ma'am," Brent says, and Sam shakes her head.

"How did I not notice you?"

"We're trained to blend in," Linc answers.

A wry laugh breaks from Sam. "*You're* trained to blend in?"

"When we're in public, yes, ma'am." And Linc's right. If Tucker hadn't told me they were assigned to Sam and Hannah, I don't think I would have noticed them. "Think of us like shadows."

"Shadows." Sam repeats the word and leans against my side, covering her eyes. "God. This is crazy." Brent glances over at Tucker before focusing back on Sam. She lets out a shaky breath. "And in all this time you've never seen anything? No one following us? Nothing?"

"No, ma'am."

Sam tilts her head. "And what if you had? What happens then?"

"Then we get you to safety, and take out the threat," Linc says after clearing his throat.

Sam's mouth drops open. "You can't mean . . ."

"It's our job to protect you, ma'am. Simple as that," Brent replies.

Sam throws her hands up. "There's nothing simple about this. And, *take out the threat?* You can't possibly mean—"

"Only as a last resort," Tucker interjects, moving beside Brent. "Sam, this is our job. Me and my guys, we know what we sign up for."

Sam straightens, looking between Brent and Linc. "I don't want anyone getting hurt because of me."

"And we don't want you getting hurt, either," Tucker says. "Look, it's just for a while, until we're sure there's no threat."

"How does this work exactly?" Sam asks.

"Ma'am?" Linc looks like he'd rather be anywhere than here.

"You're following me, I think I deserve to know what that looks like, don't you?" She plants a hand on her hip, staring both Brent and Linc down. My feisty girl is back.

"Um . . ." I kind of feel sorry for Linc and Brent. I don't think they've had to answer to anyone outside of Tucker on what they do or why in a long time. This is a job for them, one I know they take seriously, or Tucker would never let them on his security team.

Brent jumps in, saving Linc from the interrogation. "It's a pretty standard routine. We make sure the day care and the arts center are clear, keep an eye out. We usually switch out the night watch between us."

Sam just stares at Brent in silence. It's heavy and awkward. "You're in a black SUV, aren't you?" I saw one on the corner the other night." I smile down at Sam when she glances up at me.

"Yes, ma'am." Brent nods. "That's us."

She takes a step toward them and they both lean back slightly. She's dwarfed by their sheer size, but right now, she's the strong one. "I know it probably doesn't mean much, but thank you. What you're doing . . ." She takes a deep breath. "Just thank you."

♪ ♩ ♪ ♩

# *samantha*

THE CAR DOOR SHUTS WITH a soft thump, and I sigh in relief. Home, finally. Well, Cam's home. Not my home. Right.

The streetlights are beginning to wink on, making the new snow sparkle. Christmas is in two weeks and some of Cam's neighbors' homes have decorated trees in their front windows. They make the already picturesque street look even more inviting.

"Hey, you okay? I promise that the vultures didn't follow us." He shoulders our bags and looks at me with concern. The clown car Sean had insisted on for the trip to Vermont had finally earned the scorn bestowed on it by the band's more circumspect members; paparazzi had followed us from Ludlow, so Cam insisted we drive first to the Fairmont, where everyone else was staying. There, the three of us switched to a more discreet town car driven by Brent in the underground parking lot so we wouldn't be tracked to Cam's home.

"Yeah, I'm just glad to be out of a car for a while." I give him a smile and take Hannah's backpack from an obliging Brent. I'm still can't believe we have a security detail. It's not something I ever envisioned needing, but I can't help but feel grateful that we have it—even though I'm still irked it was done behind my back. Brent and Cam exchange a few words, and then he gets back in.

"Momma, I'm hungry!" Hannah pulls on my free hand, her head lolling back in an apparent show of desperation. I know it can't be that bad, since she was snacking on fruit in the van.

"Well, let's go inside and see what we can find in the kitchen, hmm?" She releases me and wades through the unmarked snow lying on the steps to the front door. Cam's warm voice in my ear sends a tingle down my spine.

"If whatever we find is even half as good as the spaghetti you made last night, I'll die a happy man." I flash him a grin in thanks and follow him to the door, where he fiddles with the keys before unlocking and opening it. Since Abby had made dinner the first night, I took over the second night. Cam and Hannah "helped," although his help consisted mainly of groping me when Hannah wasn't looking. I'd made my mother's homemade sauce, and you'd think the Redfall boys hadn't eaten in a million years by the way they scarfed it down. Tucker alone had three helpings, prompting Hannah to force him to pull up his shirt afterward so she could examine his belly to see where it all went.

After disarming the alarm system, Cam volunteers to carry our bags upstairs with Hannah while I look through the refrigerator. But I'm not really seeing the contents. Now that we're back in his home, with his scent and things surrounding me, all I can think of is my whispered promise to him. Thoughts of waking up wrapped in his arms, seeing his tousled hair and sleepy smile . . . Giving up, I shut the door and lean my forehead against the cool stainless steel. I laugh and close my eyes. Actually, being with Cam is all I've thought of for the last day and a half. Between building a snowman army with Hannah in front of the chalet, enduring more ski "lessons" with Sean, and generally trying to get to know everyone, we hadn't had another chance to steal away. And like a starving person who's been given a taste of a banquet, I'm hungering for more.

"What's the verdict?" Cam asks from the doorway. I turn to see him with a beaming Hannah perched on his shoulders. Between the two of them, they must be eight feet tall. Her head is almost brushing the ceiling.

I crane my neck to grin up at them. "How do you feel about pizza?"

"Yay, pizza! Pizza, pizza, pizza!"

Staggering slightly from the enthusiastic cheering and fist pumping going on above his head, Cam reaches over to a drawer and pulls out a take-out menu. He gives me a wink as he hands it to me. "We can worry about groceries tomorrow."

CLIMBING THE STAIRS TO PUT Hannah to bed after dinner, I stop when I see my bag still in the hallway outside our bedroom door. Cam's hand squeezes mine. "I, uh, wasn't sure whether to put your bag in Hannah's room, or . . . in mine."

His words seem to hover in the air between us, and I catch my breath. Looking up into his hazel eyes, I nod, every inch of me suddenly alive with possibility.

"Momma? Are you ready to hear my prayers?" Hannah calls from the bedroom, rousing me from my inertia.

"Yes, sweetie." Minutes later, prayers heard and teeth brushed, I settle Hannah under the covers and frantically try to figure out how to do this. I'm not sure why I'm so nervous; I'm a grown woman, after all. I can sleep anywhere—and with anyone—I want to. But . . . I quickly wipe my palms on my thighs as I sit beside her.

"Hannah, you know how you have your own little bed in our apartment?" I begin, trying to sound sure of myself. She nods, tilting her head. "Well, how would you like to sleep in this big bed by yourself while we're staying with Cameron?"

Settling herself against the pillows, she casts a glance across the empty expanse of bed. "Where will you sleep?"

"I'll be just down the hall, in Cam's room." I sense him stepping closer to me and take comfort in his presence. "Close enough to hear you if you need me, I promise."

She looks at Cam over my shoulder. "Where will *you* sleep?"

"Um, I'll sleep in my room too," he says, his voice tinged with nerves. I'm glad I'm not the only one feeling anxious. Although, I doubt he'll account to a four-year-old for his sleeping habits very often.

After a moment that feels like a million years, her face brightens. "Oh! Like a sleepover?"

"I . . . I suppose so," I reply, surprised—and a little relieved, if I'm honest. "What do you know about sleepovers?"

"Uncle Sean told me." She shrugs.

My eyes shoot open and there's a strangled snort behind me. "What exactly did 'Uncle Sean' say about that, sweetheart?" Cam asks.

"He said that you and Momma would want to have sleepovers when we gots home because old people don't sleep very good by themselves, and because they don't get naps like I do. And *I* said that Momma must sleep good even though she's old because she sleeps with me. And then *he* said that's right, but you don't have anyone to have sleepovers with, and that I should loan you Momma so you sleep better because you're even older than she is."

I rub a hand over my mouth to hide my smirk, not sure whether to hug or hit Sean the next time I see him. "He said all that, did he?"

She yawns and rubs her eyes. "Yep. He also said that I'll go on sleepovers when I get old, too."

"Well, we'll see how that works out when you're older," I say dryly, ignoring Cam's chuckle. "Goodnight, sweetie."

"G'night, Momma. G'night, Cam." She turns over and snuggles in, and I can't resist leaning in and kissing that soft cheek.

Rising, I follow Cam back to the hallway, leaving the door open a few inches. I take a second to listen to Hannah's regular breathing, and then turn to see Cam with my bag in hand.

"Shall we?" he whispers, nodding toward his door down the hall. I walk ahead of him, taking a deep breath when we enter. Moonlight floods the room through the open curtain. It strikes me as a very masculine space, with walls in colonial blue and heavy dark brown furniture. Very in keeping with the age of the building, but like the guest rooms, it's been enlarged and an en suite added.

I hear the door close with a quiet click behind me. Cam steps past to set my bag on a chair and turns to me. "What's wrong?" He runs his hands up my arms. "Are you okay?"

I chuckle and shake my head, trying to release my sudden nerves. "I'm not sure why, but this feels more official somehow."

He smirks and smooths my hair back over my shoulders. "Because we have permission?"

"Maybe," I whisper, sliding my hands up his chest. There's nothing like the feel of cashmere. "Is that weird?"

"No." He pulls me tight against him, his chest vibrating with a silent laugh. "I think I need to thank the Brit the next time I see him though."

I hum at the feel of his lips on my forehead, my earlier nerves turning to heat. "I don't want to talk about him now," I murmur, tugging on his sweater.

He takes the hint. We undress each other, taking the time we didn't in Vermont to explore with lips and hands. By the time he pulls me down to the bed with him, my pulse is thrumming in my neck. As before, he lets me take the lead, so I straddle his hips and savor the feel of his skin under my palms. His chest is firm, not overly muscled, and his strong arms are a testament to the years spent holding and playing his instrument.

"I love that you only have this one tattoo." I trace the words circling his bicep, trying to recall my high school French. "The secret of . . . liberté? Freedom?"

"The secret of happiness is freedom; the secret of freedom is courage."

The truth behind the words resonates within me. I hum in approval, tucking my hair behind my ear and out of my face so I can see him. "When did you get it?" My fingers explore the curve of muscle between his neck and shoulder, and he trembles beneath me.

"Just after I met Kennedy." His voice is low and strained. "We were playing in dives and crappy clubs for a bunch of drunks, but I'd never been happier. I felt like I'd finally found my place, playing music, with him. Despite what my parents thought."

"They weren't happy with your choices?" I toy with his chest hair and his fingertips dig into my hips, as if to anchor himself.

"You've met my mother. Does she seem the type to approve of the sex, drugs, and rock-and-roll lifestyle?" He huffs a hoarse laugh. "She probably wouldn't have minded if I'd become a concert pianist instead of joining my father's business, but that would've been the limit of her tolerance."

I lean down and press a soft kiss to his chest, and he lets out a pleasured sigh. "So the freedom and courage . . . that was a statement about your parents," I murmur against his skin. His stomach is flat with an enticing trail of silky chestnut hair leading south. I sit up and grind against him, trapping his hard cock between us, and he lets out a desperate groan.

"Um, yeah . . . Can we stop talking about my parents now?" He's panting and staring at me like I'm his last meal. "God, I want this . . . I want this, you, always." He pulls me down to him and rolls us over, crushing my breasts against his chest. "Is this okay? Are you all right like this?"

The concern in his voice warms my heart, but what feels even better is that I'm fine. Since the mountain, with *him*, I'm finally free. Cupping his face, I press my lips against his, trying to tell him everything I'm feeling but can't express with words.

Another groan escapes him and suddenly, it's like he can't touch me enough. His hands are everywhere. Kissing his way down my body, his lips leave a trail of fire behind. I arch up off the mattress when he reaches between my legs and buries his face. He's muttering to himself—I can't make out all the words, but it doesn't matter because when his mouth finds my clit, all my nerve endings explode. A strangled cry leaves me; I can hardly draw breath.

When my head clears and the spots fade from my eyes, I see his smiling face hovering over mine. "Welcome back." He swiftly sheaths himself with a condom and then kisses me deeply, stealing my breath. "Ready for more?" he murmurs against my mouth. I barely have a chance to nod before he thrusts inside. Pinning my hands to the mattress, he gasps near my ear. "Tell me if it's too much."

"I . . . I will."

It's raw and wild and delicious. Cameron is a tall man, and he's a perfect example of the old wives' tale about the size of a man's feet correlating to . . . other things. I cling to his shoulders, my nails digging in, and hang on for dear life. Just before I tip over the edge again, he peels one of my legs from around his waist and throws it over his shoulder. Oh . . . so much *deeper*! I'm dimly aware of a high-pitched moaning in the room and am only a little embarrassed to realize it's me. It doesn't matter. The only thing that matters is this incredible man with the incredible heart, and what he can do to me.

My climax hits without warning. I feel like I'm being turned inside out, and I take a handful of his hair to keep from disappearing. It seems to trigger his own release, and then we're both falling together . . . down, down into a deep pool from which I don't care if I ever resurface.

"MOVE IN WITH ME."

We're awake again. The moonlight has given way to that early morning darkness that engenders whispers. I've rarely slept so well, although we haven't slept much. I'm as much to blame as he is, I'm happy to admit. I raise my head from his shoulder so I can peer at him over the flap of blanket in the way, but his eyes are closed. He is, however, wearing one of the most contented smiles I've ever seen. I can't blame him. I may never walk again, but it's been worth it.

"We're living with you now," I murmur. I'm hedging, I know. I've been afraid of this.

"I want you to move all the way in. Hannah can have her own room, and you can have a place to play as often as you want without having to worry about bothering the Finnegans."

I frown to myself; I knew I shouldn't have mentioned that to him. "Hannah doesn't need her own room."

"Maybe you do." He opens his eyes and shifts until we're looking at each other across the pillow. "Maybe you need this one."

"You're going to give me your room?" I try for teasing, and see I'm mildly successful; a wry smile emerges from the darkness.

"I think you know what I mean." His hand glides down to cup my ass. "Move in with me."

"My apartment is close to the bar." It's a weak excuse. Although the tips are a vital boost to my income, I'm tired of spending so much time away from Hannah. I had planned on calling the Finnegans tomorrow to ask how the repairs were going on their store, and, in truth, I dread the answer. I love being with Cam. His home is like living in a mink-lined fortress; here, I know Hannah is truly safe. On the other hand, I'm afraid of becoming too dependent on him.

"Quit the bar. You can take on more students instead. Or you can just spend the time rehearsing. Whatever you want. There's a great school for Hannah two blocks over. We can walk her to school and meet her afterward."

Blinking, I stare into the mossy depths of his beautiful eyes. "But, but you won't always be here. What about the band? You're only partway through this tour, aren't you?"

"We only have two more months of dates on this run." He trails his fingers up my back, and I shift closer, craving his touch. "There'll even be a few opportunities I can come home between shows. After that, we're taking a break for a year. Kennedy's got a commitment to do something for Landon Ravine in New York, Sean's going to be busy freaking out about his sister's wedding, and Matty's . . . well, he'll be with Tess. And I can be here with you."

I gape at him, momentarily speechless. He's really thought about this. Visions of family dinners, the three of us gathered in his TV room watching whatever Disney movie is popular, and Hannah's room adorned with Redfall posters and American Girl fluff swirl in my mind, and my heart skips a beat. And then I laugh at the thought of him, an internationally known rock star, wanting to walk Hannah to school. "You'd be mobbed by all the soccer moms," I giggle-snort. "Tucker wouldn't be happy."

"I don't care about making Tucker happy," he murmurs, his breath warm against my cheek. "You're the only one I want to make happy. Well, you and Hannah."

My heart melts a little. "Cam . . ." The truth is I'm not only afraid of becoming dependent on him. I'm also afraid of falling in love with him.

He pulls our hips together, and I can't suppress a shiver of pleasure. I automatically loop my hands around his neck, letting my fingers toy with the hair at his nape. There is no way I can be in love with him already—it's too soon. I've only known him a few weeks. It's impossible to fall in love that fast. Yes, it's hard to envision my life without him, but we're doing fine now, right? It's not love.

Although it's hard to think about the future when you're living day to day, I promised myself next time I'd take my time before committing to a man. What I feel for Cam is so different from how I felt when Ray first started wooing me. Then, it was the rush of young love, that heady feeling that seems so all-encompassing at the time, but in reality is just a flood of excited hormones. With Cam, it's a deep sense of completeness overlaid with a bone-shaking physical need. Everything about him, his kindness, his generous, talented soul, speaks to my heart, and the mere touch of his hand can set me aflame.

But it's not love. *Yet.*

He nibbles on my shoulder and my eyes close reflexively as another jolt of desire shoots through me. "Just think about it, Sam. Okay?"

I sigh as his hand closes over my breast. "Okay."

I NOD TO A FEW of my fellow musicians and set my violin in my locker for a moment. We've just finished the last rehearsal of the year. The orchestra will be dark now until almost the end of March. It's been two days since Cam asked us to move in with him, and although he hasn't pressed, I feel I need to decide soon. The Finnegans' store is almost finished, and then we can return to our little apartment. If I want to.

Pushing that decision aside—I'm getting good at that—I pull my coat on and pull my purse over my shoulder, looking forward to tonight. Cam promised Hannah a night before the fire with Christmas carols and tomorrow we're going to get a tree—

"Samantha McKenzie!" I jerk around from my locker to see Olivia barreling into the room. A couple other people shake their heads at her and scuttle out of the way. Most of us are used to Olivia's histrionics and take it in stride. But, considering the outrage on her face, I don't think that's the problem.

"You've been holding out on me." She thrusts a mangled magazine into my hands.

I try to smooth out the creases and look at the cover photo, unimpressed. "Seriously, Olivia? You think I knew that superhero was boinking that chick from *The Walking Dead*?" She frowns and jabs at a square in the bottom corner of the page.

"Here! I knew there was something going on with you and the mysterious Mr. Chapman!"

The blood freezes in my veins as I stare at the crumpled page. It's a teaser about photos inside of Redfall's Cam Chapman's mystery girl. I quickly rip open the magazine to the advertised page and gasp. There are two photos, both taken during the Chapmans' Christmas tree party. One is of me and Cam dancing—he's looking down at me with a tender expression while I smile shyly at my feet. The other is of us from behind, holding hands with Hannah between us. In this one, my face is more visible as I'm looking up at him, laughing. It's a little blurry, but anyone who knows me could recognize me. Clutching the magazine, I can't look away. They don't look like professional photographs. There were photographers there, but Cam told me they ignored us. These look like they were taken with someone's phone. Who the hell would have done this?

"Where did you get this?" I choke out when I can breathe again.

She grins, flipping her blond hair over her shoulder. "I got my hair trimmed yesterday and this was sitting on the counter. It's all over the Redfall fan Twitter feed, too. So, spill, girl! How long has this been going on? Since the concert or before?"

It's online. Of course it is. Panic brings life to my frozen limbs, and I slam my locker, forgetting to grab my instrument. I walk past an incredulous Olivia and head toward the door. "Sam!" she pleads, grabbing my arm. "Hey—what's going on? Don't be mad."

"I'm, I'm not mad." Terrified, but not mad. Yet. I grimace at the floor, unable to look into her eyes. "But I can't talk now. I have to go—I'm sorry." Turning, I rush out of the locker room and then slam open the alley door. As I start to run for the bus stop, I can only think of getting to Hannah, packing a bag, and . . . I skid to a stop at the corner of Boylston and grip the lamppost to steady myself. No, I can't run yet. First, I have to talk to Cam, tell him what's happened. I owe him that much. My heart twinges at the thought of leaving him, but Hannah is my first priority. What else can I do? I can't take the risk. If it's on Twitter, it's online, and possibly on those TV gossip shows as well. Ray always kept up on Twitter and other messaging sites as part of the illegal crap he did. I have to assume that hasn't changed.

I look around but, as usual, I can't see whatever security is following me. But I know they're there. It's a comforting thought that helps ease the tension in my shoulders a bit. Running a hand through my hair, I take a deep breath and blow it out, watching the steam dissipate in the frigid air. I'm not alone this time. Feeling a little more in control, I decide to splurge and hail a cab; I can't take the time to wait for the bus.

I have to get to Cameron.

# chapter fifteen

## cameron

"IT'S LIKE A DOLL NIRVANA," Sean mutters, tucking his sunglasses into his jacket pocket as we step into the American Girl store. I feel Hannah tug on my hand, the sound of excited squeals drifting to us from somewhere at the back of the store.

"I had no idea," I mumble, following as Hannah propels us forward. The place is packed and buzzing with excitement. A sea of pink, purple, and red as far as the eye can see. Displays of dolls, houses, clothes, you name it everywhere. It's total chaos in here. I get pushed from behind, and turn to see a group of girls babbling away and an exhausted-looking woman trailing behind them with an armful of boxes.

"Watch where you're going, girls!" the woman shouts, casting me a bit of a hopeless look. She must be one of the girls' mother. "Sorry about that. It's spa time."

"Spa time?" Sean scans the store. "Just what kind of a doll shop is this exactly?"

"Hi. Welcome to American Girl." I turn in the direction of the perky voice. It's a twentysomething girl with long, dark hair. *Oh shit. Please don't know who we are.* "I'm Emily and—" Her eyes widen as she glances at Sean, and I see the telltale signs of a die-hard fangirl. Her cheeks heat as she blinks at Sean and then at me. "It's not really . . . oh my God!" There it is. The high-pitched squeal we've come to know.

Sean moves closer to her, his voice lowering. "Shhhhhhh. Breathe, Emily, is it?" She nods, her hand coming up to cover her mouth. "Emily, we're here with our friend Hannah." Sean reaches down to pull off Hannah's knit hat and Hannah giggles as he messes her hair. "We're about to spend an obscene amount of money getting her whatever she wants. So, we'd like to focus on that for a while, yes? And after, we'll take whatever pictures you want, darling. Deal?"

Emily nods, dropping her trembling hand from her mouth. "Deal," she whispers.

"Brilliant! Now, where do we start?" Sean turns back to Hannah, rubbing his hands together. "What kind of doll would you like, Poppet?"

I tug Hannah's jacket off as she squirms out of it, and she blinks up at me with those big, blue eyes. "I asked Santa for a Hannah doll," she says quietly, hugging her tattered Josie doll. "I don't want to make him mad."

My heart tugs, listening to her. "Santa would never be mad at you. Maybe your Hannah doll could use a friend to play with?" I hear Sean snort and I glare over at him. "Or some clothes?"

"I put clothes on my list, but Momma says sometimes Santa doesn't have room for everything in his sack." Everything stops as I stare at her. The fact that Sam can't afford to get Hannah the things she wants kills me. I'd buy the entire fucking store just to never see this pouty lip of Hannah's again.

"How about we look at some clothes then?" Hannah's eyes brighten, her infectious smile growing as she nods.

"And a friend, too. The more the merrier, I always say," Sean pipes up.

"We know you always say that." I give Sean a punch in the shoulder but he ignores me, continuing on.

"What kind of doll would you like as a friend then, Poppet?"

Hannah glances around the huge store. "Do you have one with blue hair?"

Sean lets out a loud laugh. "Now there's the question of the day. Emily, darling, where do you keep your dolls with blue hair?"

"Um . . ." Poor Emily is still shell-shocked, her eyes the size of saucers. "None of them have blue hair."

"Well, that's just not on." Sean folds his arms across his chest. "Take us to the dolls and then we'll visit this spa of yours. Surely we can get hair dye there." Hannah giggles, making me smile.

"I don't think they'll do that," Emily says, her voice all breathy. "But we do have colored highlights you can clip into their hair."

"Hmm. That has potential." Sean slings his arm around her shoulder as she turns to lead us through the store. "You just show us to the dolls, and I'll worry about the hair." Hannah skips along after them until we arrive at a large doll display with stacks of boxes lined up underneath. It doesn't take long for Hannah to pick one out, and I shove the box at Sean, along with a few other pieces Hannah picked out for one of her friends at day care.

"Make yourself useful."

"I'm just the pack mule, yeah?" He shakes his head, wandering off to another display.

"At least you're good for something," I call after him.

"Look! Look!" Hannah takes my hand, trying to tug me with her. "It's a horsie!" She stops, peering up at the display case that houses a tan horse and a mini stable. "It's just like the ones at your house."

"Yes it is. I bet Josie would love to play with your new doll and the stable. What do you think?" Hannah claps her hands excitedly and then darts off to another display. "You can give him the stable and horse to carry too." I nod in Sean's direction and Emily laughs.

"Cam! Come here!" Hannah's practically vibrating next to Sean as she points to a music display. There's even one with a violin. "I asked Santa for the violin, just like Mommy plays."

Chuckling, I glance over at the dolls arranged around a boy doll behind a set of drums. "What the hell is this nonsense?" Sean asks, glaring at Emily.

Emily smiles, moving to the display. "This is Logan. Our first boy doll. He's a drummer. He's quite popular."

"I can see that. And of course he's popular, the drummer always is, but that doesn't answer my question."

Emily looks panicked as she glances over at me, likely thinking I can solve whatever insanity is currently running through Sean's head. I put my hands up in surrender.

"First of all, why isn't a girl doll the drummer?" Sean rants, his voice raising.

"I don't—"

Sean plows on, not giving Emily time to try to come up with an answer. "You've got girl dolls with guitars, a piano, even a flute, but you've put the boy as the drummer?" People are starting to stare, which is typical when Sean's around, but the warning bells fire as they never have before. If pictures get out of Hannah with us, a shitstorm is going to follow that could send Sam running when

I've just started to gain her trust. I try to step in front of him, but even at my height, I'm only a bit taller than him.

"Secondly, who the hell did you collaborate with on this joke of a drum set?"

Emily looks at the display. "I'd have to ask—"

"I want to speak to the owner," Sean demands, hands on his hips as he glowers at the poor girl.

"You mean the manager? She's not in until two."

"No. I mean the owner of American Girl. Who is it? Because this . . ." He flicks his hand at the display. "Stops now. That's a subpar drum kit, not worthy to be—Ow!" Sean scowls at me after I hit him in the chest. "That hurt."

"Good. It was supposed to. You're causing a scene." I dart my eyes to Hannah and back to him, and he clamps his mouth shut. Unfortunately, that doesn't last long.

He leans closer, getting in my face. "Fine. But I want the name of the owner. This isn't over, Three. I'm fixing this shit."

Two hours later, we've had tea in the café—another experience that didn't meet with the Brit's approval—and are finally stacking the purchases into my car. Sean is still muttering about a proper tea service, while Hannah straps her new doll into the back seat beside her. We got lucky today. Sean's outburst aside, people ignored us for the most part. Only Emily and a handful of other employees took pictures, and I made sure Hannah was nowhere near a camera.

"You want a lift to the hotel?" I ask, moving around the front of the car.

"Thanks, Three, but I've got my own shopping to do. Syd's given me a list." He rolls his eyes, but I know Sean loves doing things for his twin sister. She's probably got him hunting down wedding supplies with hers coming up next year.

"All right. Just don't traumatize any more salesgirls."

"When have I ever traumatized anyone?" he asks with a grin.

"You want a list?" I open the door, dropping into the seat as Sean knocks on the window to get Hannah's attention. I press the button to lower the window beside her.

"I'll drop 'round to see you before I go home, Poppet," Sean says, crouching down to stick his face in the window.

"Home?" Hannah turns to look at Sean.

"I live in London. It's a long way from here. We'll take you one day," Sean says, and Hannah's smile grows.

"Do they have an American Girl store in London?"

"If they don't, they should." He gives her hat a little pull before stepping back from the curb. "See you soon." I catch sight of him in the rearview mirror, waving like a lunatic from the sidewalk as I pull into traffic.

Hannah yawns, and I hear her quiet, sleepy voice just before she nods off. "Thank you for today, Cam. I had the best time ever."

"I CANNOT BELIEVE YOU DID this." Sam's trying to keep her voice down and failing. Usually I love her feisty side. It's something I don't see often, something I think she's kept buried from her asshole of an ex for years. But Sam is pissed. She's been pissed since we came home and paraded in the bags and boxes from the store. She stayed pissed right through dinner and amped up the cold shoulder when Hannah asked for me to tuck her in.

"It's just a few things." I try to reach for her, but she's not having it. She stalks across the room, her hands on her hips as she glares at me.

"This isn't just a few things." She spreads her arms wide in the living room where doll paraphernalia seems to have taken over.

"How much did you spend?"

"It doesn't matter."

"Of course it matters! I can't . . ." She closes her eyes. "I can never pay you back for all this."

"Hey." I cross the room, cupping her soft cheek. "Look at me." Slowly, her eyes open, a painful mix of fire and sadness. "I'm not asking you to pay me back. Call it part of my Christmas present to Hannah."

She shakes her head, letting out a frustrated sigh as she removes my hand from her cheek. "It's too much, Cameron."

"No. It's not. It'll never be too much. Did you see how happy she is?"

"I know, and thank you. Truly, it's beyond extravagant, but we can't accept it."

"Yes you can. It would break her heart to return this." *And mine.*

Sam moves to the fireplace, staring at the flames as they crackle. "You don't get it."

I move behind her, pulling her against my chest, hating that she's upset. Not having the first clue as to why. "Then help me get it. I didn't do it to make you angry," I whisper, pressing my lips against her neck. She lets out one of her sexy moans as I press against her, and I feel her start to relax.

"I know you didn't," she says, tracing her hand along my arm. "That's what makes it worse."

"I don't understand. I know I should've told you we were going, but it was kind of last minute, and we were with Sean."

"Don't put this on Sean." She turns in my arms, her eyes searching mine. "I have a Hannah doll on hold for her there. All the extra shifts at the bar, the violin lessons—it's to pay for it. It's what Santa's bringing her for Christmas."

"I'm sorry, Sam. I didn't know until Hannah told me at the

store. She wanted to make sure Santa wouldn't be mad." It kills me when a tear escapes, trailing the curve of her cheek. "Don't cry. If I had known it would make you this upset, I never would've taken her."

"I wanted to give that to her, you know? She's had nothing for so long, and I wanted to see her face light up when she opened the box. To know that I did something right for once." She lowers her chin, staring at the hardwood. Fuck, just when I think I'm making progress, the walls go up again.

I tilt her chin up until her eyes meet mine. I need her to believe me, to see what I see. "Everything you do is right, Sam. When are you going to start believing that?"

"And there's no way we can haul all this with us when we have to go." She glances down to the stable and horse set up beside the fireplace.

I take a step back from her. "What are you talking about? You don't have to go anywhere. You can stay here, with me. I wouldn't have asked you to move in if I didn't want you here. I thought that was pretty clear."

"You haven't seen the pictures, have you?"

My heart stops. She's found out about those blurry pictures making the rounds.

She folds her arms across her middle, and in the light cast from the fire she looks so vulnerable, so lost. "There're pictures of us from your parents' party. Only a couple, but they're out there now. It's only a matter of time before he finds us." Her voice is hollow, all the feisty fire gone.

I pull her into my arms where she belongs, pressing her to my chest. Even though she feels so small against my frame, I know she's strong. Everything she's done has been to protect Hannah. But who has been protecting her? I want to take this agony away. I want to shoulder the pain. I want to be the strong one. "He's never going to find you. I won't let that happen." She looks up at me, her hands tracing along my arms, the little crease on her forehead deepening with worry. "And . . . I knew about the photos."

She rears back, her worry changing to outrage in an instant. "How? And for how long?"

"Tucker mentioned them that day in the gym."

"Cameron!" She pulls away, throwing her hands on her hips as she glares up at me. "That was almost a week ago. First the security, and now this? Why didn't you say anything?"

I clutch at my hair and take a deep breath, tamping down my rising anxiety and guilt. Shit. "I didn't want you to worry. I didn't actually see them; Tucker said they were blurry. He didn't think they were that bad. I'm sorry. I'm an idiot." Spreading my hands in supplication, I take a step toward her; my heart twinges in fear when she takes a step back. "I should have told you. I'm sorry, Sam. But I honestly didn't want you to have to worry about it. The security was in place . . ."

The hurt and betrayal in her eyes is killing me. What the fuck was I thinking? I should have fessed up as soon as I knew about those damn photos, no matter what Kennedy and Tuck said. "Cam, you've said I can trust you," she whispers. "You should have told me. If not right away, at least when you introduced me to Brent and Linc."

I hang my head, feeling two feet tall. "I know."

"Good." She presses her fingertips to her temples, as if fighting a headache. "I'm sorry, too. This shouldn't be a big deal. You shouldn't have been in the position to begin with. I shouldn't have to worry about a few innocent photos. But I do."

"No, you don't." I step forward again, feeling a surge of relief when she lets me take her in my arms again.

"I wish I could believe that. You don't know what he's capable of, Cameron. And I'm tired. I'm so tired of living like this. Of thinking the worst." I brush her hair back, feeling her start to shut down on me. It's a panicked jolt to my heart to think that she could just disappear one day.

"Sam—"

She presses her fingers over my mouth. "Don't. Okay? Please don't. I should be thanking you for taking Hannah to the store today. I should be happy that she's happy. That you want to spend time with her. That you've gone to all these lengths to try to protect us, but the only thing that I can think of is how I'm going to pack up all this when we have to run. And how disappointed she's going to be when we can't take it all."

"You don't have to think about any of that. You never have to run again. I told you I would protect you and I will." I hope she feels the sincerity in my words because I mean every single one of them.

"I just want this to end. God, it's agonizing to live like this. Not knowing. Expecting the worst. Never knowing if he's going to pop up somewhere. And now your friends are involved." She shakes her head. "And you?" Her hand tightens against my arm. "How can this be what you want? Don't you want someone normal?"

"You've seen my family. You just survived over forty-eight hours with the crazy of my best friends." She gives me a half smile, and I take her face between my hands. "Normal took a detour a long time ago."

## samantha

"HANNAH! IF YOU EAT ANOTHER pancake, you'll turn into

one." My admonishment is met with a sweet giggle and a warm chuckle.

"Listen to your mother." Cameron stands from the kitchen table and clears the dirty breakfast plates while Hannah beams at him like he hung the moon. A tiny part of me—the part that's still smarting over the fact he can buy my daughter anything her heart desires and I can't—would like to say it's because he bought her affection, but I know it's not true. She's liked Cam since the minute she met him, and her fondness for him has only grown.

I can't really blame her.

I turn away from the stove-top griddle and lean against the counter just as he sets the dishes in the sink and faces me. "Mother knows best, after all," he murmurs, tucking my hair behind my ear. He cups my cheek and I lean into him, savoring his touch. Showing affection in front of Hannah is becoming easier, despite my lingering worries about what our future holds. After the Great Doll Debacle, he'd led me upstairs to the room I share with him and showed me just how serious he is about sticking with me regardless of my screwed-up past.

"She does, does she?" I peer at him through narrowed eyes. "Still sucking up after yesterday?"

His chin quivers as he tries to stifle a grin. "Do I need to? I thought I'd done a thorough job of *that* last night."

I shiver involuntarily. He certainly had. Taking a handful of his T-shirt, I pull him down to me so I can place a soft kiss on his smiling lips. His hand skates from my cheek to sink into my hair, while his other hand skims around my back, holding me to him. I'm lost in the sensation of his warm lips moving gently with mine, claiming me absolutely and without shame. It's frightening how much I need him now, how I need his touch, his warmth, and the strength of his arms around me. It's happened so fast, and yet sometimes I feel as if I've always known him.

Another giggle reminds me we're not alone; I pull away from his mouth, only to rest my head against his chest. My heart is racing. He gives me one more squeeze, and then we turn to face my tittering daughter. "Okay, giggle-puss, time to get cleaned up so we can go," I say, making shooing motions with my hands. I plan on taking her with me to pick up my violin that I'd accidentally left at the theater in my haste to leave yesterday, and to get some more groceries. Now that I have a real kitchen at my disposal, I've been excited to revisit some of my mother's favorite holiday recipes, with Cam's wholehearted encouragement.

"Oh, but, Momma," she says, hopping in her seat like a jack-in-the-box. "Cam needs me to go with him again today! He needs my help!"

"He does?" I look at Cam, surprised to see the tips of his ears turn red.

"Well, yeah. Christmas is coming, you know." He rubs the back of his neck, squirming a little. "I need help selecting gifts for, uh, my family. And the guys, of course."

"Hmm." I fold my arms and fix him with a fishy eye. "Do I need to remind you of our talk last night?" There's no way I can accept any more gifts for Hannah. Even if we aren't forced to run—which I'm still not convinced won't happen—she doesn't need any more extravagance. I won't have her spoiled any more than she's already been.

He spreads his hands. "Trust me," he says, with an innocent blink that does nothing to reassure me. A small tug on my arm draws my attention to a pair of pleading blue eyes gazing up at me.

"Please, Momma? You can trust us!" she echoes, jumping up and down, and I feel myself giving in.

"Oh, all right. You'd better run upstairs and brush your teeth then. And get your coat and hat!" I call as she disappears out the door. The sound of her eager feet pounding up the stairs makes me smile.

Cam gives me a quick kiss and puts the dirty plates in the dishwasher. If he only knew how sexy the sight of a man helping clean up is . . . Well, maybe he does. "You'll keep an eye out, right?" I murmur, not wanting to give voice to my fears, but unable to prevent it. He immediately straightens and takes me in his arms. His light spicy scent blends deliciously with the lingering smell of maple syrup in the room.

"Of course. And remember to take Brent with you." I avoid his concerned gaze and instead watch my finger draw a line down his bicep, weighing my options.

"If it would make you happy," I concede. While I'd love to be able to take the bus on my own, knowing I have my own shadow looking out for me is comforting.

"It would." He bends to kiss me again, but the shrill ringing of his phone interrupts. I think it's the ringtone he uses for Sean. With a grimace, he glances at the screen; his frown grows. "Damn. I have to take this. Can you wait for a minute?"

I give him an understanding smile and leave to collect my purse and coat from the peg in the foyer. Tugging my hat down over my ears, I wince when his bellow bounces off the walls. "Are you fucking kidding me?"

Yeesh. God knows what Sean has done now. I don't know the blue-haired fiend very well yet, but what I do know makes me shake my head in sympathy with Cam. Based on his tone of voice, this could take him a while. Not wanting to interrupt, I tug a scrap of paper out of my pocket and scribble a quick note for Cam. Then I hitch my purse up over my shoulder and head out the front door to the ever-present Brent. Linc must have the night watch.

"Miss McKenzie." Brent gives me a nod, and I immediately feel sorry for him having to stand guard. It's freezing out and the snow has kicked up in the past hour.

I cinch the top of my coat together, hunching down from the chill. "I'm so sorry. I didn't realize it was coming down so hard. You shouldn't be out here in this."

"I'm right where I'm supposed to be, ma'am." I can see his breath when he exhales.

I cringe slightly. Brent and I are probably the same age. Him calling me *ma'am* seems wrong in so many ways. "Please call me Sam." His steely expression doesn't falter. "Ma'am makes me sound ancient. And no more standing out in the freezing cold. If you have to be here, you can at least be warm inside."

I see a hint of a smile. "Were you headed out, Miss McKenzie? Can I take you somewhere?"

"The arts center, Brent, if that's okay. I need to pick up my violin."

"Of course." He offers me his arm and helps me down the snow-covered path to the waiting SUV. It's so foreign to me, having this kind of attention and help. It's been Hannah and me on our own for so long, I'm not sure I'll ever get used to it. I also don't want to *need* it. Having Brent and Linc hover is a constant reminder that Ray is still out there, controlling me even though he's over a thousand miles away.

The drive takes longer than it should with the state of the slick roads, but we're surrounded in the warmth of the luxury car, so I shouldn't complain. I remember being on the streets in this kind of weather last year with Hannah, before I made the decision to go to the shelter. I glance out the window, squeezing my eyes shut, not wanting to be swamped by that horrible feeling of helplessness again.

So much has changed since then, and I want to focus on this year, on making it a Christmas that Hannah will never forget.

Brent waits at the corner for a few bystanders on Boylston and then follows my instructions to turn down the alley that runs behind the theater. The car slides a little on the packed snow and ice. I hope Hannah remembers her hat today. A smile teases my lips, knowing Cam will remember, even if Hannah doesn't. He's so good with her. My heart beats faster as my mind turns to my other dilemma—Cameron. I can't pretend anymore. It's love. Whether for good or ill, I'm in love with him. And I have absolutely no idea what to do now.

With pictures circling of Cameron and me, the threat of Ray looms. I *should* leave. It would be safer for Hannah *and* for Cam. I know what Ray is capable of, and I would die if something happened to Cameron because of me. I'd be lying if I said I *wanted* to leave. The temptation to stay with him and try to have a normal life is so strong I can taste it. He's been perfectly clear about what he wants. It wouldn't be easy, obviously; his mother thinks I'm a gold digger, and there's the small issue of him being a world-famous musician. I roll my eyes at myself. He's a friggin' *rock star*, Sam. It's too ludicrous to contemplate, but I can't help it. I love him.

Do I dare stay?

Brent pulls the SUV next to the theater side door, and I shove my quandary aside, unbuckling my seat belt when he cuts the engine. "I'll do a scan first, Miss McKenzie." Brent turns to me and my eyes widen. "Just to be safe."

I glance up at the darkened theater. You'd be lucky to find a mouse stirring. "There's no one in there, Brent. Even the cleaning staff is gone for the holidays."

"Then it won't take me too long." Damn stubborn man.

"And you just want me to wait in the car?" His eyes narrow

to slits before he scans the empty alleyway.

"Fine. But let me go in first." It's a minor victory but I'll take it. Brent is out quickly and hauling my door open to the frosty air. "Careful, it's slippery, Miss McKenzie."

His hulking form shelters me from the wind as I quickly key in the security code. Inside, I grope for a light switch and breathe a little easier once I can see. The silence of the empty building is ominous. Shrugging off my sudden apprehension, I push open the door, and Brent steps in front of me.

"It's the first room on the right." I nod in the direction of the instrument room, and Brent takes the lead down the short hall. The fresh smell of floor varnish fills the space. It feels like we're high school kids sneaking around in the school after hours. I shake my head, but wait as he ducks into the instrument room.

I see a light flick on in the room. "All clear," he says, emerging to the hall. "I'll just check these two." He motions to the two practice rooms further down the hall, and I fight the urge to roll my eyes.

He's being overly cautious, but I suppose that's his job. Still, I don't like feeling useless, just standing like some damsel in distress in the hall. I march into the instrument room and pull my violin case out of my cubby just as my phone rings in my purse. Before I can answer it, I hear a heavy thud followed by an eerie silence. Panic spikes, and then a floorboard creaks behind me.

"Hello, Sandy."

The breath catches in my throat. I whirl around, eyes opening wide in terror as I behold my worst nightmare.

"Ray," I choke out, clutching my case tight to my chest like a shield. He's leaning against the doorframe, blocking the way between me and freedom. My phone finally stops ringing, leaving my stuttered breathing the only sound. "What . . . what are . . ."

"You look good." His cold, pale gray eyes roam over me and the hair rises on the back of my neck in response. "I like the long hair. I almost didn't recognize you."

Regular haircuts were just one of the things I gave up when I ran from him. Safety, shelter, and food for Hannah were much more important than stylish hair . . . or morning lattes, fast food, new clothing, my own car. None of it was as important as keeping Hannah safe.

And I've failed.

A lazy, sinister smile spreads across his face that doesn't meet his eyes. "I told you in Chicago that I'd see you again. I admit it took me longer to find you than I thought it would, but here I am."

"How did you get in here?" I manage, my voice barely above a whisper. The violin case slips a little in my sweaty hands. I look behind him to the alley door down the hall, my mind racing. It looks like it's ajar, caught on something at the bottom. But that's not what stops my heart. No. It's the sight of Brent's hulking form crumpled on the hallway floor that freezes the marrow in my bones. I blink back tears at the sight of pooling blood staining the gleaming hardwood floor. It hurts to take a breath.

Ray follows my gaze before his stone expression flickers back to me. "Your friend here? He won't be bothering us for a while now." He lets out an annoyed huff. "Didn't even hear me catch the door behind you. It's the first slipup he's had."

"What are you—" Can I get past him? If I can make it to the alley, someone might hear me scream.

"Oh, I've been watching you for a while now. Ever since I saw those pictures." The light glints off his shaved pate. He's wearing a ratty gray hoodie and faded blue jeans that look like they haven't been washed in weeks. He pushes off the doorframe and takes a menacing step closer, making me step back in response. "Imagine how surprised I was at the grocery store to see my wife on the front of a fucking magazine with another man."

"I'm not your—"

"I've been waiting for a fucking chance to catch you alone." Slowly he taps the tip of a serrated knife against his palm.

My stomach roils and I have to bite back bile. He must have left Florida as soon as he saw the photos. A quick scan of the room increases my dread; there's nothing I can use as a weapon. I take a step to the right, trying to get enough room to maneuver, but he mirrors my movement. "What do you want?"

"What do you think?" He snorts out a laugh, spreading his arms wide. "I want what's mine. You, of course. And my daughter. Where is she?"

My heart almost stops. "It's none of your business. Just leave, Ray. We're divorced, and you have no right to see her. You gave her up."

"Do you think that matters?" He snorts again and strokes his patchy goatee. He never could grow a decent beard. "You're gonna like Florida, Sandy. Or should I call you *Samantha* now," he taunts. "I knew it was you in those photos, despite the bullshit caption. Christ. Did you honestly think changing your name and growing your hair out would help?" His dark expression is unnerving as he takes a step closer. "I told you I'd find you. You really think you can run from me?" I back up, but it's pointless. He's got me trapped. "I almost had you at that grocery store, but I've got you now, don't I?"

Anger lessens my fear, and I clutch my case harder. I decide not to point out that it *had* helped; if it hadn't been for the damn photos, it would've taken him longer to find me, if ever. "I'm not going anywhere," I grate, but he ignores me.

"Is Hannah with your 'boyfriend'?" He steps closer and I manage to slip behind one of the benches lined up by the lockers. "I almost shit myself when I saw you'd hooked up with someone from Redfall. Of all the dumb luck. How you managed to snag a rich fucker like him is beyond me. You're not that good in the sack." He waves the knife at me, eyeing the hem of my coat where the stitching has come loose. "I hope you weren't dreaming of some kind of Cinderella shit with him. The guy has probably fucked actresses and models—hell, maybe a princess or two. There's no way you could ever compete with high-class pussy like that."

Icy doubt flickers through my mind, but I glare in defiance. "You know *nothing* about Cam, or about us." I stick my chin out. "Just leave, Ray. We're through. Get the hell out of my life."

"We'll be through when *I* say we're through," he screams, and I jump in spite of myself. "Now, where the fuck have you stashed my daughter?"

"She's not your daughter! You never wanted her to begin with—"

Lunging forward, he darts around the bench and loses his grip on the knife. It hits the floor with a metallic clang and slides beneath the bench. He grabs my arm, making me wince. The stench of his cheap cologne makes me gag. "Of course she's mine!" His eyes burn with rage. "Just like you are."

"Not anymore!" I scream back, my courage suddenly blazing—but my bravado freezes when I see the familiar switch flip in his eyes. Time seems to slow. In my periphery, I see his other hand begin to move, but terror slows my reactions, and I can't duck in time. I hear the crack of his hand against my jaw a millisecond before a sea of red and black stars explodes in my vision. My face is on fire. Jerked off my feet, I have the sensation of flying just before my head and shoulder crash into the brick wall. My legs give way and I slither to the floor. I drop my case as I frantically try to brace myself; I just manage to keep my head from bouncing off the hardwood.

Then a hoarse cry tears out of me as his boot slams into my hip. He always knew where to hit me where it wouldn't be seen. I squeeze my eyes shut, trying to hold back the memories of beatings from the past; strategic kicks to the ribs, punches to the kidneys. I curl into a ball and gasp for air, excruciating pain radiating throughout my body.

"Now look what you've made me do." He digs his fingers into my shoulders, making me whimper. He hauls me up onto a bench, reaching for the knife and trailing the edge against my cheek—not enough to cut the skin, just enough to terrorize me. "You think he's going to want you when this pretty face is scarred?" My head is throbbing, my thoughts sluggish; I'm not sure I can stand. "You're always so fucking selfish." He pushes at my shoulder and moves away in a huff. I gingerly pat my temple and my hand comes away bloody. Everything hurts. When my vision clears, I see Ray has my case on another bench and opens it. He pulls my bow and instrument out and tosses them on the floor; they skitter across the scuffed hardwood and come to rest at my feet, while he looks at the empty case thoughtfully.

"Hmm, this has potential." He pats the interior and nods to himself. "I could easily fit a couple kilos in here. And no one would look twice at a little kid carrying a stupid violin case. Nice."

When his words finally penetrate the fog in my head, I stare at him in horror. I knew he'd still be involved in drugs somehow. And he's thinking of using Hannah? As some kind of, of, drug mule?

Over my dead body. If that's what it takes.

Cold resolve flows through me as I reach for my violin and bow. Rising to my feet, I hear Tucker and Cam's voices in my head. The soft spots . . . nose, ears, eyes . . . knee, crotch. A stab of pain in my hip makes me stumble, and I pause to regain my balance. I can feel one eye beginning to swell; I swipe at my streaming tears and swallow down my fear.

Ray glances at me, but looks away in disgust when he sees me sway unsteadily. "Oh please. None of that melodramatic crap now. You're fucking fine. Wipe your face—you look like shit. Then we're going to go get that brat and leave. For good." He pats his pockets, as if looking for something, and jeers. "And if your rich boyfriend knows what's good for him, he'll stay out of my way."

Rage. So much rage. Despite the pounding in my head, I know exactly what I need to do. This may be my only chance and I can't waste it. I can't let him get to Hannah—or Cam. He could kill them both. With my bow in my left hand and violin in my right, I tighten my grip and adjust my feet . . . and then I strike.

Whipping my bow through the air, I land it with a crack across the bridge of his nose. His howl of pain echoes in the room, but I don't give him any time—with all my might, I swing the hard edge of my instrument into his ear and temple.

"Fuck!" He hunches over, clutching at his face, and giving me my next opening. He yells again as I drive a wicked kick into his knee, and his legs buckle. The next kick nails him in the groin, and it's his turn to cower into a whimpering ball. A red haze colors everything. On my knees, I straddle his body, wielding the broken violin until it disintegrates into splinters.

My throat is raw; I'm screaming at him. It's a continuous stream, a declaration of independence and litany of grievances. "Never again! Do you hear me? Never. Again!" It's a reclaiming of my strength.

He can't hurt me any longer.

The realization clears the haze, and I see his pathetic face, bloodied and frantic. Suddenly coming back to myself, I lower my hand. I'm better than this. I'm not Ray.

Then a strong arm is pulling me off him. "Sam! Baby, it's me. It's me!" Cam's soothing voice fills my head, and I slump against him. Tears blur my vision as I look up into his worried eyes.

He turns me to face him and chokes on a breath when he sees my face. "Fuck. What has he done to you? Can you see? Can you walk?" Panic and fear are written on his face. Gentle fingers explore my jaw until I recoil, and he snatches them away. "I'm sorry! Did I hurt you?"

"No," I croak, swiping my sleeve across my runny nose. I'm a mess. He pulls me carefully into his arms, pressing a soft kiss on my noninjured cheek.

"Sam, I'm so sorry." His hoarse whisper tears at me, and I realize he's shaking. "I'm sorry I wasn't here faster. I'm sorry I wasn't with you. I love you, Sam. I love you so much."

A relieved sob tears out of me, and I cling to him, my heart swelling with love for this man. "Cam—"

A groan from the floor interrupts me. "You broke my nose, you fucking bitch!" Ray snarls and Cam's head snaps toward him.

"Shut the fuck up, asshole." Cameron's face hardening into barely contained rage, he steps away from me and aims a couple vicious kicks into Ray's stomach. Ray coughs out a curse, prompting Cam to draw back his foot again, but I grab his arm.

"Don't! He's not worth it." His jaw clenches, but he lets me pull him back. Dragging a hand through his hair, he blows out a breath and looks back at me, his expression softening.

"Come on. Let's get you out of here." He slips an arm around my shoulders and ushers me into the hall.

My breath catches as Cameron lifts me as if I weigh nothing over Brent's limp body. "Brent . . ." But there's only a pained groan from Brent, and there's no stopping Cameron. We're out the door, and our breaths billow around us in the frigid air.

"What about Ray?" I look around in confusion. There are sirens in the distance . . . or is it in my head? I can't tell. My temple throbs with unrelenting pain. "And Brent? He's hurt . . . wait, we need to call 911. Cameron, where are we going?"

My hip complains as Cameron's arm tightens around me, supporting my weight. "To the hospital."

I clutch at his hand, stopping us again. "Hannah! Where is she?"

"With my sister. She's fine, beautiful, I promise." He pries my hand off his arm and raises it to his lips. "Now, please, let me get you into the car, Sam." His fingers gently swipe over my temple and he swallows thickly at the smeared blood on his hand. "That fucking son of a bitch." I sway slightly against him, my mind foggy. "We have to get you to a hospital and get you checked out." Hearing the stubborn note in his voice, I look into his eyes; he's on autopilot. In shock? Maybe I am, too.

I let him steer me down the alley and across the street to his car. There's a lot of traffic, but it barely registers. It's like a kaleidoscope of color and noise. I feel like I'm floating, a confused haze taking over. My adrenaline is still firing; I'm babbling at him almost nonstop, but he listens patiently, murmuring soft assurances. We reach his car, and he swiftly opens the door for me to get in—

"Sandy!"

I freeze, one hand on the car door, and both of us spin to see Ray, blood smeared across his face, tripping down the alley toward us. Cam swears and tries to push me into the car, but I can't move. Ray reaches the corner but doesn't stop running, his eyes wild and glued to mine.

My scream is masked by the squeal of the bus's brakes on the icy road. I stare in horror as my ex-husband's body goes flying.

# chapter sixteen

## cameron

"AND YOU HAVEN'T HAD CONTACT with Mr. Mitchell since the incident in Chicago?" I want to throttle the police officer. It's one invasive question after another. Questions Sam is in no condition to process, much less answer.

Sam shakes her head, her eyes wide and vacant as she stares at the wall in a private room at the hospital. Despite squeezing her hand, I get nothing back. It's limp and lifeless, and it's scaring the hell out of me.

"You sure about that?"

Sam shifts her eyes to the officer, my heart taking a dive at the bruise that's formed on her jaw, the bandage on her temple. *Fucking bastard.* It's tearing me apart that he got to her. The hum of the fluorescent lights in the room seems louder than it should. For the past couple of hours, everything seems heightened for me.

The smell of Sam's blood, the shrill sound of sirens, the fucking flash of cameras. It's all playing like some twisted funhouse loop in my head.

Finding her note after Tucker had called about a possible sighting of Ray in Boston took years off my life. Sam and Brent not picking up their phones when I tried to reach them terrified me. It's all a maddening blur after that as I flew through the streets of Boston to the arts center, praying that Tucker's intel was wrong for once.

"What possible reason could I have to be in contact with him?" I glance up at the two police officers who share some sort of unspoken conversation between them.

"It's a standard question, Miss McKenzie. We're just trying to do our job here." At least the pair of cops look uncomfortable, as they fucking should asking these ridiculous questions.

"He violated a protection order. I have sole custody of Hannah. The last time I spoke to Ray he said he was going to kill me and my daughter. We've been hiding from him," Sam answers, her voice hollow. "I had no idea he was here. If I had known . . ." Her shoulders slump and she buries her face in her hands on a sob as I tighten my arm around her. So many tears, it's hard to believe she's got any more to cry out.

"Enough. All right? No more tonight. She's been through enough," I growl, feeling Sam lean against me.

I get a sympathetic smile from one of the officers. "Thank you for your time, Mr. Chapman, Miss McKenzie. We'll be in touch if we need anything further."

The door closes, Sam's hand tightening against my shirt. "They're gone. It's okay," I whisper into her hair as her body shakes. But I know it's not okay, even though the bastard that caused all this is gone forever. It might never be okay again.

"HOW THE FUCK DID YOU let this happen?" I'm barely hanging on as I rant at Tucker in the private waiting room. I've been kicked out of Sam's room while the nurses and attending physician examine her once more before we're allowed to go home. I give Tucker's chest a shove.

"Keep your voice down," Kennedy mutters, his hand tightening on my shoulder. "We don't need more attention." I shrug out from his grip, fisting Tucker's leather jacket.

"He could've fucking killed her."

"He didn't, all right. He didn't. And he's dead now." Tucker mirrors my own movement, gripping my jacket and pushing me against the wall. "Brent will be okay, by the way," Tucker adds, reminding me that Sam wasn't the only one injured. "He was doing his job, checking the rooms, and the bastard hit him in the head from behind. Thank God he didn't use the pointy end of the knife. He lost a lot of blood, but he'll be okay. He's more upset with himself than anything."

"Fucking hell." I feel the adrenaline fire, leftover rage and fear over what could've happened simmering just under the surface.

"Cameron, mate, you need to take a breath. She's safe, and Poppet is safe. That's what you need to focus on."

"Don't fucking lecture me, Sean. Not you. Not now," I snap at him, trying to push the wall of muscle that is Tucker away.

"Everybody just calm the fuck down!" Matt's voice pierces the waiting room, and we all turn to look at him. Matt taking control of a room, of our group, is a rarity. "This isn't Tucker's fault. It's not Brent's fault, or yours." Matt flicks his hand at me as he continues, "The only person to blame is no longer breathing." Tucker releases my jacket, and I lean back against the wall, needing it to hold me up. "And you know what? I think that's a good thing. I think this bastard wasn't going to stop," Matt says firmly and I hear Tess gasp under her breath. "He wasn't, Cardinal. This would've hung over Sam for the rest of her life, and that"—he shakes his head—"that's no way to live. Not for Sam, not for Hannah, and sure as fuck not for you."

Silence descends between us, and I let the back of my head hit the wall. "I'm sorry, Tuck. I know it's not your fault. Matty's right."

"Always am," Matt mumbles, taking Tessa's hand.

"I'm sorry you're all mixed up in this." I glance between my bandmates and see Sean shrug.

"I didn't have a thing planned for the holiday anyway." He shoves his phone back into the pocket of his jacket. "We are going to have to deal with the press though. It's bedlam outside."

I let out a frustrated groan. "Not tonight. I can't. I need to get Sam home. We'll lay low for a while until this blows over. I'll talk to Nic about a statement." I pinch the bridge of my nose, feeling my head start to pound. I can't deal with calling Nic now. What the fuck time is it in San Francisco now, anyway? Shit. My brain is all over the place.

"I'm already on it," Kennedy says, moving back to Abby now that they've determined I'm not going to lose it. "She's working with the hospital's communications manager and they'll release a statement in the morning."

Thank fuck for Kennedy and our PR manager, Nicole. "Thanks, man."

"Anything for you, Three," Sean pipes in.

"Anything?" I grin over at him, and he spreads his arms wide.

"I'm humbly at your service." Matt snorts as Sean bows like some courtly knight.

I tilt my head at him. "You in the mood to hog the spotlight so I can get Sam out of here?"

Sean flashes me a smile. "Three, when am I not in the mood for the spotlight?"

"Cameron?" I'm shocked to see my father, larger than life, having to duck his six-foot-eight frame to get into the room. Just when I thought the night couldn't get any worse.

"Who called my father?" I growl as he stares at me; impeccable suit, not a wrinkle in sight, when I look like I've been run over by a truck.

He chuckles under his breath. "Having the children I do, you're all on my media alerts." He pauses, looking between us all. "And my PR director did call me. He's coordinating with the hospital, police, and your band's representative. Nicole, yes?" At my surprised nod, he continues. "We're working on an angle."

I can only stare at him, dumbfounded. I have to swallow the lump in my throat to speak. "What possible angle could you put out to spin this?"

"It was a tragic accident; it was mere coincidence that you happened to be there. It shouldn't be a surprise that you were visiting the arts center that bears your family name. No one else needs to be mentioned. A simple explanation is usually the best. The fact that you don't know this is one of the many reasons you're not part of the business." He levels me a blistering glare that shuts me up quickly. I hadn't even thought of the fallout of this for my family, the business.

"Fuck," I mutter.

"Hmm. Indeed." He turns to my bandmates. "Boys, it's good to see you again." He gives each of them an obligatory nod, pausing to cast a glance over Abby and Tess.

Kennedy is the first to step in. "Mr. Chapman, this is my . . ."

Kennedy glances down at Abby with a look I now know and understand, even if I didn't before.

"She's your One," my father says, shocking the hell out of me.

"Yeah. She is," Kennedy replies, pressing Abby closer to his side. "Abigail Walker." My father holds his hand out for Abby to shake.

"Abigail. I've heard wonderful things about your foundation. That was an excellent article about What's Your Dream in *Esquire* last month." Abby's mouth drops open slightly as my father looks over to where our bass player is glowering at him. "And Matt. I'm glad you've recovered from the accident." Matty gives him a wary look. I'm sure he's as shocked as I am that my dad knows about the near-fatal motorcycle accident Matt had a year or so ago. My father has said more in the last few minutes to my bandmates than he has in the fifteen-plus years we've been together.

"Thank you. This is, ah . . . my Tess. Tessa Baker." My father shakes her hand before stepping beside me.

"Nice to meet you. Now if I could have a moment alone with my son." There's no question, no apology for showing up unannounced. My father is just in command of the room as he always is, and the group doesn't hesitate for a second.

"We'll see you in a bit," Sean says as my father claps him on the shoulder while they file out.

"I can't believe you came all the way down here. I can't take one of your lectures right now."

He nods to one of the waiting chairs. "Relax and sit down. I'm not going to lecture you. Much."

I drag my bone-tired body to the closest chair, sinking down. I'm fucking exhausted and in no mood to deal with whatever bullshit he's about to spew.

"I hear she's going to be okay." He loosens his tie as he takes a seat across from me.

"She will be. Eventually. She's pretty shaken up."

"She's the one your mother said you brought to the party. I didn't get a chance to meet her." The guilt trip. Apparently, my mother is finally starting to rub off.

I take a quick glance up at him. "Her name's Samantha, and I didn't even see you at the party. What were you doing? Working?"

"I probably deserve that," he says quietly, staring down at the floor in a rare break in his usual controlled behavior.

My knee bounces and I grip the armrests as I wait for him to continue. "You know when I met your mother, my family was dead set against her." I stare at him; I've never heard this before. My father rarely shares anything remotely personal with me. Our entire lives revolved around appearances, schedules, how to act when the governor of the state was visiting. Not this. My skin prickles listening to him. "She wasn't from our level."

"Dad . . ." I shake my head, and he lifts his gaze to me.

"Say what you want, son, but you know how you grew up. The same way I did. Privileged. With servants and cars and whatever you wanted. I met your mother at a frat party in university. She was playing the piano." He leans back in the chair, looking out the window. "She was the most beautiful thing I'd ever seen, and I just knew. I knew she was it for me." He pauses, fixing his eyes back to me. "Is that what this is with Samantha?"

It's without hesitation I answer, "Yeah, it is."

"You sure? Because your actions, they don't just impact you, no matter how much you want them to. You're a Chapman. And what you do matters. More than you think."

My fingers pull at the material on the chair. I don't know how much more of this I can take from him. "You didn't see what I saw today. You don't know what it was like to find her like I did."

I rake my hand through my hair. "He was going to kill her, Dad. I can't even imagine what that would've done to me, to Hannah."

He lets out a huff but gives me a half smile. "Just had to go and fall in love with a girl with a child, didn't you?"

"Did you expect me to follow some formula?"

He laughs, leaning forward. "If your mother had her way, yes. But I knew as soon as you picked up that guitar in high school you weren't going to fit any plan she had. I don't say it often, Cameron, but you forged your own way. And I'm proud of that. All a parent wants is for their child to be happy." He pushes up from the chair, all business once more, buttoning up his suit jacket. "Bring her around to the house when she's feeling up to it. I'd like to meet her." I stare at him, unable to answer. Floored that he's shared more with me in the last five minutes than he has my entire life. He leaves me with a nod and a squeeze to my shoulder, never looking back.

"THANK YOU, SWEETIE." SAM'S VOICE cracks a little as Hannah presses a kiss to the bandage on her temple. We told Hannah that Sam fell on the ice. A lie she believed without any questions. I wish life could be as simple as it is to a four-year-old. I never want Hannah to know what really happened. The reality is too ugly, too twisted.

"Your kisses always make my boo-boos better, Momma." I can see Sam's chin quiver as she fights to hold back tears. I pull the blanket up higher around Hannah and her dolls.

"Sleeping time now, Hannah. Your momma needs some rest, too." I press a kiss to Hannah's forehead, taking Sam's hand to help her stand up from the bed. She leans against me, and it feels like she could break apart if I'm not careful.

"I'll be back in a little while," Sam's quiet voice drifts through the room, but Hannah's eyes are already closed, sleep taking her quickly. I know the feeling. A few hours with my sister will tire anyone out. I owe Kat big time for tonight. For a lot of things.

Sam pauses at the door, turning back to look at her daughter. "If she would've been with me today . . ." She tries unsuccessfully to hold back a sob, and I guide her out to the hallway, closing the door to the room before I pull her into my arms.

"She's safe. And so are you. You always will be with me." Her nose presses against my chest. I can feel her tears soaking through my shirt, her body wracking with sobs as she clings to me. It's easy to lift her into my arms and carry her downstairs to the living room. I sink down to the couch, and she melts against me, the crackling fire silencing her cries for a few minutes.

I tighten my arms around her and just hold her. Hold her so she doesn't break apart. Hold her so I can breathe her in, convince myself she's safe, so I can feel like I'm doing something, anything but feeling helpless.

"She's never going to know who her father was," she chokes out after a few agonizing minutes. "I feel so . . . I don't even know." She fidgets with a button on my shirt. "Even though I know what he was going to do, without him, I wouldn't have Hannah." Her red-rimmed eyes kill me. This look of loss and fear is one I can't bear to see again. "And I don't know how to process that. How to put this behind me. Behind us."

She's looking to me as if I have the answers. The sad reality is that I don't. I brush her tangled hair behind her shoulder, gently caressing her cheek, careful not to press on the spreading bruises. "I wish I knew. I want more than anything to fix this." Her eyes drift back to the fire. My chest constricts as she stares vacantly at the flames.

The thought that I could've lost her tonight rips me up inside. Those agonizing minutes of getting to the arts center seem like a nightmare. I'm not sure I'll ever get the sight of her bloody and bruised and fighting for her life out of my head. My grip tightens around her, and I rest my forehead against her shoulder. Her heart beats, steady and strong. I can feel her breaths, inhale her scent. She's safe and that's all that matters. Life can turn on a dime. Given what I've been through in the band, with my father's heart attack, I know this. But none of it has hit me like this. I just want to hold her and never let her go.

"I think we just take each day as it comes," Sam says finally. "Right now, I just want to stay here. In your arms where I know I'm safe. Is that okay?"

My throat tightens as she leans back to look at me. "That's all I want."

♪ ♩ ♪ ♩

## samantha

"MOMMMMMMA." HANNAH'S SINGSONG VOICE PENE-TRATES the hazy, warm cocoon around me. When I finally pry my eyes open, I see her kneeling next to me, walking her fingers up and down my arm.

"Hey, sweetie," I croak and clear my throat, before trying again. "What time is it?" I raise my head to look around, disoriented, and see that I'm still on the sofa. Morning light is peeking through the front curtains, bathing everything in a warm glow. The scent of coffee wafting from the kitchen makes my mouth water.

"I dunno. Morning." She shrugs. She's still in her pajamas, her sleep-tousled hair forming a reddish-gold aura around her head.

"Cam!" she yells in the direction of the kitchen, and I cringe at the sudden noise. "She's awake!"

"Hannah, use your inside voice, please." I plop my head back on the throw pillow. I must have slept down here all night. The last thing I remember is stretching out on Cam as if he were my own personal body pillow and playing with his chest hair that poked out between his shirt buttons.

"But he wanted to know when you woked up," she says matter-of-factly.

Rubbing my forehead, I will my reluctant synapses to start firing. "Then you should go into the kitchen and tell—oh, never mind." Lectures can wait until later, I guess. "Have you had breakfast yet?"

"She's had some yogurt, fruit, and only slightly burnt toast." Cam's soft voice comes from above, and a coffee cup appears next to me. "How do you feel, gorgeous?" I sit up, ignoring the twinge of pain in my hip, and swing my feet to the floor next to Hannah before eagerly taking the offered cup.

"Better, now. Thank you." I inhale the heavenly aroma and let the heat of the mug warm my hands. Cam's boots are sitting neatly next to the couch. "Did you sleep here, too?"

"Of course." He sits carefully on the coffee table facing me. The sturdy oak creaks under his weight, but otherwise shows no signs of buckling. He's still wearing his button-down and jeans from yesterday.

I take a sip and savor the slightly bitter brew. "That must have been uncomfortable." I shift on the cushions, a little embarrassed I inconvenienced him. "You could've gone upstairs to bed without me."

He frowns. "There was no way I was leaving you last night. I love you and you needed me."

My heart pounds at hearing those three little words from him again, but a small, happy gasp from the floor reminds me we're not alone. Hannah's eyes are trained on her fingers as she toys with the laces of Cam's boot, but she's also listening as hard as she can. Little imp.

"Sweetie, why don't you go upstairs and get dressed for the day, hmm? Don't forget to brush your teeth." A scowl flickers across her face, giving me a taste of what I'll have to deal with when she's a teenager. *Yeah, I know—I send you away just when the conversation is getting good.* She further telegraphs her displeasure by stomping up the stairs.

"How are you feeling, really?" he asks once we're alone. His usually sparkling hazel eyes are dark with concern as he examines my face. The side where Ray struck me no longer burns, but it's black and blue under the two Steri-Strips that adorn my cheek. "Do you need another ice pack? Pain pill?"

I tentatively prod my aching cheekbone. "No, they can wait." There's another good-sized bruise on my hip, but nothing's broken. "As to the rest . . . I'm not sure how I feel. Everything and nothing, if that makes sense." Running a hand through my hair, I grimace, frustrated. "Hollow. Sad. Relieved that it's over. And guilty because I'm relieved."

"Guilty?" He's taken aback. "There's no reason for you to feel guilty. It was an accident."

"I know, but . . ." I scoot forward a little, sloshing a bit of coffee on my knee. The liquid quickly soaks into the denim, but luckily it's cooled enough that it doesn't burn. "I never wanted him dead," I whisper, my voice breaking a little. I close my eyes, trying to shut out the memory of Ray's last seconds. "I just wanted him to leave me alone!"

Cam's big hand covers my coffee-decorated knee, squeezing

slightly. "I know, Sam. I know." I automatically cover his hand with mine, grateful for the comfort of his touch. He doesn't try to rationalize what happened or dismiss what I'm feeling. He simply lets me know without words that he's there for me, in whatever way I need him. I can count on him and have been able to since the beginning.

It's just one of the many reasons I love him.

"Kat thinks it was Darcy who let the photos out," he says after a minute, sitting back.

I almost spit out my mouthful of coffee. "Really? But why would she do that?" Darcy definitely wasn't happy with me during the party, but I can't see her sparing me a second thought afterward.

"Who knows what goes on in that pea brain of hers?" Cam scowls down at his bare feet and wiggles his long toes on the area rug. "Whatever her reason, I'm sure she had no idea what she was setting in motion."

Pursing my lips, I look down at my own feet, warm in their wool socks. Maybe she was simply being bitchy, or maybe she thought the exposure would rattle me. Well, I was rattled, but Cam's right—she couldn't have known why or what would happen as a result.

After a moment, he chuckles and glances up the stairs, where the sound of Hannah singing to herself drifts down to us. "I think that's the first time I've seen her give you attitude."

"Oh, you haven't seen anything yet. She can throw a first-class tantrum. You've just been lucky so far," I assure him. Nervously, I pull my sweater down where it's ridden up a bit. "Does that change your mind about us moving in?"

"Nope. Does that mean you'll do it?" He shifts, making the table squeak, and grips his mug with both hands in front of him, like a protective shield.

Stalling, I blow across the surface of my coffee and take another sip. To be honest, I haven't wanted to think about moving back into my apartment above the Finnegans' store. I love being with Cam, and Hannah's happy here. However, the main reason for us moving in doesn't hold any longer. "We don't have to worry about our safety anymore," I murmur, staring into the depths of my cup.

"You think that was why I asked?" He frowns and dashes his hand across his eyes. "Sam, I invited you to stay because I want you to stay. I want to wake up every morning with you and go to bed with you every night. I want us to make dinners with Hannah and take her horseback riding. I even want to learn how to deal with her tantrums. I want you to stay with me because you want to, not because you think you need to."

Sincerity rings in his deep voice and my heart melts, breaking through the sorrow and guilt sloshing around inside me. "I . . . I want that, too." His gaze snaps up to meet mine, and I set my mug down on the table beside him. "But I'm a little afraid of losing myself . . . my independence. I don't want to become dependent on you. And I don't want Hannah to be spoiled."

He wrinkles his nose. "Why would you lose your independence? Sam, you can do anything you want to do—teach, perform, volunteer, do handsprings down the street . . . whatever. Just because you'll no longer have to choose between buying Hannah a winter coat or putting food on the table doesn't mean you'll lose your sense of self." His jaw tightens and he drums his fingers on the tabletop. "I don't want Hannah to become spoiled and end up like Darcy."

I tilt my head. "You think bringing all those shopping bags home wasn't spoiling her? A child can't go from zero to sixty—having nothing to everything—in a blink. She's not a BMW."

He stifles a laugh. "Did she tell you that some of the things we bought were for a friend of hers at day care? I gathered that they tend to stick together because neither of them have much compared to some of the other kids. She wasn't complaining," he hurries to assure me, holding a hand up. "She just wanted to share her good fortune with her friend. Does that sound spoiled to you?"

"No, it doesn't." I smile at the thought of my daughter. She really is a sweetheart. "It must be Maya. She's another orchestra kid; her mother plays French horn. She's really good—" I gasp, suddenly remembering. "Oh my God—Cam! I broke my violin!"

He startles at my non sequitur—God, I'm all over the place today—and then takes my hand in his, pressing a soft kiss on my knuckles. "I don't think *broke* is the right word for what happened to your violin, love."

He's right. Disintegrated would be better. Demolished. By the time I was done with it, it was just a pile of expensive toothpicks and some twisted strings. Thank God my students are on Christmas break. How could I teach them now? I pass a hand over my eyes and groan in frustration, my heart suddenly pounding. How the hell am I going to get another one before the season starts again in January? "What am I going to do?"

His soothing voice breaks me out of my mental spiral. "We'll get you another. It'll be okay, Sam. Please don't worry. We'll figure it out."

And just like that, my burgeoning panic subsides. His confidence covers me like a warm blanket. How does he do that?

One of his sleeves has slid down his arm, and he pushes it back up, revealing his toned forearm. "How long have you had your violin?"

"My parents gave it to me as a high school graduation present. They were so proud of me." A bittersweet glow fills me as I picture their happy faces when they presented the gleaming instrument to me during the small party they threw for my graduation. I was shocked; it had to have cost at least five thousand, which is average for a violin of that quality, but it must have put quite a dent in their ledger. You can make a good living owning a bar in Telluride, but it's not a luxurious life by any stretch. If I hadn't won a performance scholarship, I'm not sure I would've made it to college.

I blink back tears. "God, I miss them," I whisper. "What must they think of me now?"

"They would still be proud of you." I meet his fierce gaze. "I know it, Sam. They know you did what you had to do to survive, for yourself and for their granddaughter." He squeezes my hand, holding it on my knee. "And now they'd want you to do whatever you need to do to live your life and be happy."

Happy. Rubbing my thumb over his, one thing is clear. "I'm happy with you," I murmur, looking up at him through my lashes. His answering smile makes my heart skip a beat. "Aren't we moving too fast though? Won't people think we're crazy? We've only really known each other a month."

"I don't care what people think." He sets his mug down next to mine. "It only matters what we think."

I trace the coffee stain on my knee, struggling with the hope growing in my heart. "Your mother won't be happy."

"My mother is rarely happy with my decisions," he grumbles. "I see no reason to start worrying about that now. I know it's fast." He scrubs his hand through his hair, making it stand on end. "She'd probably say it's too soon to love you but I do."

"I love you, too."

My voice is barely a whisper, but he hears me. His eyes flare, and then his face lights up like Christmas. We lunge at the same time; he pulls me onto his lap and crushes his mouth to mine. Electric joy joins the jumble of emotions swirling inside me. My fingers are buried in his hair as I hold his face to mine, and his arms are squeezing me so tight I can barely breathe. Desire surges and I make no protest when he starts to lay me out on the hard surface—

A sharp crack is our only warning before the whole table collapses, dumping us on the floor with a crash.

"Oh my God!" I gasp through our laughter. "Your poor table!"

Keeping one arm around me as we struggle to sit up, he holds up a dripping, but thankfully not broken, coffee mug. "I was thinking of getting a new one anyway. Are you all right? How's your hip?"

I squirm in his embrace so I can pull a split table leg out from underneath my ass. "I'll live." Tossing the chunk off to the side, I look back up at him and cup his cheek. "I love you." His warm lips descend once more, and my heart races. I don't know if we're crazy or not, but we're happy. And that can't be bad.

We're lost in each other until Kennedy's hesitant voice breaks into our bubble.

"Uh, we heard a crash so we let ourselves in," he says as our heads snap toward the sound. He's standing beside Linc, whose gun is drawn, and a wide-eyed Abby at the base of the stairwell. "Are you guys okay?" Above their heads, Hannah gapes at us from the stairs.

I wave a weak hand in their direction. "We're fine." I start to get up off the floor, but Cam holds me fast.

"She loves me." Cam informs him, a silly grin on his face. My daughter snickers, while Abby hides her laugh behind her gloved hand; Kennedy merely rolls his eyes. "Duh. I knew you were gone over each other back in Vermont," he says. Linc gives us an exasperated smirk and reholsters his gun, walking back towards his post outside. Kennedy continues as if he sees us sprawled on the floor every day. "Hey, we brought you a Christmas tree. We wanted to get you something to celebrate the season before we head back to

Cali tonight. It's a nice big one that will handle anything you want to put on it." He gives me a gentle smile. "I hope that was okay."

Tears fill my eyes again, this time from happiness, as Hannah scampers down the stairs, runs past Abby, and joins the hugfest on the floor. "It's more than okay. Thank you."

I rest my head against Cam's shoulder and brush my daughter's hair out of my face, with a growing confidence that everything—eventually—really will be all right. As Sean said in Vermont, I'm part of the family now, and they take care of their own. It's a good feeling.

We aren't alone anymore. And we're loved.

# chapter seventeen

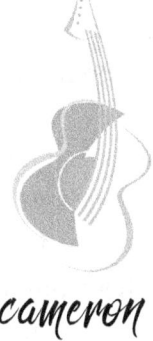

## cameron

"YOU GUYS GOT A TREE?" Helping Sam up, I watch as Hannah races over to the door, peering outside. A little squeal from her is the only answer I need.

"Yeah. Sean's been leading the paparazzi on a wild goose chase in the pink tornado for the last hour. Gave us time to pick a tree out at one of the lots," Kennedy answers, slinging his arm around Abby.

"Pink tornado?"

Matt laughs at my question. "Apparently, the clown car VW the Brit bought has its own Twitter account now," he answers.

I shake my head, watching as Hannah grips the door, opening it up wide. Tucker pokes his head in before hauling the tree in behind him.

"Where do you want it?" Tucker drags the tree into the living room, a gust of winter air blowing in behind him. He glances at the demolished coffee table on the floor. "Do I dare ask?"

"No." I glance down at Sam, who's studying the floor. "Where would you like the tree?"

"Here, Momma! Here!" Hannah races to the fireplace, waving her arms frantically.

Sam lifts her chin, and I can see her eyes dart nervously to the crowd growing in the living room. "Is beside the fireplace okay?" she asks quietly.

"Of course it's okay. We can put it up wherever you—"

"Oh my God. Sam, are you okay?" I glance up at the sound of Tess's voice as she enters the room, her eyes focused on Sam's face.

Sam immediately sets her palm over her bruised jaw with a slight nod. "Yeah, I'm—" Tess reaches for Sam's hand, and I see Sam's eyes brim with tears. "No," Sam whispers. "I'm not okay."

Tess wraps her arm around Sam's shoulder, steering her out of the room. "Abby, you're with me. Matt, you and Hannah are in charge of where that tree goes."

"You got it, Cardinal," Matt says with a mock salute, guiding Hannah toward the tree. Hannah seems too excited by the sheer size of the massive pine that fills the room to catch on to Sam's sudden change in mood.

"Wait, what—" I start to ask, but Abby places her hand on my chest, stopping my forward motion.

"She needs girl time," Abby whispers, looking up at me. "Keep Hannah occupied, we'll be out soon." I try to move to the stairs to follow them, but Kennedy steps in front of me, blocking my way.

"Just let them do whatever it is they do." I frown at him, and he shoves me in the shoulder.

"I don't get it. I thought she was doing okay." I glance over my shoulder, watching as the girls disappear up the stairs.

"She will be. I've learned not to ask a whole lot of questions. There are some times when the less you know, the better. This is one of those times."

"Look, Cam!" I turn my attention to Hannah as she claps excitedly, watching Tucker steady the tree in the corner. "Santa will see it if it's right here."

I smile at her, crouching down to move the broken pieces of the coffee table away from the tree. "How could he miss it?" Disjointed pounding on the door has me heading over to open it up again.

"About time, Three," Sean's voice carries behind a stack of containers piled high in front of his face. I recognize these. They're from my parents' storage room. "A little help here before I drop the lot of it?"

"What's all this?" I ask, taking two of the bins from the top of the pile.

He grins, pushing his way past me. A scan of the street shows no sign of the pink VW van, and I wonder where he's left it. "Ah, the lovely Kat thought you needed some decorations for the tree."

I scowl, pushing the door shut. "How did you get my sister's number?" I ask warily as he kicks his boots off, stomping into the living room.

"Kat and I are on very good terms, mate." He sets the boxes down on the floor. "Poppet! Come see what we can put on the tree." Hannah races over to join us, and Sean pops the lid off one of the boxes. Hannah pulls out a star-shaped snowman, hurrying back to the tree.

"Put this one on the top, Tuck!" she hollers.

I hear Tucker laugh from under the tree, before he calls out, "Got to give me a minute to get the tree in the stand, Hannah, and then we'll decorate it."

"You keep your hands off my sister," I growl, leaving the boxes on the couch, but not before I cuff Sean in the back of the head.

"Relax. Kat and I share love you can never understand." I glare as he waves a reindeer ornament at me. "Not that kind of love. Christ, mate. I know the golden rule. I helped make it. Don't get involved with anyone's sisters or exes." I relax only marginally. "It is possible to have a friendship with a woman and not want to bed them, despite what every movie ever made tells you."

"Famous last words," I grumble, watching as he tugs out a jumbled strand of white lights.

"How are you holding up with all this, Three?" Sean starts working on the mess of cords.

"Does it make me a bad person if I say I'm glad he's dead?"

Sean pauses, glancing over at me. "No. It makes you human. Matty was right in the hospital. He wasn't going to stop."

"Of course I was right," Matt chimes in, dropping to the couch beside us. "Tucker says Brent is going to be discharged later today. Have you been online to see what people are saying?"

Frowning, I recall the report I caught on the early news before Sam woke up. As my father promised, his press team did a good job keeping the worst of it quiet. The reporter focused on the fatal bus accident, which took the life of a tourist from Florida. His reason for visiting Boston was unknown and he had no next of kin. I was listed as a witness taken to the hospital to "rule out shock." Sam's presence wasn't even mentioned, thank God. "Yeah. Thanks to Sean's bait-and-switch bit at the hospital that gave them photos they could use, and Nicole's collaboration with my father's PR team, I think it should die down in a day or two. I was in the area after visiting the music hall named after my family and happened to witness an accident—that's it."

Sean grunts. "Good."

I watch Hannah for a few minutes as she chirps away to Tucker and Kennedy, giving them instructions, oblivious to the nightmare of the last twenty-four hours. "She's never going to know her father," I mutter so only they can hear.

"Bullshit." Matt's eyes cut to mine. "Being a father has nothing to do with biology. Tom's my father in the only ways that word matters. He's the reason I am who I am today. So don't give me some bullshit about her missing out, because she's not." Matt's voice drops a bit. "She'll start to see you as her father. Hell, she's already starting to. It's as easy as breathing. Trust me on this one."

Matt's reassurance strikes a chord; of all of us, he should know. Matty had a tough childhood—to put it mildly—but when he was a teenager, he was adopted by Tom Logan, one of the most solid guys I've ever met. Matty's always said that in doing so, Tom saved his life.

Sean assumes a solemn expression. "He's our official wise man for the holiday season, Cam. Best to listen to him." Matt tosses one of the snowmen decorations at Sean, and he ducks out of the way as it sails past his head. Sean laughs, pushing the mess of cords in my direction. "Bloody things. You give it a go."

"That's your job. You untangle those, genius."

He scowls at the lights. "I always get the best jobs."

"Oh, by the way . . ." I fish my wallet out of my back pocket and pull out a few bills that I slap in Matt's hand. "I'll give you the rest later, and I'm never making a bet with you again."

Sean barks a laugh as Matt pockets the cash with a grin. "Yes you will, loser." He ruffles my finally-no-longer-bleached hair, and I bat his hand away, not needing the reminder of another lost bet. "Was it worth it?"

I cast a glance up the stairs, and then at the bubbly little girl bouncing around the tree. "Oh yeah. Totally worth it."

It takes us the better part of an hour of arguing, but we finally get the tree secured in the exact place Hannah instructed us it should go. Sam, Abby, and Tess join us just as Sean is plugging the lights in to an excited shout from Hannah. "Momma! Look! Uncle Sean got the lights to work!"

Sam bends to pick up Hannah, and I can see her wince slightly under her weight. Taking Hannah from her, we look up at the tree. "Uncle Sean knows what he's doing," Sam says, smiling over at him.

"Thank you, Sammy. At least someone here recognizes my talent." Sean folds his arms across his chest.

Hannah squirms in my arms, and I let her down, watching her take off back to the boxes of decorations. Kennedy and Matt relax back on the sofa, taking in the mayhem her and Sean create.

I whisper so only she can hear. "Everything okay?"

She leans into my side, and I feel her wrap her arm around me, her hand fisting the back of my shirt. "It will be. I was just a little overwhelmed for a moment." I loop my arm around her shoulders, savoring the feel of her body next to mine. "The girls say Brent is being discharged today," she murmurs, and I look down to meet her watery gaze. "We need to do something to thank him. Bake him cookies, buy him a car. Something. I don't know the protocol for thanking someone who risked their life for mine."

Hugging her to my side, I press a kiss to her forehead and send another silent thank-you to the angels who protected her. When she'd mentioned to the police in the hospital that Ray said he'd been watching her, but hadn't been able to get past her guards before . . . I'd almost been paralyzed by all the what-ifs. "Don't worry, we will," I assure her.

"Good." She nods her head in the direction of the living room where my bandmates have made themselves at home. "They're really good friends of yours. You're lucky to have them."

"No. *We're* lucky to have them. They're your friends now, too. Like it or not."

She looks up at me, her eyes brighter, a little less tension in her delicate features. "I like it. I like it a lot."

"REMEMBER WHEN I SAID I liked your friends?" Sam asks in a tired voice, leaning up from her relaxed position on the couch. I press my thumb into the curve of her foot, continuing the massage I started after we put an exhausted Hannah to bed.

"*Our* friends. Yes." She smiles, closing her eyes, the lights from the tree highlighting the perfect curve of her cheek.

"I do like them but, holy cow, quiet is nice too!" I can't help but laugh.

"Quiet doesn't exactly happen when Sean's around." Her answering moan when I start to work over her calf muscle causes my dick to spring to attention.

"No kidding. How do you guys do it? I mean, seriously? The man never stops talking."

"You just learn to tune him out. You'll get used it to. Eventually."

"I'm looking forward to that." I lean forward, gathering her up into my arms. She wraps her arms around my neck as I take the stairs. "He's really just a big softy. I may be mistaken, but I'm sure I saw a tear or two when he hugged Hannah good-bye tonight."

"You're not mistaken. Sean wears his heart on his sleeve. He always has. What you see is what you get from him."

"She's going to miss him, too," she says, her lips skimming my neck.

"Mmm. I've been instructed that we're having daily video chat calls with them all so they don't miss out on anything."

She laughs loud, covering her mouth as we pass Hannah's room. "Did you ever think a group of badass rockers would be charmed by a four-year-old?"

I smirk at her. "No. But I'm glad we are. No more talk of them," I whisper, quietly turning into my room . . . *our* room now. That's got a nice ring to it. *Our* room. *Our* house. No, our *home*. That's what it feels like now with Sam and Hannah breathing new life into this place. Home. "Let's just you and I enjoy the quiet for a while."

"Please," she answers, pulling me down with her to the bed. It starts slow, with Sam's hand exploring my back, then tugging on the buttons of my shirt. I gather her hands in mine, leaning back.

"You should be resting," I whisper as she hooks her leg around mine, trying to get closer.

"No. Please . . . please, Cameron." She grips at my shirt desperately. "Make me forget. Please." Fuck, she's killing me. I brush her hair from her face, tracing the angry bruise on her jaw, and press my lips to her forehead.

"You need to rest. I don't want to hurt you. You've been through—" Her fingers cover my lips, and I see that flash of determination in her eyes.

"I need you. And I know you'd never hurt me. I need this. I need to feel wanted." I drop my forehead to hers, my jaw clenching as I try to hold it together. Her lips press lightly over my cheek, her words whispered and shaky. "I need to feel loved. Like everything is going to be okay."

"It will be. I promise." She tugs on the back of my neck, bringing my lips to hers. "I promise." Her answering little moan breaks me down. I can never deny Sam anything. I never want to be the reason she's angry or upset—or worse, questioning what

I feel for her.

It's tender kisses, soft touches, and whispered words as we give and take and share. Her body fits to mine like it's made to be there. Her lips caress and tease the most intimate parts of me, and I do the same. When she comes apart, her warm, panted breath on my neck, her legs wrapped around me, it's not quiet. It's the most beautiful thing I've ever heard.

I've been awake for an hour, studying her, tempting myself by ghosting my fingers along each delicious curve of her body. I've felt the silky thickness of her hair, savored the softness of the dip of her stomach, dropped featherlight kisses on the angry blue bruises that cover her hip.

That I couldn't get to her faster is always going to haunt me. That she's had to suffer again from that bastard is a darkness that I know will take a long time for her to get away from.

"Mmm. Feels nice." Sam's sleepy voice drifts while I trace a pattern across her stomach, and I press a kiss to her lips.

"You know you have twenty-seven freckles on your face." One eye blinks open and she lets out a laugh.

"You counted my freckles?"

I answer with a gentle palm against the underside of her breast. "A few times."

"You're a bit crazy, you know that, right?" she teases, her hand roaming over my back. It feels so good to have her like this; so close and beautifully sated. I wish I could keep her like this forever.

"Only a bit crazy. Tell me about your last Christmas."

She leans back, both of her beautiful eyes open now, the vibrant green a bit darker in the light cast from the moonlight spilling into the room. "We were at one of the shelters." My stomach drops, and I feel horrible for prying.

"Shit, Sam. I'm sorry."

She shakes her head, gently brushing her fingers against my lips. "Don't be sorry. We were lucky. It was safe, and we were warm." I press a kiss to each of her fingers as she continues, her voice quiet, "There're a lot of good people out there, Cameron. A couple of companies donate Christmas stockings every year to the shelter, and they were on the end of the bed when we woke up." My heart hammers listening to her. "They had the basics, you know? Toothpaste, soap, mittens." She lowers her hand, lacing her fingers with mine. "Tampons, little chocolates." Fucking hell. That's what she got for Christmas last year. I feel like a jackass for bringing this up. I had no idea. "Hannah's had a little coloring book and some crayons inside. She loved it. Then Santa came to the dinner later on." I feel the loss of her hand in mine before she cups my cheek. "I know what you're thinking, but it was a good day for us."

Leaning into her touch, I keep my eyes on hers. "I promise this one will be better."

"It already is."

I close my eyes, feeling her fingers trace the bridge of my nose. "Do you think they'd still be taking donations?"

"They can always use help," she answers, her lips brushing against mine.

"Good. We'll get in touch with them tomorrow. I want to donate."

I hear her sigh, and then she's pushing me onto my back, straddling my waist. I lean up, palming her ass with a needy groan as she grinds against me. "How did I get so lucky?" she asks, breathless when she leans back and reaches for a condom.

Tightening my hands against her hips, I lift her slightly, feeling her stretch around my cock as she lowers over me. "I ask myself that every day."

I GLARE AT THE THICK door in the luxury residential apartment building on Stuart Street. It's a far cry from the humble flat where we picked up the rest of Sam and Hannah's belongings yesterday. The irony isn't lost on me that my family owns the building Darcy lives in. It's fucking tempting to have her kicked out. The thought has crossed my mind more than once over the last few days.

I clench my fists to the sound of the lock clicking open, and then she's there, dressed like she's late for a pageant show, full-on makeup at eight thirty in the goddamn morning. "Cameron." She blinks at me, opening the door a bit wider.

"You're not the only one who can get an address."

"Won't you come in?" she purrs like a cat in heat, taking a step forward to skim her fingers over my jacket.

I suppress a shudder, taking a step back. "No. This won't take long." She doesn't seem to catch my gritty reply.

"I just called for breakfast to be delivered, but you know how those services can be." She waves her manicured hand dismissively. "So unreliable. Come in and join me." She motions to the open foyer, utterly clueless.

"A little bird told me you were responsible for sending pictures to a certain trashy magazine."

Her eyes widen, and she fiddles with the gaudy emerald around her neck that probably set her father back twenty grand. "I don't know what you're—"

"Don't even bother. Do you have any idea what the fuck you've done?"

Cue the watery eyes and crocodile tears that likely work on any other unsuspecting men. Her lip even wobbles right before

344      B.B. MILLER AND LESLIE CARSON

she bites it in a way I'm sure she means to be seductive. "I never meant to hurt anyone. I didn't think—"

"No. You didn't think of anyone but yourself. You just do whatever the hell you want and you don't give a shit about how your actions might affect someone else." I know I'm fighting to hold it together, but I need this. I need to let her know this ends now. No more pictures, no more interference.

Her grip falters on the door. "I'm sorry, please don't hate me," she whispers.

"You know, I don't hate you. I actually feel sorry for you. You're going to have to live the rest of your life with the knowledge that your little stunt put a woman through the worst hell you can even imagine, and cost a man his life." She gasps, staring back at me. "Was it worth it?"

Her tears spill over but I can't stop. "Answer the fucking question. How much did you get for those pictures? Five grand? Ten? Are you really that desperate for money? For attention? Is Daddy not giving you enough allowance?" She rears back at that. "And how did you think I'd ever give you the time of day after you pulled something like that?"

"I don't know," she says through a hitched breath.

"If you knew anything at all about me, you'd know I keep my private life private. And you've fucked with that. I'm only going to say this once. Stay away from me. Stay away from my band, and stay away from my family. And just in case you were confused, Sam is my family. She's everything to me, and you? You're nothing." Her hand covers her mouth and she drops her head.

"Please don't tell my father," she squeaks out, and I shake my head in disgust. "Please, Cameron. I'm sorry. If that's worth anything."

"Yeah. I'm done here." I don't hesitate when she tries to stop me, when she practically begs me to listen as I wait for the elevator. And I don't bother wasting energy even to look at her as the doors close.

"YOU SURE YOU WANT TO do this?" I ask Sam as we sit in the BMW, idling in the circular drive at my parents' estate. It's Christmas Eve, and as per Chapman tradition, the family who's in town is converging.

"Can't turn back now," Sam says, glancing up at the lit mansion where Henry's already standing with the doors open, waiting for us.

Cutting the engine, I turn back to a sleeping Hannah. She always seems to fall asleep in the car, and she looks so innocent. Her biggest worry of the night is whether she'll get to see Midnight in the stables later on. I see Sam shiver and I take her hands between mine, warming them up.

"Just remember no matter what happens, I love you, Samantha McKenzie."

"Why does that sound so ominous?" She leans forward to press a slow kiss to my lips.

"It's not meant to. It's just that my family is . . ." I glance up at the house, seeing my brothers joining Henry on the step. "Difficult sometimes."

"I think we can handle it, don't you?"

"I think we can handle anything." I brush my palm against her cheek, thankful that the bruising is finally starting to fade. Physically, Sam gets better with each passing day. Emotionally, we have a long way to go. There are still times that she shuts down on me, lost in her own thoughts, fighting against nightmares that keep coming back. I've learned to give her distance, even though it kills me. I never want her to feel like I'm crowding her, forcing her to talk about something she's not ready to. There are some things I know I can't fix. Some things I'm not sure I could bear to hear. It's one of the reasons I'm thankful for Kat setting Sam up with a counselor.

They've been spending more time together, Kat and Sam. They're meeting for lunches or coffee every couple of days. Kat's even taken Sam to the spa—something Sam objected to at first—but she was blissed out and refreshed when she came home. The more spa time the better if I can get a thank-you like the one I got that day.

"You ready then?" I unbuckle my seat belt.

"Wait." Her hand tightens on my arm. "You're not hiding presents in there, are you?"

"No, gorgeous, I'm not." I shake my head, amused.

"Because you promised no presents for us," she reminds me.

"I remember." I press a kiss to her forehead, grinning at how she's going to react when she finds the violin I bought her under the tree tomorrow morning. Technically it's not a present per se. It's a replacement for her destroyed violin. At least that's the story that I'm sticking to.

Sam's been a little lost without her violin these past couple of weeks. I would've given it to her sooner, but it didn't arrive until last night. I'm looking forward to hearing her play again. To play this time, just for me, when she doesn't have to hide any more. It's the best present I could ever have.

"Let's do this then," she says, opening up the door, but I reach over and close it, and she turns back to me, her eyes wide.

"You forgot something."

She turns to look in the back seat. "I did?"

"Mhmm."

"What did I forget?" Her eyes light up.

"See, I say I love you and you're supposed to say . . ."

She cups my face between her hands, resting her forehead on mine. "I love you, Cameron Louis Chapman the Third. More every day."

Her words warm my heart, and it's all I need to hear. "Music to my ears."

## samantha

AFTER EXTRACTING HANNAH FROM THE back seat, Cam shifts her so he can still take my hand while carrying her. Our fingers entwine; the warmth of his hand filters into my heart, calming my nerves. I've never met his father, and I'm afraid he'll be as impenetrable as his frosty wife. It won't scare me off if he disapproves of me, but it would be nice—for Cam's sake—if I could forge a pleasant rapport with at least one of his parents.

Snow crunches under our feet as we approach, and Henry beams back at me. Before I can greet him, one of the tall men at his side steps forward. "So, this is the woman who's stolen my brother's heart," he says, boldly looking me up and down before addressing Cam. "Have to say, I almost didn't recognize you with the whole domestic thing you've got going here." He waves his hand at all three of us. "Wonders never cease."

I fix him with a steely gaze, and smile to myself when he takes a startled step back. *Jerk.* Cam's jaw clamps shut on whatever response he was about to let loose, no doubt due to Hannah's presence. "Sam, this is my brother, Nathan," he says instead, and then smiles innocently at him. "Speaking of domesticity, where's

Ellen?" Nathan stiffens, his leer morphing into a scowl.

"We ended our engagement." His eyes narrow. "But you knew that."

"No, but I can't say I'm shocked." Cam gives him a grin and escorts me past his fuming brother. "Henry, how are you this evening?" He nods at the brother I remember from the party, who's standing behind Henry. "Brooks. How's tricks?"

"The trick this evening will be keeping my son from ripping into his presents before dinner." He laughs and bumps fists with Cam. Then his inquisitive eyes land on me. "Samantha, right? I didn't get a chance to say hi at the party. Nice to meet you."

"And you." Brooks shares his hazel eyes and height with Cam, but the rest belongs to his mother. He gives me a grin and turns to eye his other brother.

"Chill out, Nathan. It's not Cam's fault that Ellen dumped your sorry ass." A nervous titter from Hannah and a harrumph from Henry draw his attention, and he steps back with a sheepish smile. "Sorry. Come inside so we can close the door. It's wicked cold."

Once inside, we shed our coats and I try not to gawk. The other times we've been here, we've entered from the rear of the house. Coming into the grand foyer from the front is a different experience. It's the type of beauty you usually see in magazines. Holiday greenery adorns the wrought-iron balustrade on the twin staircases and the wall sconces. Between the scent of fresh fir and cedar, and the aromas of cinnamon and clove wafting from somewhere, I feel like we've walked into a Christmas card.

"You're just in time, sir." Henry gestures toward an arch off to the side. "Drinks are being served in the main salon."

Brooks claps Cam on the shoulder. "Perfect timing, Henry," he declares, then mutters for only Cam and me, "After listening to Ethan sing 'Joy to the World' at the top of his lungs the entire drive here, I need a few drinks." Brooks and a still surly Nathan follow Henry through the arch, as Cam crooks his elbow out for me to take.

"Shall we, my lady?" He grins down at me, eyes twinkling. Instead of starched khakis like his brothers, Cam's wearing jeans and black boots with his dark cashmere pullover and looks like something out of *GQ*. "I think I hear a glass of champagne calling your name."

"Which is Samantha, I presume?" Startled by the deep voice that sounds so much like Cam, I swing around and come face-to-stomach with the infamous Cameron Louis Chapman, Jr. Good God, were these people descended from giants or something? I crane my neck to look up at him. Cam's six-five, and his brothers seem about the same, but their father blows them all out of the water. I feel like a pygmy.

"Sam, this is my father, Louis. For being so big, you certainly move on little cat feet, Father," Cam drawls, rubbing his eyebrow with a thumb. His father huffs a chuckle.

"So I've been told. I hope you're feeling better, my dear." A faint frown of concern flickers over his stern countenance. "We were horrified by what your—"

"It was just a fall," I say quickly, glancing down at Hannah. He nods, obviously understanding our deception for Hannah's sake.

I feel the warmth of Cam's hand on the small of my back. "We're lucky she only got a few bruises," he adds, flexing his hand against me. "But her violin was a total loss."

"I heard that, too. But Christmas is a time of renewal." His father rubs his upper lip with a long finger. "You never know what Santa might bring you."

I shoot a suspicious look at Cam, but he simply gazes at me, not giving anything away. He's promised me no gifts, since there is no way I could afford anything else besides Hannah's doll. If he were to give me a violin . . . I have to be honest, I'd accept the gift. There's no other way I can get one. And I *need* a violin. I take a deep breath and vow to put my pride in the back seat, for now.

"Are you a giant?" Hannah pipes in. The elder Chapman chuckles, his eyes warming as he smiles down at her.

"No, little one. Aren't you a pretty little thing? You look like a jewel." She beams at him, and then Cam lifts her effortlessly into his arms between us.

"She's a hungry little jewel, according to her growly stomach." He pretends to nibble at her neck, making her squeal. "We'd better get her some food before she eats the house down."

His father gazes between them, startled, and then rumbles with a low hum of satisfaction. "I think we can manage that," he says, straightening. "I presume you remember the way?" With a secret smile in my direction, he turns and strides off under another archway.

I smooth down my camel sweater over my black wool skirt. "Well. That was interesting."

Cam shrugs. "I don't know what the h—er, heck is going on with him lately. He's said more to me in the last couple of weeks than he has in years." Shifting Hannah in his arms, he pecks her on the forehead and then grins at me. "Actually, I think it's you. You can charm the birds out of the trees with that smile."

Warmth runs down my spine as I look into his twinkling eyes. Who could've predicted mere weeks ago when I met this incredible man that he'd be the one to turn my world upside down, in the best of ways. "We can't eat charm, so I suppose we should join them."

Leaning down, he presses his lips to mine in a sweet kiss I feel all the way down to my toes. "I know what I'd like to eat," he murmurs against my lips and I gasp.

"Cam!" I pull back and give him a playful shove, my cheeks heating, my eyes darting to Hannah's. She giggles, but it's the normal giggle she always makes when she catches us kissing. Thank God she's too young to understand.

"It's about time you two got here." I peek past Cam to see Kat practically skipping forward. She's wearing a green and red plaid taffeta cocktail dress with gold ribbons in her long blond hair. She's like a Christmas package come to life.

"Aunt Kat!"

She reaches up to ruffle Hannah's hair. "How are you, punkin?"

"Nice dress." Cam smirks down at his sister. "Always know how to make a statement with Queen V, don't you?"

She tosses her head and adjusts one of the red laces on her knee-high black boots. "I felt festive, that's all." Linking her arm with mine, she steers me into another beautifully appointed room, Cam following with Hannah. "Let's have a drink."

"EVERYTHING ALL RIGHT? YOU DIDN'T eat much." Cam's hand flexes on my side as he escorts me out of the dining room and into a sitting room. Hannah skips ahead of us to plaster herself against one of the huge picture windows next to Ethan. The little boy is gesturing wildly, showing her the exact route he expects Santa will take in just a few hours. They run over to inspect the fireplace, and then back to the window, where they sink to the floor, peering out at the falling snow.

I smile up into his concerned eyes. "I wasn't very hungry. I had my hands full keeping Hannah's attention on her dinner."

"Ah, yes. Another Chapman man succumbing to the charms of a McKenzie woman," he whispers with a chuckle. Brooks, his wife Paige, and son Ethan were seated across from us. Ethan remembered Hannah from the Christmas party, and as soon as he saw her, he made it his mission to make her laugh by creating sculptures with his food and making faces at her. "Poor Paige had her hands full, too."

He guides me over to a sofa across from the fireplace. "You know, it actually made dinner feel more normal. It was a nice counterbalance to all the servants." It was almost like being in a restaurant, with someone setting plates in front of me and someone else removing them in a never-ending cycle. My glass was never allowed to go below half-empty, and I always had the right fork available. Conversation swirled; Cam's father and brothers mainly discussed business, Kat and Cam chatted about his upcoming tour dates, and Victoria kept an eagle eye on all us. She was surprisingly quiet during dinner. It was sad to see how reserved she was with her grandson; besides a few indulgent smiles and one half-hearted hair ruffle, she seemed content to let Paige handle the little guy. It was unnerving when her speculative gaze landed on me. Luckily, thanks to my daughter and Ethan's antics, I didn't have time to feel out of place.

"You'll get used to them." Cam leans back and accepts a glass of sparkling water from another helpful staff member. I decline a glass of champagne with a shake of my head.

"I don't think I want to," I murmur, watching as the man moves on to where Paige and Brooks have settled in some plush chairs. "I don't think I can live like this."

His arm slips up to my shoulders and he pulls me close as he leans in. "We won't. We don't have any regular staff at home, if you've noticed." That's true. Other than the cleaning service that comes in every two weeks, it's just us. He places a kiss on my temple, just as his parents and Nathan enter. I try not to stiffen when

I see his mother's eyes dart toward us.

I face Cam, ignoring his parents. "We can do whatever we want. Live however we want."

"Yes, we can," he whispers, giving me another kiss before straightening. Kat plops down on my other side, a glass of champagne in each hand. She hands one to me.

"So, now what are your plans? I still think you should make a run at concertmistress. I heard that auditions are in a couple weeks."

"I have to find another violin before I can do anything," I remind her and take a sip. The bubbles make my nose twitch. "After that, I want to resume teaching, I think. I like it. And I wouldn't have time to do that and be concertmistress. However, I'm not wild about teaching in their homes. Not every student lives near a bus line."

Cam huffs. "Well, that's not a problem. I can have a car take you—"

"Why don't you rent a studio?" Kat interjects and her face lights up. "I have a brilliant idea. You know the stairs in the vestibule of the childcare center? They lead to a room upstairs that I thought would be my office, but the only thing I keep in it is the filing cabinet where I store staff personnel files and the children's enrollment papers." She grabs my hand and leans forward with an eager smile. "Why don't you use it as a studio for lessons? You'll have all the space you need, and there's a small bathroom, too. And the separate entry from downstairs is perfect."

Hope flares and my mind is awhirl. "That would be fantastic. It's a great location for students—especially if some of the kids from the day care want lessons—and it's convenient for me, being so close to the Center." I tap a rhythm on my knee, thinking. Cam's parents settle into chairs on each side of a massive fireplace. His regal mother smiles benevolently at her grandson, who is still chattering with Hannah about Santa and elves. Biting my lip, I somehow know that Victoria's benevolence wouldn't extend to me sponging off her daughter.

Before I can voice my hesitation, Kat continues, "I'll even cut you a break on rent for the first few months, until you can establish more students."

"Rent?" Cam scowls at her. "You know as well as I do that you don't need—"

"Yes, rent." She gives him a hard look. "Not much. Just enough so that Sam doesn't feel like she's taking advantage of me." She turns back to me, a triumphant gleam in her eye. "We can work out the details later. Deal?"

"Thank you, Kat. Deal." I hold out my hand, but she grabs me in a hug instead, making me laugh, and I squeeze her in return. Kat has been wonderful since the "accident." She's listened when I've needed to talk and has distracted me when I've needed it. Cameron is everything to me, but he loves me too much to be able to listen to me talk about Ray. I've seen the effort it costs him to try to appear calm, to keep from balling up his fists in anger toward a dead man. It hurts him to hear how it was for me.

So I tell Aisha, my counselor. Another thing I'm thankful to Kat for, and one thing I'm happy to have Cam pay for, since I obviously can't, and I need it—for my daughter as well as for myself. It's exciting and a little scary to think about all the options I have now that I don't have to hide.

I lean close to Cam's ear. "What happens now?" The Chapmans are settled around the Christmas tree—a smaller tree than the one in the ballroom, but still impressive.

"We exchange a few presents. Nothing for ourselves, usually. Mostly gifts in each other's names to our favorite charities. We have enough—Christmas is for giving back," he explains as envelopes are passed around and graciously received. Cancer research, animal shelters, and Abby's charitable foundation, What's Your Dream, are among the recipients. I'm staggered by the amounts of money represented—another thing I'll have to get used to if I'm going to be with Cam. At least it's going for good causes. I know how generous Cam and his sister are; it must be a family trait.

Hannah is happy to sit with Cam and me, watching the proceedings. We've assured her that we'll be home in plenty of time for Santa to arrive. I give Cam a kiss on the cheek, surprising him, and he beams at me in return. That my daughter can wake up to a few meaningful gifts—including her Hannah doll—with a real Christmas tree is something I'm deeply grateful for. Most of it wouldn't have happened if I hadn't met the amazing man holding me close.

Suddenly, I realize that everyone is looking at me. "I'm sorry, what?" Victoria eyes me patiently.

"Our stable manager, David, says that Hannah has been most enthusiastic about riding the times you've taken her, and she is the right age to learn, so . . ."

"You're not giving her a horse!" I blurt, unable to school my shocked expression. Victoria's lips twitch and Cam chuckles beside me.

"I hardly think that's appropriate," she says dryly, but then her expression softens as she regards Hannah. "However, we thought perhaps Hannah might enjoy learning to ride. We recently acquired a pony so Ethan can begin lessons, and Louis and I thought it a good size for Hannah, as well." She sits up in her chair and gracefully crosses her ankles at a perfect angle, smoothing her dark wool dress over her knees. "We could send a car to pick her up and deliver her back to you on whatever day you choose for weekly lessons."

I'm stunned. I shoot a glance at Cam, but he's obviously as

surprised as I am. "How long have you been thinking about this?" His gaze swivels between his parents. His mother simply shrugs and lifts the delicate champagne flute to her lips.

"Long enough." She takes a sip. "You were about the same age when you began lessons, Cameron. Surely you remember that."

My instinct is to decline, but one look at Hannah's face stills my tongue. I've rarely seen such a mixture of hope and longing. How can I deny her this? So instead, I find myself saying, "Hannah, sweetie, what do we say?"

Instead of simply thanking her, Hannah approaches Victoria warily, as if she's a bomb about to go off. "I'd get to ride the horsie by myself?"

Lowering her chin, the older woman returns her serious expression. "Yes, if you would like to learn." Then her cool gaze widens in shock when she suddenly has her arms full of excited little girl, spilling her champagne.

"Thank you, thank you, thank you!" Victoria looks like she's about to pass out, but then her lips twitch in an embarrassed smile, and she pats my daughter on the back with awkward, rusty motions like the Tin Man after being oiled. It's a Christmas miracle. Kat laughs behind her hand, while Cam, Brooks, and their father smile at their feet. I wonder how long it's been since Victoria shared any physical affection with any of them.

"Hannah," Louis calls, beckoning her over. Cam leans forward, but relaxes when his father merely whispers in her ear and hands her an envelope. It's my turn for concern when she skips over and thrusts it at me.

"Take it, Momma." She wiggles the envelope until I accept it. With shaky fingers, I open it and scan the sheet of paper inside. *A donation has been made in your name* . . . It's only when I feel Cam's hand on my knee that I realize I've been gaping at the words.

"What is it?" he whispers.

"I don't understand." I look up at him, and then at his parents. I'm not a member of the family. Why would they do this?

Cam lifts the paper from my unresisting fingers and reads as his father explains. "We talked to the women's shelters in town, and it seems the greatest problem most of the residents face is not having a way to make a living on their own. Some don't have marketable skills, some simply lack direction. It often leads them to either return to their abusive situation or to rush into another relationship that may not be healthy for them." He leans back in his chair and tents his hands on his chest, watching me over his fingertips.

"So we decided to create a place to fill the gap. Women who want to learn a trade will be connected to educational courses or even journeyman programs. There's nothing wrong with a female electrician, after all, and they make good money. Scholarships will be available for those who can't pay. And for those women who have had careers and are starting over, there will be assistance with résumés and job applications, a chance to practice their interviewing techniques, and donated clothing for their job search. If it's as successful as we hope it will be, we'll augment its services over time, depending on need."

Cam stares at his father. "Did you start this before or after the atta—"

"Before," Victoria answers him. Still sitting regally in her chair, she adjusts the single strand of pearls adorning her long neck. "Anyone who finds themselves in such a place should have the help they need to make a better life for themselves." Her eyes meet mine. "And their children."

Louis hums in agreement. "We're calling it McKenzie House."

The lump in my throat makes it hard to swallow. My hand

closes convulsively over Cam's. I can't believe my ears.

"I don't . . . You can't . . ." I stammer, my eyes blurring. It's such an amazing thing that will help so many women, but for them to do it in *my* name? Unbelievable.

A small hand on my shoulder startles me; Kat has gathered Hannah onto her lap, and my daughter is frowning at me. "What do we say, Momma?" I can't help my chuckle. I pull her onto my own lap and hug her to me as Cam's arm pulls us both to his side. Smiling at his parents through watery eyes, I say the only thing I can.

"Thank you. Truly."

"WHERE ARE YOU TAKING ME?" When Kat corralled Hannah and Ethan to the kitchen to assemble cookie plates for Santa, Cam took my hand, saying he had something to show me.

He gives me a shy smile that melts my heart and opens a door to another large room. Moonlight floods through the floor-to-ceiling windows, lighting everything inside with an unearthly glow. A sleek, black Bechstein grand stands in the center of the room like a statue, just waiting for someone to bring it to life.

Our footsteps on the hardwood echo in the silence. I pause in front of the windows, but Cam continues toward the piano. "Who plays?" I ask softly.

"My mother." He runs a fingertip along the edge of the open lid. "She's good. Concert-level good, although she's never performed."

The snow lies peacefully beyond the windows, and I rub my arms. Since the heavy drapes aren't drawn, the room is markedly cooler than the rest of the house. "So that's where you get your musical talent?"

"I guess." He snorts a laugh, bracing his hands on the piano. "Not that she'd ever admit it."

"She knows, Cam. She may not say anything, but she knows. And she's proud of you. How could she not be?"

He grimaces and looks down at his hands, pale against the black surface. "I used to spend hours listening to her play when I was small. I loved watching her hands float over the keys and the music she made. I took lessons, of course, but it never really clicked for me like the guitar did. She was horrified—thought the guitar was such a 'common' instrument in comparison. For a while, I think she thought I did it to spite her."

"She may have just been disappointed that you didn't follow in her footsteps. You look so much like your father; maybe she was hoping to be able to share something of herself with you."

His hand stills. "Hmm. Maybe." He sits on the bench, straddling it, and holds a hand out in invitation. When I take it, he pulls me to sit sideways in front of him, draped over his thighs. "That's one of the things I love about you; you make me think about things differently."

Looping my arms around his neck, I nestle in his arms. "One of the things? There's more?"

"So much more." He smiles against my forehead. "Shall I make a list?"

My laugh bubbles up. "No!" I glance around the room. "So is this what you wanted to show me?"

"I really just wanted a moment to ourselves. That was a pretty amazing thing they did." He shakes his head. "How do you feel?"

"Why did they do it?" I still can't believe it. "I mean, it's fabulous, and it will help so many people, but why—"

"Because you're my One." His arms tighten around me, and I wonder if he can feel how fast my heart is beating. Nodding toward the piano, he smiles gently. "My father first saw my mother when she was playing at some party, and he knew then she was it for him. I went to what I was sure was going to be another boring society event for my family, and instead I found this beautiful auburn-haired violinist I couldn't get out of my mind."

Those sparkling hazel eyes that I've loved since I first met him smile down at me. "I found my One."

"I love you," I whisper. "What I feel for you, I've never felt before, for anyone. It's important to me that you know that. You're my One, too." He smiles and pulls my left hand from his neck, holding it between us.

"One day, Sam, one day soon . . ." He raises my hand and presses a kiss against my ring finger. "But for now, we should probably fetch your girl and get her home to bed before Santa arrives. What do you say?"

I don't think I could love him more. His intent is clear. And we both know that now isn't the time, not yet. But soon.

And I know what I'll say.

Cupping his cheek with my free hand, I kiss him firmly. "I say yes. Let's go get *our* girl."

# *five months later*

## *cameron*

"AND YOU HAVE THE NERVE to have a go at me for some of the shit I wear." Sean shakes his head with a laugh that echoes off the rafters of the stable as I lead Mystic from her stall at the polo club.

It's early May, and the band has converged in Boston for the first annual polo match in support of McKenzie House. The idea was actually my mother's. She's been working with Sam on the event for months. I was worried at first about Sam spending too much time with Queen V—my mom has a way of grating on your last nerve—but Sam says she's been amazing to work with. She's been squeezing time in on planning this event between her full schedule of students. Now that she doesn't have to hide, Sam's also moved up to first violin where she can really shine.

All the event planning has also brought them closer. Mom and Dad came over for dinner a couple of weeks ago, which is a foreign concept. It was the first time they had set foot in my townhouse since Mom renovated it four years ago. The ice queen seems to be thawing the more time she spends with Hannah, too. Not that I expect her to get down and dirty in the princess castle sandbox that now sits in my yard anytime soon, but we're making progress.

A princess castle sandbox . . . in my yard. Not something I ever thought I'd be seeing at my place, but one look at Hannah's face when I surprised her was all I needed to see. In the months since Christmas, Sam and Hannah have taken over my life and my heart. I trip over American Girl accessories constantly, find endless amounts of barrettes and hair ties everywhere, and I wouldn't want it any other way. It means they're finally comfortable, and safe. It means we've made our home together.

The bulk of the upper echelons of Boston elite are all in attendance for the event, decked out in their classy and sophisticated spring best to raise money for finishing the women's shelter my parents named after Sam. With tickets going for a couple of grand a pop, along with the silent auction and our concert being held after the match, I hope they'll reach their goal of an additional two million being raised.

I tug the reins back to bring Mystic to a stop in front of my bandmates. "What's wrong with what I'm wearing?"

"Please. I mean the white pants alone." Sean slings his arm around Kennedy's shoulder. "And riding boots up to your knees? Are we in the middle of filming a Ralph Lauren advert?" Kennedy laughs at Sean, hitting him in the chest.

"You wish you had this outfit. And you could have if you didn't all pussy out on me." They all thought I had lost my mind when I floated the idea that we have our own team. Sucks for them. They'll never know the rush they're missing.

Matt's eyes widen as he takes a look at Mystic. "I'm good on the ground, thanks."

"Says the man who rides a steel horse death trap," Kennedy says, reaching over to stroke Mystic's muzzle.

"Hey, my motorcycle is safer than any horse ever will be."

"Mhmm." Kennedy glares at Matt. "You must have suffered some memory loss, you know, from the accident you had on your precious motorcycle that almost killed you." Matt flips Kennedy off.

"Did you wear the three for me?" Sean asks, poking my chest where my number sits. "You really do love me."

I swat his hand back. "You're an idiot." Mystic huffs beside me, pushing closer to Kennedy.

"How safe is this, really?" Tucker asks, folding his arms across his chest from his spot in the doorway of the stable.

"Not even remotely." Tucker scowls at my answer.

"And when's the last time you did this?" he asks, lifting his chin at the horse.

"An actual match? When I was sixteen." Tucker rolls his eyes. "But I've been practicing."

"Jesus," he mutters.

"It'll be fine, Tuck. Stop worrying and come and meet Mystic." He mumbles something I can't quite hear under his breath, but takes a tentative step forward, eyeing the chestnut mare like she's some covert threat. "She's harmless."

"Bullshit," Matt says. "Horses hold grudges."

I choke out a laugh, dangling the reins in front of him. "That's the most ridiculous thing I've ever heard."

"True fucking story, man. Don't say I didn't warn you." He holds both hands up, backing away. "You're on your own there."

"Is our grasshopper afraid of a little pony?" Sean goads Matt, which is one of his favorite pastimes. "Had a bad experience, did you?" Matt's response is to haul off and punch Sean in the shoulder.

364 B.B. MILLER AND LESLIE CARSON

"That fucking hurt!"

Matt smirks at him. "Good."

"Are you guys behaving in here?" As always, the sound of Sam's voice causes my heart rate to kick up. She's a fucking vision in her flowing green dress, heading into the stables with Tess and Abby.

"As much as we ever can, Sammy," Sean answers.

"I'm surprised Mom let you out of her sight." Sam slides her arm around my waist and I lean down for a kiss. She gives me a chaste peck on the lips, leaning into my side. While she's still not a big fan of PDA, at least she doesn't live in fear of pictures of us getting out any longer. And there will be pictures today—lots of them. It's a paparazzi dream with the number of celebrities, politicians, and jet-setters in attendance.

"If she ever wants a job, we could use her skills at the Foundation. She's like a drill sergeant with the volunteers," Abby says, moving beside Kennedy.

"Don't I know it."

"Cardinal, don't get too close to the horse," Matt says, his voice hard.

"You mean like this?" Tess grins, sidling right up beside Mystic.

"Christ, woman." Matt squeezes the back of his neck, his eyes darting from the mare to Tess. I don't know what he's so worried about. Mystic is a gentle soul until she gets onto the field. Then, she transforms. She's lightning fast with incredible endurance. I've got eight other horses here today that I'll switch out for between chukkers to give her a rest, but Mystic is definitely my favorite. "The fucking things I do for you guys," he grumbles as Tess moves away from the mare to take his hand.

Sean swipes the mallet from me, swinging it above his head. "Seems like an insane idea. Chasing a little ball around on a horse at forty miles an hour. I've been to a match or two back home."

I grab the mallet before he knocks someone in the head. "Good. Then you can explain it to the clueless crew over here." I point the mallet to Kennedy and Matt.

Matt backs up as I start to lead Mystic out toward the field. "Just don't kill yourself, Ralph Lauren," Matt says, looking back over his shoulder at me.

"Just avoid the steaming divots during the stomp at halftime," I fire back at him, and he scrunches his nose.

"Cheer up, grumpy," Tucker chimes in, clapping Matt on the shoulder. "It's for a good cause."

I watch Tucker lead the group away to their VIP seats where Kat is currently keeping Hannah occupied. Pausing just before we exit the stable, I tighten my arm around Sam. "I missed you this morning," I whisper, leaning down to press a kiss to her neck. "You left early."

She lets out one of her little sighs as her soft lips find mine. "Your mother had us here at oh-dark-hundred. I love her, I really do, but I'll be glad when this is over." I chuckle, squeezing her waist.

"Believe me, I understand." I glance out to the packed stands and the stage set away from the field that I'll take later tonight with the band. "It will be worth it, though."

"I know. Did I say thank-you again for doing all of this?" She curls up on her toes, setting her palm against my cheek.

"You did, but I'll always accept your type of thank-you." She gives me a playful hit to my chest. "And you don't have to thank me. It'll be fun to play again."

"Just be careful, please." I press my lips to her forehead, trying to ease her worry.

"Don't you worry about me."

She leans back, tilting her head up with a gentle gaze. "I love you. It's my job to worry about you, you know."

I'll never get tired of hearing Sam say those three words to me. They fill me up and make me whole. "Keep talking like that and I'll be late for this match. We have time, don't we?" I waggle my eyebrows at her and she shakes her head with a laugh.

"Later. I promise." She backs up from me slowly with that knowing smile that I crave. "Maybe in one of the empty stables, or backstage?"

Such a little tease. I love it. "I'm holding you to that promise, McKenzie."

She watches as I place my foot in the stirrup and lift up into the saddle. She bites down on her lip a little. "Just so you know, you look incredibly hot up there." Her gaze roams over me, hot and hungry.

"So, you're saying I should keep the boots on later then?" She laughs, walking beside Mystic as I lead her to the field where the rest of the team and horses are waiting.

"Lose the shin guards and maybe." Giving me a wave, she turns for the stands, and I watch her go. The sweet sway of her hips, the sun kissing her pale skin . . . She's fucking perfect for me, and today I'm hoping she'll say yes—not just to the stables or backstage, but to forever.

The Redfall adventures continue. A sneak peek at "Wildest Dream," the final book of *The Redfall Dream Series*, coming in 2018. *Content subject to change.*

**Murphy's Law No. 261**—*If your bandmates get girlfriends, they quickly become dull and boring.*

*AKA- Being the seventh wheel sucks.*

# chapter one

## sean

"I'M GOING HANG GLIDING." MY announcement—an epic one in my opinion—is met with the typical apathy I've come to expect from my Redfall bandmates over the last several years.

Kennedy Lane—lead singer and guitar genius, Cameron Chapman—our kick-ass rhythm guitarist, and Matt Logan—fierce bassist extraordinaire, look more like teenagers unable to avoid the temptation of their smartphones than one of the biggest rock and roll bands on the planet right now.

Only Cam has the decency to lift his nose from the wonder of his beloved phone. "You're not going hang gliding," he grumbles. Since hooking up with the lovely Samantha a few months back, he's gone and got himself an instant family, and with that the parental instincts that go along with worrying about the fragile state of a five-year-old girl. Though, there is no debating how utterly adorable Hannah is. Talk about having someone wrapped around your little finger. I think all four of us would move the earth for her.

Still, Cam's the last person I would ever expect fatherly advice from, but love apparently does things to you no one can predict.

"Damn right I am. Adventure Wars called Nic the other day."

This gets their collective attention, and I can't help but smirk as I lounge back against the sofa in the green room, stretching my arm across the back. Another interview, another city. They all start to blend together after a while. We're all feeling the toll of this tour, but there's a well-earned break on the horizon, and that can't come soon enough.

"Adventure Wars?" This from Matty, who looks more than a little impressed. "As in the one where celebrities battle it out to see which one is more stupid?" My smirk fades a little. "Last week, some pro quarterback went shark diving. The other contestant was too chicken-shit to try it. They all donate money to charity regardless," Matt adds.

"No shit," mumbles Kennedy before dropping his phone into the pocket of his leather jacket. "When's this taking place?"

"It's not," Tucker Pearson chimes in. Our head of security in his finest form lurks at the door in that menacing way he has. "No fucking way are you doing that."

"But it's totally safe." Even I can admit that I sound like a petulant child.

Tucker snorts with a shake of his head. "Throwing yourself off a cliff with only a kite holding you up isn't safe, Sean."

"Where's your sense of adventure, hmm?" I challenge them all. Pushing up from the sofa, I start pacing the room, keyed up and anticipating our next performance as always.

"I'm all for adventure, but—"

"But nothing!" I interrupt Tucker. "When's the last time we

did something wild and crazy?"

"Last night," Kennedy deadpans. "Or did you forget the eigh-teen-thousand people we played for?"

"Not talking about that. *That* is safe. It's what we know. What about pushing the boundaries a little?"

"Again, what about last night?" Kennedy continues. "Pretty sure no one has played a Stones tribute that way ever."

I grin at the memory of our latest concert. We blew the roof off Madison Square Garden for the fourth night in the row. There's nothing like that kind of adrenaline rush. "All right, I'll give you that, but I'm talking about taking real risks here. You know? Feel your heart pounding, pure adrenaline- not the kind we get when we play. I mean the unknown."

"Jesus, you need a hobby," mutters Cam, rolling his eyes.

"My point exactly. We can't all be in domesticated bliss. And what would I bring to the band if you all couldn't live vicariously through me?"

"I ask myself that question on a daily basis," mocks Kennedy with a grin, lifting his Gibson guitar from the nearby stand, and strumming a few chords.

"I really want—"

"No." There's no questioning the firmness in Tucker's voice as he cuts me off. "This wacked out show must have other options, so find one."

"White water rafting in Ecuador?" Cam offers.

"Zip-lining in Costa Rica?" Matty chimes in.

Kennedy stops playing long enough to throw his two cents in. "New tattoo on your forehead this time?"

"Yes. Yes. And are you insane? I can't ruin this pretty face for women everywhere. I'm our money ticket." Cameron shakes his head with a laugh at me.

"Whatever you do, it has to be something the insurance company will cover," Tucker adds, passing me an energy drink from the table.

"Listen to you, old man. See? This is what I'm talking about. I want to spice things up and all you lot can think about is clause twenty-four in our insurance policy."

"Finding a replacement drummer would be a pain-in-the-ass," Cameron jokes. "Maybe we should start looking now?"

I level him a warning glance. "You wouldn't dare, Three." Cameron narrows his eyes at my nickname for him. Being born into an uber-rich, country club elitist family is something I'll never stop kidding Cam about. Cameron Louis Chapman, the Third . . . what a crock of shit. Who gives their kid a handle like that? So, to me, he'll always be Three. Sure, he pretends to hate the name, but secretly, I think he loves me for it.

"Don't die and we won't have to," he fires back at me.

"Words of wisdom there," Matt adds, poking at my hair. It's dyed jet black after being varying shades of purple for the last couple of weeks. I like to change things up. Keep people guessing. "Think of the women you'd disappoint if you died. Broken hearts around the globe."

"I really do hate disappointing women."

Kennedy snorts. "Doesn't that happen every night?"

A sharp knock on the door puts a stop our limitless sparring. "Redfall! You're on in ten." Duty calls as always.

I'M NOT, NOR HAVE I ever been what people define as normal. It's a blessing and curse. My parents encouraged me to question everything, to never be complacent. They tried to do the same with my twin sister, Sydney, but she's always been the one on a more even keel; pulling me back to reality when I tended to run off the rails, which back in the day, was often.

We were *that* family—the ones who took back-packing tours to the middle of nowhere, whilst everyone else was lazing about on holiday. Sydney and I spent our tenth birthday helping my parents build a school in Tanzania. With my father being a high ranking member of the International Development Office, summer holidays were taken wherever he happened to be dispatched; Nepal, Ghana, the Philippines. More than just a talking head, Dad is one of the rare ones who actually gives a shit. He rolls up his sleeves and digs in to help. He always wanted both Syd and me to get involved in political life, so near and dear it was and still is to him.

Sadly, for him, that dream was doomed for failure the moment I turned sixteen and made the miraculous discovery that girls would do just about anything if they found out you were a drummer—bless them many times over.

Politics wasn't to be for Sydney either. The artistic gene—which we still can't seem to place—bit her early. She's now an architect with one of the most prestigious firms in London. Those countless hours of drawing and sketching with my Mum, who can't draw a straight line with a ruler, obviously came in handy.

Sydney however, has never caused family embarrassment, something which I've excelled at over the years. My stints in rehab don't shine as my finer moments. I don't think that's what dear old Mum and Dad had in mind when they told me to spread my wings and explore.

The press are brutal in ways you can't imagine when you're famous and make mistakes. Couple that with a by-the-book influential member of the British government, and you've got yourself a scandal. That may be the only regret I have—causing my Mum and Dad to be hounded relentlessly by the paparazzi, demanding their comments on my coke bender that landed me in rehab for a couple of months.

Thankfully, as these things often do, the next celebrity train wreck followed mine quickly, and my family was but a by-line on page ten within a couple of weeks.

These days, with my bandmates cozying up with their significant others, the dynamic in our group has changed pretty dramatically. I had a tea-party with Cam and Hannah a few weeks back for the love of God. A proper tea-party. Mind you, those pink sunglasses she made me wear were fantastic, but still, it's quite the change in culture from our days gone by.

All that partying we did wasn't always a good thing. I know that now. For a while there, all of us were in serious danger of taking things a step too far. We've all lost people, loved ones along the way on our journey to get here, but if you asked me a year ago if I'd be hosting tea-parties for five-year-olds, I would have told you you'd lost your mind.

But, that is the wonder of life. Its unpredictability is what makes us want to get up and see what's in store. And on days like today, when I'm held back, when I'm told I'm not allowed to do something, well, that just makes me want to do it more. Buy the shoes, wear the ridiculous outfits, take the jump. You're here to light it up, and I intend to do just that.

# acknowledgements

THANK YOU TO OUR FAMILIES for your steadfast love and support.

We have so much love for Michelle Clay. Your support and encouragement drive us, and we are forever grateful for your tireless energy and your friendship.

To the Facebook Dream Team: Your daily inspiring visuals keep us going!

To the amazingly talented Jada: Thank you for your incredible gift. We continue to be in awe of your amazing talent.

Lauren and the Write Divas, thank you for your guidance, and your patience. Navigating the complex world of commas would not be the same without you!

Christine, you make our words look beyond beautiful. Thank you so much for sharing your talents!

To our wonderful pre-readers—Corinne and Tami, thank you for taking the time to read and for your feedback along the way.

A world of thanks to the wonderful community of authors and their continued support including: Melanie Moreland and the bedazzling Harper Bentley. Spirit animals, unite!

Much love to the bloggers, Twitterloves, Facebook friends and groups, ARC readers, and review sites that continue to support indie authors everywhere. We couldn't do this without you.

To you, the reader—thank you for taking another journey with us. This story has been over a year's worth of emotional research, sweat and tears, and we hope you enjoy reading it as much as we did writing it. Rock on, friends. Rock On.

# about the authors

A LITTLE OVER EIGHT YEARS ago, an American carnivore and a Canadian vegetarian bonded over their mutual love for purses, cocktails, and swoon-worthy story telling.

From her home in Portland, B.B. Miller spends her days with friends and family in search of the perfect pear martini.

Leslie Carson lives in Ottawa, with her busy family and three cats. She's at the rink so much, Zamboni drivers know her by name.

Together, they enjoy visiting random vineyards and distilleries, and writing about the romantic adventures of good and bad boys.

They would love to hear from you.

Join our group on Facebook: The Dream Team